CW00865218

THE PAJARO
MURDER

THE PAJARO MURDER

and Other Stories

David Doglietto

Copyright © 2020 by David Doglietto.
Investigator David J. Doglietto, M.S., CSCSA

Library of Congress Control Number:		2020909230
ISBN:	Hardcover	978-1-9845-8012-2
	Softcover	978-1-9845-8011-5
	eBook	978-1-9845-8010-8

All rights reserved. No part of this book may be reproduced or transmitted in any form or by any means, electronic or mechanical, including photocopying, recording, or by any information storage and retrieval system, without permission in writing from the copyright owner.

This is a work of fiction. Names, characters, places and incidents either are the product of the author's imagination or are used fictitiously, and any resemblance to any actual persons, living or dead, events, or locales is entirely coincidental.

The views expressed in this work are solely those of the author and do not necessarily reflect the views of the publisher, and the publisher hereby disclaims any responsibility for them.

Any people depicted in stock imagery provided by Getty Images are models, and such images are being used for illustrative purposes only.
Certain stock imagery © Getty Images.

Print information available on the last page.

Rev. date: 05/18/2020

To order additional copies of this book, contact:
Xlibris
1-888-795-4274
www.Xlibris.com
Orders@Xlibris.com
807577

To all prison investigators around the world who do amazing things every day but receive no recognition. Also, to all the custodial officers who really do work "the toughest beat." Finally, to my former investigations partner; together, we made an outstanding investigative team.

Central Facility

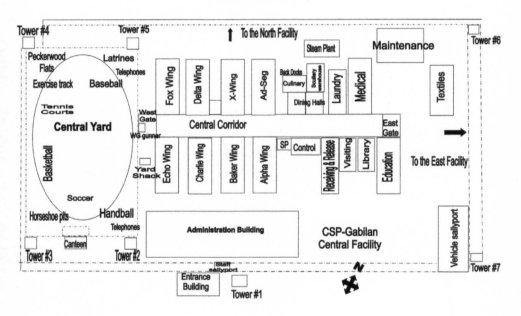

North Facility

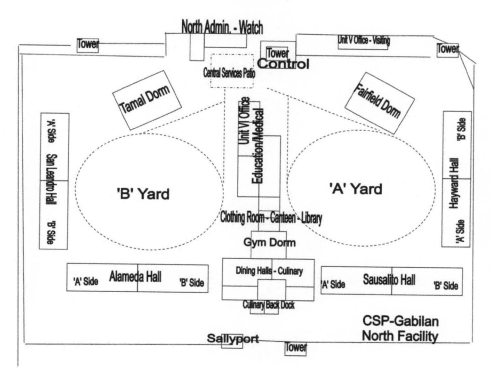

North Admin. - Watch

Tower

Unit V Office - Visiting

Tower

Tower

Control

Central Services Patio

Tamal Dorm

Fairfield Dorm

'A' Side   San Leandro Hall   'B' Side

'B' Yard

Unit VI Office

Education/Medical

'A' Yard

Hayward Hall

'B' Side

'A' Side

Clothing Room - Canteen - Library

Gym Dorm

Alameda Hall
'A' Side   'B' Side

Dining Halls - Culinary

Sausalito Hall
'A' Side   'B' Side

Culinary Back Dock

CSP-Gabilan
North Facility

Sallyport

Tower

THE PAJARO MURDER

Contents

Preface

Life in a state prison is seldom seen and even more seldom understood. It is a strange and often dangerous world. Scott Doggett is a seasoned prison investigator with twenty-eight years of experience and the goal of a comfortable retirement somewhere on the approaching horizon. Daily he accepts the challenges of conducting major criminal investigations in the custodial setting. He is twice divorced, middle aged, strong as an ox, and of good Italian stock. He lives with his cat in a small bungalow in a smaller community on the California coast. Criminal investigation is the only driving force in his life. Scott will often say, "When it comes to criminal investigations, family always comes second."

He uses good old-fashioned gumshoe investigative techniques, coupled with modern forensic sciences, to solve the machinations of the miscreant inmate population. In doing so, he helps teach the rookie investigators assigned to work with him the skills of interviewing, crime scene investigation, bloodstain pattern analysis, latent print comparison, crime scene reconstruction, and other aspects of forensic sciences. His former narcotics partner, Tyrus Phillips, a U.S. Army veteran who grew up in Detroit, has taken a promotion as the sergeant of the institutional gang investigations unit. Despite this, Scott and Tyrus maintain a very close bond and manage to devote their attention to the world of drug dealing, drug smuggling, gang influences, prison politics, and murder.

The Pajaro Murder and Other Stories is based, in part, on actual investigations conducted at California state prisons, with the greatest due deference to their investigators. The stories involve a world that is, for the most part, unknown to anyone outside the correctional system. It is, at times, an unbelievable world, but it is a real world. More than anything, these stories are lessons in investigative procedure, interview techniques, and the application of forensic sciences in solving crimes. The exact details and names of all involved have been changed to protect the innocent, as well as the guilty.

And here is the standard disclaimer: This is a work of fiction. Names, characters, businesses, places, events, locales, and incidents are either the products of the author's imagination or used in a fictitious manner. Any resemblance to actual people, living or dead, or actual events is purely coincidental.

Chapter 1

A Laugh Riot

The aging white Ford Crown Victoria bumped along the dirt service road that separated the Central Facility from the farmland to the north of the prison, kicking dust through the open windows and vents. The two prison investigators inside quickly rolled up the windows. "Doggett, I am going to write a book about all this," said Investigative Sergeant Tyrus Phillips as they approached tower no. 4. "And I'm giving you one whole chapter."

"Just one chapter?" Investigator Scott Doggett asked with his usual skepticism regarding anything Tyrus ever said. "Well, I see three problems with that, Ty. One, nobody would believe it. Two, nobody would buy it. And three, you're going to need more than one chapter for me."

"No," countered Tyrus. "I'm serious. I have a notebook, and I put everything in it. You remember that girl we served the warrant on? The one who used her baby as a shield to keep Lieutenant Kaiser from arresting her?"

"Belinda Robinson. How could I ever forget? You had to get between the two of them. What a fireplug she was," Scott responded.

"She practically threw the baby at me, Dog, and then hid behind a chair."

"Only because I blocked the door to keep her from running out, Ty, and she kicked me in the shin."

"Yeah or the girl who tried to bring the drugs into the prison in her baby's diaper."

"Sarah Hutchinson, and don't forget the sixteen-year-old who insisted we couldn't search him because he was a minor, even when we presented him with the warrant. His mother took one look at that warrant and said, 'Search him and take his ass to jail.' We searched him, and we took him to jail—"

Tyrus interrupted, "Juvie."

"Cocaine and weed were the haul, if I remember correctly," responded Scott.

"Don't forget all the dirty staff members," reminded Tyrus.

"That would be enough for a book in itself. Look, Ty, we have had a lot of fun serving search warrants up and down the state, but I just don't think it's good fodder for a book," replied Scott. "Besides, the only people who know what really goes on in prison are staff and inmates. We just don't tell the public anything that happens behind these fences."

"Well, Dog, it's all in there."

"I guess you could always self-publish, but don't expect me to buy a copy," Scott replied with a laugh.

As the dust from the gravel road drifted across the windshield and the car bounced in the ruts in the road, the radio crackled to life with a panicked voice yelling, "Code 1, Hayward Hall! Code 2 . . . code 3! *Code 3!*"

"Holy shit!" Scott exclaimed. That meant only one thing—it was the 1530 hours yard recall, and all hell was breaking loose at the North Facility. Scott made a wide U-turn in the grassy area to the west of tower no. 4 in the squeaking and grunting fifteen-year-old Crown Vic. She had 130,000 hard miles as a former transportation vehicle hauling inmates up and down the state, but she still had the spirit to sprint the 800 yards back toward the North Facility. Scott's heart was racing, and so too, he was sure, was Ty's.

Just then, they heard the three loud blasts from the Central Facility steam horn, alerting all three facilities and their sister prison up the hill to immediately lock up their inmates and prepare for an all-out staff response. "Blacks and Southerners! Hayward Hall—both sides!" came the next call on the radio, followed by, "Weapons—repeat, they have weapons."

As they passed the B Yard, the unaffected yard, Scott could see all the inmates diving for the ground and staff running from housing unit doorways. They screeched to a halt in front of the North Facility entrance building. Tyrus and Scott didn't even bother to grab any of the crime scene equipment; they just ran—and ran fast for two guys no longer in their running prime. You gotta stop the riot before you can process the crime scene. They passed through the foyer sally port and ran toward the north control room sally port. Nobody was checking IDs as they waved them through. Scott didn't think they even cared who they were or from where they came, just that they were bodies wearing green uniforms with batons and were running in the direction of Hayward Hall.

They cleared the north central services area in good speed and entered the A Yard gate, which had been opened by the tower officer. "I'm too old for this shit, Tyrus!" Scott exclaimed.

"Just run, Dog, run" was his reply. They made their way across the A Yard toward Hayward Hall, a long rectangular building containing two housing units attached in the middle by a sally port. The all-white concrete building was built in 1956 and was of the old cellblock construction with three open tiers, one atop the others, and about 150 cells on each side with two inmates occupying each cell.

Officers from every part of the facility were running toward Hayward Hall, some in groups of two and some running solo. Ahead of Scott and Tyrus were two other security and investigations unit officers, lovingly referred to as the Goons by the inmate population, and a few more were coming up from behind. All of them had Monadnock expandable batons out and at the ready.

They passed through the open front door of Hayward Hall to a scene of pandemonium on both sides. Hundreds of inmates were engaged in a riot. The hall echoed with the roar of so many inmates fighting. The housing unit staff had retreated in a daze to the protection of the sally port gunner, where they awaited the arrival of responding staff. Tyrus peeled off to the right and ran through the A side grille gate along with most of the other responders. Scott chose to run to the left and entered the B side with the housing unit sergeant Jorge Soto. As they ran to the center of the cellblock, Scott could hear the gas grenades going off on the A side, and he knew Tyrus was in the thick of it.

Sergeant Soto and Scott cleared the tables and shower area in front of the housing unit and had just passed the front stairwell when Scott saw the mess, about 130 black and Southern Hispanic inmates—some armed with shanks, crutches, canes, and broken push broom handles—getting busy in the back of the first tier and on the yard side and rear of the second tier. It was at this time that Scott realized that Sergeant Soto and he were alone. On the second tier to Scott's left, he saw three Hispanic inmates fighting with two black inmates. He didn't see any weapons, so they became low priority. He yelled up at them to stop fighting and to assume a prone position on the tier. The Hispanic inmates quickly backed off the blacks, who sought refuge farther down on the tier.

Just as the Hispanic inmates were getting into the prone position, Scott saw the telltale orange spray of an MK-9 pepper spray canister stream over his shoulder and douse the already compliant inmates, who were now crawling on the tier and now gasping for air. He looked over with disgust at the rookie cop who had run up behind him, let loose his pepper spray bottle, and then quickly beat a retreat to the open hall door. "Son of a bitch," he murmured to himself as he braced for the impending ill effects of the oleoresin capsicum (OC) spray.

The rookie officer managed to inadvertently spray the left side of Scott's face. "Great," Scott said. "Jorge now I'm half blind." The left side of his faced burned, and water from his left eye was rolling down his cheek, but he could still see well enough to observe the dozen or so Southern Hispanic inmates break away from the melee in the back of the first tier and run directly at them with seething anger in their eyes. It was at that time when Scott had one of those "oh shit" moments. He was slowly being overcome with that nasty pepper spray; he was coughing, and snot was running into his mustache. There were a dozen angry men running in his direction, and all he had was a stick.

He took one look at Sergeant Soto, who looked back at him. They both knew they were on their own, and they knew what they had to do, which was to start swinging at anything that got in range. Neither of them said a word, just faced the encroaching foe and raised their baton-equipped arms to strike. Somehow they believed the two of them alone were up to the task. They watched as these inmates climbed over the benches that separated them. The aggressors were wet with sweat, and their nostrils were flared. Within the group was one particularly thuggish-looking, bald-headed, and tattoo-adorned fellow with a stick of his own. His was wood; Scott's was metal.

The first to reach him, however, was another good-sized fellow who was shirtless and covered in blue tattoos that were the product of the prison system. Scott gave his body a slight twist to the right to give his swing that extra bit of power and aimed for the inmate's left deltoid muscle. Scott had to be quick to recover because there were three more of his comrades at his heels. Scott started his forward swing but stopped short because, to his surprise, he saw a look in the inmate's eyes that was no longer one of hate but of relief. The inmate dived for the floor, followed by every one of his charging companions.

Scott took a quick glance over to Sergeant Soto and noticed that his attackers were also on the ground, the closest a mere yard from his feet. They looked at each other and, for a brief moment, thought themselves the toughest cops on the block—that was, of course, until the cavalry swarmed past them and into the fray in the back of the hall. Well, there was no time to feel like dunderheads. Of course, the inmates didn't prone out because of the efforts of one sergeant and one investigator; they hit the floor because of the dozens of cops who were coming through the door and to their rescue. They both laughed an awkward laugh of embarrassment coupled with relief. But their work wasn't yet done.

The bulk of the inmates were in the back of the hall, and Scott could see blood on the concrete—a lot of blood on the concrete—and blood dripping from the tier above. He made his way over the same series of benches that a moment before were the enemy's hurdles, and he joined the action. The fighting was fierce, and no one was heeding staff instructions to stop.

Scott looked up on the second tier and saw a black inmate bleeding from a gash in his head, the result of being slammed headfirst into the rail by two Hispanic inmates. He saw a Southerner clasp his hands over his chest and fall to the ground, blood squirting between his fingers. There was no ascending the rear stairwell as several black inmates were using them in a scene that resembled Custer's Last Stand. Scott grabbed at one inmate at the bottom of the stairs and pulled him off balance at the same time, sweeping his feet out from under him. The inmate hit the floor hard and crawled off toward the garbage cans stored beneath the stairs.

Just as Scott was reaching for another, there was a tremendous explosion that resembled the discharge of a Civil War–era howitzer. A pall of gray smoke filled the air. When it cleared, every inmate in the place was on the ground, with the fight gone out of them. It took Scott a few seconds to figure out exactly what had happened. One of the responding officers had arrived with an antique 37 mm block gun and fired it point blank in the back of the hall. The concrete and metal construction of the building produced a chamber that magnified the report of the gun. Scott didn't think the officer hit anyone with the projected four wood blocks, but since the charge was black powder instead of gunpowder, it was the boom that counted.

Every inmate on the A side was on the ground. They didn't know what exploded, but they knew they didn't want any part of it. Once the fighting was over, it was just a matter of slipping flex-cuffs on all the inmates and finding the serious injuries. Inmates were yelling for help and beseeching medical attention for their wounded friends. Scott noted 4 gushing stab wounds; 2 massive head injuries; about 120 fat lips, broken noses, and black eyes; and a score of minor abrasions, contusions, and lacerations. Fortunately, not a single officer was hurt in the response.

Scott's first thought was to get over to the A side and find Tyrus. They had not been as lucky on their side. As Scott passed the sally port, he encountered Investigative Officer Cameron Estrada holding his bleeding arm and trying to get out the hall door. He looked tired and in pain. He was also coughing and gasping from a good dousing of chemical agents. "How many grenades did you drop?" Scott asked.

"I tossed two, and I think Ozzie dropped two T-16s." He didn't have to tell Scott, who could smell the orange and lavender scent of the chemical agent grenades; and if anyone was going to be throwing bombs, it would be former army ranger Oswaldo "Oz" Castaneda.

Now you see, Scott wore glasses, and he couldn't see a damned thing without them. So he had a choice—either don a gas mask and deal with the blur or suck it up and do without. He chose the latter, took a deep breath, and darted into the smoke to find Tyrus. It didn't take him long.

Tyrus was there on top of two black inmates, wearing his gas mask and screaming for more flex-cuffs. "Here you go, Tyrus. I have four left, and there are more coming. We need to get the fire department to bring in some fans and start clearing out this gas." The floor of the housing unit was covered in a fine off-white powder that would spring to action with the slightest disturbance, causing a burning sensation in the lungs and skin, lacrimation, and a feeling like you just can't breathe. It was not the most pleasant experience by a long shot, and it made Scott's nose run like a leaky faucet.

"They dropped seven grenades," Tyrus said, anticipating Scott's question. "It was a madhouse, Dog. They just wouldn't stop fighting."

"Let's get some fresh air, Ty. I'm dying in here." They made their way outside, and Tyrus pulled the gas mask off his head. Scott decided to return to the B side and help finish flex-cuffing inmates.

He saw Elisa Foyle, the investigator who served as the court liaison officer, yelling at a large black inmate in the back of the second tier. She had her baton raised and was ordering him off an inmate who lay beneath him. Scott ran to her side and added his orders of compliance. The inmate turned toward Scott and said, "I can't. He's my nephew, and I promised my sister nothing would happen to him in here." When the riot began, the inmate had shielded his nephew, with his back exposed to the danger.

Scott reached down with his support hand, placing it on the inmate's shoulder with a firm grasp, and said, "You, sir, are a hero. Let us protect him from here on." The inmate rolled away and from beneath appeared a young black inmate about two-thirds the size of his uncle. He lay in the fetal position, trembling like a leaf.

They spent the next three hours clearing the hall of more than two hundred combatants, placing all the Southern Hispanic inmates on the yard near the baseball backstop and the black inmates on the yard in front of Hayward Hall. The next three hours were spent dealing with the mess, aside from the interruption of a melee that broke out in Fairfield Dorm and another in the B Yard dining hall. In the latter, Scott was again doused by pepper spray as someone thought it prudent to discharge his pepper spray canister through the closed grille gate. It bounced back and hit the first three responding officers: Scott, rookie officer Adrian Kirby, and Investigator Elon Oglethorpe. Scott spent the next three minutes with his head in the sink, muttering a few choice profanities, before taking his place among the weary responders.

He rushed through the grille gate separating the steam line from the dining hall, shoving an inmate to the ground who desired to use the same gate as an avenue of egress. Scott looked around and saw Investigator Oz Castaneda, who was also the K-9 officer for the prison, jumping from tabletop to tabletop. Oz had exhausted the OC pepper spray in his MK-9 canister, so he was hopping from table to table, slamming the bottom of the canister on the top of any inmate head that came within reach. Scott jumped to the tabletop next to Oz, handed him a full canister of spray, and asked, "What are you doing, Oz, playing a life-size game of whack-a-mole?"

It was two o'clock in the morning when Tyrus and Scott got back into the trusty Vic. "Well, I guess this will be another chapter for your damned book," Scott remarked.

"It's going in" was Ty's only reply. They were both exhausted, and every pore hosted an ounce of some chemical agent or other.

There wasn't much they could do as far as the crime scene went. Scott was able to process the scene in the dining hall without too much trouble, and Oz handled the Fairfield Dorm incident because Scott had witnessed a nasty bludgeoning and therefore excused himself from the CSI team. There wasn't much they could do in Hayward Hall. Some bright lieutenant or other had instructed his staff to sweep all the evidence into the center of each hall to keep the inmates from pulling stuff under their locked cell doors in what was usually described as "fishing." There it all was—bloody clothing, weapons of every kind, trash, bandages, rubber gloves, and the lot swept into four rolling foothills. Scott collected the weapons and the bloody clothing, took a few photographs, and called it a night.

Chapter 2

Just Call Me Dog

There was an obvious reason why Tyrus called Scott "Dog." Well, it was simple really. Scott's surname was originally Doghetti when his father came through immigrations from Italy, but Scott guessed that was too hard for the immigrations official to spell, and the government gave his father a new name; Giovanni Giuseppe Doghetti became John Joseph Doggett. Scott had always been called something with a "Dog" in it. In fact, they've called him Dog since he was a pup. The male siblings always had canine nicknames. His eldest brother was a fireman; therefore, he was Fire Dog. When Scott was a tower cop, they called him Guard Dog. These days, it was just plain old Dog; but to Tyrus, it was either Dog or Doggy.

Scott had been with the department since the late '80s, and he was two years from retirement. He couldn't wait. He was tired. He was a deputy sheriff before joining the department in a small mountainous county east of Sacramento and west of Lake Tahoe. He left the sheriff's office in part because the money was better working for the state than it was in that Podunk town and also because, back then, it took a lot of guts to work in a prison. He didn't think anyone ever intended to be a correctional officer; it just worked out that way. He didn't grow up saying, "I'm going to be a prison guard when I grow up." It just didn't happen that way.

His brother was a fireman. He wanted to be a fireman since he was a little kid. Scott thought about being a fireman. It was a good life. His brother told him a fireman's worst nightmare was back draft. That was when a house was fully involved internally, but there was insufficient oxygen for fire. When you cracked a door, the whole thing would blow up. To be honest, Scott spent enough time at his firehouse to know that a fireman's worst nightmare was getting the La-Z-Boy recliner stuck in luge mode, and you can't reach the remote for the TV. Actually, on many occasions, Scott watched fire guys battle a house fire and then rip the thing apart after the fire was out. It was hard work, but that was why they got the girls. Let's face it; how often have you seen a bevy of young ladies swoon over a prison guard?

He came down to California State Prison–Gabilan in the early 1990s. Tyrus and Scott worked narcotics together for about five years, starting in 1998. Most people wouldn't think that a prison would have narcotics agents, but not only was there a tremendous problem with dope inside the pen but the criminal mind also always seemed to find a way to run his criminal activities out on the streets from the confines of his prison cell. Scott and Tyrus had served search warrants up and down the state and helped out their fellow drug agents, ranging from the bureau of narcotic enforcement to the Drug Enforcement Administration (DEA).

One intrepid inmate drug dealer told Scott that he actually looked forward to his stints in state prison because it gave him the opportunity to make far more money selling dope than when they were on the streets. It doesn't sound plausible, but this is the way it works. The value of drugs in prison is between seven to ten times greater inside a state prison than out on the streets. Therefore, inmates can make a lot more money dealing with a much smaller quantity.

Still confused? All right, look at it this way: A *pedazo*, or Mexican ounce, would be twenty-five grams of black tar heroin, which can be purchased in this state for about $750. If the inmate can successfully smuggle that amount into prison and break it down into its smallest sellable quantity, usually an eighth of a gram, he can make between $5,200 and $7,500 for that one *pedazo*. He probably would only make about $1,250 for the same amount of product on the street. A dope dealer in prison is a very lucrative profession and considered as a position of high respect by the inmate population.

Tyrus and Scott worked hard and managed to get over 250 felony convictions between the two of them. Then Tyrus decided to be promoted to investigative sergeant and moved over to supervise the gang unit. Although Scott added "certified senior crime scene analyst" to his title, he still worked dope. Once a "Dope Dog," always a dope dog. Oswaldo picked up the torch, and they still managed to "tear things up." However, every now and then, Tyrus and Scott still got into mischief.

Being a prison investigator meant you never really specialized in just one assignment. In fact, they were criminal investigators working every case from major fraud to drugs and homicide. It was like being a cop in a town of ten thousand people, and eight thousand of them were criminals. Scott was the senior investigator; ran the mini–forensics lab; did all the latent print development and comparison work, crime scene investigations, and crime scene reconstruction; question document analysis and bloodstain pattern analysis; and filled the empty hours helping Oswaldo train his dog.

Sergeant Tyrus Filmore Phillips, Scott's sometime partner—and if you asked Scott, he would jokingly say "his full-time pain in the ass"— came out to the prison just about the same time that Scott got there. Tyrus said he was named after a baseball player, a former president, and a screwdriver. He was fresh from the U.S. Army, where he was a sergeant manning the guns on an M2 Bradley crew. He saw service in the first Gulf War, where—in spite of being a mechanized cavalry—he managed to get shot in the upper thigh. Scott joked that the guy was probably aiming for his ass.

Tyrus was Motor City born and raised and was a die-hard Lions and Pistons fan. Scott and Tyrus didn't exactly see eye to eye on everything, but the other guys in the office called him Scott's "brother from another mama," and they sure had had a lot of good belly laughs together. It was hard to understand, but when you worked dope with someone as long as Tyrus and Scott did together, you knew just about everything there was to know about each other, except they really didn't know anything.

Most of all, you could say they were close friends. Tyrus was the first one Scott turned to when his eighty-year-old father was murdered in his sleep by two crackheads who wanted $20 to buy another hit of their beloved drug. Yeah, don't tell Scott dope was a victimless crime. And Scott was there for Tyrus when his father passed from cancer. Tyrus knew everything about Scott's divorces, and Scott knew about the constant troubles with Ty's sons.

One thing Scott always admired about working with Tyrus was that, in the middle of every investigation, he would stop the work and ask, "Hey, are we sure we're looking at the right guy?" No matter the momentum, they would always stop what they were doing and review all the evidence and confirm beyond a shadow of a doubt that they had their suspects positively identified.

Of course, they would always look at each other and say, "Oh, yeah, this is our guy." But they always made damned sure. Tyrus always said it was better to make no arrest than a false arrest. That was the product of growing up African American in 1980s Detroit.

He knew that Scott's motto was "A competent investigator seeks not only the evidence that proves that somebody has committed or has been committing a crime but also the evidence that will exonerate the innocent." Ty's motto was always "It ain't what you know, Doggy. It's what you can prove in court." Of course, the motto that kept them going day and night was something Scott always said: "When there is a need for an investigation, there is a victim in need of an investigator." The combination of the philosophies made for an outstanding investigative team.

Scott's current partner, Oswaldo Castaneda, was no Tyrus Phillips. Scott and Oswaldo worked great together, but Scott would say of Oswaldo, "Bless his little heart of gold." Oswaldo was born and raised in Mexico, somewhere near Mexico City. He found that the best path to American citizenship was the army and jumping out of perfectly sound airplanes. He was a solid worker, but focus can be an issue—that and a sketchy memory. His favorite sayings were either "Squared away" and

"You're golden" when critical evidence was discovered or "Two to the chest, two to the head."

To make matters more interesting, Oswaldo was the sniper on the SWAT team and a solid marksman. He was also the narcotic detection canine handler at the prison, and this was where he shone; there was no better team than Oswaldo and Ruud, his Dutch shepherd. Unlike Ty, Oswaldo called Scott "Scotty." Scott called him "Oz," an obvious reference to the movie. Somehow Scott could picture Oswaldo saying, "I am Oz, the Great and Terrible."

Don't get Scott wrong; he would do anything for the little bugger. One day Oswaldo called Scott at home and said, "Scotty, Josue Ortega just moved into my condo complex, and they haven't finished my custom .45 yet." Knowing that Josue "Trigger" Ortega was a local gang shot caller recently paroled from a northern California maximum security prison commonly known as the Bay, Scott hopped in his car and delivered to Oz one of his favorite Government Model 1911-A1s and three magazines of .45 ACP ammo. Now that was a friend.

For all of Oz's five foot seven inches and buck-thirty pounds, he can take down an inmate like nobody's business, and Scott can depend on him in a fight and when clearing a house during a search warrant. One habit that drove Scott crazy about Oz was he talked very rapidly in what Scott liked to call "five-round bursts." Oz said he developed this habit in an effort to avoid being the radio operator for his army company. "They always kill the lieutenant and his radio operator first," he would tell Scott. It worked, but the side effect was that everyone was constantly asking him to repeat himself.

Chapter 3

A Warrant Is Served

It was the morning after the riot, and Scott was blurry eyed and half asleep. "I need those riot reports, and I need them now!" bellowed his boss, Lt. John Templeton. "Headquarters is breathing down my neck."

"I'm working on it, Lieutenant, but it's going to be a twenty-pager at least," Scott snapped back, adding, "But after, I gotta run into town and get a warrant signed."

"Just give me that damned report ASAP and tell me about the warrant later," the lieutenant snorted.

Good to his word, Scott was done in three hours—twenty-two pages as promised, complete with narrative, crime scene sketches, and evidence and photo logs. "Why did I shoot 348 frames?" he muttered. Every photographic frame had to be documented with a brief description. It was like being a caption writer for a newspaper: "Frame 1—Overview of crime scene with blood-spattered, broken crutch near west corner of steam line." Even the frames where the flash misfired had to be documented. Every photograph taken in a crime scene had to be documented, whether it was in focus or not, and every photograph was subject to the rules of discovery. Scott didn't delete anything, and he didn't take a photograph that wasn't provided to the defense as evidence.

The search warrant was an easy one. Oswaldo and Scott had been watching Inmate Felix Perez for some time. A lot of money was being

15

sent from the relatives of other inmates at the Central Facility to Perla Perez, the wife of Inmate Perez. They had done surveillance on Perez for several months, and they had spotted him on the yard telephones several times and listened in on the conversations. It was your usual coded inmate drug dealer talk. "The weather is fine, although the wind is from the west. The three black tires are ready, and the wife will take the green truck to the garage on Saturday and have them installed." To the average tower officer monitoring the telephone call, it sounded like a boring conversation about a car. To the seasoned prison drug investigator, it sounded more like a dope-smuggling operation.

Now the only thing to do was to convince a judge that the wind from the west meant that his wife had made contact with a dope dealer in San Francisco and that she acquired three ounces of black tar heroin, the black tires for the car, and some marijuana, the green truck, which she would conceal in her vaginal cavity, the garage, and smuggle into the institution on the upcoming Saturday. That was where the years of training and experience paid off. Scott had the conspiracy, two or more persons conspiring to commit an illegal act, and he had the overt act—she picked up the "tires" for the car and was coming for a visit. The probable cause was sufficient to get past DDA Elizabeth Jennings, and the warrant was signed by the Honorable Judge Herbert Fielding of the superior court to be served on Perla Perez when she arrived at the institution.

On the following morning, Perla arrived at the institution for a regular contact visit with her husband. The visitor's processing center staff called Scott at his desk, and Scott went out with one of the female investigators, Becky Romero, and met with Perla. Scott informed her that he had a search warrant signed by the judge, and it commanded the prison staff to search her person, property, and vehicle. She was escorted in handcuffs to an interview building where she was provided with a copy of the warrant and instructed to be cooperative, to follow the instructions of the female officers, and to voluntarily surrender any contraband that she had brought to the institution, or she would be taken to a hospital where a medical professional would conduct an intrusive search. Perla agreed to cooperate, and the provisions of that warrant were satisfied.

Oswaldo ran Ruud through the car, and there were several alerts that told Scott that she did, in fact, pick up the drugs. In fact, Perla didn't give them much trouble. Scott thought she was glad that her nightmare was over. She was escorted into an adjacent search room where she was subjected to an unclothed body search by Becky and Elisa. Scott was standing on the outside of the closed door of the strip room with Oswaldo when he heard Becky say, "Hey, that doesn't belong in there. Take that out and give it to me right now." Oswaldo looked at Scott and held up his right thumb.

Becky instructed Perla to withdraw the large latex-wrapped, blood-covered bindle from her vaginal cavity and surrender it voluntarily. Perla complied and handed it to Becky, who immediately stuck her head out the door yelling, "Somebody take this thing now!" Scott gave Oswaldo the privilege of processing the smelly bindle into evidence. Just shy of three ounces of black tar heroin, as expected, and a half ounce of marijuana were concealed in a bindle the size of a small burrito. Once dressed, Perla was escorted back into the interview room, where Scott advised her of her rights pursuant to the *Miranda* decision. Perla acknowledged these rights and elected to make a full confession.

She informed Scott that her husband had asked her to bring the drugs into the prison but that the drugs were not for him. She said that he was heavily in debt to another inmate at the Central Facility and was smuggling drugs into the prison to resolve the debt. She did not know the name of the inmate to whom he was in debt. The amount of drugs that she had brought that day had a combined prison value of $25,000. From the investigation, Scott knew that this was likely her third load and that they had already collected somewhere in the neighborhood of $40,000.

Perla was placed under arrest for a violation of California Penal Code section 4573.6, possession of narcotics on state prison grounds, a felony, and 11352(b) of the Health and Safety Codes, transportation of narcotics across noncontiguous county lines, also a felony. And she was transported to the local jail. Inmate Perez was rehoused in the administrative segregation unit, commonly called the Hole by the inmates, pending the outcome of the investigation. All was right with the world.

Oswaldo and Scott had done it again, and the only thing remaining was to light the votive candles to the dope gods for their good fortune and to assemble the case for prosecution. This can sometimes be harder than the actual investigation itself, but they occupied the following week with the various duties of transcribing interviews and recorded telephone calls and assembling the documents into a court file for the district attorney's office.

Inmate Perez was a three-time loser. In the early '90's, he got caught coming across the San Diego border crossing with sixty kilos of powder cocaine in a hidden compartment in his Chevy step-side pickup truck. He was paroled in 1998 and promptly killed the man he thought snitched him out to the DEA. For added effect, he killed the man's wife too. Sadly, there never was an informant. The customs officials at the border found the dope from the routine detention and inspection of the vehicle; short-bed pickup trucks generally, as a rule, did not have two gas tanks. This new case would probably add another six years to his sentence with a plea agreement. Some might think that it was a waste of taxpayer money to prosecute an inmate already doing two life sentences for a "minor" dope infraction. The way Scott looked at it, you never knew when an appeals court ruling might overturn the earlier convictions or when some misguided board of prison terms panelist might grant an early parole; and therefore, they needed to protect the public for at least another six years.

Perla, on the other hand, was looking at upward of twelve years for her part. She was a convicted felon herself, having served a four-year prison term for her part in the 1998 homicides. Apparently, she lured the husband and wife to the place where her husband waited with a handgun. So if she went to jury trial on this charge and the prosecution was successful in getting a conviction, she was looking at the middle term doubled with a previous strike; that would be twelve years. That was why drugs had such a high prison value; there was an inherent risk in getting caught. After all, on prison grounds was the only place where you can still be charged with a felony for having less than a gram of marijuana on your person—at least for now.

Chapter 4

Tarantella

The next few weeks passed without anything of major significance happening. Springtime had settled on the valley, and the hills that surrounded the prison were plush with green grasses, yellow wild mustard, purple lupines, and the bright orange of the California poppies. The sunshine, mild temperatures, and pastoral beauty of the foothills surrounding the prison seemed to have a calming effect on the inmates as they spent most of their time basking in the sunshine and playing sports. It was like this every year at this time. Unfortunately, the peace never lasted.

It was Friday afternoon, and Scott reminded his lieutenant that he would be out of town on the weekend. It was his mother's seventy-fifth birthday, and he wasn't going to miss the opportunity to gather with the family, consume some Chianti, serenade Mama with old Italian songs, and dance the tarantella. His lieutenant didn't have any objections as this was a good time of year for his weary staff to have a break; the inmates were pacified with bucolic idleness, and it was the lull in the drug season before the marijuana harvest ramped up. That was when Scott made his first critical mistake: "If anything happens, Lieutenant, just call me."

Saturday morning came with a crisp sunshine that had the promise of a beautiful day that could only be found on the California coast.

As he loaded his luggage into the trunk of the car, Scott could hear the barking of the juvenile male sea lions hungry for a liaison with an eligible female counterpart. Sadly for them, all the girls had swum out to deeper water and were frolicking with the more mature males. It would only be a matter of time before the passions of the horny youth would lead to the biting and ramming that was not uncommon to the prison yard. Scott guessed he'd have to miss that because he was heading about two hundred miles inland to see the family.

Scott had a big Italian family that stayed, for the most part, in the same area. He was the only one to wander away. He was the second youngest with four brothers and two sisters. As with any Italian family, Scott spent the better part of his childhood fighting with his brothers. In fact, Scott guessed you could say that he spent the better part of his life trying to be an only child, and there were a few times when he got pretty damned close. It was funny to think about it now; back then, it was common for a large Italian family like his to settle disputes with a round of fisticuffs. The brothers were always self-disciplining. There was rarely a need for the parents to step in, that is, until it was absolutely necessary for Mama to run in with the big wooden spoon and break up the melee. Now that Scott thought about it, his mom was single-handedly putting down prison riots long before he ever did.

His dad never hit any of his children. He didn't have to; he had his henchmen, Scott's elder brothers, who were empowered with the authority to react without prior authorization. He did, however, employ a psychological warfare that was brilliant. Scott remembered one day when his brothers and he were engaged in a particularly brutal disciplinary action when his dad came home from work. He took one look at the brawling bunch and said something to the effect that they just didn't love him anymore. He promptly went down to the master bedroom, packed a suitcase, and left the house without saying another word. After the third day, the brawling brothers were in tears and assembled as a delegation to petition his mother to ask his father to come back home, to inform him that they were sorry and that they would never act like a pack of horny juvenile male sea lions ever again. Scott's mother took one look at them and said, "Are you kids crazy? Your father is on a business trip. He'll be home tomorrow." It was so masterful and yet so simple in its application.

Scott thought back on those days, and there were two valuable lessons that he learned. He was never afraid to get scrappy with an inmate, and he learned how to settle disputes with his fists instead of a gun or a knife. He thought this lesson was tragically missed by the modern youth of our communities. Of course, nowadays, if you fought with your brothers the way Scott fought with his, you'd get yourself arrested for sure.

Scott eased his 1996 green British racing Jaguar XJS onto the freeway and leisurely made his way north. Eventually, he merged onto Highway 101 and set the cruise control. After about thirty minutes, he settled into the first act of Puccini's *La bohème*, his father's favorite opera. This recording was with his favorite tenor, Jussi Björling, and mezzo-soprano Victoria de los Angeles. His father and Scott had many disagreements over tenors and just who held the title of "the second Enrico Caruso." Jussi Björling was Scott's favorite and always would be, but for his father, it was all things Mario Lanza. He would call Björling a Swedish meatball, and Scott would call Lanza a washed-up pizza delivery boy.

Opera wasn't the only thing in which they were of opposite opinions. His father always supported his beloved 49ers, and Scott was a lifelong Green Bay Packers fan. In college football, his father always took Pitt, and Scott took Penn; Scott took USC, and his father took UCLA. For some reason, they both agreed on the Dodgers mostly because of Tommy Lasorda, and neither of them gave a rat's hoop for basketball.

It was a gorgeous day, and Scott's mind was wandering far from the institution and the endless abundance of criminal activity. Scott pulled into a gas station, began pumping the gold liquid into the thirsty cat, picked up the cell phone, and called his eldest sister. "Sonya," he said, "I'm on my way. I should be there in about two hours. How's Mom?" Before she had the opportunity to reply, Scott heard the pulse of an incoming call. "Hold on a minute, Sonya. I got another call. In fact, I'll call you right back." Scott clicked over to the awaiting call.

"Dog, I'm glad you answered. It's Ty." He didn't have to tell Scott who it was; he knew the voice, and he knew that only one person could ruin his day off.

"Oh no, Tyrus, Tyrus, Tyrus, what have you done?" he asked.

"It's not what I did. It's what Inmate Pajaro did or rather what he failed to do, which was to run."

"Pajaro? Why does that name sound familiar?" Scott inquired.

"Danny Pajaro. You were helping San Diego Homicide with him last year" was his response.

"Oh, yeah, yeah, I remember," Scott said. "What happened?"

"He's dead, Dog, on the Central Yard, and the lieutenant wants you back here fast."

"Crap! Ty, it's my mother's . . . fine, fine, I'm on my way. Tell him I will be there in an hour, providing the CHP doesn't pull me over. Preserve the crime scene. I'm on my way." Scott returned the nozzle to the pump and called his sister back. "Sonya, let me talk to Mom."

The Central Facility Yard was huge. It was the largest exercise yard in the California state prison system. It measured 314,080 square feet. That was more than six regulation-size football fields placed three abreast and two deep. On this yard was an assortment of sporting venues that kept the inmates occupied during the day. These included, but were not limited to, a basketball court, tennis court, soccer field, football field, baseball diamond, handball courts, horseshoe pits, and an area with exercise equipment like sit-up benches, bar dips, and pull-up bars. The inmates lost their weight piles in 1996 after an act of legislation that banned them.

A few dear grandmother types were beaten up and robbed in the state capitol by two recent parolees. When the Sacramento newspaper showed photographs of the parolees scrawny and skinny before they went to prison and big and buffed when they came out, public sentiment over the iron piles turned ugly. The Central Facility lost its weight pile three years earlier when Inmate Juan Campos got his brains separated from his cranium with a forty-five-pound dumbbell. Poor fellow didn't heed the advice of the Asian inmates who warned him not to exercise in "their" area.

On any Saturday, there are about 1,100 inmates milling about the yard supervised only by three correctional officers on the ground and the officers in four guard towers. Generally, it was a quiet yard. There were a lot of lifers housed at the Central Facility who liked their program undisturbed. They usually kept the younger inmates from upsetting the administration who might impose a long-term lockdown. Apparently, the lifers turned a blind eye to Danny Pajaro, a lifer himself.

There was a difference between an inmate and a convict. A convict came to prison before the influx of prisoners that resulted from the advent of the violent street gangs in the mid-1980s. Convicts were more likely to be associated with the prison gangs like the Black Guerilla Family, the Mexican Mafia, the Nuestra Familia, and the Aryan Brotherhood than with the street disruptive groups they spawned. Danny Pajaro was a convict.

In the late 1970s, Danny was convicted of the kidnapping and slaying of a wealthy newspaper owner in Los Angeles. While in San Quentin, he joined the Mexican Mafia and committed two more murders in the prison yard. He was a dope dealer who was always making his presence known to Oz and Scott. As Tyrus had reminded Scott, he had helped San Diego Homicide with a cold case homicide that they were hoping to link to Danny. "I'll call them on Monday and give them the news, good or bad."

Scott stopped by the office; grabbed his radio, crime scene kits, and a camera kit; and made his way to the Central Facility. It was a lot to carry, but Scott had always been a beast of burden, and it was a balanced load. Scott contemplated bringing his bloodstain pattern analysis bag, but he figured there would be time to get it later, or maybe, just maybe, Oz would offer to help.

Although more than an hour had passed since Scott got the call, there was still much activity in the central corridor. Inmates were under escort, being led from various work assignments back to their cells. Scott could hear the slamming of gates and the distinct sound of Folger Adam keys turning tumblers in each of the housing units as they secured their cellblocks for what would be a lengthy lockdown. Once the lockdown was in effect, there would be absolutely no inmate movement outside of medical needs, which would be under direct escort.

The watch commander was busy making his notifications and getting preliminary reports from his sergeants and responding officers. "Dog, the coroner has been notified, and he is sending out an investigator," said Lt. Randall Petersen as Scott walked past. "He should be here in about thirty minutes."

"Is the body still on the yard?" Scott asked.

"What do you think?" was his reply. They had always had a problem with their medical personnel moving dead bodies from the crime scene. No matter how many meetings they had with their chief medical officer, they just didn't understand that the body didn't belong to them; it belonged to the coroner's office. If there were no lifesaving measures employed, that body must stay put. He ain't going to be any less dead in the infirmary. One of these days, a frustrated coroner's investigator was going to arrest somebody in the medical department, and Scott was going to laugh his fool head off. Served them right too. They just didn't understand how much physical evidence was being lost by moving the decedent.

"Did they at least bag his hands? What about his clothing?" Scott asked. A double negative was the reply. However, Lieutenant Petersen had the foresight to instruct medical personnel to put the body in a room and leave him there untouched. He then posted an officer at the door to make sure nobody entered.

Scott keyed the microphone of his radio and asked Ty for his location. The radio returned with "Middle of the yard."

"Ty, I need to run up to medical and deal with the body for a minute. Hold on out there for a few more minutes."

"Ten-four, but hurry" was his reply.

Scott made his way up the corridor to the medical department. As Scott was about to enter, he heard the radio call of the tower no. 1 officer informing the watch commander that the coroner's investigator had arrived. Scott decided to meet him at the East Gate sally port.

The coroner's investigator Tom Jenks was closer to retirement than Scott by about two years. Tom had been with the sheriff's office for thirty years and had been the lead investigator for the coroner's office for nearly half those years. He was a tall man, somewhat gaunt, with deep linear smoker's lines running along each side of his mouth. He had silver hair, a gray mustache, an awkwardly large nose, and a quiet, almost taciturn disposition, but he was the best in his field. "Please tell me the body is still in the crime scene" was the first thing he said as he got out of his all-white slick-top Crown Vic.

"No, Tom, sorry," Scott said reluctantly.

"Goddamn it, Scott! What do I have to do to get your staff to stop moving the body?"

"Ya want my handcuffs, Tom? It's the only way they will ever listen."

"Don't tempt me, Scott. I swear I will do it."

"I was just on my way to get some photos of our decedent, collect the clothes, and bag the hands. You showed up just in time."

"Good a place as any to start. Lead the way," he said as he gathered up the tools of his trade. Tom and Scott made their way up to the medical department. Scott filled him in with as much of the history of Inmate Pajaro as he knew, but he told him he had not yet been briefed on the circumstances of the death.

Officer Ryan Walker was standing guard in front of emergency room no. 3. The drapes had been drawn, and the lights were turned out. As they approached, Officer Walker raised his clipboard and readied his pen. "Investigator Doggett and Coroner's Investigator Jenks," Scott said. The officer made his notation, unlocked the door, and allowed Tom and Scott to enter the room.

"Has anyone else been in this room?" asked the grizzled coroner's investigator.

"No, sir, you are the first since they put him in there."

"Okay," Tom replied. "Once we are done, I don't want anyone else in this room until my assistant gets here, understand?"

"Yes, sir," was the response from the stalwart officer as he stepped to attention.

Scott closed the door and switched on the lights. He set down his equipment and lifted the Nikon D7100 digital camera from its case. Scott snapped on the bounce-flash and looked over at Tom, who was also preparing his camera in the same manner. They both turned and took their first look at the recently departed inmate Danny Pajaro. Firing off frames, they began their photo documentation of the decedent.

Tom switched on his digital voice recorder. "Male, Hispanic, approximately five nine in height, and well nourished. Approximate age is fifty-two."

Scott interrupted for a moment, "Fifty-four."

Tom continued, "Numerous stab wounds to the chest and torso penetrating the T-shirt and what appears to be an incised wound to his neck."

"That might actually be a wire or something that cut into his throat," Scott added.

"Possibly, Scott. Here are some defensive injuries on the medial crease of the right ring finger and the distal phalanx of the little finger that might have been caused by the same wire. There is also minor petechiae right here in the lower right eyelid."

"I agree," Scott said. "And look at the left eye, Tom, the start of tache noire."

"The line of death," replied the seasoned investigator, "evidence of exsanguination—he bled out. Let's get the clothes off and bagged, and we can get a better look at these stab wounds and check out his back."

Scott acknowledged his request, donned latex gloves, and secured paper bags over each of the deceased's hands. Scott then meticulously photographed, itemized, and inventoried all of Danny's clothing, wrapping each item in clean waxed butcher's paper and placing them into individual evidence bags. Scott placed the shoes in an evidence box, otherwise known as a boot box, that he procured from the clothing room. The left pant leg of the blue denim jeans, the T-shirt, and the state-issued blue chambray shirt were too blood soaked to be sealed. He would need to hang them in a forensic dryer and allow them to air-dry. In the meantime, Scott wrapped each in the butcher's paper to collect any evidence that might come loose in transport.

Tom and Scott continued the photo documentation of the condition of the body and its various clues as they moved around in a macabre dance, each knowing instinctively when to fire a flash without destroying the frame of the other. "Looks like an ice-pick-type weapon here in his chest and a double-edged, bladed weapon on the lower rib cage and stomach area," Scott said, adding, "Here, Tom, use my ABFO scale."

"I think this one pierced his aorta," Tom said thoughtfully. There was nothing of note on the back or other extremities aside from bruising and the onset of lividity.

They returned their cameras into the safety of their cases, and Scott helped Tom place the body into a white coroner's body bag. "These are nice, Tom. Are they new?"

"Yeah," he replied. "We decided it was time to switch to a disposable bag. They are expensive, but there's no cross contamination." Tom zipped the bag closed, borrowed Scott's Sharpie, and wrote "Inmate D. Pajaro—State prison" on the outside of the bag.

As Scott had his hands full of evidence bags, Tom helped him carry his equipment back to the office, where he properly processed all the clothing into evidence. Afterward, they made their way out to the Central Yard, with Tom carrying Scott's bloodstain kit. They passed through the West Gate and crossed the small path leading to the yard.

Officer Steve Rothenberg opened the yard gate and allowed them entrance. Looking to the west, Scott could see the crime scene tape Tyrus had used as a barrier, stretching from the basketball court to the canteen, an area of about sixty square yards. It was a sunny day, but a slight wind was picking up, and Scott knew it would grow stronger as the sun set. The wind picked up off the Pacific Ocean, which was only about twenty miles to the west as the crow flew. The Santa Lucia mountain range separated the prison from the ocean, but this was also the cause of the winds as the sea breezes whipped around both ends of the mountain and combined in the center into a zephyr that rolled directly through the prison.

Once Tom was finished with his inspection of the crime scene, Scott knew that he would have to move quickly to preserve any transient evidence. "How many inmates are on the yard right now, Steve?" Scott asked.

"Ninety hundred fifty—minus one" was his reply.

"Great, 949 eyewitnesses who saw nothing" was Scott's retort. Scott looked out at the yard and noticed that a half-dozen garden hoses had been stretched across the soccer field. "Are those garden hoses still running?" Scott asked.

"Been going since this morning. I don't have the key to turn them off," apologized the officer, who was already two hours past his regular shift.

"Who does?" Scott inquired.

"Shorty, my inmate yard worker. He was near the West Gate when this all happened, and they put him in Fox Wing before they brought out the code 2 responders."

"Steve, I need the water off now," he said with emphasis. "It's heading straight for the crime scene. Take care of it for me not now but right now."

"You got it, Dog," was his reply as he closed the gate behind and walked toward the West Gate.

The officers in the four guard towers were standing at attention with their Ruger Mini-14 assault rifles in the port arms position. Scott turned around and observed the central roof gunner standing in the West Gate roof gun shack. Scott gave a slight wave, and she waved back.

They then walked the seventy-five yards to where Tyrus was standing. When he reached the halfway mark, they were approached by Sergeant Robert Brandon. His uniform shirt was covered in blood. "He died in my arms, Scott. There wasn't anything I could do. He was walking straight for me, and I could see in his eyes that he wanted me to help him, but there was nothing. His eyes rolled back, and he let out a gasp, and that was it." Sergeant Brandon looked totally spent emotionally and physically.

Scott put his hand on his shoulder and said, "You did all you could do, Rob. He bled out. He knew that too. How far do you think he walked?"

"From the basketball court to the canteen. I was standing at the west corner of the building. When Pajaro saw me, he started walking in my direction. Pajaro got about a hundred feet or so when he reached out and stumbled. I caught him before he hit the ground. I'd say he walked almost forty yards."

"Forty yards," remarked Tom. "In his condition, that would have been quite an effort."

"Rob, I'm going to need that shirt in evidence," Scott added.

"I'll go do it right now, and then I have to start my report. I was already on a sixteen-hour shift when this happened. I'll be here at least another three or four hours. Man, am I tired." Sergeant Brandon walked off like a zombie toward the yard gate.

Tom and Scott stood there for a minute, looking around at the hundreds of inmates sitting on the yard. "I wonder which two are our suspects," Scott pondered.

"Or three," added Tom.

They made their way over to where Tyrus was standing. "So, Ty, exactly what do we have?" Scott asked.

"All we know right now, Doggy, is that Pajaro was walking somewhere over there on the track behind the basketball court when somebody stabbed him. He then walked south to the end of the court and then southeast toward the canteen, where he collapsed. Brandon put the yard down and called for medical, but there wasn't anything they could do."

"Then I should have a pretty good blood drip trail to follow. Anything good in the crime scene?" Scott inquired.

"I haven't really taken a good look yet, but I can tell you, most of your blood trail is gone. Somebody decided to move about seventy inmates from the southwest corner of the yard, and they walked them straight through the area that Pajaro walked to get to the canteen. And don't say anything because it happened before I got here."

"For the love of Pete, Ty, that's another thing we'll have to explain to the jury. First, they move the body and now this. And if I don't get these damned garden hoses turned off soon, we might as well just grab our gear and go home."

"Whatever we do, we better hurry," responded Tyrus. "The winds are picking up. Oh, and Alex Rowland is on his way out. He should be here in a few minutes. We might as well wait until he gets here."

The district attorney's office investigator Alex Rowland was a tall Texas native with a sluggish drawl and a friendly demeanor. Everybody, to Alex, was a buddy. He retired as a sergeant from a small police department and went to work for the DA's office investigations division. His specialty was gang-related homicides. If there was a homicide anywhere in the county, Alex was usually the first to take the call. He was also Scott's neighbor by about two blocks and a master at the barbecue grill. By his accent, you'd expect him to show up in a cowboy hat and boots, Levi's, and a buckskin shirt and pack a couple of six-shooters. Actually, you'd more likely to find him in a $3,000 Italian designer suit. He did, however, favor his eel-skin cowboy boots.

There were a few things that Alex did these days that probably wouldn't sit just right with his Texas kinfolk. He was a bodybuilder and surfer in the California tradition, which wasn't bad for his fifty-eight years, and he ran in the local marathon. It was probably the only time he didn't wear those boots.

No sooner had Tom and Scott finished taking the overview photographs of the crime scene and yard than he saw Oswaldo walking in his direction with Alex in tow. Upon their arrival and the usual "Howdy, buddy," from Alex, Scott briefed them with as much information as he had at the time. Scott told Oswaldo to assemble a crew and start canvassing for witnesses and suspects. Scott also told him to get a video camera team together and start documenting all the inmates on the yard to get eight grid maps of the yard and every inmate in position in that sector by positive identification, a task Scott knew would keep him busy for several hours. He raised the yellow crime scene tape, and Tyrus, Tom, Alex, and Scott stepped into the crime scene.

The crime scene included the basketball court, the adjacent track area, and a grassy area between the track and the first of the two perimeter fences. It also included the path that Inmate Pajaro circumnavigated on his way to the canteen, a single-story brick building where the inmates can buy various snack items using script. This boomerang-shaped path was through a grassy area between the basketball court and a volleyball sandpit. Scott selected a pathway through the crime scene that would have caused the least amount of destruction of any physical evidence, but it was already apparent that responding staff had already trudged through the area, possibly looking for the weapons. Alex was the first to notice a series of footwear impressions on the track almost at the halfway point between tower no. 3 and tower no. 4, at the southwest and northwest corners of the yard respectively. It appeared to be one stationary set of impressions that pointed in the direction of the basketball court and were surrounded by two different sets of impressions. Subsequent impressions left by the two different shoes displayed movement, and the first set changed to impressions consistent with a dragging motion that was discernable by the distinct deep heel marks of someone being pulled in the direction of the fence line.

There in the grass, directly in front of the chain-link perimeter fence, was where they found the first evidence of a bloodletting event. Bloodstain spatter was evident on the chain links of the fence, consistent with a narrow stream from a projected arterial spurt. On the grass below was spatter consistent with blood striking the ground at a ninety-degree angle. This was the spot where he was stabbed. Of that there was no doubt.

Scott noticed that where they stood, he could not see either tower. The inmates had found a blind spot in the fence line. The prison had stood for more than fifty years, but it was only now that the inmates had discovered a weakness. Because of the length of the fence, which produced a slight bowing effect and rust that had deposited on the face of the chain links, it appeared that this was the perfect place to commit a murder. A quick check with both tower officers confirmed his suspicion. They would be able to see someone going over the fence and, likewise, under because of the no-man's zone between the perimeter fences, but they could not see the four good-sized investigators who stood in that part of the crime scene. Neither did they see the assault that took place here earlier in the day.

One could imagine Danny Pajaro walking around the track that surrounded the playing fields. Perhaps he was with two people he trusted and thought were friends. Maybe he stopped to talk to them. He was facing the basketball court, where a game was being played, which prevented the officers in tower no. 2 at the southeast corner of the yard and tower no. 5 at the northeast corner from seeing. It was likely that here was where a thin wire was slipped around his neck like a garrote and that he was dragged backward into the blind spot near the inner perimeter fence, where his assailants stabbed at him with ferocious intensity.

Now which way did they go? They knew Danny walked toward the canteen. Scott's guess was that the assailants didn't go in the same direction as the victim. Therefore, they went north or northeast along the dirt track. They crossed the track, being careful not to disturb any footwear impressions, and came to the edge of the concrete basketball court. There, Scott noticed the first of a series of blood drops consistent with dripping either from the hand of one of the assailants or off the blade of one of the weapons. These blood drops were consistent with one of the suspects walking across the very top of the court where it intersected with the tennis court, perhaps around the players as they shot at the north basket or intercepted a rebound, and onto the playing field leading toward the northeast area of the yard and tower no. 5. That was where they ended.

To be sure that Scott actually found blood, he took a sample of the very edge of one of the drops and conducted a presumptive test using the phenolphthalein method. The swab quickly turned to a pink, showing a positive result for blood. The next step was to see if it was human blood. Scott collected another small sample and used the Hexagon OBTI immunochromatographic rapid test, which confirmed they were looking at blood consistent with the human species.

At this time, Tom had excused himself and left the crime scene to meet with his assistant, who had arrived to collect the body. The coroner's office was interested in the body and in having just a rudimentary understanding of the crime scene. They were not equipped to process a crime scene. "When's the autopsy, Tom?" Scott asked.

He replied, "Tuesday morning at 0930 hours, Scott. I'll see you there."

Alex too decided he had seen enough of the crime scene and wanted to take a good look at the body before it was whisked away. "Send me your report as soon as you can, buddy, and keep me updated on what you find" was his parting comment.

Scott looked over at Tyrus and asked, "You going to leave me too?"

"Not in your life. We're in this together, but I do think I'll go outside the prison and take a look in that grassy area to the west of the yard and see if I can find a weapon. You never know, they might have flung it over the fence."

"You might want to stop by the office and get a metal detector," Scott advised. "It might be quicker. That grass is pretty tall. Get old Bertha. She's the biggest detector we have, and it covers a nice swath. Bertha's been around since the 1960s. I think she saw action in 'Nam. If it's going to be found, Bertha will find it."

Scott set to work photographing, putting down evidence markers, and mapping the bloodstain patterns. After about forty-five minutes, Scott looked up and saw Tyrus on the other side of the fence. He was sweeping back and forth with big Bertha with the eagerness of a soldier sweeping a minefield. Scott went back to work prepping his swabs for collecting control samples and bloodstain specimen.

After about ten minutes, Scott looked back over at Tyrus to see how he had progressed. There he was, standing perfectly still almost parallel to Scott with a giant grin on his face. He waved his free hand, bent over, and picked up a long wire with two wooden dowels on each end that acted as handles. Scott pointed back in his direction with a smile and a nod while muttering to himself, "Okay, Ty, put the nice piece of evidence back down." Tyrus put it back among the weeds and California poppies, stuck an evidence flag in the ground next to it, and went back to sweeping.

Scott thought to himself that maybe there was a third attacker after all. Scott couldn't see any feasible way of casting the footwear impressions; the dirt track was too hard to leave a deep impression. Basically, he was looking at patterns in dust; only dust can be lifted when it was on a hard surface. This was a dirt surface and not practical for lifting. The best method of preservation would be through photography, and Scott had to work fast because the wind was against him.

Scott got out his trusty tripod and mounted his camera so that it was suspended upside down between the legs. Scott attached the flash by a slave cord so that he could direct the light to highlight different areas, and he dropped a scale. Scott liked to put a golfer's ball marker inverted in the corner of the scale to allow the analyst to know which way the flash dropped its light by looking at the direction of the shadow from the marker's peg. That way, they can tell the difference between a deep furrow and a shadow.

Then Scott tried to mist the impressions with an acrylic spray with some success. Scott mixed a batch of casting material and poured it into the casting frames that he had placed around the impressions. After an hour of drying, he pried up the casts; he was right, it didn't work. Good thing Scott had the photographs. Becky, who had been Oz's videographer, walked up and helped Scott get his triangulations and measurements for the crime scene sketch before she left to process her videotapes into evidence.

It was approaching seven o'clock at night, and the light was nearly gone. Oswaldo had finished his cataloging of inmates, and the watch commander was conducting an orderly recall of the yard. Complete strip-outs were being done in the central corridor. The officers were looking for the slightest indication of an inmate being involved in an assault. Tyrus didn't find anything else out there in his field, and Scott gave him the task of processing the garrote into evidence. That included photographing, sketching, measuring, and documenting his find.

Afterward, the three of them assembled in the middle of the yard, and a decision was made to post an officer at the West Gate and to deny entry of anyone onto the yard. To be absolutely certain that no trespassing would occur, Scott put a chain and one of his boot lock padlocks for which only he had the key on the yard gate. They would resume their inspection and processing of any evidence in the morning. The only contamination would be from the feral cats who freely roamed the yard. Hopefully, they would avoid the areas marked by the crime scene tape.

In the following morning, Tyrus, Oswaldo, and Scott met at the pedestrian gate. Scott removed the lock, and they walked out onto the yard. Nothing appeared disturbed, and the tower officers reported minimal feral cat activity during the night. They were expecting an aerial ladder truck from the local fire department to make a stop so that they could get some good all-encompassing photographs of the crime scene. It was either that or call on the highway patrol and their helicopter.

The fire truck showed up at the arranged time, and Oswaldo volunteered to brave the heights. The truck parked in the same area where Tyrus had found the garrote and extended its ladder over the perimeter fences. Oswaldo made his way out of the prison and over to where the truck was standing. Tyrus and Scott walked to the northwest corner of the yard and examined the area to the north of the crime scene between the tennis court and tower no. 4. They stood there for a few minutes, watching Oswaldo as he climbed hand over hand up the ladder and peered over the edge. He then began fiddling with the camera. "If he drops that camera, I will kill him," Scott said to Tyrus.

They slowly made their way east toward the latrines and tower no. 5, inspecting every garbage can, garment, table, and bench. Every few steps, Scott turned back to see what Oswaldo was doing. He had finished his task and, after failing to persuade the firemen to let him rappel from the ladder to the yard, was descending from the dizzying height in a mundane manner, rung by rung. Within ten minutes, he had joined Scott and Tyrus as they approached the latrine area.

The inmate yard latrines were built during the early 1980s in the grassy area among the softball backstop, the bank of yard telephones, the track, and the grassy area in front of tower no. 5 in the northeast corner of the yard. It was built in a time when it was thought to be more prudent for an inmate to have privacy while conducting his toilet business than with the ideology of a high-security prison. It was built with high walls and slats that prevented the observant eyes of the tower officer from seeing in. It was also more than three hundred yards from the crime scene.

It was here that Tyrus found two isolated drops of blood. One was on the concrete floor directly in front of toilet number three, and the other was on the toilet seat itself. Evidence of blood mixed with water was present in the sink closest to the shower area. "Well, Ty," Scott as he looked into the toilet said, "I guess we know where at least one, if not both, of the shanks went."

"Right in front of the tower too," replied Tyrus with more disgust for the construction of the latrine and the boneheaded decision to protect inmate privacy than with the tower officer himself. "I swear I am going to have this thing torn down if it is the last thing I do." He said it with determination.

"You know, Ty, let me get some photos, and we can knock it down together."

Just then, Oswaldo—who had joined them on the yard—let out a eureka-type holler. He followed it with "Hey, Scotty, look what I found in the garbage can!" Of course, he said it in five-round bursts. Tyrus and Scott walked over to where Oswaldo was standing between the latrine and the telephone bank. He tilted the garbage can back enough to let the sunlight in. He peered inside and saw the unmistakable cluster of bloodstained state-issued denim pants mixed with a bloodstained blue chambray shirt.

"Don't touch it, Oz. Let me get it all documented first," Scott said. The secondary crime scene was established, documented, photographed, mapped, and sketched complete with measurements. Scott collected swabs from the blood drops and the bloodstains mixed with water, and for extra precision, he collected the shower drain cover into evidence as well. The garbage can produced a treasure of a pair of bloodstained pants and a blood-spattered shirt.

"There's our DNA, right there, Oz. Good find," Scott said. "Just as important is what is missing."

"Uh, the weapon?" asked Oswaldo.

The answer came from Tyrus. "The shoes."

"That's right," Scott chimed in. "The bastard still has the shoes that left that print, and we need to find them. How many inmates do you think were in this grid, Oz?"

"Two hundred, maybe 230" was his reply.

"Beats 950," snapped Tyrus.

"Still, we don't know how long it took to put the yard down or how far this guy was able to walk before he changed his clothes. Jeez, Ty, he managed to get all the way from over there to here, clean up and change, and dump the clothes before Brandon put the yard down. It's amazing," Scott said.

"I don't think he would have gotten farther than here, Dog," responded Tyrus.

"Right. Then that's where we will start, with Oz's 230 inmates."

They spent the rest of the day walking back and forth over the immense yard using the grid pattern search method. They were looking for anything that would help them identify the suspects. Tyrus found a dried, blood-soaked tissue underneath the bleachers that lined the north part of the softball field about halfway between the crime scene and the latrine. It might have been discarded by one of the attackers who cut their finger, or it just might have been a nosebleed from a softball spectator. Whatever the case, it was processed into evidence. They searched every inch of that yard and turned over every garbage can, but nothing else was discovered during their search.

Scott turned the yard over to the watch commander, who assembled a battery of metal-detector-wielding officers, and they descended on the Central Yard. The warden would employ his counselors and administrators in the next few days to interview the entire Central Facility inmate population. With any luck, someone would talk, but Scott wasn't going to hold his breath.

The autopsy was held on the following Tuesday morning as promised. Dr. Fredrick Hansen was the forensic pathologist for the county. He seemed to think Scott was an "odd duck" because of his habit of photographing the internal organs that the good doctor was chopping up on the cutting board. It didn't help that Scott was always saying things like, "Hold it right there, Doc. The composition is perfect.

Look at the colors." Hearts fascinated Scott, and he was always right by
the doctor's side every time he cut into one.

According to the doc, the garrote did obstruct Danny's airway but
not to the point that he lost consciousness; however, it did leave an
abrasion furrow and a slight incised cut. This furrow was consistent
with being made by the garrote that Tyrus recovered from the field
adjacent to the area of the crime scene. It appeared that "the apparatus
was released prior to vascular compromise," to quote the good doctor.
This, to Scott, suggested that there may have been only two attackers
and that one of them let go of the garrote and got busy with a shank;
his bet would be on the taller of the two as Pajaro himself was not a
short person.

Most of the stab wounds to the lower torso were superficial aside
from two that penetrated the stomach wall. The weapon was consistent
with being a double-edged weapon with an irregularly shaped blade
that wasn't more than half an inch wide. Death, however, was caused
by exsanguination from piercing of the descending aorta and of the left
ventricle of the heart. The device was likely an ice-pick-type stabbing
weapon.

After the autopsy and after the plastic bag filled with dissected
organs was sewn back into the body cavity, Scott collected the fingerprint
impressions of the decedent inmate Pajaro. Oddly enough, Danny
would remain an inmate on the rolls of the department of corrections
until such time as Scott positively identified him by the comparison of
his fingerprint impressions with those in his central file.

Chapter 5

The Skinhead

The prison began life during World War II when the governor decided that a few loafing convicts at San Quentin State Prison could be put to use growing rubber trees for the war effort. He sent a busload of convicts and a busload of guards down to the Central Valley to a huge chunk of farmland owned by the state. They pitched a number of tents, borrowed a few tractors from local farmers, and began tilling and planting the land. They grew rubber plants, sugar beets, and cotton with the help of German POWs from a nearby camp.

In 1946, the army repaid the governor by constructing two giant Nissen huts to house the inmates and erecting a single fence line. This original facility became the minimum-support facility. A dozen Quonset huts were built outside the fence line for the staff.

In 1949, construction of the Central Facility had begun, with much of the labor coming from the convicts themselves. The North Facility was built in 1956. The prison stopped growing crops in 1961, and now the land was unused but incredibly fertile.

Scott spent five years as "the Bull" in a housing unit at the North Facility back in the early '90s. He had 312 medium maximum security inmates housed in 156 cells with three open tiers. No fancy push buttons for Scott; every door had to be opened and closed with a Folger Adam key. It was just Scott and his partner locked in a cellblock with

312 felons; just the two of them to keep order and sanity. That was a 1-to-156 ratio, Scott's kind of odds.

Back then, they didn't even have gun coverage. If something happened, the roof gunner would drop down into a secured area in the sally port, which was fine unless that something was happening to you. In fact, back then, the officers had a pair of handcuffs, a set of keys, an alarm box, and an aircraft aluminum side-handle baton. Pepper spray and protective vests came after Scott had moved onto investigations.

To make matters worse, the inmates had their beloved weight piles back then, and they spent their entire day every day pressing huge amounts of weight. This made it necessary for Scott to do his own share of weightlifting. The inmates, back then, were huge—not just huge but also huge like the cartoon character the Tick: "Spoon!"

However, where Scott had the advantage was something the inmates never quite figured out; they never developed their legs. Here would be these enormous inmates with massive chests and arms but chicken-bone legs. It didn't take Scott long to figure out that they were top heavy. All he had to do was plant his solid thigh muscles hard on the floor, bend at the waist, and swing that side-handle baton with all his strength into those tiny inmate thighs. Over they would go, and once they were on the floor, it was advantage 1 to the Bull.

Being a housing unit cop wasn't always a matter of scrappiness. It was actually a cross between being the town sheriff and being a cruise director. It wouldn't be out of the ordinary for Scott to crack a cell door open and yell at an inmate to stop beating up his cellie and in the same breath ask if the inmate had enough toilet paper.

The secret weapon Scott employed was an incredible memory for names. He memorized every inmate in his housing unit by name and cell. To top it off, he knew who their cellmates were, where they worked, who they associated with, and what job assignments they had. Scott also knew in a moment when an inmate was in his cellblock that didn't belong there. When they had mail, Scott would hand it directly to the intended inmate. This was greatly appreciated because the inmates were touchy about their cellie having the addresses of their girlfriends.

Scott would tell the young officers who worked with him to never read a magazine or newspaper that came in the mail for an inmate and never ever eat the food that was destined for their dining pleasure. The latter, of course, was for two reasons. First, Scott had been the culinary officer, and he knew the food was prepared by the inmate cooks. Let's just say that, for the most part, personal hygiene was not in their vocabulary. In fact, around the prison, *E. coli* was a condiment, and salmonella was a side dish. Second, the cops made good money, and the inmates were of the opinion that they can afford to buy their own food and not eat the food that belonged to them. It was a matter of respect.

At first, the inmates didn't particularly care for Scott's memory ability, and they made many efforts to have him assigned to another cellblock by dropping numerous death threats. When Scott received an anonymous note that said something akin to "we are going to kill you, and we know where you live," Scott stuck it up on the bulletin board with his own note: "Send your friends in groups of seven; it is so much easier to reload that way." Once they figured out that he wasn't going anywhere, the lifers especially accepted his presence and realized that they were less likely to get assaulted in the housing unit when Scott was working because he could identify their attacker; and inmates, as a rule, only attacked when they can do it anonymously. In fact, Scott remembered one night when he had about 170 inmates participating in a night privilege program.

They were milling around the housing unit and watching a movie on the one television set in the back of the hall. He noticed, at the 2030 hours courtesy lockup, that all the white and Asian inmates were going into their cells and that he was left with about 110 black and Southern Hispanic inmates in the hall. He told his partner, a rookie cop with three months on the job, to get ready for a disturbance. When they were finishing the lockup on the third tier and were on their way back down the stairs to the first tier, Scott noticed that the Hispanic inmates were on one side of the hall and the black inmates were on the other, and they were facing each other. His partner asked with a panic, "What are we going to do?"

Scott replied, "Nothing. Just follow me." And they both walked into the middle of the group, and Scott leaned with the flat of his left boot against the wall. Scott slowly looked back and forth at all the inmates assembled. After a few tense moments, the inmates started milling about, going about their games of dominoes, and watching the movie.

Scott stayed there with his foot planted against the wall, and after about twenty minutes, two inmates approached him. One was a black tier porter, Bill "Blue" Harris, and the other was the Southern Hispanic shot caller Gregorio Santos. They explained that a young black inmate had picked up a bag containing canteen items that belonged to a Southern Hispanic earlier in the day out on the yard, and he was refusing to give it back. The shot callers from the Crips and the Southerners had agreed to fight, and they were going to do it while Scott was busy with the 2030 hours lockup. What they didn't count on was that Scott figured out something was wrong in the housing unit and changed the way they did the lockup so he could have a constant vigil of the first tier. Scott went to the offending inmate's cell, retrieved the bag of canteen, procured an apology, and restored the peace.

In those five years as a housing unit officer, he learned to understand the sociopathic criminal mind, to spot instantly suspicious behavior, and most of all that humor can go a long way in resolving a dangerous situation. Don't believe me? Okay, the next time you walked past the inmate showers and you heard a bar of soap hit the floor, you should try not to laugh and say something like, "Kick it over here, man." Scott also learned that if you yell "knock it off!" at the top of your lungs, most inmates would stop what they were doing. When all else failed, he would tell the rookie cops to yell like your father when you were fighting with your brother. You'd be surprised with the results.

The inmates learned to respect Scott, and he learned to show respect to them. To get respect, you must first show respect. Scott remembered when, once, two white inmates walked up to him and said that if there was ever a riot, he should back over to their cell and let himself in, and they would "protect him." Scott was really lost for words. Finally, he looked at them and said, "Look, Schwartz, Beutler, that's very nice of you. But I'm pretty sure if there is a riot, my place is to be out here and not in there." Once Scott had their respect, however, they would often take him into their confidence. They would sometimes tell him who did what bad thing in his housing unit, especially if it would lead to further retaliation by other races. The lifers might even tell Scott who killed whom.

"Well, Tyrus, it's been three weeks and nothing," Scott blurted out in frustration.

"Not so fast, Doggy, I might have something. I have a voice mail from Capt. Geoff Sanderson. He says he has someone who is willing to talk to us."

"Inmate or staff?" Scott asked.

"Inmate" was the reply.

"What does the inmate want?" Scott inquired.

"Apparently, he's bored, and he wants a floater TV."

"A couple of weeks in a cell without a television are enough to loosen a few tongues. What have we got to lose? Set it up, Ty, and we'll kick it out today after I get back from taking all the evidence to the department of justice crime lab."

Later that afternoon, they met with their informant. Inmate Drew McIntyre was a thirty-year-old white skinhead from Santa Cruz who was on his third drug-distribution-related conviction. When he was out on the streets, he sold methamphetamines. When he was locked up, he used heroin. He tended to run up a good-sized debt, and among the first things that he lost to his dealer were his TV and radio. In any prolonged lockdown, your habitual heroin user had to first deal with the monkey on his back. The withdrawals would be agonizing for the first week. The second week was hell without some diversion from the constant desire for the chiva. Books didn't do the trick; you really needed a TV and cigarettes. McIntyre had neither. There was nothing on this earth that McIntyre hated more than a narcotics agent, except maybe an African American former narcotics agent who now headed the institutional gang investigations unit.

Scott chose to do all the talking. He opened with "A TV is possible, McIntyre, depending on if your information is good, but it has to be real good and verifiable."

"Doggett, the information is good," he replied. "I was on the yard, and I saw the shit go down."

"Where exactly were you on the yard?" Scott asked.

"I was over in Peckerwood Flats," he replied.

"At the benches by tower no. 4?" asked Ty.

"Yeah," was his terse response.

"That's sixty, seventy yards from the basketball court. How good are your eyes?" Scott inquired.

"Like a fucking hawk. I saw the two dudes who did it."

"What did you see specifically?" Scott asked.

"Dude had just walked past us on the track. He was walking with two of his compadres. I knew something was up because two Southerners were posted up in our area, I guess to catch him if he tried to escape toward us. The three of them stopped at the basketball court, and he was watching the game. That's when they dragged him over to the fence and fucked him up." He added, "I even saw one of the dudes walk across the basketball court and run toward the latrines. He reached into his pocket and pulled out a cloth and wrapped it around his finger. I saw him shove the shank in the mud by the tennis court before he started running."

"Okay," Scott said, "did you see who it was?"

"I seen him before, but I don't know who he is," he replied.

Scott continued his line of questioning. "White, black, Hispanic, or other? What flavor was our suspect?"

"One dude was short and definitely Mexican. I didn't see where he went. The other guy was tall, really tall, and dark skinned, but I don't think he was a brother."

"So this wasn't a white hit?" asked Tyrus. McIntyre ignored him.

"Let me ask you something," Scott jumped in. "How much did you owe Pajaro?"

"I ain't going to lie to you, Doggett. I was into him," replied McIntyre.

"How much?" Scott asked.

"About a grand," he replied with steely confidence.

"Looks to me like the debt is resolved," Scott said with a smirk.

"Just go out and find that shank, Doggett, and get me my TV—color, one of those small flat screens. They're nice." He got up and walked out of the Captain's office. He signaled to the officer who was standing at the door that he was ready to be escorted back to his cell.

"Well, Dog, he saw it, but he might be lying about the race of the suspects."

"True, Ty, but he also might be telling the truth. He knows who did it. Of that I am certain. At least we know two things. Danny was selling heroin to the other races big time, which is a no-no to the Southerners, and there should be a shank out there on that yard. Let's go get it."

Tyrus and Scott waited about three hours before they went out onto the yard. They didn't want it to look obvious that McIntyre had provided them with information. Any kind of snitch didn't have much of a chance on the main line. No matter how careful Scott was about meeting with an informant in a clandestine manner, there would always be the chance that he was seen with Scott or in the area near him. In the meantime, they verified with Oswaldo's diagrams that McIntyre was in the place that he said he was on the day Danny Pajaro was murdered.

A drainage ditch ran the length of the east side of the tennis court. It was about six inches wide and a foot deep, but it was filled with water, and the soil was as soft as sand. Tyrus and Scott tried the metal detector at first, but the rebar in the concrete pad of the tennis court sent old Bertha into a seizure. It was going to take a pick and a shovel to get this job done. A quick trip to the yard shack procured the requisite tools, and after a few preliminary photographs, they began their inspection of the Pajaro canal.

Scott pumped the foul-smelling water out of the canal using a bilge pump, and it was obvious that the soil underneath had reached its saturation point. Every swing of the pick sent up a spray of mud, and the impact sucked the pick head into the mire as if it were peanut butter. The shovel didn't fare much better. They resorted to using a hand trowel and a probing rod. It was dirty work, and after an hour, they had a collection of soda cans, potato chip bags, empty seasoning pouches from Top Ramen bags, and even a shoe but no weapon. "I think he was full of shit, Dog," Tyrus remarked.

"Just keep probing, Ty. We're nearly at the end." No sooner had Scott said those words than Tyrus hit something solid. "Hang on, let me get in there with the trowel," Scott said. As he turned over the mud and slopped it onto the grass, he didn't even realize that he had shoveled out the weapon. He pulled out one big clump of mud, flopped it to the side, and was digging for more when Tyrus said he had found it.

For some reason, Scott thought it would be much bigger, but there it was, covered in mud. As predicted, it was an inmate-manufactured stabbing weapon of the ice pick variety, preferred by inmate assassins. It measured only about six and a half inches in overall length with a blade that protruded about three inches from the cloth-wrapped handle. "Pity it's been under water and mud, Ty. They'll never recover any DNA from that thing. We can't say for certain, outside of eyewitness testimony, that it is the actual weapon used on Danny."

"And I doubt McIntyre is going to testify," Tyrus replied, adding, "Looks like we owe him a television though."

"Do we even have any of those small flat screens?" Scott asked.

After scraping off the layers of mud, Tyrus and Scott cornered Oswaldo and asked him for his list of inmates who were found in the area around the latrine. They eliminated the white and Asian inmates, which still left them with over 170. They then reviewed Becky's videotape and highlighted the ones that fit the description. It was going to be a long day of pulling photographs, but they were up for the challenge.

After two hours of listening to Tyrus complain, they had a stack of photographs from about 40 inmates who fit the description. They assembled the photographs into photo lineups and showed them to McIntyre when they delivered his television set. True to form, he couldn't identify any of the inmates as the one he saw leaving the crime scene. Scott didn't blame him. It was one thing to offer nondescript information to get a TV. It was another thing to offer testimony in court. In fact, it probably would have been a death sentence for McIntyre. Tyrus and Scott knew they were on their own.

The following morning, Tyrus came into Scott's office and said, "I think we can rule out the blacks in this assault. We just interviewed Inmate Wilson, the Black Guerilla Family associate. He says that nobody from the blacks sanctioned this hit and nobody even approached them about it. Took them completely by surprise, and they aren't happy about this lockdown one bit."

"Do you believe him, Ty?"

"Yes, Dog, I do. We have what McIntyre said that he didn't think it was a black. Plus, it just doesn't make sense one of the hit men was Mexican and the other black. That sort of combined hit hasn't happened here in decades."

"All right, Ty, let's work on your theory and take out all the blacks from our photo lineup. I'll rework the charts and get back to you later today."

While rearranging the photographs, Scott put his finger on the one guy he thought could possibly be the primary suspect, Hector Pena. Hector was tall, about six foot two, and dark, very dark. He was an El Salvadorian and a member of Mara Salvatrucha or MS-13. Out on the streets, the MS-13 was a dangerously violent street gang that had drawn the attention of the federal government. In the prison system, however, the MS-13 was subservient to the Mexican Mafia, and they usually associated with the rest of the Southerners. But Pena was a two-bit thug, and there had never been any love between him and Pajaro. In fact, a few years back, Pena and Pajaro mixed it up on the yard, and Pena ended up with a broken tooth and stitches.

On Scott's way over to Ty's office, Lieutenant Templeton grabbed him and ushered him into his office. "You need to call the department of justice, Scott. I just got a call from them, and they want you to cut back on the number of items you submitted."

"Oh, come on, Lieutenant," Scott replied, "I only gave them twenty-one submissions. I need all twenty-one. Can that be so hard?"

The lieutenant persisted, "They want you to knock it down to five and no more. Just give them a call."

"I'll do one better," Scott snapped. "I'll have Alex call them. If anyone can get some assistance out of the DOJ, it's the DA's office."

"Whatever you gotta do. How are you coming on the investigation?" he asked.

"Well, I think I have a suspect. I was just on my way to discuss it with Ty."

"Keep me informed," he said as he closed his door.

"Tyrus, Tyrus, Tyrus," Scott said as he swung the door to his office open.

"What do you know about Hector Pena?"

"MS-13, a.k.a. the Snake" was his response. "And he was on the yard," Scott said.

"Where?"

"Just south of the telephone bank on the bleachers, and he fits the description."

"Are you thinking what I am thinking, Doggy?"

"Yup, let's go find some shoes, Ty."

Ty, Oswaldo, and Scott walked down to Echo Wing and pulled Inmate Pena and his cellmate out of their cell. Pena only spoke Spanish, and it was a good thing that they brought Oswaldo along to translate. Immediately, Scott noticed a fresh cut on his right ring finger knuckle. "Oz," Scott said, "tell him he has some explaining to do. Ask him where he got that cut."

Oswaldo made the inquiry in Spanish, and a few words were exchanged. "He said he cut his finger playing soccer," explained Oz.

"Right, soccer. Tell ya what, Oz, why don't you take him down and put him in a holding cell? He's going to ad seg. Don't interview him without *Miranda*, but if he makes a spontaneous statement, write it down."

"What about the cellie?" asked Tyrus.

"Well, I don't know, Ty. We don't really have much of a description of the other guy except that he was shorter than Pajaro. Let's leave him alone for a little while and see what he does. In the meantime, let's see what kinds of shoes are in the cell."

Central Facility cells were nine feet wide by eleven feet in length. There were two steel bunks, one on top of the other like a bunk bed.

There was a sink and toilet assembly near the door and two standing lockers that each held six cubic feet of property. There was also room for storage under the lower bunk. Other than that, there wasn't much room. Think of two grown men living in a space the size of your bathroom. In spite of the lack of space, it still took about two hours to do a thorough search.

Inmates were packrats; they never threw anything away. They also tended to create small holes in their standard-issue urinal and DNA-encrusted mattresses. You didn't get a new mattress when you came to prison; you got an heirloom. Within these holes, they hid their hypodermic needles, weapons, tobacco, smuggled cell phones, and more illicit contraband. They also managed to hide things in places that you wouldn't even think possible to hide things.

Two hours later, they walked out without the shoes they were looking for. In itself, it didn't mean anything; there certainly was time for him to ditch the shoes. Instead, they confiscated one pair of shoes from each inmate for elimination purposes. The photographs from the crime scene had already been sent to a footwear specialist in Arizona. Hopefully, if nothing else, he could come up with a brand of shoe and size. If you got lucky, the analyst can also come up with unique characteristics that caused distinctive wear patterns like bunions, hammertoes, calcaneal bumps, or sesamoiditis. That would be "golden," as Oswaldo would say.

"Alex, it's Dog. I need your help," Scott said into the receiver of his desk phone.

"What's up, buddy?" came the response.

"The DOJ is dicking with me big time. They want me to cut the DNA submissions down to five. Five! Can you believe it? I need you to go with me over there and help me talk to their supervising criminalist."

"Just say when, buddy. I'll be your Huckleberry," he said with what Scott was certain was a wink.

On the following Tuesday, Alex and Scott sat in the office of Juan De La Torre, the senior criminalist 3 at the state crime laboratory. "There is nothing I can do, Investigator Doggett. It's not us here at this laboratory. It's the people at the DNA laboratory in Oakland. They are badly backed up and just don't have the manpower. I have talked to them on your behalf, and they can squeeze you in if you cut down on the submissions to three, five at the most. There is nothing else we can do," he said apologetically.

"Look, Juan," Scott said, "I don't see how we can possibly cut down on the submissions. I need to know who bled where to do the bloodstain pattern analysis. It would be different if you guys could just do blood typing, but you don't do typing anymore. Chances are one of my suspects bled in the crime scene. I don't need to tell you how important that would be to the investigation."

"My hands are tied," he replied. "My hands are tied. There is nothing I can do."

Scott opened his mouth for another broadside when Alex held up his hand and spoke. "Mr. De La Torre, as you know, I represent the district attorney's office, and the district attorney himself has taken a particular interest in this investigation. Surely, there is some way that we can come to an amicable resolution to this problem. This case has the potential for a death penalty prosecution." Alex was a very convincing speaker.

Juan squirmed a little in his chair, cleared his throat, and said, "Well, perhaps I can talk to them again, but twenty-one is just out of the question. Perhaps we can reach a compromise."

"Okay, okay," Scott said. "For now, we will assume that it was our victim who bled in the crime scene, but I need something that says it was him, and I need something that would link him to our suspects—the shirt, the pants, the blood from the basketball court, and definitely the tissue. That's what? Ten, twelve at the most? Oh, and analyze the garrote to see what sort of DNA evidence is on there. So twelve or thirteen."

"I'll see what I can do," responded the criminalist.

Two days later, Scott had his response: twelve would be the number of submissions acceptable to the Oakland scientists but only out of the greatest respect for the district attorney. Now there was one thing you had to know about the DNA laboratory: unlike the TV programs, you didn't get your specimen results at the end of the episode. From experience, Scott knew that it would take the better part of a year to get his results, and that would only be after calling them week after week and asking, "Is it done yet?"

The following morning, Lieutenant Templeton walked into Scott's office and asked, "So did you get that resolved with the crime lab people yet?"

"It's taken care of, Lieutenant. We agreed on twelve items of evidence for now."

"You might want to call them back," he said with a smirk.

"Now what?" Scott asked.

"They were doing another sweep of the yard and found a bloody T-shirt buried in one of the horseshoe pits. It's in one of the evidence lockers."

Scott stood up and protested, "Son of a bitch, Lieutenant, why wasn't I notified?"

"Relax, I wasn't called either. I found out this morning in the warden's meeting. The cops will be in at 1400 hours if you need to talk to them."

At 1410 hours, Officer Tim Reynolds and Officer Ben Smith were brought into Scott's office and sat in the two ancient chairs typically reserved for investigative files. "All right, fellas, I hear you found a nice bloody T-shirt for me," Scott said. "Excellent work. Now how about you guys showing me exactly where you found it."

Scott grabbed a camera kit and a crime scene kit, and the three of them made their way to the Central Facility Yard and the horseshoe pits in the southwest corner of the yard. The attentive officers pointed out the first pit and informed him the sand at first looked completely undisturbed, but when they began raking the area for weapons, Officer Smith snagged the sleeve of the T-shirt. Scott took their statements, instructed them to write reports, and photographed the area. He thought to himself that it now appeared that the other suspect walked in the same direction as their victim. Scott thought it was time to talk to the intrepid tower officers.

Upon his return to his office, Scott placed a call to Officer Pedro Garcia, who was working tower no. 3 on the day of the murder. "Pistol

Pete!" Scott bellowed. "Did I wake you? I know there's nothing to do up there without inmates on the yard."

"Yeah," he replied. "I had my feet up on the window ledge. What's up, Dog?"

"First of all, your feet wouldn't reach the window ledge. Second, I need to know what you saw the other day."

"Well, Dog, I really didn't see anything until Pajaro half-walked, half-stumbled his way past the volleyball court. There were a lot of inmates over here watching the basketball game and playing volleyball. I picked up the rifle and looked around, but I didn't see anybody at all suspicious."

"Let me ask you something, Pedro. You have the best view in the house of the horseshoe pit area. By any chance, did you see an inmate bury his bloody T-shirt in the first box?"

"Yeah, right, Dog, I think that would have been suspicious."

"Then let me ask you. Did you see an inmate over there without a shirt on?" Scott asked.

"You know, now that you mention it, Dog, there was something odd that day. The blacks were playing horseshoes, and just as the yard was going down, there was a Mexican kid who was holding the yard broom they use to sweep the sand flat. You know what else? He was wearing a blue chambray shirt but no T-shirt underneath. It didn't look right."

"Do you think you could identify him if you saw his picture?" I asked.

"I can do better. I know him. It was Cardenas, George Wing 213. I wrote him up for being out of bounds in the Indian Sweat Lodge about a month ago."

"I owe you dinner, Pedro, some place cheap. Can I get a report out of you on that?"

"For you, Dog, anything," he replied.

"Hey, Ty!" Scott yelled, "Let's go find a broom!" There were three brooms in the yard shack. Unfortunately, they were far too old and dry to get any prints from, but Scott tried anyway—no luck. Then they checked Oz's list for Cardenas, and sure enough, he was there in that area. Scott sent Oswaldo to tower no. 3 with a six-pack photo chart to show to Pedro, and he identified Cardenas as the inmate he saw holding the broom. He confirmed it; Cardenas was the second suspect.

"I feel good about this one, Ty. Let's lock the fool up and see what he has to say."

"I agree," he said, adding, "And I think we need to dig up that horseshoe pit and see what else we can find."

They walked back out to the yard shack. Scott opened the door and said, "Just so happens I have two shovels right here. Take your pick." Tyrus reached in and grabbed a shovel, Scott grabbed the other, and they made their way over to the horseshoe pits.

As Tyrus suspected, as soon as the officers found the T-shirt, they stopped raking the area. About five inches under the sand, Tyrus turned up an inmate-manufactured stabbing weapon. This one had a double-edged blade measuring about three-quarters of an inch in width and six inches in overall length. The blade portion protruded about two and a half inches from the cloth-wrapped handle. It was constructed from the aluminum flange that ran the length of the culinary hot carts that held the rubber gasket that sealed the door. It was a constant source of weapons on the yard. "This time, we're in luck, Ty. There's still blood on the handle, and I bet there is sweat on there too," Scott said optimistically.

Within an hour, the area was photographed, sketched, measured, and documented, and Ty processed the weapon into evidence. While he was doing that, Scott picked up the phone and dialed the DOJ. "Juan, it's Scott Doggett. I hate to break this to you, but we have some more evidence in the Pajaro homicide." There was silence on the other end of the phone.

The administrative segregation unit or "ad seg" can best be described as a prison within a prison. When an inmate did something that was a danger to himself or to the safety and security of the institution, he was segregated from the rest of the inmate population. Now that sounded like a broad-brush statement, so let's define it a little. You got caught with a weapon, you'd go to the Hole. You got caught selling dope, you'd go to the Hole. You killed someone, you'd go to the Hole. The Hole was not a nice place. The cells were spartan with one bunk, a toilet and sink, and a writing desk. The cell doors were not solid but bars to facilitate observation. Because of this, there was a constant din of noise. All movement outside the cell was done in full restraints, waist chains with handcuffs. The exercise yard was small, concrete, and inside a fully enclosed cage.

Most inmates hated the Hole. Some felt safe in there. Scott was beginning to think their friend Benito "Chino" Cardenas was of the latter belief. In fact, you might say it was a blue badge of courage for him. Chino was what you could best describe as your garden-variety *punk*. Scott used that word on occasion, although he had been in trouble for using that word before; but if you look the word up in the dictionary, it meant a street tough or thug. Chino was a professed Southern gangbanger who believed without reservation there was glory in gang life; therefore, by definition, he was a street tough or thug. Ergo, he was—by literal definition—a punk.

At age twelve, he committed his first crime—a carjacking—by dragging a grandmother out of her station wagon at the point of a shotgun. It didn't matter that he couldn't drive and immediately plowed the vehicle into two parked cars. He had earned status points in his clique of the South Side street disruptive group. At age sixteen, he was released from the California Youth Authority facility in Paso Robles. Shortly after that, he pointed the barrel of an assault weapon out of the back window of a Chevy Impala and shot a nineteen-year-old boy as he walked his fifteen-year-old brother home from school. The first round he fired killed the boy. The recoil of the discharged round caused him to unintentionally fire a second round that grazed the head of the driver of his getaway car. They crashed into a telephone pole, and Chino was apprehended in the area. He had conveniently left the assault rifle leaning against a fence, complete with his fingerprints. He was convicted by plea agreement as an adult to a fifteen-to-life prison sentence. He fit the description of the second suspect, being all five foot six and weighing in at about two hundred pounds. And there was no denying that Chino was "down" for the Southerners.

Tyrus and Scott went to have a chat with Chino, but upon hearing his *Miranda* advisement, he decided it would be prudent to have a lawyer present. When Scott asked him if he would be kind enough to voluntarily surrender a buccal swab, since there was no better way to prove your innocence than DNA, Chino told him to do something to himself that sounded very, very unpleasant and at Scott's age impossible. It looked to him like it was time for a warrant.

Now the nice thing about ad seg was that Scott could let a suspect cool his heels for a few months while he was under investigation without formally charging him. Therefore, Chino was where Scott wanted him, and the clock wasn't running for the DA's office. The warrant closed something like this: "Therefore, your affiant requests the issuance of this search warrant to obtain a buccal swab and two vials of blood to be drawn by a medical professional in accordance with departmental policy to determine if Inmate Benito Cardenas was a participant in the murder of Inmate Daniel Pajaro or to otherwise exclude him as a suspect." Scott insisted on adding the last part, "or to otherwise exclude him as a suspect." The objective investigator was responsible not only to prove the guilt of the criminal offender but also to exonerate the innocent.

On their way to ad seg, Tyrus and Scott first stopped in at the medical department and commandeered their old friend Bob Connors, phlebotomist extraordinaire. He had always been their go-to man when they needed blood drawn quickly from a squirming inmate. They assembled in the captain's office, and Chino was brought in, shackled around the waist and wrists. "Cardenas," Scott started, "I have here a search warrant signed by the Honorable Judge Philip Rosen of the superior court commanding us to obtain from your person one buccal swab and two vials of blood to be drawn in a manner prescribed by departmental policy. At this time, I recommend that you comply with the provisions of this warrant and voluntarily surrender the aforementioned items without incident."

"Fuck you, *puto*!" was his most cheerful reply. In the spirit of cooperation, he yelled, "I want my fucking lawyer, and I want him here now!"

Tyrus leaned in a little, put his meaty hand on Chino's shoulder, and whispered into his ear, "No, son, you don't get it. We aren't going to talk to you, and we aren't going to ask you any questions. We are going to take something from you. You don't get to have a lawyer present this time."

Scott continued with his prepared statement, mindful of the video camera placed in the corner of the room. "Inmate Cardenas, if you refuse to comply with this warrant, we are prepared to take it from you by force if necessary." Scott then softened his tone. "*Benito*, you say you didn't do this thing. What better way to prove you didn't do it than by allowing the department of justice to analyze your DNA and prove what you are saying?"

"You're going to plant it on the evidence and frame me" was his retort.

"All the evidence has already been delivered to the DOJ, and I doubt highly they have any interest in framing you," Scott replied.

Chino thought long and hard for a few minutes. He began sweating profusely, and his lower lip began to quiver. To prevent this, he rolled his lower lip under his top row of teeth and bit down. He was weighing his options among reason, rationality, and the need to impress his gangbanger brethren. He chose the latter and let out a bloodcurdling "Pinche pendejo puto!"

With that, Tyrus and Scott guided him ever so gently and painlessly—well mostly painlessly—to the floor. Bob sprang into action and drew two vials of blood in a manner suggestive of a senile veterinarian taking blood from an elderly dog. "There, there, young man, this won't hurt a bit." Once the deed was done, they lifted Chino back into his chair, by no means an easy task. "What about the swab?" inquired Bob.

"Wait for it," Scott said. With that, Chino let loose with a juicy mouthful of spit that landed on the right breast pocket of Scott's jumpsuit.

"Ah," uttered Bob as he quickly sopped up the saliva with a sterile pad.

"I think I will spare you the gassing charge, Cardenas," Scott mentioned as Chino was escorted out of the room.

While Scott was at the courthouse, he also petitioned for a search warrant for blood and saliva from Hector Pena. Scott presented the judge with the probable cause that Pena was on the yard at the time of the murder in an area where bloodied clothing was found and that he had previous conflicts with Pajaro. He did not mention their eyewitness as he gave them only a vague description of the suspect at best. Fortunately, Judge Rosen didn't need much more probable cause and signed the warrant.

Since they were already in ad seg, they had Hector escorted into the captain's office. Scott radioed for Oswaldo to join them to do the translating, and Scott presented Pena with the warrant. Unlike Chino, he was the perfect gentleman, polite and eager to assist them. The samples were collected, and Scott thanked him for his cooperation. It was unnerving.

Before leaving the administrative segregation unit, Tyrus and Scott paid a visit to the ad seg property officer Rudy Galvan. "Rudy," Scott announced as they entered the property room, "I need a big favor, partner. We need every pair of shoes that came in with Cardenas." Rudy satisfied their request and presented them with two pairs of personal shoes.

Scott turned the pair of Nike Cortez athletic shoes over and inspected the soles. "Look familiar, Ty?" he asked.

"I'll bet you two dollars those are the shoes," Tyrus responded. Scott didn't take the bet. Instead, he placed them into an evidence box.

"Well, Doggy," Tyrus postulated later in the day, "at least we have a good idea now that it was a Southern-sanctioned hit and that we don't have any other races or gangs involved. Now we just have to find out why."

"I think I know who we can talk to, Ty. I suggest we see what old Aldo Gomez has to say."

Aldo Gomez was an old-time convict with a low B number, which meant he had been down for a long, long time. He kidnapped two people in 1975, bound them, hog-tied them, and threw them in the trunk of his car for a long drive to a San Bernardino County hideout where he and his accomplice would be safe until the ransom demand was paid. Little did Aldo know that a long drive through the desert, a leaky exhaust system, and the compression of two big bodies pressed together would lead to a double homicide conviction.

For all that, Aldo wasn't so bad. In his old age, he had inherited an outlook on life that was congenial and, well, harmless. In the day, however, it was documented that Aldo held considerable influence in the Mexican Mafia, so much so that when he decided to leave the gang life behind, he was allowed to do so without the usual "blood out" requirement. Nowadays, Aldo was just an old man who repaired TVs and small appliances.

Scott had known Aldo from the early 1990s, when he was housed in his housing unit. Aldo and Scott worked up a good rapport, and although he had never before asked him to provide him inside information regarding gang activities, they did have many insightful discussions on the tier regarding life and man's inhumanity toward his fellow man. Aldo was one of the few inmates Scott had encountered who showed genuine remorse for his crime. Unfortunately, it was not a good idea for any inmate to be seen talking to the Goons. It tended to mark them as informants, which can lead to complications. Scott needed a clever rouse.

As Scott approached Aldo's cell, he was carrying a television set that looked convincingly broken. Scott asked the tier officer to open the cell door, and Scott said, "Aldo, I've got a nice project for you here."

"Mr. Doggett," Aldo remarked, "you shouldn't have. Lockdowns are so dreadfully boring. I shall, indeed, look forward to this challenge. How've you been?"

"I've been better, Aldo. I think I am getting too old for all this."

"We both are getting too old" was his reply.

"Perhaps, Aldo, when you are finished with the TV, we can have a quick chat. It would be like the old days."

"I am at your beck and call, Mr. Doggett. You were always fair, firm, and consistent as they say."

"How much time do you need for the repair?" Scott asked.

"Oh, I intend to savor this one. Shall we say the same time next week?" he replied.

"You will get a ducat for the counselor's office to work on your board hearing. I will already be there. We should still be on lockdown, so nobody will see me go in. Speaking of which, Aldo, how is your board hearing going?"

"I am getting closer, only a two-year denial last time, but I fear I will die in this godforsaken place. At least I will die among the only people that I know—sad, really, when you think of it. Oh well, until next week."

Scott handed him the television, and Aldo placed it on his bunk, sat down, and immediately began tinkering. Scott closed the door and walked down the tier and back to his office. The tier officer gently locked the cell door out of respect.

Scott was on his way back to the office from getting a well-deserved meal when he received a telephone call from Arizona. He immediately called his lieutenant. "Good news, Lieutenant," Scott said into his Bluetooth hands-free device. "I just got a call from our footwear specialist. The shoes of our victim are a match to those in the crime scene. The impressions to the left in the photograph are a Nike Cortez, size 9. Although there doesn't appear to be any individual characteristics in the photographs, our man says he can measure the ends of each chevron and see if there is a match to the shoes we just sent him. As for the shoes on the right, that's where we might get some luck. He is certain that they are a Reebok Supreme Low Deadstock Pump BB. This shoe was made in the mid-1990s, and they are a size 11. He said there are lots of small nicks and cuts in the soles that he can match if we can find the shoes . . . What? . . . No, we haven't found them yet, but I guarantee you if Pena's had those shoes since he's been down, they are still out there somewhere. How's that? . . . No, I won't repeat everything I just said. I'll be in your office in about ten minutes."

Chapter 6

The Clever CI

Scott had been waiting in the counselor's office for nearly an hour when the door opened, and Aldo Gomez walked in. The first thing he said was "Your TV is done. You can stop by and pick it up whenever you want. You are always welcome."

"Thanks, Aldo," Scott replied. "I actually broke it myself, specially for you."

"Oh, that was all too evident. I imagined you needed an excuse to come to my cell, although I did enjoy having something to occupy the hours."

"Aldo, it's this business with Danny Pajaro. I know it was a Southern-sanctioned hit, but I don't know why, and I want to know who. I know nothing gets by you, Aldo. You don't have to tell me if you don't want. If you do, your name will appear nowhere in my reports, and you have my word on that. I just need to know if I am going in the right direction. Who killed Danny Pajaro?"

Aldo sat back in his chair and looked at Scott. It had been more than a dozen years since he and Scott had their chats on the tier. Scott had scarcely said a word to him in all those years, yet that didn't seem to matter. "Mr. Doggett," he began, "why did you kill Danny Pajaro?"

"Me?" Scott exclaimed. "Aldo, be serious!"

"Unfortunately, I am being very serious," he countered. "You see, Danny was expecting a big shipment of tar heroin, and you got to it first."

"Perez?" Scott asked, adding, "You mean that stuff Perez was smuggling was for Danny? Well, I'll be damned."

"Yes, and three months before that, you also ended the smuggling career of a young man by the name of Olivera."

"Sure, Aldo, that was like an ounce of heroin and some pills," Scott replied.

"That was for Danny too. The problem for Danny was that he was collecting the money from the sales of that product in advance. The yard has been dry, very dry, and people are desperate, so they are eager to pay. Sadly, every effort he made to resupply, well, you interfered with, and the people were getting restless. They wanted their money back. They wanted to find other suppliers. Danny didn't believe in refunds. So they killed him."

"Wow," Scott remarked. "What about the money?"

"Well, 'blood for money' as they say" was Aldo's only reply. "Come by and get your TV, Mr. Doggett."

"Wait a minute, Aldo. Do I have the right guys?"

"You'll know when you get the TV," Aldo said as he walked out the door.

Later in the day, Scott stopped by Aldo's cell and retrieved the TV. Aldo didn't say a word, and Scott walked back to his office somewhat confused. Upon arriving at his office, Scott placed the television set on one of the wooden chairs, picked up the phone, and called Tyrus. He relayed the information that Aldo provided. Tyrus agreed that the information was genuine but was resolved in the fact that they had both of their suspects detained. "It's just a matter of waiting for the DNA results, and we are done," he said.

"I'm not so sure, Ty. I think we have to work this thing out to the end, or we may be missing something. Someone had to sanction this hit, someone pretty high up in the gang. What do you think about talking to Felix Perez?"

"I'm all for it," he replied. "But we better take Alex Rowland with us just in case he wants to make a deal."

"I'll give him a call and set it up. Oh, and, Ty, do you need a TV in your office?"

The following morning, they were again in the administrative segregation unit captain's office. "Perez, as you know, I am Investigator Doggett. This is my partner, Investigative Sergeant Phillips, and this is Investigator Rowland from the district attorney's office. We are not here to talk to you about your pending prosecution. Rather, we are here to see if you can lend us some cooperation in a murder investigation."

"What's in it for me?" asked Perez confidently.

"Well, let's just say certain considerations," Scott replied. "Of course, I am not in a position to offer you any inducements. However, Investigator Rowland can report your cooperation to the DA's office, and perhaps there can be some leniency."

"I want a guarantee," demanded Perez.

Alex sat forward in his chair. "Felix—I hope you don't mind me calling you by your first name, buddy—if you have information that would benefit us in this investigation, it would really be in your best interest to help us out. You are looking at a slam-dunk conviction, and I think you know that. Heroin in a prison with two prior strikes is going to get you eighteen years at 85 percent. I think we can agree to the lower term with one strike so six years."

"Lower term, no strikes and concurrent," Felix bargained.

"Not in this county, buddy. We don't do concurrent. We might be able to arrange midterm, no strike—six years at 50 percent consecutive. And it wouldn't be a strike, so you will still have one more life when you get out," Alex countered.

Perez looked at the floor for a few minutes and curled the upper left corner of his lip into his mouth. Suddenly, he looked up as if by revelation and asked, "What about my wife?"

Alex responded, "She's looking at twelve at 85 percent. We can do three at 85 percent, but the information you have has to be damned good, and you have to be willing to testify."

"Do you think she has any chance of not getting convicted?" he asked.

"Uh, I doubt that, buddy. She had the drugs in her vagina. Add to that she transported the heroin across noncontiguous county lines. I mean, come on now, even you don't believe she has a chance of walking on that one."

Felix looked down at the table and began to speak. "I told her I would get her out of this thing. It's been a nightmare, but now it is over. Fucking Danny! Fuck that asshole! I tried. I tried, and I tried to get out of this, but it was never enough for him. He found ways to keep me owing him. He said he would kill me if I didn't. After the first time, I thought I was done but no. My wife didn't want to do it. You have to believe me. She wanted to find the money to pay him, but the deal was I could give him $700 worth of chiva or $3,000 in cash."

"How much did you owe him?" Scott asked.

"It was $10,000, but I couldn't get the money in time. I would give him the drugs, and he would say that I still owed him ten grand."

"A dope debt is like a credit card debt. You really never get them resolved. The best way to resolve one is not to get the debt in the first place," Scott offered.

"It wasn't even my debt at first," he remarked. "It was my cellie's, but he left before he could pay the debt, and it fell on me. Then I used a little and a little more, and before I knew it, I was gone."

"So what can you do for us, buddy?" inquired Alex.

"Well, I heard they killed him because he wouldn't give back the money," replied Felix.

"Who did you hear that from?" asked Tyrus.

"In here. I got word through the pipes. You can communicate with the cells below you through the pipes and the cell behind you through the vent."

"I'll ask again then. Who did you hear it from?" repeated Tyrus.

"Chino. He's below me. He was bragging about how he stabbed him in the belly."

"Proud of his work?" Scott asked.

"Yeah, you could say that" came the reply.

"What about the second attacker? Do you know who he is?" Scott asked.

"Nah, nobody has claimed it."

"Have you heard of Hector Pena?" Scott inquired.

"Monkey Face Pena?" he asked.

"Uh, I guess," Scott said. "Why do you call him that? I thought his moniker was the Snake or something like that."

"On the streets, yeah. But in here, we call him Cara de Chango because he looks like a monkey."

"Did he do it?" Scott asked.

"Nah, nah, he doesn't know anything about using a shank. That's why he always gets his ass kicked. I know you have him in El Hoyo, but he didn't do it."

"All right," Scott continued, "do you know who did it?"

"No idea, but you get me outta here and put me back in my cell, and I will find out for you."

"Whoa, whoa, whoa," interjected Tyrus. "We just can't do that. It's too dangerous."

"Yeah, Sergeant Phillips is correct," Scott said. "If we took you out of here and put you back on the main line, somebody would get suspicious about why the charges were dropped all of a sudden."

"You can do it. Just say that the lab people said they weren't drugs after all," he cleverly replied.

"You know, Ty, that might work. Remember when you had that warrant, and we got that glob of tattoo ink that we swore was some kind of heroin? I think it even had a strange positive color change on the presumptive test."

"Don't remind me, but you're right, we could kick him out and then lock him back up if there is any trouble and say we resubmitted the drugs to another lab."

"Or even the same lab. Mistakes do happen," Scott threw out there, adding, "I think we can see what we can do, but you need to be straight up with us, Perez, or we'll ship you off to a supermax faster than you can blink."

"And you have to be willing to testify," reminded Alex.

"But if you do testify," Scott assured him, "we will make sure that you go to a sensitive needs yard."

"Providing you drop out of the gang and debrief," added Tyrus, aware of the requirements of a sensitive needs yard.

"Yeah, yeah, I am done with this shit. When do I get out of here?" was his parting question.

The first person they had to convince was Lieutenant Templeton, who was not in favor of their plan. Tyrus, however, was very convincing, and the second person they had to convince was the warden. Alex, however, was even more convincing. Within three days, Felix Perez was back in his old cellblock, making a big deal about how dumb the cops were that they didn't know heroin from tattoo ink. They had given him instructions on how to contact them if he had information or if he was in trouble. Of course, if he felt the other inmates were getting suspicious, he was supposed to go to the nearest officer and tell him he needed to lock up.

Scott could not deny that he wasn't just a little apprehensive about this plan. You can never really be certain about what an inmate was thinking, especially when they were being cooperative. Quite frankly, Scott wasn't convinced that Monkey Face wasn't their attacker. As Tyrus said earlier, it was all about the DNA results. Three weeks had passed, and the only information they got from Felix was an inmate appeal form on which was written the words "He's in Fox Wing."

Chapter 7

Give Inmate Rossi a Hand

The following Tuesday was a dull day with little to do. Tyrus and Lieutenant Templeton were away at a gang conference, and that left Scott in charge of the unit. He had just replaced the receiver of his desk phone after talking to a "concerned mother" who was convinced that her son's "whore girlfriend" was smuggling drugs into the institution when he heard an audible alarm emanating from a nearby housing unit. Within seconds, the central control room sergeant's voice came over the radio. "Code 1, Fox Wing. Repeat, code 1, Fox Wing."

Almost immediately, there was a call from the Fox Wing sergeant, Ron Findley. "Medical response needed ASAP!" That was all Scott needed to know. He grabbed Oswaldo, a camera kit, and a crime scene kit, and they were on their way to Fox Wing.

As they entered the central corridor, he could see that they were about fifteen paces ahead of the medical department response. "Hurry, Oz, we need to get there before medical," Scott encouraged. They walked through the housing unit door and saw Officer Jose Hernandez being consoled on the first tier by Sergeant Findley. Officer Robert Pendergrass was standing at the door of cell 238.

Findley shouted out, "He's up there, but he's definitely gone!"

Oswaldo and Scott took the stairs two at a time, and as they approached the cell, they saw a puddle of blood forming on the tier outside the cell. Pendergrass greeted them and said, "Hernandez saw the blood on the tier, hit his alarm, and looked in the cell. It's the first dead body he's ever seen."

"Oz," Scott said quietly, "get on the radio and see if there are any employee post-trauma personnel on grounds today. I think Lieutenant Bennetti is over at the South Facility. See if she can come over and talk to Hernandez."

Pendergrass stepped aside, and Scott peered into the cell. Inmate Geraldo Rossi, an E number on his second murder conviction, was lying on his back on the cell floor with his head toward the open cell door and his left shoulder against the toilet base. He was wearing a pair of denim pants and a white T-shirt—well, it would have been white had it not been thoroughly saturated in bright red blood. It was clear that no rescue efforts were needed; he was most definitely dead. A good estimate was about a gallon and a half of blood covered the cell floor. If you had trouble trying to imagine exactly how much blood that was, take a twelve-pack of twelve-ounce beer cans and pour them out on the floor. Just make sure you use cheap beer.

Scott relieved Pendergrass of his post guarding the door and established a crime scene with barrier tape. Scott asked Senior Nurse Rick Anderson to come into the crime scene and take a quick look at the body. He agreed with Scott's assessment that the victim was beyond medical attention and made the declaration of death. Finally, Scott had managed to keep a dead body in the crime scene. Tom would be very happy. Oswaldo took some overview photographs of the exterior of the cell and just a few shots of the interior with the body in situ, and they exited the crime scene and waited for Scott's old friend from the coroner's office to arrive.

In the meantime, Scott called Alex on the phone. He was up near Sacramento working on a lead in a south county homicide and would not be joining them with the death investigation. He would see what he could do about getting someone else to come out. "Oz, I am pretty sure that those shoe print impressions in the blood belong to Hernandez, but do me a favor and go check. Take a BioFoam kit and collect an exclusionary impression for me," Scott instructed before leaving the wing and making his way down to the East Gate to meet with Tom Jenks.

They were a little over an hour into the incident when Tom showed up. "Sorry, Scott, I was at lunch," he said apologetically.

"No problem, Tom, it's better that you had lunch before this one because I guarantee you won't have much appetite after. I don't think there is a drop of blood left in his body. I just did a perfunctory visual search into the cell, but it looks like someone cut his hand off."

"Which one?" asked Tom.

"Uh, the left hand" was his reply.

"Interesting. Who would do a thing like that?" inquired the veteran death investigator.

"I agree it's a new one on me. I've seen heads bashed in, my share of stabbings and slashing, and I've even seen what a .223 round can do to a head, but I've never seen a hand cut off with surgical precision," Scott replied. "Tom, if you didn't bring a Tyvek suit, let me know, and we can stop by the office and grab an extra."

"Is it that bad? I haven't had to suit up completely in years," he said.

"Trust me, you'll need one," Scott replied.

They stopped by the office and grabbed three anticontamination crime scene coveralls and headed over to Fox Wing. Scott tossed the smallest of the three suits to Oswaldo, who was guarding the crime scene, and slipped his on over his jumpsuit and equipment belt. "I hate these things," Scott said. "They make me look like the world's tallest and fattest Oompa Loompa."

"And you can never get rid of that Tyvek smell until you wash your jumpsuit," added Oswaldo.

"Tell me, Oz," Scott inquired. "Does this Tyvek suit make my ass look big?"

"Your ass is big, Scotty."

"Yeah, it's my childbearing hips."

Once they were suited and gloved, they entered the crime scene. Scott instructed Oswaldo to get complete overview photographs of the crime scene before they made any incursion into the cell. As Scott saw that he was a little perplexed on how to get good overviews without first stepping over the body, he showed him a little trick that he had picked up from his brother-in-law, who had been the head photographer at a large northern California newspaper. "Here you go, Oz. Use this monopod. Just attach your camera, adjust it so that it is shooting downward at about a forty-five-degree angle, and hoist it as high as you can get it. Set your lens at about 38 mm, which is about what the human eye sees at in the digital camera world, and use this shutter release cable or set the self-timer." It took him a couple of tries, and at one time, Scott thought the whole setup was going to take a header into the blood-soaked concrete floor, but Oz made the save.

"All right, Tom, how do you want to get in there?" Scott inquired.

"Well, the blood is starting to clot in the big puddles. What about putting down butcher's paper?" he asked.

"Hang on," Scott said. "I think I have some sterile sheets in the top part of my crime scene kit. Here ya go, this will work a lot better." They folded the sterile sheets into rectangles and placed them in the cell so that they could navigate inside without contaminating or disturbing the bloodstain patterns too badly.

"I think we better do this thing one at a time," Scott suggested. He was the first to go in. He leaned over the body and got a good look at the damage.

"All right, Tom, the hand is almost completely severed from the wrist. Man, the cut went right along the ligaments that separate the carpals from the radial and ulna bones. My god, that is some disturbing sight right there but fascinating, absolutely fascinating," Scott said with amazement. "Here's the razor blade underneath his right hand, and there are indentations in the distal phalanx of his right thumb and the distal phalanx of the right index finger consistent with the shape of the razor blade. It's one of those blades that the maintenance people use to scrape paint off the windows. Fellas, I think what we have here is the most persistent suicide of the year award."

"No way!" exclaimed Oswaldo.

"Yup, and look here, there are three cuts on his right thigh, but they are dry. He was already out of blood in his lower extremities. Now there is persistence. Look at the projected arterial gush over here by the toilet. Must have been the left radial artery because I don't think he got through the ulnar artery. Sure is a lot of gush though. It goes up the wall somewhat too. The toilet is just full of blood, and there are large drops on the toilet seat. This is where he worked on himself and then just tumbled over to where he is now. Okay, Tom, your turn," Scott offered.

"I think I will pass, Scott. Of all the bodies your medical personnel leaves behind . . . let's bag him up."

Scott stepped over the body and exited the cell. "Oz, you go inside. You're the smallest of us three. I'll get behind his shoulders and push forward. You grab his arms and pull, and Tom will slide the bag underneath. Got it?" Scott asked.

"Yeah, I got it," he replied. Oswaldo, being the smallest of the three and the youngest, could get his body between the body of the decedent and the bunk and get a better grasp on the inmate's slippery arms.

"Okay, Oz, are you ready? When I say 'pull,' pull. Pull!" Scott instructed as he pushed forward on the decedent's shoulders, and Tom began wriggling the bag underneath. Oswaldo pulled back on both forearms.

Just then, Scott noticed that Oz's eyes were opened to the size of paper plates. "What's wrong?" Scott asked.

"Dude, the fingers of my right hand are wrapped around his bone," he stated with a mild disgust.

"Suck it up, Oz. Suck it up. Just keep pulling. We're almost there. There is no crying in corrections." Scott watched Oswaldo turn a few shades of green, but he was a trooper and performed his task with zeal.

After the vinyl bag was situated, they took a closer look at the left forearm and the cause of Oz's consternation. It was apparent that Rossi was determined to end his life as swiftly as possible as he had filleted his left inner forearm open, and it looked like a raw chuck roast with a bone in the middle. Tom got out his penlight and a probe. "Well, there's where the arterial gush came from. He severed the brachial artery. It pumped out blood like a fire hose." They zipped up the bag, and Tom again utilized Scott's Sharpie.

Oswaldo went down to the first tier and retrieved the Stokes litter from the sally port. They strapped the former inmate Rossi into the litter, and the three of them carried him down the stairs and out to the corridor, where Tom's assistant was standing by with a gurney. "When's the autopsy, Tom?" Scott asked.

"Thursday at nine. Don't be late, or we'll start without you." He took off his Tyvek suit, stuffed it into a hazardous materials bag, and proceeded up the corridor to the East Gate, along with his assistant, who was wheeling the deceased inmate on the gurney.

Oswaldo and Scott returned to the cell and began their crime scene processing. "Hey, Scotty," Oswaldo said, "look at this on the lower bunk. It's a letter."

"What exactly does it say, Oz?"

"'I'm not sorry for the bitches, but I am sorry for what I did to Danny.' That's all it says."

"Well, I'll be dipped. He was tall and dark too, Mediterranean dark."

"Huh?" asked Oswaldo.

"Nothing, Oz, I was just thinking out loud. Do you remember this guy on the yard when Pajaro was killed?"

"Yes," Oswaldo replied, "I do now that you mention it. He was by the telephones at tower no. 5."

"Interesting," Scott said.

They collected the evidence and finished processing the crime scene. Interestingly, Scott found a much sharper razor blade in Rossi's locker. Rossi must have forgotten it was there. It was amazing what a person can do when he was that determined to end his own life.

As they took off their crime scene coveralls, Scott watched as Lieutenant Bennetti caringly conversed with the young officer who found the body. Scott nudged Oz's arm. "Hey, Ozzie, do you need a little post-trauma care yourself?"

"No, Scotty, I'm fine. I wonder why it is that nobody ever thinks about offering some counseling to the crime scene guys."

"Because we aren't normal, Oz. You should know that. We're machines without feelings. We turn off the emotional part and deal with the evidence. A dead body to us is just an object of evidence. The crime scene is our work site. It would be like offering counseling to a plumber or a painter."

"How do you deal with it, Scotty?"

"Well, Oz, if it wasn't for the hangovers, I'd drink heavily," Scott replied with a chuckle, adding, "I envy alcoholics. I just can't be one." Of course, Scott didn't drink heavily, and Oz was aware of that. He would occasionally, if rarely, enjoy a beer or a glass of wine, but Scott found relief in the other investigative work, opera and running. Running was a great outlet for relieving stress and purging the mind of all the bad things. Of course, Scott's days of sprinting around town had ended, but he still managed a good but slow 10K on his days off. Scott would lament he once ran like the wind but now ran like the winded.

Oswaldo watched a lot of sports on TV, and he raced motorcycles. He was fortunate in his selective memory. You might say his mind was self-cleaning.

"So, Ty, how was South Shore?" Scott asked the returning gang investigator.

"All work, Doggy, all work," he replied.

"Why is it that you gang guys get to go to all the glamour spots in the state for your meetings, and when I get training, it's in Azusa or Ontario? It just isn't fair, Tyrus."

"You could always switch to gangs" was the usual retort. "So tell me about Rossi," he inquired.

"Not much to go on right now. The note was definitely suspicious, but we haven't been able to determine if it was a plant or if it was in his own writing. We won't know until the DOJ does their analysis. I couldn't find any mention of a Danny in his central file or arrest records.

"Back in the early '80s, he killed his girlfriend, hacked her up and put the pieces in a barrel, and left the barrel in the back of his father's barn over in Riverside County. They proved that he put the body in the barrel, but they couldn't prove that he killed her. So they got him for unlawful tampering with a body or something like that. He served six years of a twelve-year sentence and got out in the late 1980s.

"He's in for a second murder that he committed in 1991. This time, it was a kid. The records aren't complete, so I sent off to Bakersfield PD for the actual police reports. He was doing twenty-five to life. They didn't have DNA when he did the first one, but they got him with it on the second."

"Any connection to him and Danny Pajaro?" asked Tyrus.

"Just the usual contact. He probably bought heroin from him from time to time like all the other lifers. Rossi was classified as a white boy, but he usually associated more with the Paisas than anyone else. He spoke Spanish fluently probably because of his father's farm. He was six foot two and about two ten and very dark for a white boy, so he fits the description, and they tell me he knew how to use a knife. There's even an early arrest where he stabbed some guy on his dad's farm, but they dismissed the case for lack of eyewitnesses, and the victim went back to Mexico."

"Why the remorse now? I don't get it," pondered Ty.

"That's what we have to figure out, but the coroner says it was suicide. I guess there was even a blood print on the razor blade that matched his right thumb."

"Another mystery for my book. I'm sorry I missed it," reflected Tyrus.

Another month had passed, and Scott was at his wit's end with the DNA lab. He had been a regular nuisance with his persistent telephone calls. "Is it done yet? Is it done now? When will it be done? Will it ever be done?" He felt like Pope Julius II inquiring if the ceiling would ever be finished. Even Alex had tried and failed.

Scott had no sooner hung up the phone from another failed attempt with the DOJ than Tyrus walked into the office, holding another blank inmate appeal form. "Another one of Perez's notes came in my mail today. Says he wants to talk to us. He says the guy who killed himself didn't do it, and he has the name of the guy that did but didn't want to write it down."

"All right, Ty, when do you want to pull him in?"

"Let's see if we can get him over to the chapel, and we can sneak in from the outside without anyone seeing us."

"Good idea. I'll get him a ducat for tomorrow afternoon," Scott replied, adding, "I already knew about Rossi. I got a packet from Bakersfield PD yesterday. The police report reflected that he killed his seventeen-year-old son, a kid named Danny. Oddly enough, it was the son that he had with the girl that he chopped up. He cut the kid's head off with a machete and buried him in a shallow grave."

"There must have been some serious relationship trouble there," replied Tyrus.

"Ya think? I guess he had also told a few of the older lifers around here that if he ever took himself out, it would be the same way he killed both of his victims. I guess he couldn't figure out how to cut himself up into enough pieces to flush down the toilet."

"Good thing he didn't because then we would have had to charge him with an escape," said Tyrus thoughtfully.

"Have I mentioned lately you are an idiot, Ty?"

Oz pushed by Tyrus and walked into the office. "Mail call, men," he said as he tossed a stack of letters on Scott's desk. "Oh, and this one's from the department of justice forensic DNA laboratory in Oakland. Looks important." He handed it to Scott, turned, and after already having lost interest walked out the door.

"Well, I'll be damned," Scott exclaimed. He quickly opened the envelope and pulled out the letter. "Ugh, why can't they write these things so that we dumb prison investigators can understand them? Wait, okay, okay, blood on fence, on basketball court—definitely Pajaro. Blood on T-shirt from the horseshoe pit also Pajaro. Oh, this is nice—blood found under the cloth handle of the shank found inside of horseshoe pit also Pajaro. DNA recovered from collar of T-shirt and handle of shank—oh, beautiful, *Cardenas*! We have him, Ty, and we have him good."

"Come on, Doggy, there's more."

"Okay, okay, blood on pants recovered from the garbage can also Pajaro. Um, blood from sink, unable to identify. Blood from toilet seat, not Pajaro, interesting . . . shank from the mud, nothing. No surprises there. Okay, blood on tissue was not Pajaro but matched the blood on the toilet seat. And get this, the DNA recovered from the inner waist of the garbage can pants—okay, where is the thing I want to see . . . *damn*! Ty, it's not Pena, not a match. Shit, Ty, we have to kick him out."

"Hey, we got one out of two so far," Tyrus said consolingly. "We'll get the other. What did your dad use to say?"

"A little hard work never hurt anyone, killed quite a few but never hurt any of them?" Scott replied smugly.

"No," he said, "the other thing."

"Patience and persistence pays off," Scott replied.

"Yup, patience and persistence," he repeated. "My father was a font of useless sayings and analogies."

Chapter 8

The Fatal Shower Scene

Scott pulled up in front of his modest little bungalow and did his usual expert job of parallel parking. He gathered up his gear and got out of the car. He walked up the path to the front door, lifted the cover on the mailbox, and pulled out the stack of bills. *Bills, it's always bills. Why doesn't anyone ever send money?*

He opened the door, walked in, and greeted the cat who was stretched out in her "love me, I've been bad" pose. Scott dropped his Sam Browne belt on the kitchen table chair and set his briefcase on the seat. He poured out a little more food in the cat dish and shook the water dispenser to let out a fresh supply.

He plugged his cell phone into the charger, sat on the edge of the bed, and kicked off his jump boots. He wondered to himself why black socks made his feet stink so much when white cotton socks didn't. He took off his jumpsuit and hung it on the hook in the bathroom. He took off his combination ballistic/stab vest and laid it out on the cistern. He could see the steam rising from the panels. He changed his socks, put on his running shorts and a sweatshirt, and thought seriously about putting on his running shoes for a chug around the beachfront.

Just as quickly, he discarded the running shoes in favor of his house slippers, went into the kitchen, and poured a glass of his favorite beer—a

Gordon Biersch Märzen. While studying the refrigerator for something to eat, his cell phone rang. He picked up the phone and said, "Doggett."

It was his lieutenant. "Get to the office now, Scott. There's been another homicide."

"Figures," Scott said. "I just popped open a beer."

"Did you drink any?" the lieutenant quickly asked.

"Nope."

"Then get in here now."

"Yeah, I'll be there in forty minutes. Who was it this time?" Scott asked.

"It's your informant, Perez. He was stomped to death in the shower. There's blood everywhere."

"Shit! Make that thirty-five minutes." Scott hung up the phone, poured the beer down the drain with his apologies to Dan Gordon, performed the above tasks in reverse, and ran out the door.

As he put the key in the ignition, he called Tyrus. "I heard," he said. "I'm on my way too."

The Central Facility was built in 1949 in the new, at the time, prison construction method in the telephone pole design, with cellblocks jutting from a centralized corridor. Each wing, as they were called, was built for containment; that is, if something should happen in one wing, it can be isolated by a series of gates and doors. Unfortunately, the construction was undertaken at a time when the state had fewer than 18,000 inmates housed in six prisons. Therefore, the original design was for a prison population of 1,300 inmates.

Today, the Central Facility housed, at times, over 4,000 inmates. The institution itself was originally built to hold 3,100 inmates. At its highest capacity, it housed over 8,000 inmates. Yes, overcrowding was an issue. The state prison system had expanded to over 170,000 inmates housed in thirty-five prisons, all of which were overcrowded. At Scott's prison, cells that were originally designed for one inmate now housed two. Gymnasiums that were built for inmate exercise purposes now housed row after row of bunk beds. Showers that were designed with a more equitable guard-to-inmate ratio were now overcrowded and inadequately supervised. Such was the case when they arrived at the Echo Wing second-floor showers.

The showers were at the back of the hall and in a place where the officers did not regularly stand to supervise the inmate activity. A fish-eye-view mirror, known as a security mirror, was mounted in a position where an officer can look up and see what was going on in the shower area should an officer conveniently be walking past. Other than that, it was an inmate-friendly area; that was where they went to shoot up dope, make their nefarious deals, and do everything else imaginable. No inmates were observed or apprehended in the area. There were, as always, no witnesses. The only eyes that they were certain observed the attack were staring at the tile.

The officer who found Perez stepped into the shower and turned off the water, checked for a pulse, and activated his alarm. In spite of the damage done to his face, Scott immediately recognized him as Felix. He couldn't help but think that he was responsible for yet another death. The lieutenant was correct in one thing—there was a lot of blood. Unfortunately, Felix was lying in the spray of the showerhead, which washed him clean. There was, however, evidence of cast-off bloodstain patterns on the walls and ceiling, and medium-velocity impact spatter was on the adjacent wall not affected by the water. He was beaten with such force that castoff was found on the other side of the second tier a distance of about forty feet.

"Boot up, Ty," Scott said as he approached on the tier just outside the shower area. "It's a bloody scene. Our path, for now, is going to be the same as the tier cop who turned off the water, one step to the left of the privacy screen, just there about three feet in. The second step will be right there on the curb, two o'clock to the body. The cop took an extra step, but I don't think we need to go that far just yet. Okay, Ty, one at a time." Scott stepped into the crime scene with Ty on his heels.

"Hey, Dog, is that lividity on the left side of his torso? What's it doing there? Has he been moved?" asked Tyrus.

"No, look, when I depress the area, it stays purple. It's a huge contusion. My guess would be a ruptured lung and a lacerated liver,"

Scott replied, adding, "antemortem unless I miss my guess, or our medical personnel have already been here."

Tyrus just looked at him.

"A joke, Ty, a joke," he said.

"Wow," Scott continued, "look at this, an indented skull at an impact point with an outward bending periphery. They either rammed his head into the corner of the privacy screen or hit him with something hard. My guess would be the latter. It looks like they knocked him down and then either jumped on him or stomped him to death. Is Alex on his way?"

"Yeah, he should be here soon, coroner's office too," Tyrus replied.

"Well, they'll be happy that, for the second time, the medical personnel didn't take the body. All right then, let's get out of here until they do what they have to do, and then we can get the crime scene. In the meantime, let's get a few preliminary photographs and map the blood on the tier. Ty? What are you doing, Tyrus?"

"Going through his pants," he responded.

"I'd rather you didn't."

"Look at this, Dog. Here is the ducat for the chapel you had sent. He got it this afternoon."

"Don't remind me, Ty. Just put it back in the pocket. Wait, let me see that. There's something written on the back." Tyrus handed Scott the piece of paper, and he turned it over to read the writing. "'Bandit,'" he read aloud.

"Bandit?" asked Tyrus. "Why does that name sound familiar? Do you know a Bandit, Dog?"

"I know of many bandits here, Tyrus, but not of a specific Bandit. Put it back, and let's get out of here. We'll collect it later when we process the crime scene."

Alex arrived about a half hour later, and he looked markedly worried. "Shit, buddy, ain't this a howdy? I guess we are going to have some explaining to do."

"No shit, Alex. The lieutenant has already given Ty and me the evil eye. He is pissed."

"I have never seen him so pissed," added Tyrus.

"Well," said Alex, "I think I can make a phone call to the district attorney himself, and we can smooth things over with your boss. There is nothing wrong with engaging Felix as an informant. We use confidential informants all the time, and we manage our informants effectively. Now, of course, we usually don't get them killed, but he was advised of the dangers, and he was told what to do if he feared for his safety. It's a terrible thing, but don't blame yourself for what happened. Prison is a dangerous place."

"One thing for sure, we'll find out in the morning. But in the meantime, we've got one hell of a crime scene to process. Who's coming out from the coroner's office?" Scott asked.

"I already talked to Tom," replied Alex. "He's not on duty this week. He's in Cancún. It's going to be one of the new guys, Dan something."

"Judging by the radio traffic," interrupted Tyrus, "he's here. There's someone at the gatehouse wearing blue jeans without his badge or credentials saying he's from the coroner's office."

"Ty," Scott said while shaking his head, "Oz is in the office. Can you ask him to take a pair of vendor BDUs out to the gatehouse and arrange for a visitor's pass for our coroner's office friend? I don't want to wait an hour for him to go back home and change."

"Will do, Doggy."

"Oh, and, Ty, stop by the watch commander's office and smooth things over."

Dan Johansen was the new investigator fresh from auto theft detail, and this was his first trip into a state prison. Tyrus explained the protocols against wearing blue jeans and apologized for the ancient vendor's pants he was asked to wear. It would appear that Oz didn't count on their visitor being six foot three and took a pair of his size 29 waist BDUs out to the gatehouse. He had to go back to the entrance building for a size 36 waist pair. After being inspected by the assemblage of investigators, Felix was bagged and tagged and removed from the crime scene.

The autopsy would be the following morning at 0900 hours. The watch commander asked Scott if he knew the location of the next of kin. Alex informed him that she was in custody at the county jail and that he would talk to her in the morning. There was nobody better at breaking tragic news than Alex. The man had a gift in such matters.

Tyrus and Scott spent the next six hours documenting the crime scene and all the evidence it contained. There were 298 inmates assigned to Echo Wing; a veritable cornucopia of DNA was present in that shower in spite of the required thrice-a-day cleaning. There were no footwear impressions to speak of, but they did manage to develop a few partial footprints in the shower itself. "Hey, Dog, look at the back of this privacy screen. Look at the water droplets. Does it look like maybe a hand had been there?"

"Sure does, Ty," Scott remarked.

"Too bad it's wet. I bet there are some prints on there," he replied.

"Well, Ty, it is stainless steel. If there are some prints there, we can develop them."

"How?" he asked.

"SPR," Scott responded.

"SPR?" he inquired.

"Yup, Ty, small particle reagent, molybdenum disulfide. My guess is that it should work. It's no different from using it on a car door or hood on a rainy day." Scott dug through his crime scene kit and found a small pump bottle on the bottom of one of the drawers. With a few pumps, it began to spit forth a dark liquid spray that trickled down the back of the screen. Within a few seconds, they could see finger and palm print impressions develop. Scott used a Nalgene water bottle to wash away the excess reagent and examined the prints with a magnifying glass.

"AFIS quality, Ty," Scott said with some satisfaction.

"How are you going to lift them?" asked Ty.

"Well, first, we are going to photograph them, and then I will lift them using tape."

"But it's wet," added Ty.

"Photography and gel lift tape, Ty, the stuff we used when we got the print off the doorknob in the library a few months ago." With that, Scott went to work documenting and lifting three good developed impressions, two fingers and a partial palm. They collected what other evidence they could and called it a night.

After booking the evidence into the lockers, Scott headed over to Ty's office. He had just started on his report. "Ty, I am not looking forward to tomorrow and sitting in there with the warden. This very well might be it for us unless Alex can pull off a miracle. All the warden is going to see is lawsuit. We're boned, Tyrus."

"Don't remind me, Doggy. Looks like it will be first-watch culinary sergeant for me."

"Well, like my daddy always said, the fun went out of law enforcement when they took the running boards off the automobiles."

"That doesn't make any sense," replied the unimaginative Tyrus. "And we still need to have these reports done."

Suddenly, he bolted from his chair and yelled, "Bandit!"

Scott jumped from his chair and spun around toward the door. "What the hell, Ty? You scared the crap out of me!" Scott yelled back.

"No," Tyrus replied. "I know where I saw Bandit. It's on that TV you gave me. Look, it's right there on the front." They both looked at the thirteen-inch color TV, and sure as shooting, there it was, scratched into the front panel of the set directly under the Zenith emblem. Inmates can obtain television sets as a purchase either through the special canteen or by having a relative buy one from an authorized vendor. When the television was received by the institution, it was inscribed on the back or top with the inmate's name and prisoner number. Scott looked on the top of the set, and the original name had been obliterated. He looked on the back and found inscribed the name of Frankie Reyes with his prisoner number. Tyrus ran the number through the inmate locater and found that he lived in Fox Wing, cell 351.

Scott sat back down in the chair, feeling like a complete idiot. All those months ago, that clever fox Aldo had told him who the killer was, and Scott was blind to see it. He had scratched the name on the back of the TV and put the moniker under the emblem.

Before leaving for the autopsy the following morning, Tyrus and Scott were summoned to the warden's office. He didn't give Alex time to talk to his boss, and he didn't want to hear any excuses. The last time Scott sat in the chair before the warden was about three years earlier.

He had just saved the life of a visitor who, upon seeing him walking in her direction, popped three small bindles containing black tar heroin into her mouth. To prevent her from swallowing the bindles and having a massive overdose, Scott instinctively reached up with his right hand and placed it on the back of her lower jaw in an effort to prevent her from gulping, a maneuver called the C clamp. It worked, and she spit the bindles out on the floor. During the interview, she thanked Scott for preventing her from swallowing the bindles. She explained that, earlier in the week, she had sampled a hit of the heroin and ended up in the hospital with an overdose. Swallowing four grams of the junk would have killed her. Even her mother called Scott and thanked him for his quick thinking, even though he had arrested her daughter and taken her to jail. Scott completed the investigation and submitted it to the district attorney's office for prosecution, with a successful court outcome for both the girl and her inmate boyfriend.

A short time later, Scott was called up to the warden's office regarding the matter. He was prepared to tell him that he did not want a commendation for his actions, but the warden had other ideas. He was having Scott charged with felony assault on a civilian and relieved him immediately of duty. Scott surrendered his badge and credentials and elected to take a four-week-long vacation while awaiting the decision not only of the district attorney's office but also of the infamous internal affairs division.

After a nerve-racking fortnight, he got word from the DA's office that they were not going to prosecute. In fact, they cited numerous accounts of officers from different agencies reacting in the same manner, and they went so far as to recommend that Scott be given a commendation for his actions. One week after that, the internal affairs investigation was completed. The finding was that Scott did not violate the law and recommended reinstatement.

Unfortunately, the suits in the legal affairs division at the headquarters didn't see things the same way. They recommended once again that Scott be relieved of duty. Eventually, the decision was made by the director of the department himself that Scott should remain on duty. The warden sat him in the chair and yelled at him at length for ten minutes. He then ordered Scott never again to touch a civilian visitor. Scott informed him that he could not promise to not react in the same way should the situation present itself. He reminded the warden that he was duty bound to save lives, and allowing the visitor to swallow what he believed to be a dangerous controlled substance would be tantamount to negligent homicide. The warden impressed on him that he didn't care what he thought. Well, needless to say, they left it at an agreement to disagree.

Scott wasn't angry or bitter—well, maybe just a little, but what he was angry about was that he had to burn over four weeks' worth of vacation time that was not reimbursed. *The bastards!* That was three years ago. Today the warden was frothing at the mouth and spitting fury. For Scott, he didn't much care because he had faced the wrath before, but this was the first time for Tyrus, and Scott felt badly for him.

The warden was the first to object to letting Felix back on the main line. While pretty much ignoring the tirade, Scott had pulled his badge out of his wallet and tucked it into his credentials case. Lieutenant Templeton represented them to good effect and soothed the frothing administrator to some extent. He told the warden that they were too valuable to the investigation to be relieved and that they were working in conjunction with the district attorney's office. He begged the warden to wait for an official statement from the DA's office before taking any drastic actions. The red-faced, apoplectic superintendent continued his rant for another ten minutes, rehashing all his arguments over and over again. They were summarily excused from the office with a foreboding doom.

The lieutenant confined them to the office for the day and sent Oswaldo to the autopsy. Scott began searching the state personnel board job bulletin for any investigator position available far away from the prison. After lunch, Scott noticed Alex walking into the warden's office with ADA Duncan Smith. Scott wished him Godspeed and good luck and retreated to his office.

They must have had some effect on the old man. This time, there would be no internal affairs investigation, but the matter would be submitted to the evil legal affairs division because of the potential for civil litigation. Tyrus and Scott were severally chastised, and once again, Scott found himself reaching for the antacid bottle and searching the job bulletins. Although Tyrus seemed relieved, Scott knew they had not heard the last of the issue.

Scott walked into Ty's office and plunked down onto a chair. "Bad news, Tyrus. All the prints I lifted from the shower belong to Perez. At some point, Felix must have reached up and put his hand against the privacy screen."

"Are you sure?" asked Tyrus.

"Distal phalanx of the left middle and ring fingers and hypothenar of the left palm, there were plenty of points of comparison. There is no doubt."

"Too bad, but it was worth the try," he responded.

Chapter 9

Bandit

Frankie "Bandit" Reyes was an up-and-coming gangbanging nightmare at age twenty-three. As a juvenile, he had already killed a man in an argument outside a bar. As an adult, he had robbed a liquor store, murdered another man, and had a litany of drug-related arrests. He was born and raised in a posh neighborhood in Brentwood, California, in relative wealth and comfort. His father was a retired army colonel who made his wealth in real estate, and his mother was from a prominent Hollywood family. He was bored as a teenager in high school and began experimenting with drugs. This boredom resulted in a number of petty crimes that introduced him to county jail time, where he mingled with the wrong element and liked it.

After the death of the drunk outside the bar, Frankie was sentenced to the California Youth Authority, where he became a member of the Southern Hispanic street disruptive group. He was released from the Northern California Youth Correctional Facility on his twenty-first birthday. Within six months, he had killed again, this time an elderly man whom Frankie happened to be robbing at gunpoint and who had decided it was the appropriate time to have a massive heart attack. He was dead before he hit the sidewalk. Frankie was captured by the LAPD running from the scene. The handgun was recovered, and a video surveillance camera at a nearby gas station sealed his fate. He was holding the old man's wallet. It contained five U.S. dollars. He was serving a fifteen-to-life sentence and hadn't even reached his twenty-fourth birthday.

He certainly was tall enough to be their suspect at 6'2" and weighed in at about 165 pounds, and he had a dark tan from months of basking in the afternoon sun instead of tidying up the West Gate, where he was assigned as a porter. He didn't seem to get into any trouble at the prison, and staff found him to be cooperative and congenial. Their main problem was that he was not in Oz's diagram. In fact, it appeared that he wasn't anywhere on the yard at all.

"Ty, I can't figure this stupid thing out," Scott said. "I have looked at all the videotapes and reviewed every diagram. He wasn't out there. In fact, I have a cop who says Bandit was in Fox Wing at the time it happened."

"Maybe he was the one who called the hit," inquired Oswaldo.

"No," replied Tyrus. "He didn't have that much juice. He would have been the hit man, sure, but he would have never had enough pull to call it."

"Where did he work?" Scott asked.

"Well, here's the thing, Doggy, he was assigned as the porter at the West Gate, but nobody will acknowledge if he was even working that day."

"What about the time sheets?" Scott asked.

"They say he was at work, but you know how that goes. Some cops just fill those things out in advance or at the end of the month," replied Tyrus.

"Well, Ty, I can't see getting a warrant for his DNA if I can't place him on the yard."

"What about showing his photograph to McIntyre?" asked Tyrus.

"McIntyre won't testify, and I don't blame him. No, we have to figure this thing out without our informants. I've got an idea, Ty, that just might work."

"Oh no, Dog, I don't like that look one bit."

"No, it's simple really. Let's go take a look in his cell and see what we can find."

"Like shoes maybe?" asked Tyrus.

"Precisely what I was thinking, Tyrus."

They wasted no time in getting to his cell and having a good look around. Tyrus reviewed all the paperwork and found certain documents that linked him to the gang and confirmed his alias but nothing in the way of orders to commit an assault. "Hey, Ty, under the bunk, I think I see an old pair of Reeboks. Hang on while I reach under there and grab them. Man, these things are ancient. What do you think?" Scott asked while turning them over.

"I don't know, Doggy. I don't think those are the shoes."

"Yeah, I agree, it's definitely a different pattern—size 11, though, and Reeboks. That helps a little."

"Those other shoes are probably long gone," Tyrus replied. "Hey, Doggy, don't you wear a size 11?" he asked.

"Yes, but I have an alibi," Scott reminded him.

"No, we have only your word that you were on the freeway."

"Okay, Ty, you got me. Do your duty, Officer. I was wearing Reeboks that day too. By the way, who is his cellie?"

"Uh, let me see what kind of mail is in the other locker," he replied as he opened the door of the cellmate's locker. "Inmate Hermano Delgadillo. Mean anything to you?"

"Nope," Scott replied.

"Well, Doggy, that's why you work dope. It is rumored that he has the keys to the yard."

"So, Ty, what you are saying is that Bandit's cellie is the biggest and baddest Southerner in the Central Facility?"

"That is what I am saying," replied the gang investigator.

"Things that make you go 'hmm,'" Scott said while rubbing his chin with his forefinger and thumb.

They finished the search without discovering any remarkable evidence. "So," Scott said in disgust, "we are back to square one and nothing for a warrant except some circumstantial evidence—size 11 shoes, Reeboks, and his cellie's status in the gang."

As they exited the cell, Tyrus noticed Bandit's supervisor sitting at the West Gate. Officer Donald Foxworthy was a twenty-eight-year veteran of the force and had been assigned to the West Gate for the last fifteen years or more. The West Gate was the portal from the corridor to the yard. Inmates must first pass through a metal detector and a search of the items they were taking with them before being allowed to proceed to the yard. They must surrender a photographic identification card known as a yard card. Two inmate porters were assigned to this area as janitors, although for the life of Scott he could not figure out what they actually did all day other than sweep a little and bullshit with staff. Frankie was one of these porters.

"What's up, Foxy?" Tyrus asked.

"Same old thing, Sergeant Phillips, just one day closer to retirement," replied the seasoned officer.

Tyrus continued, "I heard that. Hey, weren't you working on the day Pajaro was killed?"

"Oh, yeah, I was here. That was a mess. We had buck naked inmates stretched from the gate to Baker Wing. I didn't get out of here until after ten o'clock at night. Why?" he asked.

"Well, we're kinda wondering what you did with your porters," asked Tyrus.

"They both live in Fox Wing, so I just put them in there before the code 2 responders came down."

"Where were they when the whole thing started?" Scott inquired.

"Well, Castro was sitting right there at the desk, and Reyes was outside, sitting in the grassy area just outside the door." They thanked Foxy for his time and started back to the office.

"Ty, I don't know what else to do. I think this is a dead end."

"Reyes wasn't in his cell just now, and we're back on lockdown. Where do you think he is?" asked Tyrus.

"The tier cop said he was down at medical. You wanna go buzz him and see what he is wearing?" Scott asked.

"You read my mind, Doggy."

They walked down to the infirmary and asked the first-floor officer if he had seen Inmate Reyes. He pointed them in the direction of the nurse's station. To look at him, you wouldn't think Inmate Reyes was born a killer. He was young, tall, good looking, and well built. His father was of Spanish descent, and his mother came from German stock, so he looked more Caucasian than Hispanic. He had no visible tattoos, but his central file reflected he had the word "bandit" emblazed across his back, "love to kill" on his right deltoid, and "Barrios Brentwood Locos" on his chest. They walked past him and noted that he was all in state blues as they liked to say—blue chambray shirt, blue denim pants with "CDC-Prisoner" inscribed on the right pant leg, and brown boots.

Tyrus couldn't contain himself. Scott knew it was pointless from the start to expect that he would. As soon as they passed Frankie, Tyrus let out with a "How's it going, Bandit?" And he kept walking. Scott looked over at Frankie, and he had a look of shock on his face.

"Well, that'll get him thinking," Scott said, knowing that inmates became exceptionally nervous when the Goons knew their aliases.

Chapter 10

Darling Frankie

Several months had passed, and the institution was on normal program—no lockdown. Tyrus and Scott maintained close surveillance on Frankie Reyes. They intercepted his incoming and outgoing mail and listened to his telephone conversations, which although innocuous were annoying as hell, especially those with his mother. "Oh, Frankie, you are such a darling," she would say over and over again.

"What did the lawyers say about my appeal, Mom?" he would ask.

"Oh, darling, the lawyers say you will be out soon. They are working on getting you a new trial. They guarantee me that you will be home for Christmas. Won't that be nice, darling? You didn't kill that poor old man. That old man was going to die anyway. He had a very bad heart. You didn't even do it, sweetheart. They can't prove that was your gun. That could be anyone in that video, and you told them you just found the wallet on the sidewalk. They are just out to get you, but Mommy won't let them. Mommy has the best lawyers for you, my darling." Ah, a mother's love was simple and blind. The letters were just as bad, if not worse.

Scott had just finished his frozen entrée for lunch and was enjoying his midday Mountain Dew. It was his only vice, and if he didn't have one by 1130 hours every morning, he became a fiend like a crack addict. Oswaldo would tell you this was true. He'd seen the unpleasant result of a day without the Dew. He tried to encourage Scott to break the habit, but Scott told him it was his one and only vice. "If I were to give it up," Scott said, "I would be perfect, and you don't want me to be perfect. Besides, I've seen you hide a Dew in the fridge yourself."

Scott was going through a stack of inmate mail when his telephone rang. It was a single ring, so he knew it was an internal telephone call, meaning a staff member was calling. The only difference between a double ring and a single ring was whether he answered with "Investigator Doggett" or just plain "Doggett," which was what he said into the receiver.

"Dog, it's Planski. I think I have something for you."

"What's up, Cecil," Scott said cheerfully. "I haven't heard much out of tower no. 2 these days. What do you have for me?"

"Well, I got an old-time Mexican on the phone, and I think he is talking to Danny Pajaro's wife. He says that he knows how he died but couldn't tell her on the phone because it would be worth millions of dollars to her when she sues the department. He said he would send a letter to her, and she gave him her address."

"Is he still on the phone, Cec?"

"He's on number 6, but he's talking to somebody else right now."

"Okay, get him ID'd for me when he gets off the phone, and I will have a word with him. Call me back when you know who he is."

Just as Scott hung up the telephone, he heard the radio traffic from tower no. 2. "Charlie 6 Alpha, tower 2, give me a 10-21. I need you to identify someone for me, please." About twenty minutes later, Cecil called Scott back with the name of the inmate—Guillermo Rodriguez, a Charlie number out of B Wing, cell 126.

"I don't know, Ty," Scott said into the phone. "I listened to the telephone call, and it sounds legit. I don't think he's talking to Pajaro's wife, though. I think it's his mother. It might be nothing, or it might be that he made the same connection that Aldo made. We just need to talk to him and find out what he knows."

"All right, Doggy, you know what to do," he replied.

Later in the afternoon, Tyrus and Scott had Rodriguez brought to the unit 1 correctional counselor 2's office. He was a small Hispanic man in his late sixties or early seventies. He did not look at all pleased to see them and, at first, claimed not to understand or speak English. When Scott told him he listened to his telephone conversation and offered to get Oswaldo to come up and translate, he suddenly remembered that he was fluent in the English language. "Look," Scott began, "Rodriguez, I heard your telephone conversation with Danny's mother. We're not mad at you for telling her to sue the department. That's not what we are here to talk to you about. We just want to know if you have any information that will help us find the guys that killed your friend. Surely, Danny would want you to help us."

"No! No, no, no! I will not. You people killed him, and you must pay his mother money, lots of money."

"Well," Scott continued, "that is a civil matter. I do not investigate civil matters, only criminal matters. If the department did something wrong, then she is in her rights to seek a remedy in the civil courts. I am looking for a remedy in the criminal courts. I need your help to find the guys who did this and to make sure that only the guilty will be brought to justice. So what do you say? Can you help us?"

"No! You are the people who need to be brought to justice" was his retort.

Tyrus leaned into the conversation. "Okay, wait a minute, you do know that he was stabbed to death."

"Yes, this is true," he responded.

"So are you saying one of us stabbed him?"

"Not exactly, but you are responsible just the same."

"Is it because the tower officers didn't do anything to stop the attack? Because they couldn't see it. It happened in a blind spot. We had no idea there was even a blind spot there. We have fixed the problem since then. Maintenance bowed the fence outward, and now there is an unobstructed view," Scott explained.

"I do not blame the tower officers. I blame the warden," replied the old curmudgeon.

"Aw, help us out here. We can go on like this all day. Just tell us what you know, and you can go back to your house or out to the yard," responded the frustrated Ty.

The old man scratched his chin and raised his eyebrows up and down with deep thought. He then calmly placed his hands on the desktop and interlaced his fingers. He took a short breath and looked directly at Tyrus and said, "It was because of you that my dear friend was unable to break free of his attackers and run for help."

"How so?" Scott inquired.

"It is the heaters," he said with a matter-of-fact demeanor. "It is springtime and very warm, and you still have the heaters blowing hot air into the cells day and night."

"Oh no! You gotta be kidding me!" exclaimed Tyrus as he shoved himself back in his chair.

Scott reached out with his left hand and steadied the inmate's right forearm. He patted him a few times while looking at the old grizzled convict. He knew this would have the good-cop-bad-cop effect, and it was time for him to be the good cop. "I think I see your point. Yes, you know how maintenance is around here. They'll turn the heaters off sometime in September. That was always my fight with them when I was a housing unit officer. It can be miserable in the cells, and the heat doesn't just stay in the cells. It travels out to the entire housing unit. How exactly did this prevent Danny from getting away?"

"My friend complained all the time about the heat. He couldn't sleep at night because of the heat. He was sluggish, and he moved like a snail. You took his strength. Daniel was a lion. He had the strength of many men, but you took his strength away from him. To make him endure the heat like that is cruel and unusual punishment, and it is against the law, against the Constitution!"

"I understand your concern, and I am sorry for your loss," Scott interjected. "You have every right to inform his mother. Let me ask you something, were you on the yard that day?"

"Were I on the yard that day, I would have come to his rescue and fought those evil men with every ounce of strength I have in my body."

"Of that I have no doubt," Scott answered. They thanked the tired old man for his help, and Tyrus held the office door open for him.

When he was gone, Tyrus plunked himself back down onto the chair and gave Scott a look of annoyance. "Okay, okay, he's a crackpot," Scott said. "But he might just be blowing smoke up our asses, and he really does know something."

"You think he was just making something up right now and saving the true story for Pajaro's mother?"

"It is a possibility, Tyrus. You saw the way he thought hard about his response. We better keep an eye on his outgoing mail. We are, however, obligated to do a follow-up. I will call maintenance and ask them if the heaters were still on. I'm pretty sure they were still on, and I remember we activated the heat plan a couple of times during that month too. I'll do the follow-up report and put it in the investigative file just so that we can say we covered the lead."

A few days later, Scott intercepted an outgoing letter disguised as legal mail being sent from Inmate Rodriguez to the grieving mother of Danny Pajaro. Legal mail was generally considered to be of a confidential nature and therefore cannot be read by staff. However, as Mrs. Pajaro was not in the registry of licensed attorneys, Scott determined that the regulations did not apply. He opened the envelope and read the enclosed letter. It mimicked the statement provided by the inmate in every detail. The only difference was that now he was certain that her lawsuit would bring, at the very least, a one-billion-dollar windfall. Scott told Tyrus that should she win, they can always give her a prison. Scott didn't blame the old guy. He lost his best friend and was probably feeling a little guilty for not being on the yard to protect him.

Still reeling from their interesting interview with the elder Rodriguez, they decided to take a second look at all the inmates on the yard who matched the suspect description. They even tried to interview Chino Cardenas with the same results and verbal abuse as the previous interview. The only difference was that, this time, he wanted his lawyer, and he wanted him now. Okay, okay, Scott got it; he was innocent. They even had an interview with Alex and DDA Richard Rainwater, the prosecutor assigned to prison crimes, to see how they felt about pursuing criminal charges against Chino alone. Alex was resolute that their mystery stabber would be found and pledged to be more proactive in the investigation.

As they left the DA's office, Scott looked over at Tyrus and said, "We gotta get something on Bandit and at least get him locked up." When Scott got back to his office, he picked up the receiver of the telephone to check for messages. The double dial tone was always an invitation to pick up his pen, find a piece of paper, and punch in the secret code, which was not so secret as it was the number of his phone extension. Hey, Scott was a simple man, and he had no brain storage space for a lot of secret codes. He wrote on the paper "Foxy needs to talk." Scott called Officer Foxworthy at the West Gate and asked him to stop by his office after his shift.

Ten minutes past two o'clock, Foxy was knocking at the door. "Look, Dog, I have something to tell you," he began. "Inmate Castro has been my porter for almost ten years. Sometimes I give him things in exchange for information. It's never anything bad, just peaches from my tree at home or cupcakes or a candy bar. I know it is wrong, and I could lose my job because of it, but he gives me good information. He told me something today as he chewed on a Snickers bar. It had something to do with Inmate Reyes and the day that Inmate Pajaro died."

"Look, Foxy, I've known you forever. And to be honest with you, we've known for a long time that Castro is your informant. I don't care. I don't think anyone cares as long as you don't go too far. There is a fine line between overfamiliarity, which is a termination offense, and treating an informant to a Snickers bar. I won't tell if you don't. Now what the hell did he say?"

"Well, I'm kinda embarrassed because I didn't notice it myself, but I thought you needed to know," he stammered.

"Foxy, you're killing me here," Scott implored.

"Okay, okay, Castro said that Reyes wasn't wearing his state blues when he came in from outside and that when I put him in Fox Wing, he was wearing sweatpants."

"You're sure he came to work in blues?" Scott asked.

"Oh, yeah, he had to because I would have sent him back to change if he hadn't."

"Foxy, I could kiss you. Can you put that in writing for me?"

"Well, I don't want to give up Castro," he said reluctantly.

"Okay, here's what we are going to do. You got it from a confidential informant, and I will protect you under section 1040 of the Evidence Code as long as I can."

Scott let Officer Foxworthy out of the office and immediately ran into Ty's office. "Tyrus! Tyrus! Tyrus! We have our first break!" Scott yelled. He explained to him what Foxy had said, and Tyrus just sat there for a moment with his forehead crinkled and one eyebrow raised. "It means, Tyrus, that he changed."

"Yeah, but, Doggy, that's at least seventy-five yards or more from where we found the pants in the garbage can. There is no way that he could have made it that far. No way, Dog. Staff was responding through that pedestrian gate."

"Look, Ty, all the action was over there at the west corner of the canteen. All the towers were looking in that area. The first ones out that gate were the West Gate code 1 responders and then the housing unit cops from the west end. After that, it would be the housing unit cops from the east end and all the supervisors. All he had to do was keep moving closer and closer to the gate and then wait for his chance to get back to the grassy area. Nobody would have noticed him, and even if they did, they wouldn't think anything of it. You know how people get tunnel vision when they are responding to alarms."

"I don't think it can be done," Tyrus stated adamantly.

"Ty, I will prove it to you."

After a few minutes' discussion with his lieutenant and a longer discussion with Captain Sanderson, in-service training lieutenant Donny Pearson, and armory sergeant Steve MacDonnell, Scott had persuaded them to conduct an alarm response training exercise on the Central Yard in front of the canteen. The institution went on lockdown status for two hours the following day. Officers were assembled at the west corner of the canteen. A prearranged radio alarm would be announced for the purpose of the training exercise. The watch commander announced a code 2 alarm on the yard. Scott began the exercise standing in the area of the horseshoe pit.

As the commotion grew larger with the initial collection of officers representing yard staff yelling at imaginary inmates, Scott began walking in the direction of the basketball court and then toward the latrine. He observed the responding officers come out of the West Gate almost exactly in the manner described earlier. The first ones out were the West Gate and west end housing unit officers. They ran directly toward the simulated incident. Scott noted that not one of them looked in his direction. He thought to himself that even during a fake incident, they still had tunnel vision.

He delayed a few minutes at the latrine and then walked at a casual pace to the yard pedestrian gate. He watched as the east end housing unit officers and a cluster of sergeants and lieutenants ran toward the action. He slipped past the pedestrian gate and crossed the walkway between the gate and the grassy area near the West Gate just as the code 2 responders came through. He then walked into the West Gate and called Officer Stephen Kent, a veteran tower cop in tower no. 5. "Stephen, it's Dog," he said.

"Wait a minute," he replied, "how are you calling me? You're on the yard."

"No, Stephen, I'm at the West Gate. Didn't you see me come in?" Scott asked.

"You must be invisible" was his reply.

Scott called the three other towers and only tower no. 3 said that he saw him. Scott attributed this to Stephen being faster at the dial than he was. He then walked back to where Ty was standing in the center of the yard. "They didn't see me, Ty, and that was with only imaginary inmates on the yard. Just think how well I could have done that with inmates moving around, vying for the most comfortable place to assume the prone position."

"All right," he said, "I will say that it is plausible."

"You are one stubborn bastard, Ty."

"Maybe, but it still isn't enough to lock him up."

"No," Scott agreed. "But we are getting closer."

That evening as Scott drove the winding coastal road home, he got a call from Alex. After fumbling for his earpiece while negotiating the curves, he yelled into the microphone, "Doggett!"

"Well, hey, buddy, I've got some information I think you might like to know about."

"Alex Rowland, my hero, what do you have for me?" Scott beseeched.

"Well, do you remember Alejandro Bourgoin-Taylor, the guy you busted for smuggling drugs into the prison using the free person who worked in the laundry room?"

"Oh, yeah, sweet deal. We intercepted the boxes he was sending from Los Angeles to Humboldt County. The packages went to a lady who visited another inmate, and she would stop and give the dope to the laundry guy at his house before she would arrive at the prison for a visit. It took us some time to figure that one out. It was the postal inspector's office that helped us. What about it?" Scott asked.

"Well, he sent me a letter. He says that he can give us some information if we reconsider that sentence that was about to be handed down to him in that plea agreement."

"What, does he want it to go away?" Scott asked.

"I don't think he's even asking for that much, but the plea was for nine years. I think he will be happy with half of that. You want to go talk to him, buddy?"

"Go ahead, Alex, ask me twice," Scott kidded.

"Okay, buddy, do you—"
"Yes!"

It took five days for Alex and Scott to get their schedules to jive enough to interview Inmate Bourgoin-Taylor. It was almost two years since Oswaldo and Scott completed that investigation, which included an inspector from the United States Postal Inspector's Office hiding behind the counter of a very small post office in the city of Montague, California. It was the third time Scott had been involved in an investigation regarding Bourgoin-Taylor's many efforts to smuggle quality marijuana and heroin into the institution; the first was in 1999 involving a legal mail parcel filled with the smelliest weed he'd ever encountered. In that case, Bourgoin-Taylor wrestled the tier officer to the ground for the parcel. In court, his defense was that he thought the parcel was a bomb and wanted to absorb the full blast with his body and thereby saving the life of the officer. *Well done*, Scott thought, but the jury didn't believe him. He later petitioned the court for leniency in the sentence on the grounds of his heroic act, but it didn't work.

In the second case, Scott intercepted a care package sent from his faithful wife. Cleverly concealed in four cans of dace was over 660 grams of quality marijuana. The only reason the cans were detected was that Officer Karen Santiago was filling in for the vacationing property room officer. Karen was a cautious consumer of the first degree, and she noticed that the weight of the cans seemed unusually light. She weighed each can and discovered a discrepancy between the weight printed on the label and the weight on the scale. That was when she called Scott.

Scott opened the cans and discovered the weed. The labels had been removed from each can, and a hole was cut in the side. The contents were removed, and the cans were air-dried. The cans were then filled with marijuana, and the square piece of tin that had been removed from the side was soldered back into place and sanded flush. The label was then glued back in place. It was clever, indeed, but not clever enough to fool a frugal mother of three. During that trial, Inmate Bourgoin-Taylor alleged that he was smuggling the pot into the institution to assist all the terminally ill inmates who desperately needed medicinal marijuana. It didn't work.

Scott didn't think Alejandro would be pleased to see him; he wasn't. "Why did you bring him?" he asked angrily.

"Well, buddy, I couldn't exactly come moseying in here by myself, now could I?" responded Alex.

After a few minutes, Alejandro accepted the fact that Scott wasn't going to leave and began talking freely with Alex. "I was there, you know, when the Mexican guy got killed in the shower. I was just putting my clothes back on when this tall guy walked past me and hit him square in the top of his head with something that looked like C or D cell batteries tied up in a sock. Once he went to the ground, the guy jumped up and down on top of him like a trampoline, kicking him and stomping on him. I want you to get me a deal on my sentence, and I can tell you who he was," demanded Inmate Bourgoin-Taylor, formerly of Baton Rouge, Louisiana.

Alex looked over at Scott, held out his hand, and said, "Let me borrow your cell phone." And he walked out of the room.

A few minutes later, Alex walked back into the room and said, "Okay, you have a deal—three years consecutive at 50 percent."

"Two years concurrent," countered Alejandro.

"What is it with you guys and concurrent sentencing? We don't do that in this county. Consecutive, and that's my final offer."

"Wait a minute," Scott interrupted. "Do you even know who this guy was?"

"I lived right next door to him in Fox Wing for over a year before I transferred over to Echo Wing" was his reply.

"Frankie Reyes," Scott said slowly.

"Exactly," replied Alejandro, adding, "They call him Bandit."

"How did he get out of the wing?" Scott asked.

"I watched him walk out the front door when they recalled the yard. All he had to do was blend in with the inmates coming in off day yard for count."

"The door cop didn't stop him? What about the blood? He would have been covered in blood," Scott asked in disbelief.

"You aren't going to believe me, but Frankie stripped off all his clothes like he was getting in for a shower before he hit that Mexican. He beat him to death while he was naked himself. He showered off the blood and got dressed and left. I watched the whole thing. I couldn't move. I was almost paralyzed with fear and amazement. I have been doing time for twenty-six years, and I have never seen anything as vicious as that. That man is a killer."

Scott leaned over toward Alex and whispered, "Perez had a radial fracture of the skull. I saw it in the autopsy photographs. That wound very easily could have been made by a few batteries in a sock. I believe him."

Alex leaned forward and said, "You have a deal, buddy, but it's consecutive, and you will have to testify." He then shook Alejandro's hand to seal the deal.

"That's not all," added the Louisiana native. "I saw someone hand Bandit a knife on the tier in Fox Wing the night before Danny Pajaro was killed." Alex and Scott were dumbfounded. Alejandro described the knife as having an ice-pick-type blade and a cloth handle. He could not identify the inmate who handed him the shank because his back was to him. Scott didn't care.

Before they left the room, Scott turned to Alejandro and asked, "Can we knock it off with the marijuana?" Alejandro replied something to the effect that he was doing God's work for the sake of the ill and infirm. Scott reminded him that he would therefore be doing Dog's work for the sake of the public.

Chapter 11

Capone

"Well, Ty, Deputy District Attorney Rainwater says we need to try to talk to Frankie Reyes and see what he has to say before we go any further. We have to try to verify some of the stuff Bourgoin-Taylor told us. I'm thinking we interview him as a witness since he was out on the yard, and that way, there isn't a need for *Miranda* until he says something incriminating."

"Is that legal?" Ty asked.

"Perfectly, but if it will make you feel any better, I will do the *Beheler* warning instead."

Later that day, they pulled Frankie into the unit 3 captain's office. Scott set his digital recorder on the table, only slightly obscured by his departmental-issued black baseball cap with small brass hat badge. They sat Frankie down in the chair nearest the door. "Inmate Reyes, we would like to have a word with you," Scott started. "You are not under arrest or being detained. You are under no obligation to talk with us. At any time, if you wish to leave this room, you are free to do so. I am Investigator Doggett, and this is Investigative Sergeant Phillips. We are from the security and investigations unit, and we are investigating the death of Inmate Danny Pajaro."

"Why do you want to talk to me?" he asked.

"You were working on that day, were you not?" inquired Tyrus.

"Yes, I was. I was at the West Gate," he replied.

"What were you doing at the time he was stabbed?"

"I was sunning myself on the grass outside the gate."

"Did you know Danny?" Scott asked.

He responded, "Everybody knew him."

"Did you see him walking on the track?"

"Yeah," he said.

Scott continued, "Do you remember who he was walking with?"

"His two friends," he replied.

"Do you know their names?" asked Tyrus.

"Um, I think it was Flacco and Casper."

"Can you identify Flacco and Casper for us?" Scott inquired.

"Ramirez in Charlie Wing and Lopez in Delta Wing," he replied, adding, "I don't know their first names or what cells they are in."

"Can you give us a description?" asked Tyrus.

"Yeah, Flacco is a tall and skinny guy, and Casper is kinda heavy and short."

"Facial hair?" Scott asked.

"Flacco has a mustache, and Casper is bald," he replied.

"From where you were, could you see over to the basketball court?"

"Uh-huh, a little, but I couldn't see the other side because there were too many people."

"So you didn't see him get stabbed?"

"Nope."

"What about your cellie? Was he on the yard?" Scott asked.

"No, he was at school."

Scott continued, "Are you sure he went to school that day?"

"I don't know. Why don't you ask him?"

"Don't worry, we will," Tyrus responded, adding, "I hear he has the keys to the yard."

"What? No, fuck no, he's just an old man" was Frankie's retort.

"He's only thirty-eight," Scott said, only slightly offended.

"Yeah, that's what I said, old."

Tyrus tipped his hat back and leaned in a little. He gave Scott a quick wink and said to Frankie, "You know, the tower officer said that he saw you walking out of the shower area just after Pajaro was stabbed."

"Nah, it wasn't me. They won't let me go out on the yard when I am working," he replied, adding, "You can ask Foxworthy."

"We did, and that's why we are talking to you, to get your side of the story."

"Am I a suspect?" he asked nervously.

"Did we say you were a suspect?" Scott asked in return.

"No, but you're making me nervous. I'm almost out of here. My lawyers are winning my appeal. I don't need to be blamed for something else I didn't do."

"Look, Reyes, we aren't saying you did it, so don't get sideways on us," encouraged Tyrus.

"We just want to know if you saw anything since you were in a spot that was just slightly elevated from the rest of the yard," Scott said.

"No, man, no, I didn't see anything. I want to go. I want to get out of here," he said as sweat formed on his brow. He slid back his chair and stood up.

"Look, Frankie," Scott said, "Foxworthy said you were sitting on the grass, and he put you in Fox Wing himself. We're talking to everybody, so don't get so upset."

"Okay, okay, but can I go now?"

"Sure, Frankie, you can go," Scott said.

"Don't call me Frankie. It's disrespectful."

"Sure thing, Bandit. Now get out of here," replied Tyrus tersely.

He backed out the door while keeping his eyes fixed on Tyrus. They sat for a few minutes in silence to allow time for Frankie to get out of earshot. "Well?" Scott asked.

"The little fucker is lying, Dog."

"Indeed he is, Ty. Indeed he is. Let's check the mail tomorrow and see what he writes to his mother."

In the following day's mail was a letter addressed to Frankie's mother being sent by her little darling.

Mom,

These asshole pigs are trying to say that I killed someone. It's a lie, Mom, a lie! You know how much they hate me. Everybody hates me, and nobody cares about me either. I wasn't anywhere neer where the dude was when he got stabed. I was at work, Mom, and they know I was at work too. My boss says I was at work, and he told them that too because I asked him. I need you to tell the lawyers what they are trying to do to me. Call the warden and tell them I am innocence.

Your loving son,
Frankie

How sweet.

"Well, Ty, I don't think he has a very high opinion of us, my old friend," Scott said as Tyrus was stuffing the letter back into its envelope.

"Maybe not, Doggy, and there is not much of anything to help us get him locked up in this letter."

Oswaldo stuck his head in the office and announced that the lieutenant wanted to talk to them. They reported immediately to Lieutenant Templeton's office. "You wanted to see us, Lieutenant?" Scott asked.

"You guys ever hear of Inmate Delgadillo?" he asked.

"He's the Southerner shot caller on the yard," responded Tyrus. Scott added, "And Frankie Reyes's cellie."

"The warden wants to lock him up," replied their commander.

"Why's that?" inquired Tyrus.

"They found him with a cellular telephone in his cell last night."

"Where do you suppose he got that?" Scott asked.

"Rumor is that Foxworthy gave it to him," replied the lieutenant.

"No, not Foxy," Scott said, adding, "I know Foxy, and I know he has his limits."

"Internal affairs seems to think that Delgadillo found out that he was giving his porter little gifts and was blackmailing him," Lieutenant Templeton said matter-of-factly.

"Now that I can believe," Scott had to admit.

"I bet Frankie is the one that told him too," added Tyrus.

"Poor Foxy, he should have come to us first," Scott said.

Tyrus jumped in, "That is, if he did it."

"True, Tyrus, true. It isn't what you know. It's what you can prove," Scott said with a wink.

"All right," interrupted the lieutenant, "let's get him locked up."

Although Hermano "Capone" Delgadillo was a Charlie-number lifer, he never killed anyone, although he told everyone that he did in part because he thought that he killed someone. He shot the guy in the back as he was scrambling out the door, but the guy didn't die. In fact, although he was arrested for the shooting, he was never charged. Instead, he earned his life sentence by being what was commonly known as a career criminal. He spent the better part of his thirty-eight years stealing cars, doing residential burglaries, receiving stolen property, committing strong-arm robberies, and doing a litany of misdemeanors—not exactly the boy next door. He was a member of the Riverside Varrio Locos and had "RVL" tattooed prominently across his forehead, thus removing himself permanently from the job pool. He achieved his notoriety in the Southern Hispanic gang inside the prison because his father was an early associate of the Mexican Mafia in the 1970s and made his mark. It was rumored that Capone had the keys to the yard, which meant that everything—from which Southerner went to the canteen at what time and what they bought to who to when and where someone would be assaulted on the yard—had to be authorized by him.

Tyrus, Oswaldo, and Scott walked down to the education department and asked Officer Salvador Torres, the education officer, to find Inmate Delgadillo and bring him out to the front desk on some pretext like a telephone call. Oswaldo stepped into a nearby closet, and Tyrus and Scott waited in the restroom near the front door. They wanted to make sure that Delgadillo was away from any of his Southerner buddies.

"Your counselor wanted to talk to you on the phone, Delgadillo. I need to call him back. Just wait right here," instructed Officer Torres.

As he picked up the telephone, Tyrus and Scott stepped out of the restroom, and Oswaldo emerged from the closet. "Put your hands behind your back," Tyrus ordered. Delgadillo complied, and Tyrus placed him in handcuffs.

"Charlie 9. One in restraints from education," Oswaldo announced into his radio microphone.

It was followed by a radio call from Officer White. "Central Control. Charlie 9, clear the east and west corridor from the education department to the holding cells."

As they marched Inmate Delgadillo down the corridor to the holding cells, it reminded Scott of the photographs he had seen as a child of Mussolini walking in defiance after he had been caught by the resistance. His chin was out, his mouth was in a downward crescent, and he nodded to every Southerner whom they passed, who in turn bowed their heads. They weren't taking any chances. They escorted him with their batons out and pepper spray in hand. He would later be escorted from the holding cell to ad seg during count to avoid any retaliation from his lackeys.

The removal of Delgadillo left an obvious void in the leadership of the Southerners at the Central Facility. Their informants were telling Tyrus and his gang investigators that Frankie was stepping up to fill the command gap, but there was some unknown opposition from some of the other gang heavies. Only time would tell who ultimately would be selected as the overall shot caller at the Central Facility. The decision would ultimately come from Delgadillo himself.

Tyrus and Scott interviewed Inmate Delgadillo without success. He denied everything from being a gang member to being the leader of the gang to ordering the death of Inmate Pajaro. He denied that he owned a cell phone regardless of it being found in his hand, and he denied receiving it from Officer Foxworthy. On his way out of the interview room, Scott asked Delgadillo when his next parole board hearing was scheduled. He then asked him what chance he thought he would have with a cell phone rules violation report in his file. He didn't tell Scott, but Scott always liked planting the seed and giving them something to think about.

A few days later, Tyrus walked into Scott's office with a note that had been intercepted by the laundry room officer. It had been smuggled out of ad seg by Inmate Delgadillo in his laundry bag, and it was destined for Inmate Tito "Cornejo" Rosas. Tyrus had never heard of him either, but Capone was giving Cornejo the keys to the yard with special instructions to take care of a problem child whom they had already discussed. They had a pretty good idea whom he was talking about, but since Cornejo didn't get the note, they didn't think it was necessary to act quickly. They decided, instead, to have another talk with Capone. This time, they would threaten to disclose the note to the parole board, thus ending any hope of ever getting a parole date.

Needless to say, he was not happy to see them again and started off afresh with the barrage of denials, until Tyrus dropped the note down on the table. This time, it was in a plastic sleeve with a label that read "Caution: Chemically treated. Wear gloves." Scott had treated the quarter-page note using the ninhydrin method and developed at least one latent print that he could match to their interviewee with twelve individual points of minutiae or Galton's detail and ridge structure, ridge sequence, and ridge spatial relationships in agreement and distortions within acceptable tolerances. After a few minutes, Capone saw that denial was pointless and that bargaining was the better alternative. "What do you guys want to know?" he asked sheepishly.

"Quite a bit," Scott answered. "To begin with, why did you call the hit on Pajaro?"

"I didn't," he rejoined.

"Who did?" Tyrus asked.

"I don't think anyone did. If they did, it went around me, and I can tell you that I wasn't happy with it. Danny was my friend. I could have fixed everything if they came to me first."

"So it was someone acting alone?" asked Tyrus.

"Someone with, shall we say, ambition?" Scott added.

"Yes, someone who needs to be taught his place," pondered Delgadillo.

"Well, that's where we can help you, by letting you help us," Scott suggested.

"We have our own ways," he said defiantly.

"Look, Delgadillo, you can't do this the way you want to, not this time. We know it would come from you. This time, you need to let us, justice, and the courts do what is necessary," Scott encouraged.

"What do you want?" he inquired.

"A little help with the proof would be nice," Scott said.

"Like what?"

"A confession would be great," blurted Tyrus half-jokingly.

"That is not a problem. Give me a week or two, and you will have your confession," he responded.

"No shit?" Scott said, dumbfounded.

"It is not a problem," he again replied.

"Let me ask you something," inquired Tyrus. "What is the real story with the cell phone? Did you get it from Foxworthy?"

"No, the cell phone was not mine," he replied.

"Were you borrowing it?" Scott asked.

"No, it was not mine."

"But they saw you with it in your hand?" pressed Tyrus.

"Yes, but it was not mine. It was my cellie's. He put it in my shower bag. I pulled it out of the bag when Officer Chamberlain approached me. Did you find anything on that phone that linked it to me?"

"No, it was wiped clean," Scott replied.

"As I expected," he answered.

"Wait," interjected Tyrus, "you mean it was a setup?"

"Yes, Bandit told Chamberlain I had a phone. When he ordered me to hand him the shower bag, I reached in to get out my ID card. I felt the phone and pulled it out. You can ask Chamberlain. I looked as surprised as he did."

"He got the phone from Foxworthy?" Scott asked.

"Yes, he was blackmailing him because Foxworthy was giving things to Castro, and Bandit knew about it and threatened to tell."

"What else did he get from Foxworthy?" Tyrus inquired.

"He said that Officer Foxworthy gave him a grand in cash and the cell phone," responded Capone.

"I'm confused, Delgadillo. Why would Bandit plant a cell phone on you?" questioned Tyrus.

"To get rid of him, Ty," Scott replied. "Bandit wanted Delgadillo out of the way so that he could take over the yard, am I right?" Scott turned from Tyrus to Capone.

"He wanted to control everything and knew that I was friends with Danny. I told him I was sending word to the bay asking for instructions regarding his act."

"And did you?" Scott asked.

"Yes. I had told Cornejo to wait for instructions of what to do. I got my reply a few days ago."

"In the Hole?" Scott asked with disbelief.

"Our system of communication is extensive," he responded.

"What was the decision?" inquired Tyrus.

"Blood for blood" was his chilling response.

"And now?" Scott asked.

"I will do it your way for now," he replied. Inmate Delgadillo promised them he would send word regarding his next move. Scott told him that he could trust Officer Rudy Galvan to get word to him as they had worked together in the past.

As they walked out of the administrative segregation unit, Scott turned to Tyrus and asked, "What do you think he meant by 'for now'?"

"Somewhere, sometime, there will be payback, Doggy. Eventually, they will get Frankie, but it won't be here, and it won't be now. He knows that we can finger him because we have the note."

"I guess so. Poor Foxy," Scott said as he shook his head. "All he had to do was come and talk to us."

"He's done now for sure," Tyrus replied.

"Yeah, Ty, not only will he lose his job but he could also be prosecuted if Bandit used that phone for anything, uh, sinister."

Tyrus replied, "At least they can't give him the felony for accepting a bribe. He didn't get paid for the phone. In fact, he had to pay up a grand."

Two weeks to the day later, Scott got a call from Rudy Galvan. He said that he pulled Inmate Delgadillo into the property room to discuss a property issue when Delgadillo handed him a piece of paper that he wanted him to give to him. Scott retrieved the paper from Rudy and showed it to Tyrus. Written on the paper was "You will have your answer next Tuesday in the Supreme Court Reporter no. 89, 393-394 U.S., October Term 1968 on page 32."

"What the heck does that mean?" asked Tyrus.

"Well, Tyrus," Scott replied, "I think it means that Bandit is going to leave a message for Capone in the law library. Ad seg goes to the library Tuesday morning. The general population goes Monday afternoon. My guess is that Bandit will be in the library on Monday, request this book, and hide something on page 32. The inmate clerk is the one who passes out the law books, so it's a perfect communication device. That book has probably sat on the shelf since 1969 without anyone looking at it for legal reasons. Plus, do you see anything significant about the book number?"

"Eighty-nine? No," he responded.

"I do," Scott answered. "It's the last two digits of Delgadillo's prisoner number."

On the following Monday, Tyrus and Scott let themselves into the central library after the librarian had gone home for the day. They proceeded to the legal law section, which was secluded from the rest of the library. Tyrus found the volume before Scott and snatched it up. "Glove up, Ty," Scott urged, adding, "Anything we find will have to be processed for latents." He heeded Scott's admonition and donned latex gloves.

Pressed between pages 32 and 33 was a neatly folded piece of paper on which was written, "Capone—The decision was made without you because of your feelings for Danny. He did us wrong, and I was chosen the assassin. We have all agreed that I have the yard until you return. Con respecto, Bandit."

"Is it our confession, Tyrus?" Scott asked.

"It'll do, Doggy. It will do."

Scott petitioned the court for a search warrant for a buccal swab and blood from Frankie "Bandit" Reyes. Scott always requested blood, not that the DOJ needed the blood, but he enjoyed seeing the suspect squirm as it was being drawn. There was also a certain psychological victory that you got with blood over saliva. It sent the message home that we would find DNA.

The statement of probable cause included the garments found in the garbage can, the blood on the tissue, the statement by Officer Foxworthy that Frankie had changed his clothing, their demonstration suggesting the plausibility of movement, the eyewitness testimony of Inmate Bourgoin-Taylor, and the note. They did not disclose the identity of Capone, just that he was a high-ranking member of the gang. The information was weak but sufficient, Scott believed as did Superior Court Judge Timothy Buckhurst, who signed the warrant. It was filed with the clerk of the court, and Scott was on his way back to the institution to meet with young Frankie.

Tyrus and Scott went down to the West Gate, where he was working; placed him in handcuffs; and escorted him up the corridor to the infirmary, where Bob Connors was waiting. Also waiting was two of the biggest correctional officers Scott could find, and these guys made sumo wrestlers look anorexic. Scott sat Frankie down in the chair in the phlebotomy lab. He read the search warrant to him and asked him if he would voluntarily agree to submit the required DNA samples. Not only did he say no but he also lurched forward in the chair, hitting Scott square in the chest with his head. Scott fell back into the adjacent locker as Tyrus reached forward to grab Frankie. Frankie twisted out of his grasp, and Tyrus found that the more prudent thing to do was to protect Bob from harm. He pushed Bob behind him and drew out his baton, flicking it to the open position. Scott got to his feet just as Frankie raised his leg in a sideways kick. Scott threw himself into his body, and they both crashed through the laboratory door and into the hallway.

The first-floor infirmary officer activated his alarm and pushed the infirmary door open for responding staff. Although he was in handcuffs, Frankie put up a remarkable fight. He rammed his shoulder into Scott's chest and kneed him in the stomach with an incredible force, which doubled Scott over in pain. Ty had run out of the lab as Scott was attempting to regain his breath, and he drove the power tip of his baton directly into the upper thigh of Frankie's right leg, leaving the perfect contusion impression of a Monadnock expandable baton. Scott got to his feet and threw himself onto Frankie, forcing him to the ground with the advantage of his weight. Tyrus was quick to get a hold of his top half while Scott rolled over to stop the kicking of his legs.

At that point, the two oversize officers who were in waiting appeared and assisted them in restraining the squirming youth on the ground. Bob casually walked out of the lab, stuck the needle in the fleshy part of Frankie's backside, and drew the blood. "What about the swab?" he asked.

"Bob, I don't think it matters this time."

A pair of leg-irons was brought down from the control room, and Scott placed them on his kicking ankles. The four of them picked up Frankie and carried him, squirming and wriggling, to the administrative segregation unit. In fairness, they only dropped him once, but that was because he had gotten a little sweaty, and it was difficult to hold him with all that moving about. As they were picking him back up again, Scott noticed something he should have noticed much earlier. He looked over at Tyrus and said, "Put him back down."

"No, Dog, let's get him to ad seg," insisted Tyrus.

"Ty, I'm serious! Drop him!" Scott yelled. The others complied, and they set the exhausted Bandit back on the floor. All right, they dropped the exhausted Bandit facedown onto the floor.

"The shoes, Ty," Scott said, "look at the shoes. Unless I miss my guess, those are our Reebok Deadstocks. I bet they were in his locker at the West Gate this whole time. How stupid of me not to think of looking there."

Chapter 12

The Prosecution Rests

The DNA results came back six months later. The blood they submitted for Bandit was a match for the blood on the tissue and the DNA from the waistband of the pants. The footwear expert agreed that the shoes they pulled off the feet of the squirming Frankie Reyes were likely the shoes that left the impressions in the crime scene.

Inmate Chino Cardenas took a plea agreement to twenty-five years to life in state prison to be served consecutively to his present commitment. He was proud of what he had done, although the significance that he had conducted the unsanctioned murder of a fellow gang member never really manifested itself on his brain. As far as he was concerned, he had done his duty. Almost two years later, he was stabbed to death by his own gang members in an exercise yard at their sister prison on the hill. He was killed by his two best friends, which was usually the case in inner-gang-related homicides. They had done their duty. Chino had devoted his entire life to his beloved gang, and in the end, his life was consumed entirely by the same gang.

Inmate Frankie "Bandit" Reyes took his case to jury trial, which was his constitutional right. The high-priced private attorney hired by his loving mother argued the usual contamination issues that came with any crime scene. He argued the validity of their experiment regarding Bandit's ability to move across the yard undetected. He said they didn't establish a chain of custody for the evidence. He challenged the report of Officer Foxworthy that Bandit had changed his clothing and that it was hearsay evidence as Foxy was not present in court himself. He argued the relevance of the blood on the tissue. He argued all the same things Scott would have argued if Scott was hired to represent the defendant. In spite of his efforts, Frankie was found guilty of premeditated murder in the first degree. Scott believed it was the testimony of Alejandro Bourgoin-Taylor regarding seeing the weapon being given to Frankie the night before the murder that was what sealed his fate.

Two months later, he was sentenced to death and transferred to death row in San Quentin State Prison. He wasn't charged with the murder of Inmate Perez because of a lack of evidence, even though Alejandro was willing to testify in that case too. Scott thought the district attorney's office wasn't interested in spending the money on another expensive homicide trial after getting the conviction in the Pajaro case. The Perez homicide investigation remained open to this day.

Occasionally, Scott pulled the archive boxes out of the evidence vault and picked through the evidence they collected. If only Frankie had left behind the towel with which he dried himself, but even Alejandro said he remembered Frankie taking it with him. Scott pulled out the gel lifters with the footprint impressions. They sure did look like Bandit's feet. Even if it was analyzed, Scott knew it wouldn't be enough for the DA's office to prosecute. Frankie wasn't even charged with the assault on staff.

One year later, the same high-priced lawyer successfully argued that the jury was influenced by the shackles worn by his defendant during the trial. Although Scott never saw the chains on his feet, Scott could hear him jingling them throughout the trial. The appeal might have failed if not for the bailiff, who noted in her log that the defendant was making noise with his chains. A new trial date was set, but the matter was resolved by plea bargain to twenty-five years to life to be served consecutively to his current commitment, the previous murder conviction. Rumor had it that the colonel put his foot down and refused to spend the additional $50,000 the lawyer wanted to represent his darling son again. Scott was sure that someday, at some other prison, Capone would have satisfied his revenge, and what the judicial system failed to produce would end with the same result.

The warden took pity on the poor officer Foxworthy and allowed him to retire with full benefits. It wasn't the way Foxy wanted to end his lengthy career. It wasn't the way anyone wanted to see it end either. Four months after he retired, he had a massive heart attack and died alone in his house. That was why he wasn't able to give testimony in court. His funeral was attended by more than two hundred officers of the department. Scott even dug his class A uniform out of the closet. Try as he may, he couldn't get the jacket zipped. At least the hat still fit.

Alex was reassigned to the south county office owing to an increase in gang-related slayings in that area. He was replaced by Alberto Gutierrez, a good man with over thirty years' service in law enforcement but definitely without the flare of the tall Texan. Scott still heard from Alex every time there was a new slaying in the southern cities or when he wanted him to keep an eye on one of the locals who was the guest of that lovely facility. Alex also would give Scott a call from time to time when he wanted a crime scene reconstructed or the particulars of a bloodstain pattern explained.

Scott went to Tom's retirement send-off as did Alex. It was held at the coroner's office in the break room. They were just happy it wasn't in the autopsy suite. There was a cake and a battery of soda pop and ice tea but no booze. There was an appearance by the sheriff himself, and Tom was sent off into retirement with a hearty handclasp and a rather cheap-looking gold watch. Scott never could understand the watch thing. You needed a watch when you were working. God forbid you needed a watch in your retirement. Last Scott heard, Tom was terrorizing his neighborhood with his new riding lawn mower.

Tyrus was just in Scott's office. He asked Scott if he was serious about retiring in the next few years. He tried his best to persuade Scott to stay at least eight more years because that was how much time he still had to go. "I don't know if I'll stay eight more, and I'm not sure if I will go in two. The nice thing is, once you have that golden twenty-five years and have reached the half-century mark, which I have yet to reach by the way, it's always nice to know that one day when you've had too much you can pick up the phone and say I'm out of here. Besides, I can't leave my little buddy Oz just now, or should I say I can't leave the department at the mercy of Oz just yet."

Oh, and Scott occasionally got hate mail to this day from Frankie's mother accusing him of planting evidence on her "darling" son. Scott gave the letters to Tyrus for his book.

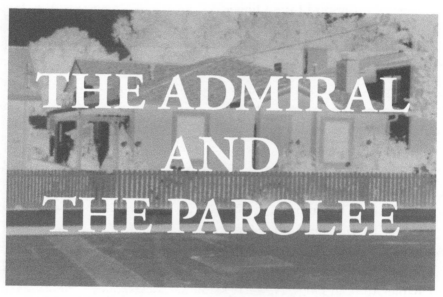

THE ADMIRAL
AND
THE PAROLEE

LESSONS IN INVESTIGATIVE TECHNIQUES

Contents

Chapter 1

The Admiral and the Parolee

"Are you doing anything today, Doggett, or are you just wasting state money?" asked Sergeant Tyrus Phillips as Scott sat staring at a stack of paperwork on his desk.

"Tyrus," Scott replied, "you wouldn't believe me if I told you the kind of day I have had. Why aren't you validating some gang member instead of chewing my ass?"

"Just finished validating Drew McIntyre as a skinhead," he responded.

"What? After he helped us with the Pajaro murder? You are one cruel bastard, Sergeant Phillips. Everyone knows he's a skinhead. Why are you validating him now?"

"He's due to get out soon. Santa Cruz PD wants him validated in case he decides to get in trouble again while on parole," answered Scott's old partner.

"Ah, the old gang enhancement. How is he taking it?" Scott inquired.

"He's not happy, mostly with you, Doggy."

"Why me?" Scott asked.

"Because I told him it was your idea."

"Thanks, Ty," Scott said with a smirk.

"He said you better stay out of Santa Cruz," Tyrus said as he walked out of Scott's office.

Just then Scott's telephone rang. It was a double ring, suggesting it was a telephone call from outside the prison. "Investigator Doggett," he answered with his official voice.

"Scott, it's me, Floyd. Are you busy?"

"Never too busy for my favorite neighbor, Floyd. Is everything all right? How is Barbara?"

"Barbara is fine, but we've had some trouble. I really don't want to talk about it over the phone, and I don't want to call the police. Can you stop by when you get home?"

"I'll be there at about 1710 hours, Admiral."

Retired rear admiral Floyd DeWitt and his wife of some sixty-five years, Barbara, were the best neighbors anybody could ever have. They were both retired navy personnel in their late '80s. Floyd commanded a destroyer during the Japanese attack on Pearl Harbor, and his five-inch deck gun crew was credited with downing one of the enemy torpedo bombers. Floyd was full of stories, and Barbara made the best sweet cherry pie in the world. They bought the house across the street from Scott's bungalow in the late 1970s, when Floyd was assigned as an instructor at the U.S. Navy Postgraduate College, which was within walking distance. They were the neighborhood watchdogs and scrutinized every person and vehicle passing by.

This was the first time Floyd had called Scott at the office, and he knew it had to be something serious. Scott pulled up in front of his house at 1712 hours, as promised, and Floyd was waiting at the gate of the white picket fence that surrounded their small battleship gray house. Before Scott could get his right leg out of the car, Floyd was on his way over. "My word, Scott, those are some shiny boots."

"Floyd, you say that every time I get out of the car. I haven't put any polish on them in over a week. What naughty business have you and Barbara been up to?"

"Maybe you should come in. Barbara is so mad at me, but I think she has a nice piece of chocolate cake waiting for you." They walked up the short path to the front door. Floyd opened the door and extended a hand as if giving permission to board his ship.

"Piping aboard!" exclaimed Scott. "Admiral on deck!"

Before they cleared the small foyer, Scott was greeted by Barbara, who was standing in the kitchen, holding a piece of cake on a plate. "Scott, I am so mad at him!" exclaimed the former navy nurse.

"All right, let's all sit down, and I'll see what I can do to save this marriage," Scott said tongue in cheek. Barbara and Scott sat on the sofa in the living room, and Floyd paced back and forth on the other side of the sofa table.

While Scott enjoyed a fantastic piece of homemade German chocolate cake, Floyd began his dissertation. "Two days ago, Barbara and I were doing our volunteer day at the reading room at the church. A well-dressed young African American man came in and started talking to Barbara."

Barbara immediately interrupted, "He was so nice. He said his name was Byron. He had an African accent, and he was telling me how he was a member of the church, and he had just arrived in the area from Nigeria. He was in the Nigerian Navy, and he was selected to attend the navy college. He said they had put him up at a motel in Salinas, and he was robbed at gunpoint the first night that he arrived. He wanted to leave Salinas and find a place here, and he wondered if the church had any way of helping."

Floyd resumed, "He didn't have any money because they took all his cash in the robbery. Barbara asked me if I would mind if we let him stay in the apartment that's attached to our garage until he could find something suitable."

"He said he had a check from the Royal Bank of Nigeria," added Barbara.

Floyd continued, "That's right, dear, it was for $5,000, but the Navy Credit Union here kept the check until it could be verified."

Barbara was back in the tale. "Floyd took him to the motel in Salinas, and he collected up a gym bag with some clothes, and he brought him back here. We took him out to dinner, and we stopped at the store and got him some toiletry items."

Floyd resumed, "The next morning, Barbara fixed him breakfast, and he and I went over to the bank to check on his money. I thought maybe I could help since I have our accounts there too, but he wanted to talk to the teller himself, and I waited in the lobby. After a few minutes, he returned to where I was sitting and said they still had not heard from Nigeria, but they expected to hear by the next morning. He asked me if I could lend him some money with the check as collateral. I asked him how much he needed, and he said $3,000 would cover the expenses of buying some clothes to attend the college in and to find a suitable apartment in the area. Well, it was a lot of money, and I knew I should have asked Barbara before I agreed to it, but I guess I just wasn't thinking.

"I filled out a withdrawal slip and went to the counter. The teller saw me talking to Byron and suggested that I write a check instead of a withdrawal slip. They are really smart at that bank, and I guess she was suspicious. This took Byron by surprise a little, but I wrote a check. He said his name was Byron White, which I thought was an odd name for a Nigerian. He showed the teller some sort of identification card, and she made him put his thumbprint on the front of the check before she gave him the money.

"Well, we came back home, and I took a nap while he went for a jog. He said he would sign a promissory note that I prepared when he got back from his run. I wasn't feeling well, and I went to bed early. When I got up in the morning, I went out to tell Byron that Barbara was going to fix him breakfast. There was no answer when I knocked on the door, so I thought maybe he went for another run. I waited and waited, but it was midmorning, and he still wasn't back. I walked over to the navy college and asked if anyone by that name was scheduled to attend this semester, and they said no. I guess I should have done that the day before now that I think about it.

"Around noon, I decided to use the key and look inside the apartment. Some of his stuff was still there, but the gym bag and his clothing were gone. I hadn't told Barb about the money yet, and I really didn't want to."

"I was so mad at him," added Barbara.

"Well, I didn't want to call the police and tell them how stupid I had been. So I thought I had better call you."

"Okay," Scott said, wiping the frosting out of his mustache, "first of all, Barbara, you can't kill Floyd no matter how justifiable. Second, if he comes back for any reason tonight, call me immediately. Third, let's take a look at the apartment. Has anyone other than you been in there today?"

"No, after I locked the door, I kept the key in my pocket," replied Floyd.

"I actually have a fourth question for you, Floyd. Does Nigeria even have a navy?" Scott asked.

"Not much of one, mostly coastal patrol boats and a few modern destroyers," he replied.

They walked out through the side door and to the back of the driveway, where Mr. and Mrs. DeWitt had built what was commonly referred to as a "mother-in-law" apartment behind the main house. It was an impressive two-story structure, with the first floor composed of a one-car garage and a studio guest room with a full bath. The second floor was a one-bedroom fully furnished apartment with a full bath and kitchen that they reserved for the use of their children or grandchildren when they were in town. Floyd unlocked the door of the first-floor guest room and pushed it open slightly before stepping out of the way. Scott pushed the door open, and the first thing out of his mouth was "Parolee."

Floyd asked, "How can you be sure?"

"Well, Floyd, you see his shower shoes by the bed with the plastic soap dish tucked in one shoe and the rolled socks in the other and the tightly rolled towel on top of the two?"

Floyd answered in the affirmative.

"Either the Nigerian Navy has the same habits as our inmate population or he is a parolee. My money is on the latter," Scott said. He took a long look around the small room.

"Could he get into this computer?" Scott asked, pointing at an old PC.

"Not without my password or Barb's password," answered the admiral.

Scott walked into the bathroom. "Floyd," Scott inquired, pointing at some items on the sink, "are these the toiletries you bought?"

Floyd responded in the affirmative.

"Have either you or Barbara touched any of the items since his departure?" Scott asked.

"No, nobody has touched anything," he replied.

"Wait here for a few minutes. I want to get something out of the trunk of my car. Don't touch anything. In fact, put your hands in your pockets, uh, sir," Scott instructed. He went back to his 1996 green British racing Jaguar XJS, retrieved an orange Pelican case, and set it by the curb. He grabbed his Sam Browne belt, threw it over his shoulder, and walked up the path to the front door of his modest bungalow. He grabbed the stack of bills protruding from the mailbox and unlocked the front door.

Through the plate glass window, he could see the cat walking down the back of the sofa to greet him as he entered. "What's my little girl been up to today?" Scott asked as she stretched out in front of him on the carpet. "Yes, yes, I see you, and I am going to step over you. I'm not done working yet, but I'll be back in a minute." He dropped his duty belt on the kitchen table chair, tossed the bills on the table, and went into his bedroom to retrieve a digital camera.

Of course, he wasn't getting back through the front door without first dropping to the ground for a minute of belly and ear rubbing. "Did you even do anything today, or was it just another day sleeping on your blanket?" he asked the little fat Russian Blue.

With this task complete and Natasha, the cat, satisfied with her moment of attention, Scott returned with the Pelican case and camera case to where he had left his neighbor. "Okay, Floyd, can you step outside for a minute while I take a few photographs? And you can remove your hands from your pockets, sir."

Scott made a lead card from an index card that he had in his pocket and began photo-documenting the crime scene. After this, he placed the Pelican case on the dresser, opened it, and removed a pair of latex gloves.

He donned the gloves and removed an ostrich-feather latent print brush from its tube and opened a jar of volcanic black dusting powder. He removed a discarded Irish Spring soap box from the garbage can and lightly dusted it with the powder. "Lots of partials on this, but nothing that I like," he said as he put it aside and began dusting the Barbasol shaving cream can.

"Oh, now I like this, and it's on the one part of the can where there is no writing. Looks like . . . let me see, yes, a complete distal phalanx and some of the medial phalanx of the right ring finger," Scott said, demonstrating to Floyd how the depositor would have held the can. He photographed the print in situ with a scale, lifted it with tape, and placed it on a backing card.

"The rest, I think, I will do in the laboratory at work, but I'm confident this print will belong to our Mr. White," he said with certainty. He collected up the toiletries, shower shoes, and other items and placed them in evidence bags.

"All right, Floyd, I'll stop by when I get home tomorrow. Now remember, if he comes back, you waste no time in calling me. Oh, and you might want to call the phone company and ask them if any long-distance telephone calls were made on that phone," Scott said as he pointed at an old rotary telephone sitting on the desk next to the computer.

"Should I change the lock?" he asked.

"First thing tomorrow morning," Scott replied. As he walked past the side door, Barbara stepped out with another piece of cake, which he was obliged to accept with the promise of returning the plate the next day.

The following morning found Scott in his fingerprint lab processing the evidence items for latents. He was able to develop a thumbprint on the plastic soap dish using the cyanoacrylate process and a second thumbprint on a Salinas street map that he collected from the nightstand using the ninhydrin method. Next step was to check with his friend and onetime mentor Calvin Brownlow at the Salinas Parole Unit. As always, he was out of the office, but Scott left him an urgent message to return his call. It didn't take him long to call him back.

"Calvin," Scott said, "I need to pick your brain. What can you tell me about a Byron White?"

"Do you have a prison number or date of birth?" he asked.

"None of the above, just the name," Scott responded.

"Let me check the system. B-Y-R-O-N?"

"Common spelling, I would assume, Calvin."

"Yeah, Byron Sinclair White, I got him right here. He's on Agent Peck's caseload" was his response.

"Fantastic! The fool used his real name!" Scott exclaimed. "Calvin, buddy, can I get a prison number, DOB, and Peck's extension from you?"

"Sure thing, Dog. CDCR no. J-908175, and you can find Agent Peck sitting at his desk, eating a breakfast burrito at extension no. 232. I will transfer you, and I'll tell him he better pick up the phone."

"Thanks, Calvin," Scott said. "I owe you one, buddy."

The telephone was transferred to Parole Agent Gerald Peck, who answered it with a mouthful of chorizo and egg. "Agent Peck, it's Investigator Doggett at the prison. I hope I didn't catch you at a bad time."

"No, no, just got in. What can I do for you?" he replied.

"Well, I am working an interesting case. I believe one of your parolees has embezzled a large sum of cash from an elderly couple over on the Monterey peninsula. They're good people, the kind that rinse their soup cans out before putting them in the recycle. I'd like to see if I can help them on this one."

"How do you know he is one of mine?" asked the hungry agent.

"Well, it would appear the bank teller took him by surprise, and he was forced to give up his real name. At least I'm hoping it was him and not somebody using his identification card. What can you tell me about Byron Sinclair White?"

"Not much," replied Agent Peck. "He just got out of High Desert State Prison four days ago. I saw him on Friday, and he said he was staying at a motel in Salinas until he could find an apartment. He's not supposed to check in for another two weeks."

"Well, I don't rightly think he's going to be checking in with you anytime soon," Scott stated, adding, "I'm pretty sure he's out of the area. Is there any chance that I can get a current photograph of him from you?"

"Sure, stop on by, and I'll give you a copy of the photograph I took on Friday. In the meantime, I'm going to drive over to the motel and see if he is still there. What do you want me to do if he's there?" he asked.

"I'm not ready to take him into custody yet. Just tell him to make sure he keeps his next check-in date, and maybe I'll be there waiting for him if everything goes as planned," Scott responded.

With that, Scott hung up the phone and made the next call to the prison teletype operator. "Maria, can you run a California Law Enforcement Tracking System and Department of Motor Vehicles records check on a Byron Sinclair White, CDCR no. J-908175, and call me when it's done?" Maria asked Scott to give her ten minutes and then just come over to her office. It worked for Scott. True to her word, she had the complete packet waiting for him when he got to her office.

Byron White was no angel, and there seemed to be a common thread in his arrest history—embezzlement. He was first arrested as an adult in 1990 for grand theft wherein he liberated an elderly woman of $1,800. He served a year in county jail and was ordered to make restitution to the victim. In 1993, he was again arrested on a felony charge. This time, he was charged with embezzlement after he stole through deception $10,500 from a vegetable packing company that was kind enough to give him a job. He was sentenced to three years in state prison and ordered to make restitution. In 1998, he was released from the Sierra Conservation Center in Jamestown, California. He was dropped off at the bus depot by prison officials who purchased for him a one-way ticket to Salinas, California. He apparently did not wish to wait for the bus and stole a car. He was stopped before he even got out of the small town. He was returned to the custody of the department of corrections and charged with a new crime. He was released again in 2001 and spent two weeks looking for gainful employment. Having failed in this endeavor, he held up a mom-and-pop store with a hammer. He was again a guest of the department, this time serving his entire sentence at High Desert State Prison, that is, until four days ago. As for all the restitution, he had only paid a little over $400. Scott was sure he had the right man as there was a noticeable trend in his criminal history.

It was time to call his buddy Tadeo Nakamuro at the department of justice, automated latent print section, in Sacramento. "Tadeo, dude, it's Scott Doggett. I need your help."

"Got something interesting for me, Dog?" he asked.

"I think I got this one, but I need some print cards. Do you think you can dig up a good set for Byron Sinclair White?" Scott inquired.

"Oh, I'm sure we can find something around here for you" was his reply. After giving him the pertinent details of the offender, Tadeo promised to send over a set by government fast delivery, which in spite of its name was pretty fast.

Scott sat down at his desk and cleared his mind with a quick game of solitaire on his laptop. He pulled out a case file folder and documented all the information he had gathered, putting it in order and completing an investigator's worksheet. Maintaining a good case file was perhaps one of the most important things an investigator can do in any investigation.

Once this task was finished, he drove out to the parole office and picked up a nice 8" × 10" glossy of his suspect and grabbed a digital copy for his flash drive. He made a quick drive over to the district attorney's office and dropped in on his old friend Investigator Alexander Rowland, the tall Texan. "Well, howdy, bud. What can I do for you?" he asked.

"Alex, there are two reasons I've come to see you. I'm working an interesting case. Do you know Floyd and Barbara DeWitt? They live across the street from me."

Alex lived two blocks from Scott and a bit closer to the ocean. "The beige house or the gray one with the white picket fence?" he asked.

"The battleship gray one," he replied.

"Oh, yeah, the old guy who was an admiral or general or something. What's going on with them?"

"Well, they got taken for three Gs by a guy I'm pretty sure is a parolee. Since I was in the neighborhood, I figured I could just pop on over, and we can use your computer to make a six-pack of photographs for the old dears to look at."

"Sure thing, buddy, we can do that in a lick," he proffered.

Using the digital image on his flash drive, they soon included it onto a collage with five mug shots of recently booked residents of the county jail who closely resembled Mr. White. "Now, Alex, for part two. Your wife is the manager of their bank. Do you think there would be any chance of getting the countersurveillance video and the endorsed check? Oh, and just for shits and giggles, ask her if there really was a check from the Royal Bank of Nigeria, of which I sincerely doubt."

"I'll see what I can do for you, buddy, but it might take a letter on your agency letterhead," he answered, adding, "I'll give you a call in an hour or two."

With that, Scott departed the district attorney's office and made his way back down to the prison. Everything was progressing smoothly. When Scott arrived at his office, he placed a call to the local police department where he lived and talked to Cpl. Randy Bitterman, a fellow narcotics detective. Scott provided him with the details of his investigation and asked him if he would mind meeting with him at his neighbor's house for the follow-up interview. Scott knew he would have a better chance getting an arrest warrant in the system if a report from the local PD accompanied his report. Randy checked with his supervisor and agreed to meet Scott at 1900 hours.

As it turned out, Floyd called soon after Scott hung up the telephone with Randy. He had been on the phone with the telephone company, and they provided him with some interesting information regarding the extension in his guest room. Two long-distance telephone calls had been placed to telephone numbers in the 772 area code. Scott wrote down the telephone numbers and asked Floyd to save the telephone bill when it arrived. He also told him he would be stopping by with Corporal Bitterman later that evening. Scott was sure Barbara would have plenty of time to bake up something tasty.

The last call of the day came from Alex. "Got some good news and some bad news for you, buddy."

"Give me the good news first, Alex."

"If you can write up a request on your agency letterhead, we can get you the countersurveillance. It won't be the entire video, but they'll give you a few good stills. Oh, and there has been no check from Nigeria or Tasmania or wherever it was you said."

"Yeah, I found out Nigeria is a federal republic so no royal anything. I'll bring the letter by your house tonight. What's the bad news?" Scott asked.

"You'll have to wait for the endorsed check to get back from the processing center. It might take a few days, and it will need to be picked up by the account holder."

"I think I can live with that kind of bad news, Alex. I'm meeting them later on tonight with Randy Bitterman. Do you want to sit in on the interview?"

"Oh, I think you can handle this one on your own, Scott." Scott didn't tell him he was missing out on Dutch apple pie.

At a few minutes past seven at night, Scott shook Randy's hand and escorted him up the path to the DeWitt abode. Floyd greeted them at the door and, after the introduction, sat them both down on the sofa. Scott set his case file on his lap, and Randy flipped out a notebook. Floyd and Barbara sat in chairs across from them and the sofa table. Scott asked Floyd to repeat everything he had told him the night before, which he did without leaving out any of the details. Barbara, of course, added her part. Scott told Floyd he had some photographs that he wanted him to look at and asked Barbara to leave the room for just a minute so that she wouldn't be influenced by his decision. She scampered off to the kitchen, where Scott heard the distinct rattle of dessert dishes.

Scott set the six-pack down on the table, and without batting an eye, Floyd pointed to suspect number five, Byron Sinclair White. "That's him. I would never forget that face."

Randy asked, "How can you be so sure?"

"Well, I spent so much time with him, right next to him. I drove him over to Salinas. I sat across from him at dinner. He was standing so close to me at the bank too." Randy seemed satisfied with the answer.

A few minutes later, Barbara appeared from the kitchen, wiping her hands on a kitchen towel. "Barbara, would you mind looking at these photographs?" Scott asked.

She put on her reading glasses and studied the series of photographs intently. "Well, I'm not quite sure. It could be either number two or number five. I would say it is number five, but this guy is much too small. He was bigger than that. I think it could be number two because he looks bigger."

Damn. Okay, one out of two isn't bad.

She made up for it when she asked, "How about a nice piece of pie?"

Floyd took Randy out to the apartment for a look around. When they returned and the pie was duly eaten, the investigators got up to leave. As Scott stood up, the 8" × 10" glossy photograph of Byron White slipped out of his file and landed face up on the table. "That's him!" shouted Barbara.

Once they were on the other side of the front door, Randy turned to Scott and said, "You did that on purpose."

"No, I promise, Randy, it just dropped out. I couldn't have done that on purpose if I tried. You'll have my full report in a few days, and then we can go over to the district attorney's office and get an arrest warrant," Scott replied.

"Do you know where he is?" asked the intrepid officer.

"I have a pretty good idea he's on his way to Florida."

"What an idiot, using his real name," added Randy.

"He didn't have any choice. The teller caught him completely by surprise when she told Floyd to write a check instead of the withdrawal slip. Although it didn't matter in the long run, I have a pretty good idea it's going to be his print on the shaving cream can. Oh, hey, I dropped off a letter with Alex Rowland to give to his wife. Can you swing by the bank in the morning and pick up the countersurveillance photographs?" Scott asked.

"Sure, I have to do some banking there in the morning anyway," he replied. It was a small town with only two banks. Scott banked at the other one.

Scott learned a valuable lesson that night. Some people can't judge depth in photographs. If someone was standing farther away from the camera lens, they appeared smaller in stature to someone who was standing closer to the lens. Therefore, if you had two photographs side by side of two guys who were exactly six feet tall, the guy who was standing farthest from the lens would have the appearance of being smaller. From that night on, Scott gave up using the six-pack photographic lineup. Now he placed individual 8" × 10" photographs in front of the witness.

In the following morning, Scott wrote a search warrant for telephone subscriber and call detail records for the two telephone numbers that were called from the guest apartment. The warrant was signed by a judge, filed with the clerk of the court, and faxed to the telephone company. Fortunately for him, both numbers were landlines, which meant that he would have real physical addresses.

Scott received the fingerprint cards from the DOJ in the afternoon, and he quickly matched the unknown fingerprint impression he recovered from the shaving cream can to the inked right ring finger of Parolee Byron Sinclair White—an ulnar loop with sufficient ridge detail and minutiae to make the most skeptic defense attorney fume. The lift from the soap dish was matched to his right thumb. He couldn't match the thumbprint from the map to Mr. White, and a follow-up call to Floyd revealed that Barbara was the likely depositor of the print. He should have gotten exclusionary prints, but he was busy with the chocolate cake at the time.

Randy gave Scott a call and told him he had picked up the surveillance photographs, a bit grainy but a match with their suspect. They agreed to meet in the morning at the district attorney's office to request an arrest warrant. Scott called Agent Peck and informed him of their progress. He asked Scott to fax a copy of his report to him, and he would use it as the basis of a parolee-at-large (PAL) bulletin and the revocation of his parole.

In the following morning, Randy and Scott met with DDA Joe Buckwalters in general felonies and explained their investigative efforts. He agreed with their conclusions and walked through an arrest warrant, which Scott in turn took to the sheriff's office to be entered into the statewide and national criminal data systems. Once back at the office, Scott placed a call to the telephone company's legal unit and explained the urgency for the subscriber addresses in association with his submitted warrants. They were happy to oblige and provided him with two names and addresses in the city of Stuart, Florida. It was apparent that, while biding time in the small apartment behind the DeWitt's house, Byron called his mother and his sister back in his hometown. Scott was playing a hunch that he was informing them he was on his way.

The Stuart Police Department was a small agency with fewer than thirty employees, of whom twenty were sworn officers. Scott gathered what information he could off their website and wrote a concise letter to the chief explaining his belief that Byron was on his way home. He implored his assistance in being vigilant to help him find justice for an elderly couple, and he warned him of his fears that Byron might defraud other elderly persons in his community. Scott included the arrest warrant, the parolee-at-large bulletin, and a synopsis of the investigation with a criminal history of the suspect. Scott dispatched the letter by facsimile and a hard copy by mail. After that, it was all about the wait.

It was then that Scott realized he hadn't informed his lieutenant that he was conducting a freelance investigation. He gathered up his case file and knocked on the lieutenant's door, gained entrance, and explained his case in full detail. The lieutenant could not have cared less but gave his blessing to continue.

"Scott, before you leave," he growled, "I need to talk to you about something. I know that you and Tyrus have been partners for a very long time, but I need to separate the two of you. The headquarters wants his validation numbers up, and he needs to do what he is expected to do, which is getting his two investigators focused on getting inmates validated for gang affiliation."

"Oswaldo is my partner, Lieutenant. Ty and I just get into mischief every now and then. I don't think I take him away from his duties that often, just every once in a while to bounce an idea off him," Scott replied.

"Oh, I know, Scott, but I've got a favor to ask of you."

"What's that?" Scott inquired.

"Well, we've got a new investigator coming in, and I want you to take him under your wings as a favor to me."

Scott knew when he said it was a favor, it was, in reality, an order. "Now you aren't going to separate Oz and me too, are you?" Scott asked.

"For the time being, yes, Scott. Oz will still work narcotics, and I intend to keep him busy with his dog, Ruud."

"But, Lieutenant, Oz isn't just my partner. He's like my kid brother. He makes up the levity in that office. I love that moment when the gears in his brain stop, but his mouth keeps going. It's classic comedy."

"He's not leaving the office, Scott. There's room for another desk in there, and I want you to take this new kid under your wings and teach him what it is to be a good investigator. His mother is a friend of mine, and I promised her I would look after the kid. Besides, he was handpicked by the warden for the job. I think you know him. His name is Adrian Kirby, and he starts on Monday."

"Oh, yeah," he said. "We shared a kitchen sink during the last riot when we both got doused with pepper spray. They say he's a good cop, young but good. I'll see what I can do."

Scott walked back to his office and noticed that Tyrus was approaching quickly. He sat down at his desk and turned to greet him as he came through the door. "Get out, Tyrus, I'm not supposed to be talking you," Scott said.

"You heard then," he replied, adding, "I understand where he is coming from. I really have to stay on these guys to get these validations done. We're getting way behind. Don't worry, though, we'll always stir things up."

"Yes, Tyrus, of that I have no doubt. What do you know about this young Adrian Kirby?" Scott inquired.

"The only thing I know is that his mother just recently retired as an associate warden at San Quentin or something like that. Other than that, he's got three years in the department, and that's all," he said.

After Tyrus left, Oswaldo came moping in like somebody had taken away his favorite Cold Steel Recon 1 titanium combat knife. Scott reminded him that he had a few Spanish-speaking investigations open, and he would need his help doing the translations and working the cases, so they were, in effect, still dope partners. It seemed to cheer him up a little, but they still had to figure out how they were going to fit one more desk in an already crowded office. After a few tries, they ended up with their two desks facing the opposite walls and the new kid's desk right in the middle of the room. Only one of the 1950s-era oak chairs that sat in front of Scott's desk survived the transition but was now relegated to the corner of the office to the left side of the desk, crammed in between the filing cabinet and a computer desk.

Scott stood for a moment in front of his bookcase and selected a battery of books that he thought would be helpful in teaching the kid the basics: Ross Gardner's *Practical Crime Scene Processing and Investigation*, Prof. Herbert MacDonell's *Bloodstain Patterns*, Ross Gardner and Tom Bevel's *Bloodstain Pattern Analysis*, the Di Maio brothers' *Forensic Pathology*, and his favorite, Vernon J. Geberth's *Practical Homicide Investigation*. He threw in Dr. Jon Nordby's *Dead Reckoning* for good measure, a classic primer on deductive reasoning. He stacked them on the corner of his desk with a note instructing him to "read and return."

On the following Monday morning as Scott slinked grumpily into the office, he was greeted by the tall bald twenty-five-year-old Adrian Kirby, who was thumbing through one of the books. "This stuff reminds me of my college textbooks," he said as he studied one of the more graphic crime scene photographs.

"Well," Scott said, "you're not in college now. We're going to put the theory into practical application." They both sat down, and the lessons began. Scott talked to him about the importance of maintaining an investigative file. He explained to him how a file was "road-mapped," highlighting important information that needed to be followed up, documented, or saved for later inquiry, as well as where to find important documentation in the inmate's central file, police reports, and visiting records. He explained to him that the investigator's worksheet should be updated every time there was any activity in the investigation. It should also be filled out in a manner that any investigator can pick up his file and automatically either continue the investigation or have the necessary information for subsequent investigations readily available. Most important was to remember that his investigative file could be subpoenaed to court. Every note that he took, even if it was on a small yellow Post-it note, must be permanently retained in the file.

The next conversation was regarding essential report writing. Adrian assured Scott he had excellent report-writing skills, or at least that was what his mother had told him. Okay, it was time for Scott's standard speech. "The English language is structured for a reason. The reader should not have to suffer for your failure to get the basic concept of composition. The reader should not have to read a sentence more than once to understand what you, the writer, are trying to convey. It may not be fair, but you will be judged on your efforts. That is just the way it is, and there is no reason why it should not be that way.

"In a jury trial, your credibility as a competent law enforcement official will hinge on three things: your appearance, your presentation, and the quality of your report. Improper grammar in your report will reflect on your competency as an investigator or reporting employee. Improper grammar in your report will reflect on your intelligence as an investigator. Improper grammar in your report will reflect on your aptitude and critical thinking skills as an investigator. Most of all, it will have an adverse effect on the way you represent your department or agency.

"During a trial, you are allowed to testify using one of two methods, by memory and by memory refreshed. This is why it is imperative that your report be accurate, detailed, complete, and descriptive. It will not be of much assistance if your report doesn't contain the facts needed to refresh your memory. It also doesn't do you much good to forget to bring your report with you. Put it in a folder and set it on the stand in front of you or keep it on your lap. If you need to refresh your memory, ask the judge if you can refer to your report to do just that. 'Your Honor, may I refer to my report to refresh my memory?' He will say yes. Now I do have to tell you that for every second you spend trying to find that particular information in your report to improve your memory, it will seem like an hour, and the sweat will begin to drip down your forehead. Read your report in advance and have a good idea where everything is on the page. Use these little Post-it flags or a highlighter if necessary. That's enough for now. Let's get to work."

Scott noticed Oswaldo was shaking his head in affirmation during his dissertation. As Oswaldo and Scott were scrounging up the accessories for young Adrian's desk, Tyrus stuck his head in the door. "Doggy," he said, "I need you to round up your guys and bring them along to the B Yard. We're going to pat down some gang associates and look for tattoos."

"Thanks, Ty. It's just what I've always wanted to do," Scott replied, adding, "Grab a camera kit, Adrian. You're riding with me. You will never leave this office without a camera kit."

Within five minutes, they joined Sergeant Phillips and his crew at the North Facility foyer. They agreed to first enter the A Yard from the central services patio, walk down the length of the track toward the dining halls, and then access the B Yard through the clothing room, which served both yards. This way, the inmates on the B Yard would not be aware of their presence on the yard until it was too late.

Unfortunately, when they entered the clothing room, they took the inmate workers completely by surprise as well. They stumbled onto a veritable playground of illicit activity. Inmates were rolling contraband tobacco cigarettes, gambling, receiving tattoos, and drinking inmate-manufactured alcohol. The supervisor, a nonsworn staff member, was nowhere to be found. They stopped all inmate movement, collected up the contraband, and began strip-searching all the inmates in the area.

After strip-searching Scott's third inmate, Tyrus called him over to where he was standing. Scott tapped Adrian on his shoulder harness and motioned for him to follow. Standing in front of Tyrus was a short slender inmate with all the telltale tattoos of an affiliation with the Northerner gang, and he was nude. "Meet Inmate Sandoval. He's going home in six weeks," Tyrus announced, adding, "Can you get me another pair of boxer shorts? There's something wrong with his." Adrian reached into a box of white Prison Industries Authority boxer shorts, pulled out a pair, and tossed them to Scott, for which he exchanged with the pair that Tyrus was holding.

As soon as Tyrus had made the exchange, Scott knew that he had been set up. "You bastard," he said, looking at Tyrus as he felt the hard metal object concealed in the front flap of the boxers. Tyrus had already handed the inmate the new pair and motioned for him to put them on.

"Adrian, cuff him," Scott said as he pulled the inmate-manufactured stabbing weapon out from an altered compartment in the fold of the boxer's flap. Adrian instinctively pulled his handcuffs from their case and instructed the inmate to turn around and put his hands behind his back. Inmate Sandoval complied and was restrained in short order, with Tyrus chuckling with self-satisfaction.

"North Control," Scott said into the radio, "clear the A Yard track from the clothing room to the patio, one in restraints under escort."

Scott then turned to Tyrus and said, "What are you laughing at, Ty? You're coming with me. Oh, and, Adrian, here's lesson number three for the day: never trust a sneaky partner who wants you to find the weapon so he doesn't have to write the report."

On their quarter-mile walk from the clothing room to the central service holding cells, Scott advised Inmate Sandoval of his rights pursuant to the *Miranda* decision. He informed him that he was charging him with a violation of Penal Code section 4502, possession of an inmate-manufactured stabbing weapon, a felony. He asked Scott how much time he thought he would get. Scott told him at least three years. Inmate Sandoval wasn't happy. He was six weeks from going home, and now he was looking at another three years at least. He told Scott he was afraid that someone was going to jump him because he was "short to the house," meaning he was going home soon, and he carried the weapon for protection. Sometimes the other inmates get jealous of the inmates who are going home, and they beat them up for no other reason than they are going home.

Scott told him the officers were his protection and that he didn't need a knife, but maybe the judge would take it into consideration and be lenient. Of course, Scott doubted highly he would get anything less than the three-year minimum. Scott also didn't tell him assaults happened so fast he doubted the inmate would ever have been able to produce the weapon from his boxer shorts holster fast enough to do much good. Scott left Adrian with Oswaldo and returned to the security and investigations unit to photograph and process the weapon and boxers into evidence. It was a short shank but lethally sharp, and it would do the job if jabbed into a neck, stomach, or eyeball.

Scott went back to his office and picked up the phone to check for messages. Floyd had called and left a message that he picked up the endorsed check from the bank. Scott called him back and told him he would stop by when he got home, and he was anxious to do the comparison of the inked print obtained on the front of the check by the teller.

Chapter 2

Big Bird from Oildale

"Thanks, Chief. I'm sorry I have to impose on your department, but I'm afraid this guy will continue to prey on the elderly, and we are anxious to get him back into our custody. You will let me know if anything develops . . . You too, sir. Goodbye." Scott rushed the telephone call because he could hear an alarm being called on the institutional radio.

"Where's the code, Adrian?" Scott asked as he slammed the phone down.

"It sounds like the North B Yard, and it sounds serious!" Adrian exclaimed. Scott agreed since it wasn't an audible alarm emitting from one of the housing units, the kind that were generally accidentally set off during shift change. This time, it was a radio alarm coming from one of the roof gunners.

They paused for a minute and listened to the next radio transmission. It was Sergeant Dave Adams. "North Control, I need medical ASAP."

The call was met by the control room sergeant. "What is the nature of the emergency?"

"I have one 10-15 with a stab wound to the neck. He is losing a lot of blood," explained Sergeant Adams. They actually didn't need to use the radio as the inmate had collapsed only a few feet from the B Yard gate, a mere sixty feet from the control room.

"Grab two camera kits, and let's move!" Scott yelled.

"Oz, take one camera kit and head directly to the north infirmary. Adrian, you are with me," Scott instructed as he grabbed his bloodstain pattern analysis kit and a few blood presumptive test kits from the refrigerator.

Within three minutes, they were in front of the North Facility, and Scott was removing the crime scene kits from the trunk of his cruiser. As they passed through the control room sally port, Sergeant Eugene Travis informed them they had already taken the inmate into the infirmary and that he had called for an ambulance. Scott sent Oswaldo to the infirmary with a camera kit, and he took Adrian with him onto the yard with the rest of the equipment. "Well, Adrian, what's the first thing you see—I mean, other than the two hundred or so inmates lying on the yard?" Scott asked.

"Everybody is standing by the latrine," he replied.

"What I see is about twenty cops standing in the crime scene. That's forty individual feet walking on top of my evidence. Let's drop our gear over by the dining hall, stretch some crime scene tape, and get these idiots out of the way."

On their way down to the latrine area, Scott met with Sergeant Adams, who was standing with a group of officers. He informed Scott he had just stepped onto the B Yard when he came face-to-face with Inmate Birdsong, who was holding a blood-soaked T-shirt against his neck. He called the code and summoned assistance, and they carried Inmate Birdsong into the infirmary.

He came back out onto the yard to see if he could find where the attack occurred and if any of his yard staff witnessed anything. He could find neither. Scott instructed Adrian to stretch the crime scene barrier tape from the corner of the dining hall around light pole no. 8, a thirty-foot pole supporting stadium lights, over to the education Department pedestrian gate—an area of about fifty square yards encompassing the latrine and track area. He then ordered all staff out of the crime scene and left only a handful of inmates lying on the track near the education gate within the scene itself. They placed these inmates in flex-cuffs and posted one officer on the other side of the tape to keep watch. There were a few white inmates by light pole no. 8, but they just scooted them over a bit to get them out of the crime scene.

Scott then began his cursory inspection of the crime scene. After a few minutes, they were joined by Oswaldo. "He's on his way to the hospital, Scotty," he said.

"Is he going to make it?" Scott inquired.

"He died once already, but they managed to bring him back. The blade must have been like an ice pick. It went straight through his neck." He motioned with his hand a horizontal movement across Scott's shoulder in a parallel manner, suggesting the blade went in the right side and came out the left.

"Wait, it went all the way through?" Scott asked in disbelief.

"All the way through," he repeated with emphasis.

"Six-inch blade at least then," Scott reflected. "Isn't Birdsong the white shot caller over here?"

"He's white, and he has all those Hitler-type tattoos," replied Oswaldo.

"That explains why the white boys over by light pole no. 8 are watching us. How far from the latrine would you say that light pole is?" Scott asked.

"About thirty feet," replied Adrian.

"Interesting," Scott mused, adding, "We'll want to check them for bloodstains. Keep an eye on them for now, Adrian."

"So you think it was the whites?" he asked.

Scott answered in the affirmative.

"How do you know?" he pressed.

"Because if it wasn't, we wouldn't have a stabbing here. We'd have a riot." Oswaldo chuckled a little at the rookie's expense. "All right, c'mon, you two, let's retrace the steps of our victim starting at the B Yard gate," Scott said as he led them up the track toward the gate.

"It's a distance of about 250 feet from the latrine to the gate. I've measured it before. So he walked all this distance with a bloody T-shirt pressed against his neck, and more than likely, nobody saw anything. Oz, go into the unit 6 lieutenant's office and call the tower cop and see what he saw. Here is where he collapsed. You can see where he stopped for a minute either to get someone's attention or to talk to Sergeant Adams. These blood drops are striking the ground at a ninety-degree angle."

"How can you tell?" asked the new investigator.

"Well, although it is an asphalt track, this area has been worn somewhat smooth by all the traffic going in and out of the gate. Therefore, there aren't too many small rocks that will alter the blood drop when it strikes the target. If you look at this drop, you will see that it is very nearly round with scalloping that goes all the way around the drop in a very uniform pattern. When the angle of the impact changes as with motion, the shape of the drop and the distribution of this scalloping around the resulting stain also change. So let's get some overview photographs of this area, and then we'll drop some markers and work in reverse chronological sequence from where he fell to where he got stabbed."

Scott instructed Adrian to take photographs from the four corners with the lens set at 38 mm, which was close to what the eye would see on a digital camera, and then from the central services patio looking out onto the yard. He then dropped an evidence marker and a directional marker showing the approximate north and instructed him to take the series of photographs again. Scott had him take a few midrange photographs of the evidence markers and bloodstains. He placed disposable scales and letter markers at the bloodstain patterns he wished documented and made sure these photographs were taken perpendicular and parallel.

Oswaldo returned from the lieutenant's office and informed him the tower officer had seen nothing. His attention was on an argument on the handball court. "Which race was arguing?" Scott asked. Oswaldo shrugged and went back into the office for another call.

"Why is that important?" asked the underling.

"It may have been a diversion to keep the gunner's attention away from the latrine area, assuming that's where the assault occurred."

Oswaldo pushed open the window and stuck his left arm out. "They were white," he said with one thumb up.

"Ah!" Scott exclaimed. "Just as I expected, it was a housecleaning hit. Our friend Mr. Birdsong must have transgressed on their rules and was dealt with."

They walked back toward the latrine area on the track that surrounded the grassy yard area. As Scott suspected, there wasn't much blood evidence as Inmate Birdsong undoubtedly had the T-shirt pressed firmly against his wound. They only found a few drops as they got closer to the latrine that had the wave castoff that showed directionality toward the yard gate. There was no castoff from the weapon anywhere. The only bloodstain Scott found was a small smudge on the Zurn Aquaflush push button in the middle toilet stall and an altered drop on the toilet seat. Scott dropped a magnet wand down the toilet bowl in the hopes of attracting a metallic weapon. Unfortunately, his efforts were met with negative results.

They photographed what there was, but there was no way to know for certain that Inmate Birdsong was stabbed in the area of the latrines. They wouldn't know until Birdsong was able to talk again and only if he was willing to talk. "Adrian, while you are photographing the latrine area, point your camera at those white inmates around light pole no. 8 and the park bench that is next to it. Try to catch their faces."

After the photographs were taken, Scott showed Adrian how to conduct a presumptive test of the bloodstains using the phenolphthalein method and Hexagon OBTI immunochromatographic rapid test, which would be useful in confirming human blood traces. Scott showed him how to properly collect blood specimen and control samples for DNA testing and how to take measurements for a diagram using the baseline method.

When they were finished, Scott summoned Tyrus and his two gang investigators; and along with Oswaldo and Adrian, they approached the group of white inmates who were lying around light pole no. 8. Assistant Institutional Gang Investigator Mark McShane identified the inmates using their state-issued identification cards and drew a sketch of their positions on the yard while Oswaldo and Scott examined them closely for blood evidence. "Nothing, Oz, not even so much as a scratch. No yard gloves around either. I give up. Let's get the plumbers out here, and they can take that toilet off. Maybe we will get lucky and find the weapon."

After an hour of waiting and watching the unit lieutenant recall the yard without doing strip searches or documentation of the inmates on the yard, the plumbers arrived. They pulled off each of the toilets and checked the pipes without any luck. They also used a fiber-optic camera device to look inside the pipe with the same lack of success. The maintenance department plumbers were always eager to go beyond normal effort to find weapons; it was like an addiction. Scott wasn't surprised. He had seen these toilets suck down an entire gray wool blanket when he was a housing unit officer. They returned to the office somewhat dejected. Scott processed the bloodstained items into evidence and downloaded the images into the digital image evidence computer. It was time to go home and try again in the morning.

Scott stopped by to see Floyd and Barbara when he got home. He collected the endorsed check and put it in an evidence envelope. He took a quick look at the inked thumbprint; it wasn't good. Byron was one step ahead of the teller on this one. She allowed him just enough freedom in placing his own thumb on the check that he lifted the volar pad clean off the paper and only deposited the print of the tip and upper third of the thumb. Scott knew he would need major case prints to make the match, and he also knew he didn't have any. He didn't want to cause any concern for the elderly couple, so he just said, "Excellent." He walked back home with a nice piece of strawberry cheesecake on a borrowed plate.

Scott's work cell phone rang at about ten thirty that night. He had only just gotten to sleep, so he wasn't his usual cheerful self when he answered. His demeanor changed when the caller announced himself as Dr. Winthrop at Stanford Medical Center in Palo Alto. He apologized for calling at the late hour and said that he got Scott's phone number from the prison. He was about to do surgery on Inmate Birdsong, and it looked like he would have to remove about a half inch of his trachea. He wanted to know if there would be any evidentiary reason to keep the part he was going to cut out. "No, Doc, I don't think that will be necessary," Scott said, adding, "I think we can just use your notes or testimony and the fact that his head will be about a half inch closer to his shoulders."

The doctor explained the path the blade took, entering the right side of the neck in front of the spine, narrowly missing the jugular vein passing through the trachea just below the Adam's apple, and exiting the other side just above the collarbone. Scott thanked him for the information and asked, "Will he live, Doc?"

The response was "If I have anything to do with it." With that, Scott went back to bed.

Chapter 3

Bird on a Wire

"Scotty, can you go with me to interview Inmate Birdsong?" asked Tyrus over the telephone.

"Isn't he still in the hospital?" Scott asked.

"They're bringing him back right now. He'll be in the second-floor infirmary under guard," he responded.

"It's been three weeks since the stabbing. Can he talk yet?" Scott inquired.

"According to the transportation cops, he won't shut up."

"What do you know about him, Ty?"

"Not much. He's a neo-Nazi skinhead, and that's about all I know. McShane says he had the keys to the yard, but I don't think so. The last white who was calling shots on the B Yard was Inmate Robert Finch. They call him Tennessee."

"Well, I guess we'll find out. What time do you want to go?" Scott asked.

"Sometime after lunch" was his reply. It was always "sometime after lunch" with Tyrus, especially if Scott was buying.

"Birdsong, I am Sergeant Phillips with the institutional gang investigations unit, and this is Investigator Doggett. He did the crime scene."

"What there was of it," Scott interrupted.

Tyrus continued, "Are you able to talk?"

"I can talk for short periods, and then I have to rest, or I lose my voice," replied the still bandaged inmate.

"Is there anything you can tell us about the attack that could be helpful to finding out who did this to you?" Scott asked.

"Not really," he answered in a raspy voice. "I didn't see the guy because he came up from behind me."

"Where were you exactly when you got hit?" Scott inquired.

"Somewhere between our table and the latrine."

"Your table is by light pole no. 8, correct?" asked Tyrus.

Inmate Birdsong answered in the affirmative.

"You know they tried to kill you, right? You have no idea why they would want to do that?" Scott asked.

"Nope, and I don't think they wanted to kill me," he replied.

"So you think you are still good with the rest of the whites at North?" asked Tyrus.

"Yeah, in fact, I want to go back. Can you send me back over there?" he asked.

"Oh, I'm sure you do," Scott said. "I'm sure you have a few debts you'd like to repay."

"No, no, nothing like that, I promise."

"Is it true you had the keys to the yard?" asked Tyrus.

"You mean was I in control of the whites? No, not me. Tennessee is still in charge," he protested.

"What do you mean still in charge? Was he not in charge at one time?" followed Tyrus.

"Well, uh, it's just that they wanted me to take over, but I didn't want to step on Tennessee's toes."

"Who wanted you to take over?" asked the persistent gang investigator.

"Well, the skins because Tennessee is a peckerwood, and sometimes his ideas aren't the same. He just wants everybody to get along."

"So you can't think of any reason why someone would want to kill you?" Scott asked.

"Nobody tried to kill me."

"Do you have any sex crimes on your jacket that might make them want to remove you from the yard?" Scott persisted.

"Nah, nothing like that. I steal cars. I like stealing cars."

"How much time do you have left?" asked Tyrus.

"Two and half," replied the gravelly-voiced inmate.

"So do you think you can do the next two and half years on the main line without getting stabbed again?" inquired Tyrus.

"No problems here. I'm starting to lose my voice. I don't think I can answer any more," he replied.

With that, Tyrus and Scott left his small infirmary room. "What happened to the good old days when inmates told on the guys who stabbed them?" Scott asked Tyrus as they walked down the central corridor.

"If I got stabbed, I'd be tellin'," he replied.

"Do we go talk to Tennessee?" Scott asked.

"I can't see any reason right now, but I'll let you know."

"Tyrus, what exactly is the major difference between the skinheads and the peckerwoods?" Scott asked.

"Racial purity," he replied. "Peckerwoods don't go in for that as much as the skinheads do. They consider themselves to be more good old boys than anything else. They don't have the hatred of the blacks and Jews that the skinheads have either."

"I'll tell you one thing, Ty. Three weeks ago, that guy was dead. Today we are talking to him. Had that been you or me who got stabbed in the neck, we'd be dead." With that said, they separated. Neither of them wanted to be called into the lieutenant's office.

Chapter 4

Tennessee

"What's up, Oz?" Scott asked. He had looked at the caller ID on his work cell phone before answering.

"Nothing, Scotty. I just got home from the gym. What about you?"

"Got my run in earlier this evening, but it's Friday night, and I'm finally going to have a beer. We still going bowling tomorrow night?" Scott asked.

"Yeah, yeah, yeah. Hey, do you want to go shooting this weekend? Adrian needs to get his off-duty qualification done. I told him I'd take him over to Markley's Indoor Range in Watsonville."

"Just say what time, and I'll be there, providing nothing happens at work," Scott replied.

Scott hung up the phone, walked into the kitchen, and opened the refrigerator door. He reached in and grabbed the foil-wrapped neck of a Negra Modelo, extracted it, popped the cap, and placed it on the countertop. He found his favorite beer mug and tipped the bottle. He thought of how nice it would be to finally enjoy a beer. It had been two weeks since he bought the stubby brown bottle and five more of its siblings. For two weeks, they had teased him each time he opened the refrigerator door. Finally, he . . .

"Doggett," he groused into the cell phone receiver.

"Scott, it's Lieutenant Templeton. Meet me at the prison in thirty minutes. There's been another stabbing on the B Yard."

"Son of a sea monkey, Lieutenant! Why can't I pour a beer without getting a call from you? I'm on my way. I'll call Oz. He ain't doing anything right now."

"Call Adrian too," he ordered.

Scott poured the beer down the kitchen sink drain and gave a salute as he turned on the faucet. He didn't know to whom to apologize. Was there a Mr. Modelo?

It was almost eight at night when he arrived at the institution. Oswaldo and Adrian were already waiting for him when he pulled up. "I grabbed your radio for you," said Oswaldo as he handed Scott his radio with a fresh battery.

"Life Flight is coming in. Those are the lights on the helicopter unless I am mistaken," Scott said as he adjusted his equipment belt and pointed toward the eastern sky. "Any idea who the inmate is?"

"Beech or Finch or something like that, white boy off the B Yard," replied Oswaldo.

"Inmate Finch. It would appear that someone is trying to kill our white inmates, Oz. Where's the lieutenant?" Scott inquired, but before anyone could answer, he was hailed on the radio by Lieutenant Templeton and instructed to respond to the B Yard with some celerity.

"Oz, drive your K-9 van onto the yard. We'll use it as a platform for the portable lights. Adrian, you come with me. We'll make a quick stop by the helipad and see if Finch is still alive. Five minutes, Oz, I'll see you on the yard in five minutes. Stretch the crime scene tape if it already hasn't been done, but don't drop any markers until we get our overview photographs first."

Inmate Finch was still alive but barely. He had been stabbed through the throat with an ice-pick-type weapon. The blade went through his trachea just above the clavicle. They loaded his gurney onto the helicopter, and it took off in the direction of Stanford. "Looks like Dr. Winthrop will have another patient," Scott murmured. "And I'll get another midnight call."

Adrian and Scott rushed to the North Facility, grabbed the equipment from the trunk of the cruiser, and proceeded to the B Yard. Oswaldo had parked his van near the dining hall vehicle gate and had stretched the crime scene tape from the rear bumper of his van, around the picnic table at light pole no. 8, and around the latrine and back to his van. He placed the flood lights on the roof of his vehicle and fired up the portable generator. The ambient light from light pole no. 8 was sufficient to illuminate the area but not in a manner suitable for forensic purposes.

They dropped their kits by Oz's van, and Scott walked over to where the lieutenant was standing. "I'm going to send Ty up to Stanford in the morning, and I want you to go with him. We need to find out what's going on," he said as Scott approached.

"That's assuming he will make it. They were doing chest compressions on him as they shoved him on the helicopter. What do we know about the crime scene?" Scott inquired.

"At about 1845 hours, the gunner saw two inmates dragging Finch from the table to the light pole. He didn't see any weapons but saw the stabbing action of one of the inmates. He fired a warning shot somewhere over there by Alameda Hall. All the inmates got down. Staff came out of the library and culinary and ran over to where Finch was lying on the ground. They tried to stop the bleeding using that jacket over there. Medical came out with the code 2 responders and got him stabilized enough to transport him to the north infirmary. The rest you know. There are four white inmates cuffed by the picnic table and two pretty close to where Finch was lying. One of them has blood on his shirt."

"Okay, Lieutenant, we've got the crime scene," Scott said, hoping the interloping lieutenant would go off to do something administrative. "Oz, go into Alameda Hall and call the roof gunner and see what he saw. And, Oz, write it down. Have him show you where he fired that warning shot and then collect the spent cartridge casing for evidence. Then call the gunner on the roof of San Leandro Hall and see what he saw."

Scott turned to Adrian and instructed him to find the initial responding officers and to write down their statements. "Oh, and, Adrian," Scott continued, "get a list of all the people who were in the crime scene, including medical personnel."

Scott grabbed the camera and walked over to the crime scene where two officers had been posted to keep an eye on the six inmates who were still lying in restraints. He took his long-range photographs, shooting from the four compass points. When he completed this task, he took a few midrange photographs capturing each inmate in their prone position. He then approached the young white inmate with the bloodstained blue chambray shirt. "You're shaking, son. Are you cold?" Scott asked the young man.

"Yes, sir," he said with his lower lip quivering.

"How did you get this blood on your sleeve?"

"I don't rightly know, sir," he replied.

"Well, you know I'm going to have to take that shirt for evidence."

"Yes, sir," he chattered.

"In fact, I am going to need your pants and shoes too, but not to worry, I've got a new pair coming and a wool blanket. But first, I need to take some photographs of you. Let's get you standing up." Scott reached down, grabbed the kid by his inner arm, and lifted him. He was surprisingly light. "What's your name, son?"

"Jacob, sir."

"And your last name?"

"Tanner."

"How old are you, Jacob?" he asked.

"Nineteen," he gibbered through chattering teeth.

"What do they call you here?" Scott asked.

"They call me Havoc."

"Are you a skinhead, Jacob?"

"No, I am a practicing Odinist. It's a religion," he stated.

"So are you a Hammerskin? I mean, you are wearing the Hammer of Odin necklace," Scott inquired.

"Yeah, I guess so," he replied in monotone.

As Scott was talking to him, he was also photographing the kid's face and hands. Scott walked him out of the crime scene and removed the handcuffs. First, he took off his chambray shirt, and Scott placed it into an evidence bag. He then instructed the kid to remove his T-shirt and hand it to him. Scott placed that in a separate evidence bag. He did the same with his pants and boots. The kid was very cooperative and performed the tasks as if he was a robot devoid of feelings. He seemed numb to everything that was going on around him. It was very suspicious to say the least. Scott photographed Inmate Tanner wearing only his boxer shorts and handed him replacement clothing. The kid was skinny as a rail. Once he put on his new clothing, Scott placed him back in mechanical restraints. He copied the identifying information from his identification card, draped a blanket around his shoulders, and had him escorted up to a holding cell.

He went back into the crime scene and placed an evidence marker to represent the position where Inmate Tanner was lying. He followed the same procedure with Inmate Aydin Campbell, who was also in the immediate area where Inmate Finch collapsed, but he could find no bloodstain evidence in the available light on his garments. They would have to be analyzed in the lab. Inmate Tyler "Jeremy" Keller, Inmate Elbert "Hammer" Jones, Inmate Mathias Volks, and Inmate Billy Morgan were the four inmates lying closer to the picnic table. Inmate Keller was wiping his bloodied right ring finger in the grass. For his efforts, he got his picture taken, his clothing collected, and his hand swabbed.

Oswaldo reappeared from Alameda Hall and provided Scott with the details of Officer Justin Walker, the roof gunner who called the code and fired the warning shot. He said he was standing near the gunner's shack over the front door of Alameda Hall when he noticed a commotion to his right. He started walking along the rooftop in the direction of light pole no. 8. He informed Oswaldo the lighting was not good enough for him to see exactly what was happening, but he did see that Inmate Finch looked like he was trying to push one of the inmates away from him while holding on to the other. He saw an inmate, whom he believed to be wearing gray sweatpants and a blue chambray shirt, come up behind Inmate Finch and make a stabbing motion with his right hand. He fired a warning shot in the grassy area in front of Alameda B side cell 109. He could not identify any of the inmates, only that one had a dark blue jacket, one had a blue chambray shirt and blue denim pants, and the other had a blue chambray shirt and gray sweatpants.

They looked around at their detained suspects. Inmate Keller was wearing a dark blue jacket as was Inmate Morgan and Inmate Jones. Inmate Tanner had the blue chambray shirt and blue denim pants, which Scott already placed into evidence. They could not see anywhere on the yard an inmate with a blue chambray shirt and gray sweatpants, but inmates were masters at quick change. "What about the bloody shirt?" asked Oswaldo.

"Oh, definitely involved," Scott replied. "It was a distinct transfer pattern on the left forearm, a void pattern if you will. Think of an oblong circle with a one-inch-wide path down the middle. One thing for sure, Finch had a hold of this kid."

Adrian also returned to the crime scene and handed Scott a piece of paper with the names of the personnel who had responded. His interview of the two responding officers, Officer Devon Luna and Officer Raymond Perez, showed they were in the north library when they heard the radio call from the gunner and the discharge of a rifle. They both exited the library together, paused for a moment to make sure that the gunner had finished firing, and then ran toward the light pole. They were primarily focused on Inmate Finch and the inmate whom he had latched onto, whom they confirmed as Inmate Tanner. Other than that, they were only concerned with stopping the effusion of blood.

Unit 4 lieutenant Doug Metcalf responded from his office and made sure that all the inmates remained where they saw them now. Not much information could be had from the medical personnel other than it was their latex gloves that dotted the crime scene. Scott instructed Adrian to do a grid pattern search in the crime scene area with a metal detector in a futile hope that the weapon would be found. Scott knew it was pointless because the ground was hard, and it would have been unlikely that someone would have been able to bury a shank, but if it didn't get done, there would be questions.

Lieutenant Templeton approached Scott as he was talking on his cell phone. He raised his chin from the phone and said, "He was stabbed twice or rather stabbed once and slashed once. The slash is on his right chest. I'm thinking two attackers."

"Not necessarily," Scott said, adding, "I'd have to see the wound. It might have been the result of withdrawing the shank from his neck and then slashing the chest as the attacker made his escape."

"No, I said two attackers," the lieutenant obstinately replied. "Finch is still alive, although he died twice on the helicopter. They rushed him into surgery at a trauma center in San Jose. It was a thin, pointed weapon like an ice pick."

Just then, Scott noticed Oswaldo standing in front of Alameda Hall. He was waving his right hand in the air. "He found either the weapon or, more likely, where the bullet struck." It was the latter. Oswaldo marked it, documented it, photographed it, took a trajectory measurement, and retrieved the bullet from the hole. In a prison, you had to find that bullet. If the soil was soft and it didn't become shrapnel on impact, an inmate could find it and manufacture a zip gun to accommodate the projectile. Scott found three zip guns in his career, all crudely made but functional. All it took were a metal tube, such as a quarter-inch copper or brass pipe from the plumbing shop; a projectile; and matchstick heads for a propellant.

They documented the crime scene, photographed it, collected all discarded garments as evidence, took triangulated measurements, and prepared a diagram. Near the picnic table, Scott stood looking at a single cotton glove that was lying on the bench. He picked it up and inspected the blue and white work glove. He noticed the smallest drop of blood, perhaps 2 mm in diameter, on the palm of the glove. The nearest inmate would have been Keller, he thought. He documented the glove and collected it as evidence. They bagged up all the evidence and collected their gear. Oz's van carried the equipment back to the office, but the evidence remained with Scott.

Chapter 5

A Chat with Tennessee

"You're looking pretty good for a guy with a shank stuck in his throat two days ago," Scott said as he entered the hospital room.

"They almost killed old Tennessee this time," said Inmate Finch as he gasped for air and the strength to talk.

"I don't want you to do much talking today, Rob, but I do have some photographs that I want you to look at." Scott laid out one at a time some photographs of various white inmates from the North Facility. Included in this group were photographs of the inmates who were in the crime scene.

"Havoc," he said while tapping the photograph of Inmate Tanner with his right middle finger. He took a deep breath. "He did it. I had a hold of him. I looked right at him, right into his eyes." As he spoke, a greenish-brown bile dripped, gurgled, and occasionally splashed from the tube that was inserted in his neck. It turned Scott's stomach and that of the two hospital coverage officers.

"Okay, Rob," Scott said, "I don't want to go into detail today. You need your rest." The suggestion was more out of a desire to shrink from the bile than to save his larynx.

"We'll talk with you when you get back to the prison," added Tyrus.

Scott shook his hand, wished him well, and turned to depart, noting that the bile had shot clear down to the inmate's feet. He nudged Ty's arm and whispered, "Remind me not to stand in front of him."

It took about a week before they brought Finch back to the institution and placed him in the second-floor infirmary next door to Inmate Birdsong. "Hey, Ty, we can kill two birds with one stone. Don't look at me like that. We can go talk to Finch and Birdsong and show them the photographs again."

"Yeah, we need to find out if Birdsong can identify Tanner as being on the yard when he got hit because we have absolutely no idea who was and was not on the yard on that day," replied the still pun-disgusted sergeant.

Later that afternoon, they showed the photographs to Inmate Birdsong. He paused for a minute at the photograph of Inmate Tanner but continued without making even the hint of a positive identification. "Nope, sorry, I don't remember if any of these guys were on the yard. Like I told you, I was talking to my road dog, and then I just got blindsided. Everything went black, and I couldn't tell you who it was or even what race."

"So exactly who is your road dog again?" Scott asked.

"McGregor. They call him Highlander," he replied.

"Right, right, I remember you telling me that," Scott added.

They left Inmate Birdsong's infirmary room, and before entering Inmate Finch's room, Scott looked over at Tyrus and said, "At least we have someone new to interview. He never told us about McGregor before."

Inmate Finch was propped up in his hospital bed, watching television. The plastic tube was still in his neck just below his Adam's apple, but this time, there was an absence of the percolating bile. In fact, aside from the tube, you wouldn't have known anything had happened to him.

Finch was in his early fifties and had been incarcerated since the mid-1980s. He was about Scott's height and of average build and carried himself in the tradition of a gentleman of the South. He spoke with a slow Tennessee drawl and pondered carefully about his thoughts before engaging his mouth so as to never say anything in the least bit offensive unless provoked.

He was serving a twenty-five years' to life sentence for a 1984 homicide after killing a man in a bar fight and beating the bartender near death just because he watched the killing. He had served more than thirty of his fifty-four-year sentence in prison. He had transferred to Gabilan State Prison seven years prior from the infamous Corcoran State Prison Security Housing Unit. This gave him the prestige to have control over all the white inmates on the North Facility B Yard. Actually, Inmate Finch was placed in the Security Housing Unit with a group of white inmates who were present during a small riot between white and black inmates. There was no clear indication that Finch was involved in that riot.

"You feeling better, Rob?" Scott asked.

"Yes, sir, much better. Thank you for asking," he replied.

Scott placed the photographs down on his bunk one at a time. Again, he pointed to the photograph of Inmate Tanner and said, "That's the bastard."

Scott asked him if he could identify any of the other inmates who were near him at the time of the stabbing, to which he responded, "No, sir. I am telling you, it was Havoc who stabbed me. I looked right at him, and I could tell he was scared. As soon as I felt that metal hit my neck, I grabbed on to him, and all I could do was ask why. He just looked at me with those wide eyes."

"Why do you think you were stabbed?" interrupted Tyrus.

"Well, Mr. Phillips, I have heard that they didn't like the way I was spending so much time with Captain Trenton. But hell, they were the ones who kept giving me all these problems that they wanted resolved— visiting, packages, canteen, you name it. Every time I went into the captain's office, it was because they all had some complaint or problem that they wanted me to fix. It just don't make no sense nohow."

"Yeah, that doesn't make any sense," Scott quipped, adding, "But whatever does make sense around here?"

"Do you think there is any connection between you and Birdsong?" asked Tyrus.

"I don't think so. I heard that Big Bird was buying marijuana from the blacks, and he had accumulated a sizable debt. That, in the philosophy of the skinheads, is a no-no. You know, I also intervened on a few occasions between the blacks and the skinheads over drug debts. It seems those guys just can't get enough of the stuff, and the blacks are always willing to sell it to them. You know, the Paisas cut them off because they weren't paying their debts. I'd have to negotiate settlements, and I even gave the blacks $300 of my own canteen just to clear one of the debts. Man, I have told them they had to knock the shit off, but they won't listen."

"What about Jacob Tanner? Was he ever in debt to the blacks?" Scott asked.

"Not to the blacks. He uses meth. His cellie gets it for him."

"Who was his cellie?" Scott inquired.

"Mayer. They call him Santa."

"How does Tanner pay for the—"

Finch quickly interrupted Scott, "Well, uh, Mr. Doggett, it's rumored that, uh, well, you know, we don't talk about that in polite society. Santa likes the young neo-Nazis. It gives him a sense of control, power."

"So he . . . oh, oh, *oh*!" exclaimed Scott's former partner.

"Yes, Tyrus," Scott confirmed, "I am afraid it is what you are thinking, not confirmed but rumored." He looked back over to Inmate Finch. "This is going to take some sorting. It's likely this whole thing is over dope debts. Again, we have this completely perverse aberration of logic where it is against the rules of the skinheads to use dope, buy dope from the blacks, and get dope debts, even potentially engaging in risky sexual behavior to resolve debts, yet a large number of them are engaged in these practices every chance they get. So what do they do? They take out the guy who is trying to get them to stop and make examples of those who are doing the same thing. Yes, this is going to take some figuring out. Look, Rob, if there is anything else that you can think of, even if you don't think it's that important, get word to me. Is there anything that we can do for you?"

"Yes, sir, you can check on my property. That would be nice. Oh, and can you do me an enormous favor?"

"What's that?" Scott asked.

"Can you call my wife? She is mad at me something fierce. Just tell her I'm going to be all right. Here, I'll write down her number."

"Sure thing," Scott said. "But I'm not making any guarantees she'll be any less mad. It seems of late that I am making it a practice to be a marriage counselor."

Chapter 6

Havoc

Scott's father would have described Jacob Tanner as "a *ragazzo birichino* or knucklehead." He was a nineteen-year-old skinhead from Reseda, California, who one day thought it would be a good idea to carjack a vehicle using a replica pistol. Unfortunately for Jacob, his intended target was an off-duty California Highway Patrol officer who had a real pistol of his own. He was charged with second-degree robbery, brandishing a firearm replica, and carjacking and was sentenced to five years of not-so-hard labor. He was short and skinny, about 5'6", and 120 pounds if he was lucky, just a little smaller than Oswaldo. The only difference between the two was that Oswaldo could use his size and weight to take down the biggest foe, whereas Jacob would probably just piss his pants.

Adrian and Scott decided to pay Jacob a visit since he had been chilling his heels in the administrative segregation unit since the incident. He had written a few letters out to his girlfriend and mother but professed his innocence and that he had no idea why he was sent to the Hole. The escort officers brought him into the conference room and sat him in the chair next to Scott. He was in full restraints pursuant to ad seg procedures. His thin head and face were clean shaven, and the only features remaining were his blondish-white eyebrows and steel-gray eyes, which made for an eerie sight. Outside of his appearance, he had an amiable disposition. "Hello, sir," he said with a soft voice.

"Jacob, are they treating you all right in here?" Scott asked.

"Yes, sir, I have no complaints. You get more food, and I think it's better."

"Okay, Jacob, you know I have to ask you a few questions regarding what happened the other night."

"Yes, sir," he timidly replied.

"Before I do that, I want you to be aware of your rights pursuant to the *Miranda* decision. You have the right to remain silent. Anything you say can and will be used against you in a court of law. You have the right to an attorney and to have an attorney present during questioning. If you cannot afford an attorney, one will be appointed to you free of charge. Do you understand these rights as I have explained them to you?"

"Yes, sir, I understand my rights."

"Fantastic. Having these rights in mind, do you wish to answer questions at this time?"

"No, sir, I would rather not."

"You'd rather not speak to me, or you want a lawyer?" asked Scott.

"Talk" was the brief reply.

"Well, Jacob, I can't talk to you anymore then. I was hoping that if you were innocent, you would help me and tell me what actually happened that night so that I could help you prove that you didn't do anything wrong. I don't want you to think that I find your lack of cooperation in the least bit suspicious. Why don't you think about it and then I'll come back and talk to you? If you change your mind and just want to talk, send me a note, and I'll come back and see you. Oh, I do have one question for you that you can answer. Why do they call you Havoc?"

"It's my temper, sir. They say I am out of control just like I'm causing havoc," he responded. Scott looked at him and pictured this skinny kid in a fit of rage, but somehow he felt that it would be more like a tempest in a teapot. A good swift kick in the ass was probably all it would take to settle his outburst.

Scott called for the escort officers to return and take Inmate Tanner back to his cell. Once they had escorted him out of the room, Adrian turned to Scott and asked, "So he did it?"

"The jury is still out," Scott replied.

"Why is that?" asked the junior investigator.

"There may be other reasons why he doesn't want to talk. He might be afraid to identify the actual perpetrator, or he might not want to be labeled an informant. He may be suspicious of me and think I might turn anything he says into an admission of sorts. It could be anything really. The fact of the matter is that just because he didn't want to talk now doesn't mean he won't talk or just wants to have his lawyer with him. Remember, just because you have a suspect who invokes his rights pursuant to *Miranda* doesn't mean that you can never talk to him. You just have to do it with the lawyer present or, if he's still in ad seg, wait a fortnight and try again. I'm not afraid of questioning a suspect with their lawyer present, and you shouldn't be either."

The next day, Scott saw the letter going out to Inmate Tanner's mother wherein he asked her to find him a good attorney in the area. He told her that she was not to worry, but he needed the attorney to clear his name in something serious that happened when he was at the North Facility. About six days later, Inmate Tanner received a letter back from his mother saying that an attorney would be coming to see him shortly. Scott went out to the entrance building and put a memo in the computer that he was to be notified immediately if an attorney came to call.

"Who is his attorney?" Scott asked the entrance building officer who had called to inform him that an attorney was at the institution to represent Inmate Tanner.

"James Calloway" was the response. Scott thanked the officer and informed him to escort the attorney to the Central Facility visiting room and that he would be there in five minutes.

He then turned to his new partner. "Adrian, his attorney is James Calloway. Here is where you are going to learn a lesson. Mr. Calloway is a gadget head. When I give you this signal where I point at you like I am shooting a gun, I want you to compliment him on his briefcase. Ask him where he got it and if his laptop fits in there. Tell him all about your laptop and ask him to show you how big the briefcase is and whether he thinks your laptop will fit. As soon as he starts going on about his laptop, keep him going and then ask him about his iPhone and whether he thinks it is better than your Galaxy. Just keep him engaged about all his electronic toys and ignore what I am doing. Got it?" Scott asked the bewildered rookie.

"Yeah, but why?" replied Adrian.

"Trust me on this. Sergeant Phillips and I do this to Mr. Calloway all the time. You have to be convincing, or I'll take him or Oz instead. Can you pull it off?"

Adrian pursed his lips and said, "I can try."

They met Mr. Calloway in the visiting room and talked briefly about the circumstances of the incident while they waited for the administrative segregation unit staff to bring Inmate Tanner into the small attorney conference room. Scott had placed four chairs around a small table. Jacob sat directly opposite him, and Adrian sat across from the attorney. Scott started his digital recorder and placed it on the table as did Mr. Calloway. He gave his spiel that he was representing Inmate Tanner in any criminal inquiries, and Scott gave his spiel that Inmate Tanner was not under arrest at this time but being interviewed in the matter of the attempted murder of Inmate Finch.

During the introductions of the people in the room, Scott pointed at Adrian and pulled the trigger on his finger gun. It was a blank; Adrian just stared at him. Again, Scott fired his finger gun and this time gave Adrian a little wink. Scott saw the gears turning in his head, and once they had engaged his brain fully, he leaned forward and looked at the nice metallic briefcase at the right leg of Mr. Calloway. He commented on how nice and durable the briefcase appeared and that he was looking for one exactly like it for his new laptop. Immediately, the attorney engaged Adrian on a litany of briefcase options, computer accessories, and the fine quality of his new laptop.

Taking advantage of this opportunity, Scott leaned forward and put his right hand on Jacob's left knee and said, "Okay, Jacob, I am glad that you got your attorney here. Now I can ask you a few questions about what happened that night. Can we begin?"

Jacob looked over at his attorney, whose entire attention was focused on Adrian's new Galaxy, and then looked back at Scott, saying, "Uh, I guess it's all right."

"Fine. So tell me what happened that night, and how was it you ended up with Tennessee's blood on your shirt?"

"I was standing there. I was supposed to be the lookout, but I didn't know for what. They just said that I had to stand where I was standing and stop Tennessee if he ran in my direction."

"Who told you?" Scott asked.

Jacob looked again at his attorney, but somehow the topic between Mr. Calloway and Adrian managed to drift to dress shoes. "I don't want to tell you. They will have me hurt, and I want to go home to my mother and my girlfriend."

"Look, son, you want me to help you, right? Then you need to tell me the truth." Laughter erupted from the Adrian and Calloway conversation.

"I can't," replied the nervous felon.

"Okay for now. How did you get the blood on your shirt?" Scott asked.

"I froze. Tennessee turned to me right after he got stuck. He had his hand on his neck, and then he reached out and grabbed my shirt. I went numb with fear. I don't know what happened after that. All I remember is being on the ground and then you asking me questions. I don't even remember them putting me in handcuffs. I was cold. It was like there wasn't any blood left in my body either."

"Was it the first time you saw someone stabbed?" Scott asked.

"No, I was there when Birdsong was stabbed too. I hope I never see it again ever. I believe in Odin, and I believe in Thor, but I don't believe in the rest of what they are saying. I have friends at home who are black. My grandmother was Jewish. I just want to go home."

"Do you mind if later I come back to see you and get a DNA sample from you to help me prove your innocence?"

"No, I don't mind. Will I need my lawyer present?"

"Only if you want him there, Jacob, but I don't think he will mind. He hasn't objected to anything yet."

Mr. Calloway put his laptop back in its case and turned to Scott, saying, "I don't think my client has anything to say at this time."

Scott thanked him for his attendance, turned off his recorder, and escorted Inmate Tanner back to the awaiting ad seg officers. Before they took him away, Scott counseled him about the evils of methamphetamines and how they would destroy his life and the lives of the people he loved. Jacob thanked him and said that he would quit. Scott doubted it highly.

Adrian and Scott walked Mr. Calloway back to the entrance building and bid him a good day. As they strolled back to the office, Adrian turned to Scott and asked, "What did I miss?"

Later that day, Scott went back over to the Administrative Segregation Unit and collected a buccal swab from Jacob. He didn't seem like a bad kid. If he had the right influence in his life, he might not have made the decision that put him behind bars. Then again, he did come from the "right kind of family," and it didn't do any good.

Chapter 7

The Experiment

"Adrian, how tall are you?" Scott asked.

"Six feet" was his response.

"Oz, how tall are you?" Scott inquired.

"Five foot seven and a half," replied Oswaldo with an emphasis on the half.

"Okay, Inmate Finch is six foot one, and Tanner is five foot six. You two will do. Come with me to the forensic lab," Scott instructed.

His two wards followed him faithfully to his small laboratory, where he had a video camera in an elevated position and a digital camera on the desk. "Adrian, stand here and face the camera. Good, just like that. Now, Oz, take this dowel in your right hand and stand behind Adrian. Okay, good. Let me get my cameras ready. Oz, stab Adrian in the throat just below his Adam's apple." As the end of the dowel touched Adrian's neck, Scott stopped Oz and told him to hold his position. He documented the angle of the dowel in an upward trajectory at forty-two degrees using a flat board on Adrian's shoulder and a level for accuracy.

He then instructed Oswaldo to pull Adrian back toward him and try to bring the dowel down on his throat as straight as possible. The first thing they noticed was that Adrian automatically put his right arm up as he was being bent backward. The second thing they noted was that as Adrian came back on Oz's left shoulder, the horizontal angle of the dowel changed drastically. The only way that Oswaldo could get the dowel in a straight vertical and horizontal line was to stand on his tiptoes and pull himself up slightly with his left hand on Adrian's shoulders.

"Well, that's it for me," Scott muttered, adding, "The doctor said that the blade of the weapon went into Finch's neck on an almost perfectly level plane. I don't see Tanner pulling this thing off."

"So he didn't do it?" asked Adrian.

"Doesn't look like it," replied Oswaldo.

"Not with our demonstration here. Plus, the bloodstain void on his sleeve suggests that Finch placed his hand against his throat before grabbing the kid by the arm. The blood transferred to his right hand, which in turn was transferred to the shirtsleeve. I think that is exactly what happened. The kid froze, and Finch grabbed him. Since he was the first one he saw, he got it into his head that young Havoc was the stabber. Don't get me wrong, he might be an accessory, but he's not our prime suspect.

"On that note, I already talked to Inmate Jones. He said he was on his way back to his cell when they put the yard down. He didn't see anything because it was dark. He went up to medical to get his medication. He's only been at the institution for a few days and goes home the week after next. The gunner verified that he was walking across the yard and wasn't close enough to Finch to be involved. So that leaves him out too.

"Inmate Campbell had just been released from his assignment at the dining hall. He said he was walking over to the picnic table to put down the food items that he had smuggled out of the kitchen. He never made it past the fire hydrant. His supervisor confirmed that he had just let him out, and to be honest with you, Campbell is near sixty and pretty short. He really doesn't fit the profile either. The three that remain are Inmate Keller, Inmate Volks, and Inmate Morgan, and let's not forget Keller was bleeding from a cut on his knuckle."

"Have you interviewed any of them yet?" asked Oswaldo.

"Morgan had nothing to say. He says he was waiting for his friend to come out of Alameda Hall and was looking in that direction. He said that when he saw the gunner running across the roof in his direction, he instinctively hit the ground. Volks said he was sitting at the picnic table and hit the ground when the gunner started yelling. He said he saw Tennessee holding on to Tanner but didn't know anything was wrong. He thought they were playing. I need one of you to go with me to interview Keller."

"I'll go," offered Adrian.

Inmate Keller was already sitting in the X Wing interview room when they arrived. X Wing was the overflow ad seg unit for the prison. Most of the inmates housed there were newly arrived and waiting for their initial placement classification hearing. Prison officials didn't like having ad seg inmates housed in X Wing because they utilized Central Facility mainline inmates for feeding and clerical work unlike the actual ad seg unit. Therefore, the inmates who were supposed to be removed from the general population still had some contact with other inmates who were still on the main line. They gave them notes to take back to their buddies, or they would ask a clerk to make telephone calls on their behalf.

Inmate Keller seemed cordial but unconcerned with their visit. Scott advised him of his rights pursuant to the *Miranda* decision. He replied, "Sure," when asked if he wanted to talk.

Scott showed him the same photographs that he showed all the other suspects and witnesses. The photographs included one of himself looking up into the camera. "That's cool," he said as he admired his image. "Can I have this one?"

"Maybe when we're done with the investigation or during discovery," Scott replied. The reference went over his head.

"I want to send it to my mom," he added.

Scott had to admit it was a good photograph and one he was sure his mother would appreciate, an eight-by-ten photograph of her beloved son in handcuffs with blood on his hand in the middle of a crime scene. "Tell you what, if you cooperate and tell the truth, I will make sure you get the photograph at the end of the investigation," Scott bargained.

"Cool," he replied, adding, "What do you want to know?"

"In brief, I want to know who stabbed Tennessee," Scott asked.

"I don't know, but it wasn't Havoc," he insisted.

"How do you know?" asked Adrian.

"I saw Tennessee backpedaling toward the light pole, and then he grabbed Havoc, but he was already gettin' dragged before he got him. He held on to him until he hit the ground."

"Where were you exactly when this all happened?" Scott asked.

"Pretty much where you found me. The gunner was yellin', and I just lay down."

"How did you get the blood on your hand?" Scott inquired.

"I cut my knuckle on the side of the desk in my cell earlier. It started to heal, but I must have opened it up again when I hit the ground."

"Did you notify staff of the injury?"

"Nope."

"Mind if we collect a buccal swab from you today?" Scott asked.

"What for?" he queried.

"To prove your innocence or mark your guilt, take your pick. If it's your blood that I swabbed that day, then you have nothing to worry about. If it was Tennessee's blood, you might want to get an attorney. I will be getting a warrant," Scott advised.

"It'll be my blood," he said with confidence.

"Great, I'll have a consent form and swab brought up. Adrian, see if Oz or Becky Romero can bring that up." Adrian turned in his chair and picked up the phone that was on the counselor's desk.

"So did you see who did the stabbing?" Scott asked.

"No, it was pretty dark, and all I saw was somebody behind him, dude, but I couldn't see who it was or where they went after."

"What about Inmate Morgan?" Scott asked.

"Who?"

"Morgan, he was on the left side of Tennessee, to your right, toward the table," Scott replied, pushing a photograph of Inmate Morgan over toward their apparent "surfer dude" witness.

"Billy," he responded.

"Could he have been the stabber?" Scott asked.

"No, he was by the fire hydrant when I saw him last," he replied.

"How did he get over here?" Scott pointed to Morgan's position in the crime scene.

"Maybe he went to help Tennessee. He's a peckerwood too."

"And you?" Scott inquired.

"Newport Beach, dude," he said with bravado.

"And Havoc?"

"He's into that Thor shit."

"What about Inmate Volks?" Scott said as he pushed another photograph toward the surfer.

"We call him the Nazi."

"Why's that?" Scott inquired.

"He's all into that Hitler shit too. He's all proud of being German. He speaks it too."

"Where was he when Tennessee got hit?"

"He was sitting at the picnic table."

"How old are you, Keller?" Scott asked.

"Twenty-four," he replied.

"When are you getting out?"

"Two more years."

"What did you do to find yourself in here?"

"We had a tagging crew, and we mixed it up with some nonlocals. I busted one of them up with my skateboard. I guess I busted him up good. They say he's in a wheelchair now."

"Was it worth it?" Scott asked.

"Locals only, dude. Wrecked a good board though."

Becky brought the consent form and buccal swab kit. Inmate Keller signed the waiver, and Scott collected the DNA sample from his inner cheek and gums. "What about the pic, man?" he asked before being escorted to his cell.

"Like I said, when the investigation is finished," Scott replied.

Chapter 8

The Scullery

The audible alarm blared over the North Facility kitchen like the baying of a giant hound dog with lungs the size of a gray whale. Responding staff had run into the A and B Yard dining halls and converged in the kitchen, which was in the middle. Some had already walked back outside and were standing in the open air in amazement at what they had just witnessed. Some had been shaken to their core and were sitting on benches, shaking their heads in disbelief.

Adrian, Oswaldo, and Scott walked past them, carrying every piece of crime scene equipment they possessed. They entered through the A Yard dining hall and walked into the kitchen, dropping their gear near the culinary sergeant's office door. Only one inmate, an elderly black gentleman, was in the kitchen area. He appeared to be in shock and was being attended to by a nurse. Only a few officers remained in the building, posted up at the entrance of the scullery to keep out the curious.

Sergeant Vernon Akers was the culinary sergeant on duty. He walked over to Scott, shaking his head. "Dog, I've been here almost thirty years. I have never seen anything like this ever. Man, I have seen some nasty shit, but this is the worst!"

"Do we know who he is, Vern?"

"No, no, I don't even know how we are ever going to know other than he's a white boy," replied the shaken supervisor.

"Fingerprints most likely," Scott responded.

Just then, Oswaldo walked up to Scott and said one word. "Wow!"

"Oz, let's get some crime scene tape up here and get everybody out. Have them take the inmate who found the body up to the infirmary and make him comfortable. We'll talk to him up there shortly." Scott turned to Sergeant Akers. "Vern, have they started the emergency count yet?"

"Not yet, but they will pretty soon," he replied.

"Okay, well, that'll be our first clue in finding out who this guy is or was rather. What time did they find the body?"

"They come in and turn on the tray washing machine and dishwasher every day at 1530 hours to get them warmed up for the evening meal. When the dish washing machine started up, that's when Inmate Davenport noticed the blood running out from under the door. He switched it off and raised the side door, but he had trouble getting it open. However, he managed to open it partially. When he saw the hand fall out, he immediately ran into my office as white as a ghost. I called over Tony Padilla, the kitchen officer, and had him stay with Davenport while I went in and opened the machine up the rest of the way. There was no doubt in my mind that he was dead. Half his head is missing."

"A dead body stuffed into an industrial dishwasher. That is a first for this department," Scott mused.

"Medical department wants to move the body to the infirmary," announced Adrian.

"Get them out of here!" Scott roared. "I want everybody other than the three of us out of here now. That body stays where it is. So help me, if they even try to move it, I am going to start arresting people myself. Everybody just stand down until the coroner's office and district attorney's office investigators get here. Oz, stretch the crime scene all the way out to include both dining halls. That'll keep them back."

Scott turned to Sergeant Akers, "Vern, can you stay in your office while we process this crime scene? I might have some questions for you. Oh, what time did they last use the dishwasher?"

"I wasn't here this morning, but they would have used it after the breakfast meal. They're usually done using it around nine thirty or ten o'clock."

"Thanks. Oh, and, Vern, can you cancel that alarm? It is giving me an incredible headache."

"Oh, man, I forgot all about it."

Scott stepped out onto the loading dock and placed a call on his cellular telephone. "Alex, it's Scott. I really need you to come out on this one. We have a crime scene in a scullery. The room is tile and stainless steel, and everything is washed clean. The body is in a giant dishwasher. This one is going to take some effort. And, Alex, someone is killing our white inmates, and I need to figure out why."

"I'm already on my way, buddy, but it's going to be me and Alberto Gutierrez, and we'll be there in about twenty minutes."

Scott thanked him and put the phone back in its holster. "Adrian!" Scott shouted. In good order, Adrian appeared on the loading dock. "Adrian, take my keys and go back to the office. Go into the lab and bring back the ALS, goggles, and a long extension cord."

"ALS?" he asked.

"Alternate light source, Adrian, the big silver thing on the counter. Make sure you bring orange and yellow goggles and filter plates. Also, bring back the bloodstain kit and get several bottles of Bluestar and spray bottles and bring as many Hexagon OBTI kits as you can. Get Becky Romero to help you if she isn't doing anything else. Ask Oz to call over to plant operations and see if they have a blueprint sketch of the north scullery room and get them to send it over with someone. We'll use that as our diagram. Tell Oz to make copies." Adrian acknowledged his instructions and disappeared back into the kitchen. Scott stood on the loading dock for a minute longer to collect his thoughts and then stepped back into the crime scene.

However, before he could take two steps, his phone rang. He looked down at the screen and saw it was Tyrus. "Doggy, I'm on my way with the coroner's investigator."

"Who is it, Tyrus?"

"Dan, uh, Johnson," he replied.

"Dan Johansen maybe?"

"Yeah, that's it," Tyrus replied.

"Too bad Tom Jenks retired. He would have loved this one," Scott said.

"What have you got?" inquired Tyrus.

"It appears that someone decided to bash in the skull of some kid and stuff him inside an industrial dishwasher. It looks like the murder weapon is in there with him."

"Wait, the dishwasher or the tray washer?" asked Tyrus.

"The dishwasher, the one they use for the pots and pans."

"Tight fit?"

"It's bigger than you think, Ty, maybe fifty-eight square inches. You'll see it when you get here."

"Okay, we'll be there in about five minutes. I just passed Adrian in your Crown Vic."

"He's going back for supplies. Ty, when you guys get here, can you check on the status of the count and go to the infirmary and talk with Inmate Davenport? He's an elderly black inmate. He's the one who found the body. You might want to get a statement from him now before he goes catatonic or something. The body can wait a few more minutes. He's already had his bath."

"You mean they turned the machine on?" asked the bewildered sergeant.

"At least once and very likely twice," Scott responded.

"That water is scalding hot, Dog. I used to be a culinary officer."

Scott agreed, hung up the phone, and walked back into where Oswaldo was standing guard. "Tyvek up, Oz. This one is going to be a project."

Oswaldo acknowledged these instructions and dug through the bag of white coveralls, locating the only size medium in the pile. He selected a triple extralarge and tossed it to Scott. Scott threw it back at him with zest and requested an extralarge with an expletive. After a futile attempt, Scott stuffed the extralarge suit into the garbage can and reluctantly asked for the triple extralarge. "Shut up, Oz. It's my hips."

"There's a leg missing from the back of the machine," Oswaldo advised.

"It's not missing, Ozzie. It's in the dishwasher. Who did the initial photographs, you or Adrian?"

"I did" was his response.

"Did you get good photos of the place where the leg was missing from?" Scott inquired.

"Yeah, yeah, of course," he replied.

"Crap, we're going to need a tripod and remote shutter release. Get Adrian on the radio and make sure that he brings those with him and my camera filters," Scott instructed.

"Howdy, buddy!" exclaimed the dapper Texan from across the dining hall. Next to Alex was a short round Hispanic gentleman with day-old salt-and-pepper stubble and a blue vest that read "DA Investigator" on the back. He had a round face, a kind smile, and a leprechaun's twinkle in his eye.

"Buddy, this is Alberto Gutierrez, one of the finest investigators in the DA's office," Alex made the introduction.

"Pleased to meet you," Scott said, extending his hand and adding, "I've got a fantastic crime scene for you." They shook hands.

"You must be the Dog I hear so much about. Just call me Bert."

"Coroner's investigator here yet?" asked Alex.

"Dan Johansen is here with Ty, but they are up in the infirmary interviewing the inmate who found the body," Scott responded.

"Do we know who the deceased is?" asked Bert.

"Not yet. They are right in the middle of the count. We'll know when they are done, and then I will make the verification by fingerprints," Scott replied.

"And you say he's in a dishwasher?" asked the portly investigator.

"Indeed he is, waiting for the rinse cycle." Scott chortled.

"Well, we might as well wait for Dan to get down here. Did they say how long it was going to take them?" asked Alex.

"They should be on their way down. I'll have my ALS ready to go once they move the body. You sticking around for that?" Scott asked.

"Wouldn't miss it for the world, buddy, you and your fancy doodads."

It only took about ten minutes of small talk before Tyrus and Dan walked through the A Yard dining hall door. Scott briefed them on what they had in the crime scene, and Tyrus informed Scott of what Inmate Davenport had to say, which wasn't much different from that which Sergeant Akers had already told him. Preliminary information from the emergency count stated that Inmate Dana Higgins was missing from his cell in San Leandro Hall. Scott sent Becky to the records department to pull his central file before they lost it to the unit 6 lieutenant.

Scott walked the three investigators over to the scullery and recommended they put on boot covers and masks at the very least. The scullery was a large square room with a tile floor, a tile wall, and a forty-eight-inch-tall stainless steel wainscoting. Two drains were in the center of the room, and a series of garden hoses hung on the wall. A small utility room was attached, and a dozen dirty string mops hung on pegs over a sink. It was the same sink where Scott and Adrian soaked their heads after being doused with pepper spray during the riot.

The dishwasher was on the south wall at the end of a counter that had two large sink basins and a drying table. The dishwasher itself was a large square stainless steel box with a rolling door on each end. The entire unit and sinks sat on top of a large stainless steel table of sorts with numerous round steel tubes that acted as legs, each measuring about thirty-six inches in length and two and a half inches in diameter. One was missing from the back underneath one of the sink basins.

The tray washing machine was a much larger appliance that was mounted to the west wall. It was about the size of a small car and was open on both ends, except for rubber strips that kept most of the water inside the machine, with a conveyor belt that pulled the meal trays through a series of soap, steam, and hot water rinse nozzles. The perpetrators selected the dishwasher over the tray washer for obvious reasons; it had doors. The unmistakable smell of bleach was in the air.

Three digital cameras clicked off frame after frame, documenting the room and various appliances. Scott slowly opened the dishwasher door in the manner described by Sergeant Akers and Inmate Davenport while camera flashes sparked. The body was in a seated position with its knees tucked up to its chest, supporting the head, and his right arm and hand stiffly by the right thigh. Lividity had settled in the lower extremities, and rigor mortis was present in the neck, shoulders, and arms. The tip of the metal post could be seen behind his back. The body was clad only in socks, boxer shorts, and blue denim pants, which had been pulled down probably from the efforts of placing him in the machine. An avulsion was visible on the right forehead. Blood mixed with water streamed down the victim's wet chest like red food coloring.

There were three things that were immediately obvious: he was dead, the left side of his head had been bashed in, and he was a young white inmate. "Looks like someone finally figured out how to actually kill one," Scott said half under his breath. Oswaldo looked over at Scott and smiled.

"What?" asked Bert.

"We've had two of our high-profile whites off the B Yard stabbed this month. They did their best to kill 'em, but they both pulled through. I was waiting for them to succeed with one," Scott replied.

"How the heck are we going to get him out of there?" asked Alex as he inspected the door.

"Well, I think if we can get in from the other side and turn him sideways, we can jockey him out as if we were moving a sofa through a doorway," Scott offered.

"Flashlight and forty-five, Scotty," said Oswaldo as he hopped up on the sink side of the unit, opened the door, and leaned almost his entire body inside the dishwasher.

"Gutsy kid," commented Bert.

"Flashlight and forty-five?" asked the coroner's investigator.

"That's our code. If he was old enough to have been in Vietnam, Oz would have been a tunnel rat. So any time I need him to crawl into a tight space, I just say 'flashlight and forty-five,' meaning a U.S. Army angle-head flashlight and a government-issue .45-caliber 1911A1 pistol," Scott clarified.

As Scott said that, he observed the decedent slide back from his perch deeper into the dishwasher and take a header toward the assembled investigators. The skin of the deceased inmate was reddish as if boiled by the extreme temperature of the water. Scott reached in and slid him partly out while Oswaldo jockeyed his legs back and forth until he cleared the dishwasher completely. "Becky's here with the central file. I'm going to take a look," said Tyrus as he left the scullery for the sergeant's office.

"Geez, look at those crushing blows on the left side of the skull. You can see brain matter," said Oswaldo as he crawled out of the dishwasher on the side where the investigators stood.

"Nice, Oz, no sense going out the way you went in," Scott remarked.

"Had to get the pipe," he said with a smile.

"Okay, I forgive you. Get the camera, and let's get some photographs before we load him into the body bag," Scott instructed.

"How the hell are we going to get him into the bag?" asked Bert.

"It'll take four of us to straighten him out," replied Dan.

"Definite bruising on his right chest, side and upper arm," remarked Alex.

"Defensive wounds to his inner left arm and left hand," Scott added.

"Also here on his right forearm," stated Bert.

"They must have knocked him down first, kicked him, and struck him with the metal leg or pipe thing," Scott reflected.

"They?" asked Bert.

"Yeah, I'm saying it took at least two to get him down, but I could be wrong. Then again, these are inmates, so they usually don't act alone," Scott said.

"The skin on the shoulders is erythematous from the hot dishwater," observed Dan.

"Is that a bite mark on the upper right trapezius?" asked Bert.

"Sure is," replied Alex.

"Kinky devils," Scott jibed.

"I wonder if he did some biting of his own," asked Alex.

"We'll find out at the autopsy," responded Dan.

"Might have just been a method of control used as a means of dominance," contributed Bert.

"No sense swabbing," Scott said, adding, "However, I can get some nice photographs with and without an ABFO scale. Too bad I didn't bring the UV-IR camera, but what I do have is my extruder gun kit."

After a few minutes of rummaging through his crime scene kit, Scott returned with a black case that contained the casting gun and a tube of medium-viscosity casting mix. "It'll have to do," Scott said as he screwed the unit together. Oswaldo provided the towels, and they dried the area around the bite as best as they could. Scott gave the trigger a couple of good pumps, and the casting material squirted out like he was caulking a shower. He smoothed out the compound using a tongue depressor. After about fifteen minutes, the compound had dried sufficiently to be lifted, revealing a reverse image of the actual bite mark.

"Not too bad, very few bubbles. Good enough for our local forensic odontologist," Scott reflected as he pulled bits of dead skin from the casting.

Just then, Tyrus walked in with a photograph from the central file. "Yeah, that's him, all right, Inmate Dana Higgins," he said, adding, "And get this, Doggy, he's a white Rolling '30s Crip."

"Well, that would explain the tattoo on his upper left arm," suggested Oswaldo as he photographed the blue image of a hand shaped into the letter C and the words "rolling" and "'30s" emblazoned above and below.

"This is getting interesting, Ty. We have a skinhead, peckerwood, and white Crip in the bad news mix. What do you make of it?" Scott asked.

"I know what to make of it, but I'll keep it to myself for the time being," he replied.

"How old was he?" asked Dan.

"Twenty-two," replied Tyrus. "And he was in for an armed PC 211 at a gas station in Whittier."

They straightened Dana out as best they could and zipped him into the body bag. Dan wrote the name and prisoner number of the deceased inmate on the outside of the bag with Scott's Sharpie and wheeled in the gurney. Tyrus, Oswaldo, and Scott helped slide him onto the wheeled carriage. It was obvious that he had retained some water from his postmortem baptism. "The autopsy will be the day after tomorrow around nine. We don't do autopsies on Thursdays. We'll see you there," chimed Dan as he wheeled the recently departed out the door.

Scott happened to notice that Inmate Higgins's legs were starting to return to their tucked position within the confines of the bag. As Dan exited the dining hall doors, he was met by Adrian, who was carrying enough forensic equipment to burden a mule. "Good man," Scott encouraged. "Bring it over here, and then you and Oz go over to the maintenance paint shop and bring back the biggest canvas drop cloth you guys can find. Oh, and, Oz, let's not mention anything about the bite mark in our reports just yet. We'll do a supplemental report later. I'll just put down 'casting' right now as evidence collected."

"Why is that?" he asked.

"Because, Oz, our initial report will go to the unit 6 lieutenant to be faxed off to the headquarters in the incident package. All the reports will be handled by the inmate clerks who undoubtedly will read them and then disseminate the information to the rest of the inmate population. If our suspect finds out that we have a casting of his bite mark, he will do something to alter his teeth. We'll keep that tidbit secret until we can develop a suspect and get a warrant for his bite impression."

Chapter 9

Forensics

"Welcome to Forensics 101," Scott said to Adrian as they taped cardboard over the windows of the scullery. "We need to get this room as dark as possible, ergo the canvas drop cloth for the entry."

"How are we going to get it to stay up?" he asked.

"Nails and Gorilla tape, that stuff will hold anything," Scott replied.

Once the room was sealed from as much of the ambient light as they could, Scott placed the SPEX Mini-CrimeScope on a wheeled cart and handed Oz the UltraLite unit with the UV Magnum head attached and a dedicated 415-nanometer flashlight. "Start at 405 nanometers' wavelength with yellow goggles and then switch to 450 nanometers with the orange goggles," Scott instructed, adding, "I want every inch of this room examined, including the ceiling. And pay close attention to the grout between the tiles."

As soon as Scott turned on the forensic light from the heavy SPEX unit, Adrian pointed at a glowing stain and exclaimed, "Look at that!"

"That's probably just a cleaning chemical. Cleaning chemicals that contain phosphates often fluoresce like that. We'll know when we see blood," Scott advised. "In fact, here, let me put the light on the interior of the dishwasher." Adrian carefully studied the detail of the diluted bloodstains under the forensic light. "Now switch your goggles to the orange pair, and I will bump this up to 450 nanometers." Again, he carefully studied the stains.

"It's even more pronounced with blood that is not diluted," Scott advised. Alex and Bert stood quietly in the corner and observed the proceedings, each wearing orange goggles.

"Found something over here under the sink," remarked Oswaldo. He worked his way underneath the table. "It's a skull fragment or something with some hairs on it."

"Leave it where it is and drop an evidence marker," Scott instructed.

"Got some blood over here by the sink too, but it looks diluted," Oswaldo said as he crawled out from under the table.

"Not surprising," Scott said, adding, "Check the garden hoses over there too. You might get lucky and get a handprint or something. We have some castoff over here on the tray machine. Look, Adrian, they tried to wash it off, but most of it is still here, castoff going up right here, one swing going down, and then another going back up again. So how many blows were delivered?" Scott asked.

"Two?" he answered with a question.

"Two or more," Scott replied. "The first blow does not generally produce blood on the downswing. Take the number of castoff patterns that you see and add one, but be aware that it may have taken more than one blow to produce bloodshed. Never commit to an exact number of blows because you very likely will be wrong. It's all an estimate."

"Got blood over here on the hose and spray nozzle," chimed Oswaldo.

"Sweet," Scott responded, adding, "We have some blood on the drain over here too. Of course, we are assuming it is blood. We'll have to conduct some presumptive tests to be sure."

Oswaldo found additional castoff bloodstains on the ceiling using the handheld 415 nm forensic light. It was the one place their suspects neglected to wash down. They switched back on the lights once all their markers were dropped. Examining the patterns, they determined that Inmate Higgins was struck with the metal leg as he was in proximity to the tray machine and near to the ground, perhaps on his hands and knees. The upward swing of the castoff pattern was forty-two inches above the floor. The blow shot a fragment of his skull skidding underneath the sink.

Scott placed a fluorescent magnetic scale on the side of the tray machine in the area of the castoff patterns and affixed a reflective letter sticker in proximity to the scale to designate the bloodstain mapping area. "Oz, get some good photographs of the crime scene with the evidence markers. Shoot the four corners and the flats," Scott instructed.

"What's next?" asked Adrian.

"Two things actually. First, we photograph the crime scene with the evidence markers. And second, I give you this bottle of Leucocrystal Violet and send you in to the mop room so you can spray the mops," Scott said as he mixed the two chemicals into a spray bottle and handed the bottle to Adrian. "Wear gloves, safety glasses, and a mask and use it sparingly."

"What do I do with this?" he asked sheepishly.

"Spray the mopheads, the stringy part. Keep spraying until something turns violet and then stop spraying and move on to the next one."

Adrian diligently proceeded into the mop room, spray bottle in hand. In short order, Scott heard the sound of atomized spray being pumped through the spray nozzle. "It's turning purple! What do I do now?" bellowed Adrian.

"Stop spraying and move over to the next mop!" Scott hollered back.

Turning to Oswaldo, he said, "Go in there and photograph what he found."

Oswaldo marched into the mop room and dropped a marker by the second mop from the left. Now Scott saw the flash of the camera illuminate the small room. After a few minutes, Oswaldo returned to where Scott was standing and said, "It was just the one mop. There was blood on the strings and the handle."

"Excellent. Was our young ward impressed?"

"He's still standing there with his mouth open."

"Smoke and mirrors, Oz. It's all magic. Wait until he sees what's next. Speaking of which, put the camera on the tripod, attach the remote shutter release, turn off the flash, and set it for bulb, f/16, ISO 400. You know you're going to have to be quick, and it needs to be manually focused. Adrian! Get in here!"

"What's up?" he replied as he emerged from the mop room.

"How long have we been in these Tyvek suits?" Scott asked.

"I don't know, maybe a little over an hour."

"Right then, it's time for a break before we get started on our next project." They found their way out from behind the canvas drop cloth and stepped into the A side dining hall, where they peeled off their white coveralls and removed their latex gloves. They each grabbed a bottle of water and walked outside. Oswaldo and Adrian disappeared into the north dormitory to utilize the restroom. Scott, on the other hand, had the bladder of a camel. Alex and Bert decided they had seen enough and wanted to get back to the office. Therefore, they bid them a good night and left.

Darkness had descended on the institution, and the tungsten lights atop the tall light poles dropped their yellow hue onto the white buildings and green yard. It always reminded Scott of a parking lot for some reason or a night game at a minor league baseball playing field. There were no inmates and only a few correctional officers making their rounds, collecting count slips from each housing unit. The tower officers had unslung their Ruger Mini-14s to have a quick meal and were moving back and forth in their confined spaces.

A feral cat introduced herself and asked if Scott had any morsels. "Sorry, old girl, no food here."

But this is the dining hall. There is supposed to be food. There are supposed to be inmates with food, she mewed.

Crap, Scott thought with a sense of urgency. *Food! We have to feed three thousand inmates.*

Scott scurried back into the dining hall and made his way back to the sergeant's office. "Vern, what are we going to do to feed these inmates?" he asked.

"We'll be cell-feeding tonight. We're trucking in the food from central. We'll use paper trays to serve and then truck the pots and pans back to central to get washed. Don't worry, Dog, you have all night if necessary."

"That's a relief. We have at least two, maybe three hours to go," Scott replied.

On his way out of Vern's office, he procured a package of tuna fish. He walked outside, opened the pouch, and presented it to Her Scruffiness. She purred as if completely out of control of her emotions as she gulped down huge chunks of the fish. She was joined by a brave seagull that patiently waited just out of her reach for its turn at the scraps. "I could kill a cheeseburger," said Oswaldo as he watched the pair.

"Man, that does sound good. Raymond's French burger and fries would hit the spot," Scott reflected.

"Yeah or a queen burger with bacon and cheese. We should see if Sergeant Phillips or Becky can go up to the snack bar and get some food," requested Oswaldo.

"What time is it?" Scott asked.

"It's 1835 hours," returned Adrian.

"I think Raymond is closed, Oz. We'll have to tough it out," Scott responded.

"Shit" came his reply.

"C'mon then, back to work," Scott said as he stepped back into the dining hall. They suited and booted as it was called in the business or, as Scott would say, "bunny suit up." They donned masks and latex gloves on top of cotton ones and stepped back into the crime scene.

"Ready for this?" Scott asked.

"Ready for what?" replied Adrian.

"Bluestar Forensic," Scott said, holding a bottle. "This reagent is designed to reveal bloodstains that are washed, wiped, or otherwise unseen by the human eye. The nice thing about this stuff is that you don't need total darkness, which makes it easier to photograph than luminol, and it doesn't alter or destroy DNA either."

"What does it do?" asked the fresh investigator.

"It glows," responded Oswaldo.

"No way," challenged Adrian.

"Watch and learn," Scott advised. With that, he mixed the catalyst tablet with the reagent, and Oswaldo assumed his position behind the camera, which was perched atop the Giottos tripod.

"Manual focus, Oz," Scott asked as he switched off the lights. He began spraying the floor in front of the tray machine. A soft blue glow developed between the drain and the machine.

Suddenly, Scott was blinded by a brilliant light. "Oz! Turn off the flash!" he yelled.

"Sorry!"

After a few adjustments, they tried it again. "Wow! Look at the floor!" exclaimed Adrian.

"Well, we have to keep in mind that Bluestar will react with a 5 percent bleach solution and oddly enough potatoes, tomatoes, horseradish, and a few of the legumes. I'm sure they've had their share of those in here, but with a little practice, you can tell the difference. However, I find Bluestar Forensic reagent glowed brighter and lasted longer than luminol, which has been around since the 1930s," Scott commented. "See the swirling pattern underneath the tray machine?"

"Yeah," replied Adrian.

"That's a wipe pattern. An object was dragged through blood that was already present, thus altering its appearance. That's where they used the mop to clean up. You good, Oz?"

"Yeah, I'm good. What's next, Scotty?"

"I'm thinking first the side of the tray machine with the castoff and then the dishwasher. It'll be very effective with the jury to see the glowing blood dripping down onto the conveyor from under the door and the inside of the tray machine glowing."

"Don't forget the sink and hose," reminded Oswaldo.

"No worries, not to mention the drain and the ceiling."

Once they had captured all the revealed stains in the scullery, Scott went back around the room with the Bluestar and an adhesive photographic scales and arrows to show the areas he wanted swabbed and tested. His efforts to develop latent prints on the dishwasher using small particle reagent were not successful. Even the developed prints that he could attribute to Sergeant Akers were distorted beyond recognition owing mostly to the textured pattern of the brushed aluminum doors. The metal table leg was a complete wash for prints—pardon the pun.

However, Scott did manage to lift a partial palm print from the leg that was in front of the missing leg underneath the sink. He developed it using black powder and an ostrich-feather brush and lifted it with a large lift tab. It looked like part of the thenar, but palms were definitely not his specialty. It did have sufficient ridge detail to send off to his good friend Tadeo at the department of justice.

Within two hours, they had documented, tested, swabbed, and processed all the evidence in the crime scene. Within an hour after that, Oswaldo and Scott were on the prowl for a cheeseburger.

Chapter 10

The Interviews

"So the last time you think the dishwasher was run yesterday was about eight o'clock in the morning?" Scott asked Officer Theresa Watkins, the second-watch culinary officer.

"Yeah, they was done about then. They only use the dishwasher for the pots. The pans are rinsed in the back and then run through the tray machine," she replied.

"And what time were the inmates finished cleaning up?"

"I had let everybody out by eleven. The only inmate that stayed in was Forman. He's the leadman. He was in the kitchen for a while, but he spent most of his time in the dining hall writing a letter. He left when I left at one."

"Do you recognize this guy?" Scott asked as he showed her a photograph of Inmate Higgins.

"No, he don't work for me."

"Yes, well, he doesn't work for anybody right now. Was there anything suspicious about any of your workers yesterday?" Scott inquired.

"No, nothing that I can think of. I just let them out, and that was it," she replied.

"Who was your sergeant?"

"It was a part-timer. I think his name is Bergmann. He was here for the morning meal, but then I didn't see him the rest of the shift."

"What time did the supervising cooks leave?" Scott asked.

"They were gone after the meal. They had a meeting up in the Administration Building. Um, I think Cook Perry came in just before I left."

"Who was working in the dining halls?" Scott asked.

"Margaret was on the A side, and Adam was on the B side."

"Margaret?"

"Swift, Officer Swift and Officer Adam Burgess," she corrected.

"How were your white inmate workers behaving yesterday? Did you notice anything different?" Scott asked.

"No, I only have two right now, and they haven't been acting any different from what they always do," she replied.

"And they are . . ." Scott inquired as if pulling teeth.

"Inmate Lacey and Inmate McGregor. They both live in Alameda Hall on the A side," she said as she wrote down their information on a piece of paper.

"McGregor. Where have I heard that name before? Do you know what they call him?" Scott asked.

"Highway or Hightower or something like that," she replied half-heartedly.

"Highlander perhaps?" Scott inquired.

"Maybe that's it. Are we done because I have to do the time cards?" she informed Scott.

"Yeah, I suppose so. If you can think of anything, let me know. Before I go, can you give me a list of all your workers who were on shift yesterday, including all volunteers?" She reluctantly provided him with a hastily drafted list of her inmate workers and dismissed Scott with a grunt.

On his way out of the kitchen, he ran into Officer Burgess and asked him if he had a few minutes to talk. He responded in the affirmative, and they went into his rather small office. He informed Scott that he and Officer Swift were required to release their assigned inmates before eleven o'clock and report to the north education department to assist in a search of the classrooms for a missing pair of scissors. He and Officer

Swift left together, and all the inmates assigned to the kitchen were still cleaning and putting things away from the morning meal. He did not observe or notice anything out of the ordinary. A conversation with Officer Swift produced the same information.

As Scott finished up the staff interviews, including Cook Perry, who was more interested in the evening meal than providing any useful information, Scott ran into Tyrus, who was walking back from San Leandro Hall. "Doggy," he said as he approached, "the only thing I could find out from his cellie was that Higgins had a ducat to the central infirmary at 0830 hours."

"That's easy enough to verify," Scott said, adding, "I wonder what time he came through sally port no. 12?"

"That is right behind the culinary back dock. They may have seen him coming back through the sally port, grabbed him, and dragged him into the scullery."

"My thoughts exactly, Tyrus. Let's go and have a word with Officer Vargas."

Officer Ignacio Vargas was a twenty-eight-year veteran of the department and had worked sally port no. 12 since the early 1990s. In fact, he worked that sally port when Scott was a tier officer in the early 1990s in Sausalito Hall on the A Yard. He knew a great deal more than running sally port no. 12, however, as he was number three on the seniority list and therefore worked a tremendous amount of overtime shifts anywhere and everywhere in the institution.

"Vargas, my old friend, how are things?" Scott said as Tyrus and he walked through the pedestrian gate.

"Fine, fine, and how are you, guys?"

"We come seeking your wisdom and detailed record keeping," responded Tyrus.

"Anything I can do to help you fine, gentlemen, it would be an honor," replied the silver-haired officer.

"Do you remember an Inmate Higgins coming through the sally port for a central medical ducat yesterday?" Scott asked.

"The white Crip?" he asked in turn.

"That's the guy," replied Tyrus.

"Yes, yes, he came through at about 0810 on his way to central."

"Was he wearing state blues?" Scott asked.

"He has to wear all blues, shirt, and pants to go to central," replied the seasoned officer.

"What time did he come back through?" asked Ty.

"Oh, I'd say about . . . oh, he came back at about . . . here, let me see the logbook. He came back through at 1035 hours on the dot. Is he the one that got killed?"

"Yes, Ignacio, that was him," Scott said.

"The poor kid, it is very sad," he replied.

"Did you notice him talking to anyone on the back dock?" asked Tyrus.

"No, no, but I had a culinary truck go through at the same time, so I was busy with that."

Tyrus and Scott thanked him for his assistance and walked back toward the culinary. "Well, Ty, that should give us a time of death," Scot remarked.

"Yeah, I'd say between ten thirty-five and eleven."

"Wait, wait!" cried out Officer Vargas.

Tyrus and Scott stopped and turned to address him. "It wasn't when he went back through but when he went out. Two white inmates said something to him from the back dock of the culinary before he got to the sally port on his way over to central. I didn't hear what they said, but it upset him very much, I could tell."

"Do you think you could recognize the white inmates if I showed you some photos?" Scott asked.

"Certainly," he replied.

Again, Tyrus and Scott thanked him for his information and left with a promise to return with photographs. "Tyrus, according to Officer Watkins's list, we have two white inmates, two Paisas, and the leadman, Inmate Forman, a black, working in or around the scullery at the time. Inmate Lacey and Inmate McGregor were the whites. McGregor was with Birdsong when he got stabbed. What do you think about making another run on Birdsong and Finch?"

"You want to do that now?" he asked.

"Might as well. We can go back through sally port no. 12 and walk over to the central culinary back dock and cut through the central kitchen to the infirmary." It was a longer walk than expected, but within ten minutes, they were in the central infirmary. They were unable to talk to Inmate Birdsong as a staph infection had developed in his throat, and the medication they were administering made him sleep. Inmate Finch, however, was in good spirits. They found him talkative and appreciative of the company.

"They're going to let me out of here soon, but I think they are going to move me to another pen," he informed them.

"Anywhere you'd like to go?" Scott asked.

"Well, I'd like to stay here or up at CSP–Monterey Bay because my wife lives close, and I don't think she wants me to move too far away because of the visits. You know how women are. Did you ever call my wife?"

"Yes, Rob, I called her," Scott said. "You are right, she is mad at you. I tried my best to calm her, but she is concerned and rightly so."

"I have been writing to her, but it just isn't the same. Once I get out of here, I will be able to talk to her face-to-face, and everything will be fine again."

"Rob, something happened at north yesterday, and I am wondering if you can shed some light on it for us," Scott asked.

"I don't get any news in here. What happened?" he inquired.

"Inmate Dana Higgins, the white Crip on the B Yard, was murdered," replied Tyrus.

"Oh no! Not that kid! They call him White Chocolate as corny as that may sound. I thought that whole thing was over and done with."

"What whole thing, Rob?" Scott asked.

"Well, six, seven months ago, Big Bird came to me and said that the skinheads were unhappy with this kid being on the yard."

"Big Bird?" inquired Tyrus.

"Birdsong. They said the kid was a disgrace to his white heritage. Big Bird said they approached him and asked him to consent to an assault just to get him off the yard. Big Bird said he would talk to me about it because I had the yard. I told him to let it go. These days, you have all kinds of races mixing in these gangs. It's all about where you grow up and not what the color of your skin is. We had to just accept it as part of the times. You've got blacks who are Southerners and Asians who are Bloods. We sure have enough white Northerners. Heck, the kid Lobo ran the Northerners on the B Yard, and he is whiter than you and me. So I didn't give them any green light on the kid at all. In fact, I told him that the peckerwoods would not back them, and there would be trouble if they did anything to him. We didn't want any trouble with the Crips. It just wasn't worth it. I told them they had to leave it alone, and that was final."

"Did they accept that?" asked Tyrus.

"I thought they had. I didn't hear nothing about it again after that."

"Did Birdsong say who was behind the effort to assault the kid?" Scott asked.

"Yeah, it was Highlander and Santa. You know Highlander wanted control of the yard."

"Rob, I want you to think about this carefully. Is it possible they hit you to remove you from the yard and that would clear the way for the assault on Higgins?" Scott asked.

"And maybe that's the same reason they hit Big Bird?" added Tyrus.

"No, no, I just don't see it. I woulda had some warning. Someone would have told me," he stated adamantly. With that, they thanked him for his time and departed back to the North Facility.

"What's next, Dog?" asked Tyrus.

"Let's pull McGregor into the captain's office and interview him as a witness in the Inmate Birdsong incident."

As they walked past the culinary back dock, something blue caught Scott's eye underneath a dumpster. "Hang on a minute, Ty," Scott said as he walked over to the dumpster and got down on his hands and knees. He reached under with his extended baton and snagged a blue chambray shirt complete with a long-sleeved white T-shirt inside. "My guess is that's the shirt Higgins was wearing when he went to central.

Better take it as evidence." Tyrus found a brown paper bag in the kitchen and brought it to Scott.

They continued on to the unit 6 captain's office, and within fifteen minutes, Highlander was escorted to where Tyrus and Scott sat waiting. "McGregor, have you got your ID card with you?" asked Sergeant Phillips. Inmate McGregor reached into his blue chambray shirt pocket, withdrew his state-issued inmate identification card, and set it on the desk.

"Have a seat McGregor," said Tyrus, accepting and reviewing the ID. "I'm sure you know what we are here to talk to you about."

"Probably that dude that got killed in the kitchen" was his reply.

"Actually," Scott interrupted before it was necessary to issue a *Miranda* warning, "it's about Inmate Birdsong. We just found out you were walking with him when he got stabbed. So we are interviewing you today as a witness in that assault."

"Who told you I was there?"

"It was Big Bird himself. He said he was walking on the track with you when he got stabbed."

"Nah, he's wrong. I wasn't there. I was in my cell. I heard about it, but I wasn't there."

"What if I said he wasn't the only one that said you were there?"

"Then I would say they are all lying because I wasn't there."

"Were you on the yard when Inmate Finch got stabbed?" asked Tyrus.

"Nope, I wasn't there either. I can't go out on the yard at night because I am on C status. I got a write-up for possession of tobacco."

Tyrus continued, "So are you a skinhead?"

"No, man, I ain't no skinhead."

"Neo-Nazi?"

"What is this?" he queried the questioning.

"Who do you run with?" Tyrus persisted.

"Nobody," he proclaimed.

"So," Tyrus said, playing his ace, "these 'oi' and swastika on your forearm aren't neo-Nazi symbols?"

"Man, I got nothing to say to you or him," he said, pointing at Scott.

"Just one more question," Scott said while leaning forward on the table. "Exactly where were you yesterday between the hours of ten thirty and eleven?"

"At work. Ask my boss," he said, standing up. "And I want to go back to my cell now."

"You are free to leave," Scott stated as he motioned for the escort officer.

"Well, that didn't get us anywhere. Now what?" asked Tyrus as they left the captain's office.

"I'm not sure, Tyrus. I think we need to sit down and go over all the evidence that we have so far, make a chart, and look at all the information we've developed thus far in the investigation."

Chapter 11

The Case Thus Far

They assembled in Scott's office—Tyrus, Oswaldo, Adrian, and Scott. He had procured a three-panel dry-erase board from the procurement warehouse, which he promised someday to return, and balanced it on top of two easels. "This is the case as we know it thus far," Scott said. On the left panel he wrote "Inmate Birdsong" at the top. On the right panel, he wrote "Inmate Finch" at the top. The center panel he labeled "Inmate Higgins."

"How do we know they are all connected?" asked Adrian.

"We don't," Scott replied, adding, "However, they all occurred on the B Yard, they happened within a reasonable amount of time of one another, and they all involved white inmates."

"Except Inmate Higgins was a Crip," piped Adrian.

"Exactly!" Scott exclaimed, much to Adrian's consternation.

"So," he continued, "what do we know about Inmate Birdsong's case?"

"Not much," replied Tyrus. "Evidence-wise, you are correct, but we do have some circumstantial evidence. We know that he was the first to be attacked. We know that he had some influence with the skinheads and asked Inmate Finch for his permission to allow the skinheads to attack Inmate Higgins. He may have had a substantial drug debt to the blacks, which is not good. And we believe that he was with Inmate

McGregor at the time of the incident," Scott stated as he wrote each item on the board.

"And the assault took place over in the whites' area," contributed Oswaldo.

"Precisely, Oz, well done," he encouraged.

"What does that have to do with it?" asked Adrian.

"It means that it was likely a white assault. No other race would be bold enough to attack a white in the whites' area. That would be an automatic invitation to a riot," observed Tyrus.

"Thank you, Gang Investigative Sergeant Phillips." Scott applauded. "Last but not least, it was an ice-pick-type weapon delivered at neck level," Scott added. "Now for Inmate Finch, we know that he was the white shot caller on the yard. He refused Big Bird's request to allow the skinheads to assault Inmate Higgins. He was attacked in the white area by a white inmate."

Scott was immediately interrupted by Adrian. "Again, how do we know?"

"Because if it wasn't a white, the other whites in the area would not have let the attacker get away," noted Tyrus.

"Continuing," Scott said, "he was stabbed with an ice-pick-type weapon in the neck. They also may have been mad at him for spending a lot of time in the captain's office. Oz, what am I forgetting?"

"Uh, Inmate Tanner?"

"No, not Tanner, although he is a witness. I know there is something that I am forgetting. Well, it will come to me. On to Inmate Higgins, white inmate who is also a Crip and living with a black, beaten to death presumably with a metal table leg, or at least that is what I expect they'll tell us at the autopsy tomorrow. He was challenged by two white inmates behind the culinary back dock, which upset him greatly. Coincidentally, he was killed in the scullery of the same culinary. Interestingly, we have two white inmates who work in the scullery—Inmate McGregor, the same Inmate McGregor, and Inmate Lacey, whom we know very little about at this point."

"Speaking of which," interrupted Tyrus, "I showed the photographs of McGregor and Lacey to Vargas, and he said he couldn't be sure of

Lacey, but it was definitely McGregor who was standing on the back dock that morning."

"We do have a partial palm print that I will be sending off to the automated fingerprint identification system people. Of course, at this point in the investigation, it is only circumstantial evidence. Oz, can you pull the central files for both inmates McGregor and Lacey? And, Ty, any information you might have on these two in the gang database would be helpful."

"Hey, Scotty, there is one thing though," offered Oswaldo. "I don't remember either of these guys out on the yard when Tennessee was stabbed."

"You are correct, Oz, but there still might be a connection, and I'm thinking it might have something to do with Inmate Mayer. What say we pay his cell a little visit?"

"I don't mind," replied the sniper-slash-K-9 handler.

"But first, Oz, go get those C files." Shortly after their meeting convened, Oswaldo returned from the records department with two large gray central files.

Jimmy Lacey was a twenty-four-year-old second-termer from Atascadero in San Luis Obispo County with a long and varied criminal record. It appeared that he had a thing for high-speed vehicle chases with the local authorities and had served jail and prison terms for his adventures. He also had a conviction for assault with a deadly weapon not a firearm for which he managed a suspended sentence and three years on probation. Two years later, he was again arrested for the same offense and sentenced to five years in state prison. He had about a dozen arrests for possession of marijuana and ecstasy. Each charge was either reduced to a misdemeanor or dismissed outright. Their informants stated he had progressed from marijuana to methamphetamines, which he was reportedly receiving from Santa.

Inmate Sean McGregor had a rather unique criminal history going back fifteen years. His arrest history began as an eighteen-year old in San Bernardino County with arrests and convictions for possession of marijuana for sale and receiving stolen property for which he received

120 days in jail and three years formal probation. He progressed to various possessions of methamphetamine and heroin charges, driving without a license, and a DUI arrest and conviction. On his thirty-fourth birthday, he was arrested on five counts of annoying or molesting a minor under the age of fourteen for which he was given a five-year sentence in state prison. Obviously, that was a conviction that would not bode well with the other skinheads if disclosed. He was due to be released in three months. Scott often found the so-called chesters were usually the ones who stirred up the most trouble as a means of deflecting attention from themselves.

Inmate Mayer was not happy to see the Goons arrive at his cell door with Ruud. He was not happy when they put him in handcuffs and had him escorted to the holding cells. He was especially not happy when they found his cache of methamphetamines in his mattress and the two ice-pick-type weapons he had concealed in a Doritos bag, on which he did a good job. For all intents and purposes, it appeared to be factory sealed. However, when they found the tube of silicon sealant that had been smuggled out of the plumbing shop, they took a closer look at all the unopened canteen items. Ty was happy to find a plethora of neo-Nazi and skinhead propaganda. Who knew Santa was a neo-Nazi? Santa wasn't on his way to the North Pole; instead, he was on his way to the Hole.

As Scott was collecting their equipment from in front of Santa's cell, he discovered a small piece of paper that had fallen from the tier above and landed near his feet. He opened the paper and read it cautiously. "I needs to talk to you but not here." Scott casually walked across the tier and stood with his back against the wall opposing Mayer's cell. He carefully looked up and noticed Inmate Forman, the culinary leadman, standing by his cell on the second tier. He nodded and disappeared back into his cell as the tier officer closed and locked his door. Scott walked over to where Tyrus was standing and showed him the note. They agreed to meet with Inmate Forman on the following Monday under the pretext that he was to see his counselor about his appeal.

Chapter 12

The Autopsy

"Okay, Adrian, let me lay the ground rules down to you seeing as how this is your first autopsy. If you feel at all queasy, sit down immediately. If you faint or throw up, be advised that I will take your photograph. I will enlarge it, and I will post it everywhere in the institution and email it to your family and friends. Do you understand?"

He acknowledged Scott's instructions while protesting its severity and guaranteeing that he was as solid as a rock. "We shall see," Scott noted, adding, "The roughest part for me is still the snapping sound the rib cage makes as it is being cut with a pair of gardener's loppers. I will admit I generally sit in the corner until they are done with that part. I don't know if it's the sound that bothers me or the fact they are using gardener's loppers. Other than that, it's all about the photographs. Keep in mind things tend to fly when they use the bone saw, so don't get too close. Most important is to stay out of their way."

Alicia, the coroner's technician, wheeled in the steel gurney with the body-shaped white bag. She unzipped the bag and worked it out from underneath the deceased inmate Higgins. "I'm going to say 165 pounds," Scott guessed as he studied the deceased. "What about you, Adrian?"

"What about what?"

"Guess the weight. Loser buys lunch."

"That's disgusting. I cannot believe you are wagering on the weight of a dead guy," he responded sanctimoniously.

"No money involved, lunch only. As a peace officer, you must be good at judging a man's height and weight."

Adrian looked for a moment and entered his guess. "All right, I will say 174 pounds."

Dr. Fredrick Hansen, Scott's favorite forensic pathologist, merely shook his head. Alicia wheeled the gurney out into the next room. After a few minutes, she wheeled it back in, saying, "Who had 162?" Scott raised his hand.

"I suck at this," Adrian murmured. Dr. Hansen again shook his head.

Scott handed Adrian the lead card bearing Inmate Higgins's information and instructed him to hold it underneath the decedent's chin while Scott snapped his first frame. Dan followed suit before rolling out a ladder that resembled the kind you wheeled up to an old airplane when you boarded from the tarmac. He climbed up first and took an overall photograph of the body. After he dismounted, Scott scaled the rickety treads, careful not to lean too far forward as he had been on this ride before, and it was front heavy.

Alicia shaved the deceased's head with noticeably short ginger-blond hair. While she performed this task, Adrian pointed out all the tattoos on the various parts of the kid's body. "Whittier" was tattooed on his chest, "Crip" on his left breast, and "thug life" on his right bicep, and there was the previously photographed tattoo on his left arm. Scott wasn't accustomed to seeing these specific tattoos on a white background. Regardless, Scott photo-documented the blue-ink images.

Doc Hansen made note of the external description of the body. He documented the degree and distribution of rigor and livor mortis, hair and eye color, skin, scars, congenital malformations, and the appearance of the eyes and recorded the periorbital ecchymosis. He worked silently, methodically, and meticulously. Once he was finished with this, Alicia drew a vitreous solution from the left eyeball.

Doc then examined the teeth carefully, looking for any evidence that the young man sank them solidly into the limb of one or both of his attackers. His search was inconclusive. He therefore returned to his inspection, looking for the presence of vomitus in the nostrils and mouth. After checking for evidence of surgical scars or medical treatments and external diseases, he recorded in detail the external injuries to the scalp and skull and the defensive injuries on his arms and back. He recorded the bite mark that was still clearly visible on the upper right trapezius area.

Dan and Scott danced around the body, adeptly handling their cameras in a symbiotic relationship, and Dr. Hansen as he pointed out the various areas of importance. "Interesting," he said as if to himself. "Something under the fingernails of the middle and ring fingers on the right hand. We better get some clippings." He clipped, scraped, and swabbed the area. He pushed the clippings and scrapings into a small evidence envelope, sealed it, and set it aside. Alicia placed a sticker bearing the pertinent information of the deceased on the outside of the envelope.

Satisfied with this, Dr. Hansen made the standard Y incision. He then stepped aside and selected his cutlery while Scott went in the corner and sat down. After the rib cage was removed, Scott returned to his position, hovering near the pathologist, who removed the internal organs, weighing each one and recording the data. Upon finishing, Dr. Hansen said but one word. "Unremarkable."

While he did this, Alicia was busy sawing off the top of the decedent's skull with the bone saw. Adrian stood uncomfortably close during this process, close to Scott, that is to say. Dr. Hansen removed the brain and carried it to the cutting board. He sliced it with a series of "interesting" and "as suspected" comments. While Doc Hansen hosed down his cutting surface, Alicia returned the plastic bag containing the dissected internal organs into the open chest cavity and began sewing up the opening using a very wide needle and sinewy thread.

Dr. Hansen turned to Scott and explained his preliminary findings. "He died from severe head trauma. There are multiple fractures of the skull in the frontal bone as well as subdural and subarachnoid hemorrhaging. He took one very severe blow to the lower left occipital, which lacerated a basilar artery. Death would have been within minutes. The metal table leg that you brought is consistent with the injuries. You'll want to submit the nail scrapings to the department of justice for analysis."

Dan walked up to Adrian and congratulated him on managing to get through his first autopsy without incident. He added, of course, the story about the young female "guard" who passed out during an autopsy and hit the floor so hard that they had to call an ambulance. The incident occurred long before Dan ever joined the sheriff's department, but it still made the rounds as if it happened yesterday. He then walked over to Scott and quietly said, "I see you have a Klingon."

"Yeah, I get it, a cling-on. He was a bit clingy there for a minute. Let's see how he does with the fingerprints."

Alicia wrapped a towel around the left wrist of Inmate Higgins and pulled his body across the gurney onto a second one that had the body bag laid flat. Once he was back in his cocoon, she pushed the gurney over toward where Adrian and Scott were standing. Scott had finished preparing the fingerprint cards and had loaded a strip into the postmortem spoon. Scott grabbed a stack of paper towels and wiped the fingers and hands of the decedent. There was little rigor present in the arms, and the hands moved without much difficulty. Scott inked up the fingers with a Porelon pad and obtained a good set of fingerprint impressions. He then instructed Adrian on the process and let him roll a few sets himself. His first set was fair but didn't include a sufficient portion of the medial phalange for Scott's liking. His second set was spot on. "Good job, Adrian," Scott commented.

"His hands are cold" was all he said in return.

Chapter 13

Inmate Forman Grilled

Inmate Forman stood on the North Facility central services patio and pressed his face close to the window that separated the counselor's office from the patio. Scott put a suit jacket on over his jumpsuit and removed his hat to give the appearance that Forman was talking to his counselor through the small window. Scott handed him papers that appeared to be official on a clipboard through a slot underneath the window, and he pretended to sign the documents and handed them back. "So what did you want to tell me?" Scott asked.

"Look," he said apprehensively, "I don't like to tell on anyone, but what they did was dead wrong."

"What who did specifically?" Scott asked.

"Them two whites in the back of the kitchen. Look, look, I know Miss Watkins didn't say nothing, but I saw them washing down the scullery and pouring out bleach and mopping the area, but they wasn't just mopping the floors and shit. They was mopping the walls and all that shit. I saw them, but I didn't know they put that poor white boy in the dishwasher. I didn't know that. And when they left, they was all wet. They was all wet from head to toe. They clothes was wet. They boots was wet. They faces was wet. Everything was wet, and they smelled like bleach. Miss Watkins watched them do it from her office. She told them later that she liked the way they cleaned."

"Don't you usually get wet in the scullery?" Scott asked.

"Not like that. You always wear the apron, the rubber apron, and rubber boots and rubber gloves, and you wear a hat."

"Can you identify the two white inmates?" Scott inquired.

"One they call Highlander. The other is Jimmy."

"These two?" Scott asked as he showed him the photographs of Inmate McGregor and Inmate Lacey.

"Them two," he replied. "Look, I can't see my name on any paper over this. You can't tell anyone I told you."

"No, I appreciate your letting me know, and I won't use your name. Let me ask you something, did Officer Watkins ask why they were wetter than usual?"

"She asked them why they was so wet when she let them out. They said they got into a water fight with the hoses. She just laughed."

"So, Forman, why are you telling me this?" Scott inquired.

"I just don't think I could look at that dishwasher ever again knowing that poor boy was in there dead. I'm going to see if I can get a job change."

"We'll talk to your counselor about getting an assignment change since we are here."

Tyrus and Scott watched Inmate Forman leave the patio area and return to the B Yard. They waited about thirty minutes, had a chat with his counselor, and then entered the North Facility and walked down the A Yard to the dining hall. They met Officer Watkins at the sergeant's office. This time, Tyrus asked the questions. "Is there any reason why you didn't tell us about Inmate Lacey and Inmate McGregor?"

"About what?" she asked, feigning ignorance.

"Did you not think that it would be important to our investigation that both inmates were soaked to the bone and smelled like bleach?"

"Who told you that?" she answered with yet another question.

"They were observed by staff after you let them out of the dining hall," Scott quickly interjected so as not to reveal their source.

"So what?" she replied. "Maybe I just forgot."

"Well, maybe you should just remember and put it in a report," suggested the sergeant.

"I don't see what good it would do," she said stubbornly.

"How about you consider my suggestion a direct order? And if you do not want it to turn into an insubordination charge, you comply." Reluctantly, she reached into her desk drawer, pulled out a blank incident report form, and started writing. Tyrus was clearly annoyed with the young officer, and Scott noticed his back teeth clenching, which was a sure sign that he was angry.

They exited the culinary on the B Yard and began walking back to the central services patio, where they could exit through the control room sally port and leave the facility. As they passed the edge of the yard, Scott stopped and looked over the area where Inmate Finch was stabbed. Scott nudged Ty's arm and motioned him to follow him over to the former crime scene. They reconstructed the series of events as they believed they occurred, and Scott stood back in deep thought. "What are you thinking, Dog?"

"I'm thinking I'm getting old and tired, and there is something I am missing or forgetting."

"Details-wise or evidence-wise?"

"Empirical, Tyrus, empirical—something I saw that night, I just don't know. I can't remember right now. Come on, Ty, let's get back to the car."

As they continued their walk toward the patio, Scott observed an inmate standing under a chin-up bar in the exercise area. He reached up and grabbed the bar that was over his head and began to lift himself off the ground. Scott stopped and watched him for a minute and then turned to Tyrus and said, "The frickin' glove, Ty, like the one that inmate is wearing right now. I forgot about the frickin' glove I recovered from the picnic table. We need to get it to the lab."

Chapter 14

The Forensic Odontologist

"Dr. Foster," Scott said into the telephone receiver, "it's Scott Doggett out here at the prison. I've got something you might be interested in."

"Scott? Scott, I haven't seen you in the office in a number of years. You know you are way overdue for a checkup and a cleaning."

"Doc, I'm way overdue for a lot more than just a checkup, but you know we have the worst dental insurance in the state, and I'm still paying for my last divorce."

"Ouch, how much do you have left?"

"To pay or left in my savings? If I know you, Doc, you want what's left in my savings, and there ain't much. As far as how much I still need to pay, thirty Gs, and I get one of my testicles back. I promise, Doc, I'll come in before the summer is out."

"Well, if you want to keep your original teeth, Scott, you'll come and see me. What do you have for me?"

"Well, we had a homicide victim who looked mighty tasty to one of our suspects."

"A bite mark, splendid. You haven't brought me one of those in four or five years."

"Yeah, I remember, the Cartwell rape case. Your testimony was flawless. He got twenty-five to life for that."

"It is always my pleasure. May I ask how you preserved this nice piece of dentition evidence?"

"Photography with and without an ABFO scale, parallel and perpendicular, and I made a casting," Scott replied.

"Great, that's fantastic. Bring everything by, and we can talk about it during your examination."

"You're a hard man, Doc. How about Thursday morning?"

"I think I can fit you in at nine o'clock, or is that too early?"

"No, Doc, that'll be perfect. I'll see about getting a loan."

Dave Foster was not just the only forensic odontologist in the county; he was probably the best forensic odontologist in California. Of course, if you asked him, he would say he was the best in the country. Scott hated going to the dentist. The pain he can take; the cost he could not. However, he couldn't alienate the only bite mark specialist in the county. *The sacrifices he made for his job*, he thought.

Thursday came entirely too soon. "Rinse and spit. Three cavities, and we definitely need to talk about this root canal I have been telling you about for how long now?"

"Oh, Doc, about ten years now," Scott replied cautiously.

"Well, you're the one who will end up with dentures before you are fifty."

"Doc, I think you and my ex-wife have the same time-share in the Bahamas. But enough talk about my mouth. What about the mouth of our suspect?" Scott asked, changing the subject.

David M. Foster, DDS, leaned over his open mouth and concentrated on filling two of the cavities. "Well, I like the photographs, and I can certainly make a nice mold from your casting. Do you have any suspects I can match them to?"

"Aw, haw, we hafth woo," Scott managed.

"Interesting. Can you get me samples of their bites?"

"We can twy. I uill hafth ew geth a wawant."

"Great, just let me know when you have something for me to compare, and I will make my analysis. In the meantime, I will make a mold and get started. Rinse and spit."

"Thanks Doc, we owe you one for this."

"Root canals are my only reward. Make another appointment for two weeks on your way out. Oh, and you need to update your insurance information."

"How's your mouth?" asked Oswaldo as he handed Scott an ice-cold Mountain Dew, which he had purposely chilled in the freezer.

"You are a bastard, Oz, an absolute bastard. I'll just have this slightly warm water for now, but thanks."

"What did he say about the photographs?" asked Oswaldo as he put the soda back in the refrigerator.

"He seemed to like them, but we have to get warrants for exemplars of our suspects' teeth."

"How are we going to get them to give us that?" inquired Adrian.

"Well, that's the tricky part. You can serve them with a warrant, but that doesn't mean they are going to comply. Even if they do comply, they could grind the mold with their teeth or purposely try to alter their teeth by banging their mouths on a countertop or something dumb like that. No, we definitely need to get the warrant, but we need to be tricky about how we are going to get the impressions," Scott replied.

"Any ideas?" Adrian asked.

"Yup," Scott replied. "I'm thinking we need to get a warrant for any dental records we have here at the prison and hope they are recent enough to be useful. If not, well, I don't know what we're going to do just yet, but I will think of something. I can tell you one thing, Adrian."

"What's that?"

"The one who didn't bite him will give up his jaw impressions without any problem."

"What about the glove?" asked Oswaldo.

"It went to the department of justice as did the fingernail clippings of the late Inmate Higgins, but we really don't have any suspects right now other than inmates Keller, Tanner, Morgan, and Volks. We have buccal swabs from Keller, Morgan, and Tanner. Morgan is a peckerwood, and I can't see him being the stabber, not to mention he gave up a buccal swab when I asked for it.

"Volks, on the other hand, is a man of mystery. He's a German national who came over on a holiday and decided to rob a bank and two gas stations. He's one of the young neo-Nazis on the yard and stirs up a lot of shit according to the gang guys. He was also one of Santa's old cellies. We seem to think once these youngsters reach a certain age, Santa kicks them out in favor of even younger skinheads. As they say, Santa likes them young."

"So do you think he's our suspect?" asked Adrian.

"Not sure. He gave up a DNA sample when I asked for it. Either he's not guilty or he's bluffing. There's only one way to find out. It's in the hands of the DOJ now. They have the two weapons from Santa's cell too. Hopefully, there will be some traces of blood on one or both of them."

"What about the palm print we got from the kitchen?" inquired Oswaldo.

"Tadeo Nakamuro has it right now. Hopefully, I will hear from him soon. At least now I think we are sure about the motive. They wanted to purge the flock of undesirable white blood, and they had to go through Birdsong and Tennessee to do it."

"Hey, does anybody know anything about a Myron or Brian Wright?" queried Lieutenant Templeton as he stood in the doorway of Scott's overcrowded office.

"Nope, doesn't sound familiar," Scott said. Oswaldo shrugged as usual.

"Is he one of our informants?" asked Adrian.

"No, I don't think he's here, and I really don't know anything about it," admitted the lieutenant. "All I know is I got an email from the district attorney's office, and they got a letter from this guy demanding to know why he was arrested and if there were any charges he wanted them dismissed immediately. There's something about Florida too. I guess I'll email back and tell them we don't know anything about it."

"Uh, Lieutenant, did you say Florida?" Scott asked.

"Yeah, hang on, I have a copy of the letter he sent. It says they took him from Florida across the country in a van, and he's in San Quentin on a parole violation. He's demanding to know why he is being charged with a crime in our county when he has never been in the Monterey area."

"Byron Sinclair White by any chance?" Scott inquired.

"Yeah, that's his name."

"Lieutenant, let's go into your office, and I will give you all the details. Then I need to place a telephone call to the Stuart Police Department and thank them."

Chapter 15

Floyd's Victory

"Are you sitting down, Floyd? I have some good news for you and Barbara. I just got off the phone with the chief of the Stuart Police Department in Florida. Those wonderful folks there set up surveillance on the house of Byron White's mother for the past three months. I guess one of their officers lives just a few houses down from her and across the street, so it was the perfect place to do their surveillance. Wouldn't you know it, old Byron finally came home to see his mommy, and he got swooped on by a half-dozen cops. He even had an ounce of weed in his pocket when they patted him down."

"Oh, Scott, that is fantastic news. Barbara will be so happy. Maybe she won't be so mad at me now."

"It gets better, Floyd. They waived prosecution on their marijuana charge so we could extradite him back here as quickly as possible, and they put him in a transport van and drove him clear across the country. It took them a week to get him back here because of all the stops they made on the way, but he's here now in San Quentin for the parole violation, and he is pissed. He wrote a nasty letter to the district attorney demanding to know why he was being charged with a crime and demanding that all the charges against him be dropped. He says he has never been in our county ever. Of course, this is his original county of commitment, but I guess he doesn't think that counts. I just talked to Joe Buckwalters, and they are going to send an order to produce to San Quentin for his arrangement next Tuesday. Joe wants to meet you, Floyd. He's anxious to get this guy prosecuted."

"He wants to meet me? Oh, I suppose that's all right. Does he want me to go to his office?"

"Don't worry, Floyd, I'll pick you up tomorrow morning, and we'll both drive over there together."

"Will I have to testify in court?" he asked.

"I'm sure you will. Is that all right?"

"Oh, yes, Scott, I'll testify. I'm not sure about Barb though."

"Well, I don't know if he will need her. But knowing Barbara as I do, I don't think there's not much chance you'll have of keeping her from testifying against Byron. In fact, you might not be able to keep her from jumping over the defense counsel's table and punching him. I'll stop by and pick you up about 0800 hours, Admiral."

"Why don't you come over for breakfast at seven? Barb makes a wonderful breakfast strudel."

"How is it the two of you are so thin?" Scott asked his neighbors as he pushed aside his breakfast dish. "Bacon and eggs and a wonderful strudel, are you sure you can't adopt me?"

"I think we have," replied Barbara.

"Well, you know, as the lead investigator in this investigation, I'm not sure I can continue to accept these gratuities."

"Oh, we hadn't thought of that. Are you going to arrest us?" lamented Floyd.

"I won't tell if you don't. All right, Floyd, the day of reckoning is neigh. Let's go see the prosecutor."

With that, Floyd got up and kissed Barbara on the cheek. He put on his sport jacket and donned his gentleman's driving cap. He was expecting to find Scott's green British racing Jag waiting to drive him the seventeen miles to the district attorney's office. Instead, he had brought home his faithful old Crown Vic from work the night before. "Oh my, you are going to arrest me!" exclaimed the Admiral.

"Not this time, Floyd. You can sit up front with me, but if you want, we can shove Barbara in the back in the cage."

"No, she's a good girl, but I'll keep it in mind." With that, they climbed in and sped off to their predetermined destination.

"So this is the intrepid rear admiral Floyd DeWitt. Sir, it is a pleasure to meet you. Gunner's Mate Second Class Joe Buckwalters. I hear you were at Pearl," he said as he stood up from behind his desk and extended his hand.

"Oh yes, sir, I commanded a little tin can that managed to swat a fly," replied the proud navy man.

"Someday I'd like to sit down and talk to you about your career, sir. But right now, we need to talk about Mr. Byron White. Tell me what happened," said the prosecutor as he sat back down in his chair. Floyd retold the story with incredible care, not missing a single detail.

Joe looked over at Scott and said, "Dog, your report sure is thorough. Everything is in there. Mr. DeWitt, do you think you can repeat that story in front of a jury?"

"Well, I've never been in front of a deputy judge advocate general of the navy, but I sure have been one a time or two. I think I can manage. I've also been on my share of juries. Will you need my wife to testify too?"

"No, I don't think so, unless the defense subpoenas her for some reason," he speculated.

"Do you think he will go to prison?" asked Floyd.

"That's where he belongs, Admiral. This is a career criminal, and he preys on the innocent," replied the grizzled prosecutor.

"What's your offer, Joe?" Scott asked.

"My offer is twelve at 50 percent. Unfortunately, he only has one strike, but it was in 1999. If he comes at me sideways, I'll go for career criminal and see if I can get that time doubled. It's a hell of a case, and I think we can get a jury to agree with us."

As Scott drove Floyd home, Floyd talked at length about humanity and charity. He said if Byron White had just asked him for enough money to get back to Florida, they would have given it to him, bought him a ticket on the train or something. Scott thought about his father and how he was murdered by two people who only wanted twenty dollars to buy crack. He would have given them the money had they asked, but it was just easier to kill an eighty-year-old man in his sleep. Scott wasn't there to save his father, but he wasn't about to let his guard down with his elderly neighbors.

"Floyd, if anyone ever tries to get money from you ever again, you call me right away. If anyone breaks into your house, you waste no time calling me or getting across the street. Put me on speed dial, and when I answer you, just yell '911,' and I will come running. I will get there before the cops can get there, and I will bring more firepower to bear than a battleship. I promise you that."

Scott thought he took the poor old guy by surprise because, for the rest of the trip home, he sat silently listening to the classical music playing over the radio mixed with the squawk of the county communications radio traffic. Scott couldn't help himself. His frustration over being absent when his father was murdered pushed him to react in that way. He cared about Floyd and Barbara, and he was serious. He closed his eyes for a moment and wanted to cry.

In fifteen minutes, they were home. As he got out of the car, Floyd gave Scott a salute and said, "We'll be expecting you for dinner tomorrow night. Barb is doing a pot roast and a strawberry pie. Do you think it would be appropriate for us to write a letter of thanks to that police department in Florida?"

"I've already taken care of that, Admiral, but if you want, I think it would be very appropriate and a nice gesture. I'll get the address to you this afternoon. Give my best to Barbara and tell her strawberry pie is my favorite."

As Scott nosed the car back toward the freeway, he said to himself, "It is no wonder I had three cavities."

Chapter 16

Old Dogs, New Tricks

"So I'm afraid the print didn't match your Inmate Lacey, but we don't seem to have a palm print on file for your Inmate McGregor. Do you want me to run it through our database anyway, or do you want me to wait until you get an exemplar from your suspect?" asked Tadeo on the telephone.

"Well, T., I think you're going to have to run it through your database anyway, but I'll get an inked print sent off to you today," Scott replied.

"Can't you Live Scan?" he asked. "Can you send me $80,000 to buy the system?" Scott returned.

"Inked will be fine," he responded.

Scott hung up the phone and looked over at Oswaldo, who was sitting at his desk with a vapid expression like he had just turned his brain completely off. "Looks like we need to get palm prints from McGregor. I'm sure he's a PC 296 candidate because of his sex offense," Scott remarked.

"Let's go get him," replied Oswaldo in knee-jerk fashion.

"Not so fast there, Speedy. I don't feel like wrestling with this guy today. I'm thinking of a little deception. Let me call over to the PC 296 desk and see if they've already collected samples. If not, this is as good a time as any to get it done, and he won't even know it was us."

After a few minutes on the telephone to the records department, Scott again turned to Oswaldo and said, "As I suspected, he is required to register as a sex offender and provide DNA, fingerprints, and palm prints. Records hasn't sent the packet over to the DNA collection folks yet. So I'm going to go pick it up. Have you got an old class B uniform in your locker?"

"Sure do, and it still fits, unlike yours."

"Ouch but true. Do you think you can pose as a DNA collection officer?"

"I don't see why not. I'll go change."

"I'll go get the DNA packet. Do me a favor and roll two sets of palm prints and get two buccal swabs. We'll send one set of prints to AFIS, send one of the buccal swabs to the DOJ, and send the others with the packet. Take Adrian with you," Scott instructed.

"I don't have a class B here," stated Adrian.

"Just put your class B jacket over your jumpsuit and zip it up, take off your hat, and unblouse your boots. He'll never know," Scott advised. Oswaldo went into the locker room and changed into the standard khaki and green uniform of a correctional officer, collected a fingerprinting and palm-printing kit, took the DNA packet from Scott, and drove over to the North Facility with Adrian.

"What's this about?" asked Inmate McGregor as he walked into the small room on the North Facility central services patio.

"DNA and palm prints," replied Oswaldo, adding, "It's for your PC 296 registration."

"I already did this at the reception center."

"You may have, but I don't know that because I wasn't there, and they sent this packet to us, so here we are," responded Oswaldo in his rapid-fire talking mode. Inmate McGregor just stood there looking at him while trying to find a way to argue with the logic. He couldn't and therefore submitted to the collection of another DNA packet. Within thirty minutes, Oswaldo was back in their office.

"Take the DNA packet over to records, and I'll send the extra palm print card to Tadeo by government fast mail and ask Becky to drive

the second buccal swab over to the DOJ laboratory," Scott told him.
"Then get changed. We need to go over and talk to the dentist at the
North Facility."

"Dr. Henry, I am Investigator Doggett from the security and
investigations unit, and this is my partner, Investigator Oswaldo
Castaneda. What I want to talk to you about is of the utmost
confidentiality and cannot be repeated to anyone."

"Yes?" asked the bewildered dentist.

"Do we have any dental records on these two inmates?" Scott asked
as he passed the information sheet containing Inmate McGregor and
Inmate Lacey to the doctor.

"Let me check," he said as he rose from his chair and walked to
a series of standing filing cabinets while holding the piece of paper.
He walked back holding one large folder. "I have records on Inmate
McGregor. He was just in three weeks ago for an extraction, and I
repaired a broken canine. I don't have anything for the other gentleman.
Is that what you wanted to know?"

"Yes, Doc, thanks, that's all we needed to know," Scott replied,
reminding, "As I said, Doc, please do not tell anyone about our
conversation. You will be hearing back from me shortly."

They exited the North Facility and drove back to their office. "Well,
Oz, that's it. I'm going to need a search warrant for the dental records for
Inmate McGregor and a warrant for bite impressions for Inmate Lacey.
The bad thing about McGregor's records is that he has had an extraction
and some dental work since our homicide occurred. Hopefully, they did
a before and after set of X-rays."

"No, ma'am, as far as we can tell, your grandson is not being
extorted for money, nor is he paying tens of thousands of dollars on
attorney fees. In fact, there is no record of his attendance in the legal
law library or any record of him sending out any legal materials through
the mail room. Pure and simple, Mrs. Belhaven, your grandson has a
drug problem, a serious drug problem, and we recommend you stop
paying his dope debts before he drains you of every penny you have in
your savings.

"Well, ma'am, I'm sorry you feel that way. I've been doing this for more years than I care to think about, and I cannot tell you the countless number of times I have seen inmates suck their relatives completely dry of their life savings and income. They don't care. All they want is their drug debts resolved, and they don't care how they go about doing it. If you listen to the telephone conversations over here, you'd think we have the clumsiest officers in the world. Every day dozens of television sets that didn't belong to the inmate caller or that they were borrowing from another inmate have been accidentally broken by an officer during a cell search, and now he has to send money to some guy's girlfriend so that he can get a new one.

"No, ma'am, the TVs aren't getting broken. They have drug debts. I *am* trying to do something about the drug problem. We have almost 8,000 inmates and 1,600 employees. Every weekend, we have 2,000 or 3,000 visitors each day. There are packages, mail, drop-offs, and a scarce few of us to go through everything to try to stop the drugs from getting into the prison.

"Yes, ma'am, I am saying exactly that. Your grandson is a habitual drug user, and you should stop enabling his drug habit. If you stop paying his debts, he won't get his drugs . . . Well, as I said, I am sorry you feel that way . . . Yes, ma'am, you have a nice day . . . Holy crap, Oz, next time I get a phone call like that, you get to talk to the little old dears."

"Who was that you were talking to?" he asked.

"Mrs. Elizabeth Belhaven. Of all people to call me, it was Inmate Lacey's grandmother. Apparently, she has already spent $20,000 for his 'legal work,' and now she is beginning to think that he is being extorted. I was just calling her back to tell her what I found out."

"Is he?" asked Adrian.

"Nope, he has a nasty dope debt. He developed a strong appreciation for methamphetamines, thanks to Santa."

"Do you think she'll stop?" asked Oswaldo.

"Nope, that's her cherished little grandson, incapable of doing any wrong. However, speaking of Lacey, guess what we get to do today?"

"Search his cell?"

"More exciting than that, Oz," Scott said. "As soon as I get back from the courthouse, we get to figure out how we are going to get an impression of his teeth."

Later that afternoon, Scott, Adrian, and Oswaldo assembled in the North Facility dental office. Dr. Henry was apprehensive about their visit. He sent his lab technician off somewhere with the large folder containing the dental records of Inmate McGregor with instructions to make copies of everything in the folder to include all the X-rays. "Okay, Doc, here is the tricky part. We need to get a mold of the teeth of Inmate Lacey. I have a search warrant signed by a judge compelling him to comply. Hopefully, he will do so willingly. But failing that, we will be using force. Do you have any suggestions?" Scott asked.

"Not a clue," he replied. "Getting the mold is fine. I have the trays and material here, but he has to remain perfectly still until the medium sets."

"Prepare your trays, Doc, we're going to give it a try. Oz, you and Adrian go down to his cell and bring him back, in restraints if necessary."

Twenty minutes later, Oswaldo and Adrian returned with a handcuffed Inmate Lacey, who was instructed to sit in the dental chair. "What's this about?" he asked, somewhat vexed by the experience.

"Lacey, I have a search warrant signed by a judge of the superior court. It commands us to obtain a bite mark impression of your teeth. Will you comply with this order?"

"Fuck you and fuck that piece of paper!" he exclaimed.

Scott turned to Oswaldo and gave him instructions. "Strap him in, boys." Oswaldo produced a set of leather medical humane restraints that had been stashed in a medical cabinet for immediate access.

Scott turned on a video camera to document the service of the search warrant and began to narrate, "On this date, we are serving a search warrant signed by the Honorable Judge Velasquez of the superior court. Inmate Lacey has refused to comply with this warrant, and therefore, the provisions of the warrant will be satisfied by the use of physical and mechanical restraints and the least amount of force necessary to satisfy the warrant."

With that, Adrian approached the legs of Inmate Lacey with the leather straps while Oswaldo and Scott grabbed his forearms. "He's kicking! He's kicking!" screamed Adrian as he avoided having a tooth knocked out himself. Oswaldo had one leather strap attached to Lacey's left arm. There was nothing Scott could do to help Adrian until they got the second arm restrained. Inmate Lacey was trying to get out of the chair, and Oz was doing his best to pin him down while Scott pulled the strap around the back of the chair.

The thought that Scott had brought an insufficient number of staff to affect the successful service of this warrant had crossed his mind on more than one occasion but increased tenfold when he saw Adrian fall to the floor. Dr. Henry had backed up to the counter and watched in amazement, unsure if he should activate his personal alarm or just watch. Instead, he did nothing. Adrian recovered from his fall, grabbed both of Lacey's legs, and with every ounce of strength he had pushed both legs forward into Lacey's chest, somewhat pinning Oswaldo in the process. Oz caught on to the idea and helped Adrian manage the legs while Scott threaded the leather strap through a slot in the back of the dental chair and then around to Lacey's right arm. With his arms restrained, the three of them concentrated on gaining control over his legs.

Breathing heavily and gasping for air, Scott returned to his narration, "Inmate Lacey is now . . . restrained." He turned his attention back to Inmate Lacey. "Lacey, now that you are restrained, I hope that you will be sensible and cooperate with the rest of this warrant."

"Fuck you and fuck your warrant!"

"How nice," Scott replied. "Doc, I'm going to get my hand on his forehead while Oz pulls down on his jaw. Do you think you can get the trays in his mouth as we do that?"

"I can try."

Scott stood behind the dental chair, put both of his hands on Lacey's forehead, and pulled back. As Scott did this, Oswaldo pushed down on his chin. It worked for a second, but Lacey was able to slam his jaws shut, and try as Oswaldo could, he could not reopen them. "This guy's got more bite pressure than Ruud!" ejaculated Oswaldo as he retracted his fingers.

"Let me try," offered Adrian. They repeated the operation, and Dr. Henry shoved the top tray in the mouth of Inmate Lacey as Adrian's grip gave way, and the tray was pinned firmly between Lacey's jaws.

"It won't work," stated the doctor. "He's gnashing his teeth and moving the tray back and forth in his mouth. It's just not going to work." They waited a few minutes for the upper tray to harden enough to remove. Dr. Henry pulled out the tray and set it on the countertop as a failure.

"I've run out of ideas, Doc!" Scott exclaimed in defeat.

"What do you want to do with this tray?" he asked.

"I'm going to book it into evidence. I'm charging him with assault on a peace officer for kicking Investigator Kirby and for interfering with a peace officer in the performance of his duties, not to mention hindering a criminal investigation. Inmate Lacey, you are going to the Hole."

Chapter 17

Itaque Relinquit Inmate Volks

"Scott, how far away from the institution are you?"

"About ten minutes, Lieutenant. What's up?" Scott asked.

"Inmate Volks hung himself in his cell this morning."

"Where's the body?"

"He's in the central infirmary . . . I know, I know, don't start with me. Nobody was there to stop them," replied the flummoxed lieutenant.

"As soon as I get to the pen, I'll grab Adrian, and I'll be right there."

"Good. I have Oz standing by at the cell. I'll talk to you when you get here."

Scott hung up the phone and depressed the throttle. He met Adrian in the parking lot, and they walked into the institution together, stopping to pick up their crime scene equipment and radios. "Let's go down to the infirmary first and get some photographs of the victim," Scott said to Adrian as they entered the Central Facility corridor. When they found the deceased inmate Volks, he was in emergency room no. 3. He wasn't hard to spot, lying beneath a white sheet, but the sheet was partially levitating.

"What the!" exclaimed Adrian.

"I call this the Captain Morgan pose," Scott said as he pulled the sheet aside. Inmate Volks was lying on his back with his arms at his side. His right leg was raised stiffly as if in death he was standing on a keg of rum.

"How come that happened?" asked Adrian.

"Usually, it's because he got it caught on something, or he was suspended and partially supported by an object or stepped off something with one leg and left the other on the object he was standing on. It's usually something like that. He's pretty stiff. Lividity is set in the lower extremities. Rigor is fixed. He has the deep V notch in his neck with a wide ligature mark, consistent with a sheet and being suspended as opposed to manual strangulation. The ligature mark is predominant, meaning he had been suspended for quite a while. Notice how his tongue is sticking out of his mouth. See how black it is? That's caused by drying. Blood has pooled in the dependent areas of his legs and forearms. There's a lot of congestion in his face, and right here on his eye is petechiae conjunctivae and facial petechiae on the eyelids. The mechanism of death is likely going to be occlusion of the vessels supplying blood to the brain, thereby depriving it of oxygen."

"Dog, Dick Welsh is here from the coroner's office," announced Frank Lewis, the first-floor infirmary officer.

"Dick, nice to see you. Does Dan have the day off?"

"Dan is golfing today. He got some ticket to play Pebble, and he called in sick. Lucky me. I haven't been out here in a decade."

"Well, we like to keep things interesting for Dan, but I'm afraid this one is pretty much by the books. Adrian, can you go down and spell Oz for a bit. Tell him to come down here, and you post up on the cell until we get there." While they waited for Oswaldo to come up with the details of the discovery, Dick and Scott discussed the particulars of the decedent and took their forensic photographs.

"Here comes Oz now," Scott remarked. "What do we have in the cell?"

"Pretty basic. The ligature is his bedsheet. It's tied to the bars about eight feet off the ground. The first-tier officers found him suspended by the neck at about 0445 hours and immediately called the code and cut him down. They did CPR for about fifteen minutes before the doctor called it."

"Four forty-five? What time is it now?" asked Dick.

"Seven thirty," Scott noted. "Why'd they wait so long before they called us?"

"They didn't call me until 0615," responded Oswaldo.

"Shit, it was six thirty when I got the call," Scott stated.

"Was he celled by himself?" asked Dick.

"Good question. Was there a cellie, Oz?"

"Yes."

"Crap, who was his cellie?" Scott asked.

"Billy Morgan."

"Shit," Scott groaned. "Where is he now?"

"Ad seg holding cell," replied Oz.

Oswaldo looked at the body and exclaimed, "Hey, it's Captain Morgan!"

"Did he leave a note?" asked Dick.

"Two words, 'heil Hitler,'" replied Oswaldo.

"Where is the note now?" Scott inquired.

"On the upper bunk."

"Has anybody touched it without gloves?" Scott asked knowingly.

"Yes, they have," he replied, "everyone who went in the cell."

"Shall I shoot you now or later? Shoot me now. Shoot me now. I demand you, shoot me now," Scott murmured.

"Do we know his next of kin?" asked Dick as he made notes in his notebook.

"There's a mother, father, and sister, uh, in Hamburg, Germany. I'm willing to fly over there if you need someone to go," Scott replied enthusiastically.

On their way down to the cell, Scott briefed Dick on the particulars of the attempted homicide of Inmate Finch and how Inmate Volks and Inmate Morgan were suspects. Scott told him how Inmate Morgan was a peckerwood and likely was trying to assist Inmate Finch against, Scott suspected, a skinhead attacker, and Inmate Volks was a skinhead. Dick stopped in the ad seg captain's office and spoke to the officer who discovered the body. He told him basically the same thing that Oswaldo had already told him.

They then went down to inspect and photograph the cell. One of the first responders accompanied them. "Was it this warm last night?" asked Dick.

"Yeah, it doesn't cool off that much on this side because the sun sets on this side, and it heats up the wing, and it stays hot," replied the officer.

"The first-watch officer said he passed the cell twice doing the counts. At 0245 hours, he was still in bed. But at the 0400 hours count, he was standing with his back to the bars," informed Oswaldo.

"He was probably dead at that time but just looked like he was standing. With the ligature tied so far up on the bar, his right foot was probably on the footboard of the lower bunk, and his left foot was barely reaching the floor. If the officer didn't look up and see the noose, he probably would have thought he was standing," Scott explained.

"Well, that's a good story anyway," remarked Dick.

"Excuse me for a minute while you guys get the photographs over here," Scott said as he walked back to the captain's office, where he noticed the ad seg mailbag sitting on a chair. He dumped the contents of the bag onto the conference table and began sorting through the pile of outgoing mail. He found what he was looking for, a letter bearing the familiar legend "Mitt Luftpost" by airmail: Helga Volks, Kampstraße 7, 20253 Hamburg, Germany. "Saint Pauli Girl country," he said to himself. He opened the letter and examined it—German as Scott expected.

Scott walked back over to where Oswaldo and Dick were standing with their cameras in action. Scott held up the letter. "In the mail last night. It's in German," he said.

"We'll have to get it translated," replied Dick.

"No need, I may not be fluent, *aber mein Deutsch ist nicht so schlecht. Ich kann es lessen*," Scott responded.

"Dog spent a lot of time in Germany working on a winery," advised Oswaldo.

"It is to his sister and says he is sad, and Jesus hates him. It says that his father is a big disappointment to him, along with a few other choice words. Jesus apparently hates his father too. He calls his mother a whore. How nice. He says that he is surrounded here by people who say they are of the master race but are the farthest thing from it. 'Sie ermorden ihre Leiter ohne Ursache.' He also says, 'Ich muss mich selbst töten, rein zu sein.' Loosely translated, that means he has to kill himself to make himself pure or to make things correct. It's something like that. And thus exits Inmate Volks."

Inmate Morgan was crouched in the bottom of a very small metal cage, an ad seg holding cell about the size of an old-fashioned telephone booth. He was shivering. Scott unlocked the door, helped him up, and walked him into the captain's office. Scott took the handcuffs off the young man and poured him a cup of coffee. Dick and Oswaldo were sitting on one side of the conference table. Scott sat on the other side, with Billy Morgan sitting on the end.

"I was asleep, man, sound asleep. I woke up when they turned on the lights and hit the alarm. I was still rubbing my eyes when they opened the cell door and rushed in. One of the officers ran to get a knife, and I held up my cellie while the other officer tried to untie the knot. He couldn't do it, but the other officer came back with a tool and cut the sheet. They told me to get out of the cell while they tried to resuscitate him, but he was dead. Next thing I know, the nurse is asking me questions, and I find myself sitting in a cage."

"Billy, did your cellie try to kill Tennessee?" Scott asked.

"No, Mr. Doggett, it was him I knocked out of the way when I saw Rob getting pulled back, but then I heard the gunner yelling, and I didn't want him to think that I was trying to hit Mathias, so I hit the ground."

"Mathias?" asked Oswaldo.

"Inmate Volks," Scott replied. "They called him the Nazi, but his name was Mathias."

"Did your cellie seem strange of late?" asked Dick.

"He's been acting all weird for the last month. He kept talking about Germany and how he would be going home soon. Hell, I told him he still had nine years to do, but he kept saying he would be home before Christmas. He also said some foul things about his parents, especially his dad."

"We'll get you into a clean cell here in a minute, Billy. Just be patient," Scott said.

"Have you seen Tennessee?" he inquired.

"In fact, I have just recently," Scott replied.

"How is he?" he asked.

"He's doing good, healing. I'll tell him you send your regards."

"Well, Oz, I think we can eliminate Inmate Volks as a suspect in the Tennessee case."

"How so?" he asked.

"*Sie ermorden ihre Leiter ohne Ursache.* They murder their leaders without a reason. Plus, Morgan said he knocked him down as Tennessee was being dragged backward. What time is the autopsy, Dick?"

"I don't think there will be one. I'm satisfied that it was a suicide. Give us a call in the morning, and we'll let you know for sure."

Chapter 18

Puzzle Pieces

"Sorry, Dave, I tried to get a good bite mark impression from Inmate Lacey, but it was impossible. He was practically chewing on the mold tray. We don't even have any X-rays or anything, and I have not been able to find out who his dentist was out on the streets. I do, however, have all the dental records for Inmate McGregor with some really good X-rays. And when we brought McGregor in for the search warrant, he voluntarily gave up a full set of uppers and lowers. Dr. Henry made a casting of the mold. It's in this box. One thing, though, he's had an extraction and a broken tooth repaired since the homicide."

"All right, Scott, at least I can do a comparison of McGregor's dentitions, but my guess would be that Lacey was your biter. Why else wouldn't he give you his impressions?" speculated Dr. Foster.

"Yeah, Doc, I am inclined to agree with you there. How much time do you think it will take you?"

"Maybe a week at the most. I have to work on it after my practice hours. I've got a full week of patients, and I think you are one of them," he reminded.

"Yeah, Doc, Thursday afternoon, thanks for reminding me," Scott grumbled. "I should have it done by then so you won't have to make another trip, that is, until your root canal."

When Scott got back to the office, Oswaldo was waiting for him with the results from the DNA laboratory in Oakland, California. The blood on the outer shell of the glove was positively matched to Rob Finch. The DNA collected from the sweat inside the glove, however, did not match any of the suspect DNA that was submitted. The only thing they could tell them was that it was a male contributor. Gee, thanks. It was, after all, an all-male prison.

Interestingly, the DNA from the nail clippings taken from Inmate Higgins at autopsy matched the DNA from the interior of the glove. It was, however, not Inmate McGregor's profile. Inmate Keller was telling the truth. The blood specimen swabbed from his finger was, in fact, his own blood. The blood specimen swabs that they collected from the scullery returned positive results for Inmate Higgins's blood. No blood was detected on the weapons found in Inmate Mayer's cell, nor were there any fingerprints recovered from the weapons or tortilla chip bags.

"Well, it's a mixed blessing here, Oz. Our work is not done. We still have a mystery attacker who was present when Rob Finch was stabbed and when Dana Higgins was bludgeoned to death. Wait a minute, Oz, let's take another look at the photographs of the Finch crime scene. Do you still have the diagram that you drew?"

"Yeah, yeah, yeah, yeah, yeah," he replied in staccato. Scott retrieved the 8" × 10" glossy photos of the crime scene from the file and scattered them on Adrian's desk. It was the only desk in the room that wasn't cluttered with files and paperwork, and he was out of the office at the time.

"Man, these photographs sure are dark. We really need a better lighting system for nighttime crime scenes," Scott bitched.

"Here's the diagram," said Oswaldo as he handed Scott his original document.

"Nice stick figures," Scott remarked.

"Hey, it was late," he justified.

"Okay, I see our first problem. Not everybody on the yard is on your diagram. Look at this overview photo. There are three white inmates not in the immediate crime scene. You don't have these guys on your diagram either."

"They weren't in the crime scene," he again justified.

"Yeah, that was my bad. Question is, who are these guys? The photo is too grainy for magnification, but it is a digital image. Let's take a look at it on the computer," Scott said as he booted up his laptop. After a few minutes, he found the file and the photograph. "Here it is, Oz, frame number 36. Let's click on this and then use the magnification bar to find our suspects."

"They look Mexican," replied Oswaldo.

"Perhaps two of them do, but the one in the middle is definitely white, and he's wearing a blue chambray shirt and gray sweatpants, which is what the gunner saw. Unfortunately, there is no way to tell who he is, but I have a fiendishly clever plan to find out. You want to go with me to do some interviews in ad seg?" Scott asked his eager partner.

"I wouldn't miss it," he replied.

"Let me just go make some copies of a few photographs, and we will be on our way." Scott walked over to the room containing the digital image evidence computer and printed three photographs.

They proceeded to the X Wing interview room and requested that Inmate Keller be brought down for an interview. Within a few minutes, he was brought down by a rather large escort officer and seated in the chair across from where Oswaldo and Scott sat. "Keller, what's your first name?" he asked.

"Tyler, but I go by Jeremy. It's my middle name," he replied.

"Yeah, I have a cousin named Tyler who goes by his middle name too," Scott said, adding, "Are you ready to get out of here, son?"

"You bet I am. I told you I didn't do it."

"And I believed you too, but we are tasked with investigating, and your blood had to be confirmed by the department of justice. I do have one question for you though," Scott said as he spun the overview photograph around toward him. "Who are these inmates right here?"

"Southerners, I think," he replied. "But I can't tell who they are."

"Your eyes are younger than mine, Jeremy. But if I am not mistaken, the one in the middle isn't a Southerner," Scott said as he handed him the enlargement of the area.

"No, that's Jimmy. You can tell by his ball cap. See how it folds up in the front and has that writing on it? You can't make out what it says, but it's a rebel flag."

"A rebel flag? I thought he was a skinhead?" Scott asked.

"Yeah, he is. There's a Nazi flag on the other side, and there is a pair of Doc Martens on each side of the rebel flag," he clarified.

"Yeah, but you can't tell that from this photograph, can you?" Scott asked.

"No, but I know that hat. I like to duck-bill my hats, but Jimmy folds his up like a goober."

"Who is Jimmy?" asked Oswaldo.

"Inmate Lacey, correct? We are talking about Inmate Lacey?" Scott inquired of Inmate Keller.

"Yeah, Jimmy Lacey," he replied. "Hey, I hear they killed that white Crip."

"What do you know about it, Jeremy?" Scott inquired.

"Nothing. I was in here remember?" he said with a smile.

"All right, I believe you. So I'm going to cut a release chrono and send you back to North today. Is there any reason why you can't go back to North?" Scott asked.

"Nope, send me back," he replied. "Oh, and . . ."

"What, Jeremy?" Scott asked.

"Oh, nothing, it's just that . . . oh, never mind."

"I didn't forget," Scott said as he slid the photograph across the table and added, "I managed to crop out the handcuffs."

"Cool, dude. It's for my mom for Christmas."

"He's going to put up a fight," stated Oswaldo as they walked back to the office.

"Who is?" Scott inquired.

"Lacey. If he puts up any kind of fight like he did with the tooth thing, we need to bring a lot more staff."

"You're right, Oz, I didn't bring enough staff that time, but I don't think we are going to have any trouble with Lacey."

"Why not? You think he'll just give you a DNA sample?" questioned Oswaldo.

"Because we already have his DNA," Scott replied.

"Oh, he's in the DNA database?"

"Well, probably, but that's cold case DNA only. We can't use it for current investigations. No, Oz, we have something already in evidence that is loaded with his DNA."

"Something from the crime scene?"

"We have something from a crime scene. We have the upper mold tray that was in his mouth, and he was chewing on it, I am sure sufficiently to deposit tons of DNA."

"Can we use that?" asked Oswaldo.

"I don't see why not. It was in his mouth, and we have four people who saw it in his mouth. We'll use it, and if they challenge it, then the court can order him to give up another DNA sample." Scott made arrangements with Elisa Foyle, the evidence control officer, to retrieve the upper mold tray from the evidence locker. He filled out the department of justice evidence submission form and sent her on her way to the lab. He picked up his phone and checked for messages.

There was a voice mail left by Tadeo Nakamuro; the palm print matched Inmate McGregor's left hand, and he was returning the evidence with his report. Oswaldo and Adrian seemed pleased to hear the news, but Scott reminded them that Inmate McGregor worked in the scullery, and it would not be unusual for his palm print to be found there; the evidence was circumstantial at best. Their exuberance was slightly abated. "You keep saying that, but how is it circumstantial?" asked Adrian.

"All right, let's say you ask me to pass you this piece of paper. After I hand it to you, you write a note telling the teller at a bank to hand you all the money. Later, Oz develops my prints on the paper. Does that mean I had anything to do with the crime?"

Adrian objected, "No, but this is different. His palm print was on the table leg."

"But it wasn't the leg that was used as the weapon. It was the leg that was still attached to the table. Granted, it was the leg directly in front of the missing leg, but it still wasn't the weapon."

Adrian looked confused. "Cheer up, fellas. We're on the right track," Scott encouraged.

Scott sat in the dental chair with incredible angst, and he wondered how many dental hygienists it would take to get the leather medical humane restraints on him if they were intent on performing a root canal. The one that cleaned his teeth the last time looked considerably brutish, he thought. "Hey, Doc!" Scott hollered as he saw Dave Foster walking past the room.

He stopped, backed up, and looked into the examination room. "Oh, hi, Scott, it won't be but a minute."

"Doc, do you think we should have anesthetized Lacey to get the impressions?" It was too late; he had ducked into his office. Scott pondered if maybe he should have made that a part of the warrant.

While Scott pondered, he fidgeted with the tools hanging near the chair. "Oh crap," he muttered as he fired a stream of water across the room from the hose attachment near the basin.

Just then, Dr. Foster walked through the door and skidded slightly on the back of his heel, "What the heck?" he exclaimed as he steadied himself on the countertop.

"Watch the water, Doc," Scott offered too late.

"What sort of mischief have you gotten into? I can't leave you alone for one minute," he harped as he wiped up the floor with a towel.

"Sorry, Doc, my mind was wandering, and you know what happens then."

"Apparently, you destroy my examination room."

"Hey, Doc, what do you think about putting Lacey asleep to get that impression?"

"It would be the best way, but didn't I tell you?" he interjected.

"Tell me what, Doc?"

"Your bite mark was a match to Mr. McGregor. I thought I left you a message."

"No shit, Doc? That's great news!"

"He has a very distinct central incisor."

"What about all the dental work he had done?" Scott inquired. "Well, there is a difference in the canine postrepair, but we can see in the early X-rays that it is the same tooth, and of course, the tooth that is missing can be accounted for as well. No, I'm certain that you have the right man there."

"I'm looking forward to reading your report, and I'm sure the district attorney will be interested in it as well," Scott implied.

"It'll be ready by the time we are finished here. Now what was it again today, root canal?" he mentioned as he leaned over Scott's mouth.

"Nice try, Doc. It's the last two cavities."

In the following morning, Adrian and Scott drove over to the North Facility and briefed unit 6 captain Larry Trenton of the evidence against Inmate McGregor. They asked that he be escorted to the captain's office so they could advise him that he was under arrest for the murder of Inmate Higgins. Captain Trenton dispatched two stout officers and a sergeant to fetch Inmate McGregor and bring him to his office. Scott watched as they walked him across the yard toward the unit 6 office complex.

Once inside the captain's office, Scott motioned McGregor to sit down on a wooden chair. Captain Trenton excused himself and exited the office. "What's this all about?" asked the Highlander.

"Inmate McGregor, I am Investigator Doggett, and this is Investigator Kirby. You are under arrest for the murder of Inmate Dana Higgins. You have the right to remain—"

Inmate McGregor suddenly stood up and grabbed the wooden chair, lifted it, and flung it in the direction of Adrian and Scott. "To hell I am!" he exclaimed, using another chair as a shield as if he was taming a lion.

Scott continued, "You have the right to remain silent. Anything you say and, at this point, do can be used against you in a court of law. You have the right to an attorney and to have an attorney present during questioning. If you cannot afford an attorney . . . ouch!" Scott took the chair directly to his left knee. "An attorney will be appointed to you—son of a bitch, that hurt—free of charge. Do you understand these rights as I have explained them to you?"

He thrust the chair upward toward Scott's face. "I'll take that as a yes," Scott said as he ducked to the side.

Adrian had drawn his Mark IX pepper spray canister and was pointing it at the irate inmate. "Don't you dare, Adrian!" Scott exclaimed while drawing out his Monadnock expandable baton and flicking it to the open position. "Captain will be pissed if you bomb his office with OC."

Inmate McGregor swung the chair like a baseball bat in an attempt to hit both Adrian and Scott. "Fuck it," Scott said. "Douse him!" With that, Adrian let loose with a full can of oleo capsicum resin spray. McGregor dropped the chair and put both of his hands to his face. Scott grabbed him and pushed him out the door into the open air and onto the B Yard track; Adrian followed closely. It took both of them to get McGregor in handcuffs. It's a funny phenomenon in the cops and robbers game; once the handcuffs go on, it's game over.

"So, Highlander, do you have anything to say?" Scott asked as he gasped for breath and wiped the tears from his eyes.

With nasal discharge streaming down his fire-engine-red face, Highlander managed a "Fuck you!"

Scott replied, "Fair enough. You can join your buddy Jimmy over in ad seg." They escorted Inmate McGregor over to the central services patio area, where he was decontaminated and seen by the medical staff for injuries before being placed in a holding cell for placement in ad seg. To say Larry Trenton was not happy with what they did to his office would be an understatement.

Scott turned the ignition of the faithful Crown Vic, and the old girl roared to life. "You smell like pepper spray," he said, looking over at Adrian.

"A chair? I mean, what the fuck, a chair?" he replied as he shook his head.

"Did you see the look on Captain Trenton's face when he found out you hosed the inside of his office?" Scott cajoled.

"Do you think he will ever stop hating me?"

"I've known Larry Trenton for years," Scott replied. "He was the worst sally port officer I ever had. No, he will never forgive you."

Chapter 19

The Proverbial Nail

"Well, that clinches it for Jimmy Lacey," Scott said as he read the DNA laboratory results. "The DNA recovered from under the fingernails of Inmate Higgins and the sweat from the interior of the glove were matches to the DNA they swabbed from the dental tray. It looks like the case is finally closed. Who wants to go with me to tell Lacey the good news?"

"I'll go. Maybe we'll have another chair fight," replied Adrian.

"He's in ad seg and will no doubt be in restraints. So no pepper spray," Scott reminded.

A half hour later, Scott advised Inmate Lacey of his rights pursuant to the *Miranda* decision. When he asked if he had anything to say, he replied, "Not to you. I'll do my talking to the DA." Scott informed him he was placing him under arrest for the murder of Inmate Higgins and the attempted murder of Inmate Finch. He shrugged.

"I noticed you have a recent scar on the back of your left hand," Scott mentioned. "Can you tell me just how you got that scar?"

"I don't remember. Maybe I got it playing football."

"I hope you don't mind if we photograph it," Scott said as he called Oswaldo on the radio to bring up a camera kit. Reluctantly, Lacey complied.

"I just have one question for you. If you knew you weren't the one who bit Higgins, why did you put up such a fight?" Scott inquired.

"Because I hate you fucking cops. I've always hated cops."

"You hate cops, but you love Hitler's SS and Gestapo. Where's the logic in that? At least we maintain order and keep anarchy in check, and we do it without the jackboot tactics of your heroes. What makes you so perfect? What makes you the master race? Nothing. You don't have an advanced education or intellect. You are drug addicted and dependent, just like your beloved Führer. You're not even the blue-eyed, blond-haired Aryan that Himmler and Goebbels claimed were the purest humans. You are a failure by your own standards. You embody all the same qualities you hate in other people. Oh, and in case this little gem hadn't crossed that little brain of yours, Jesus *was* a Jew!"

"Jesus was not a Jew! He hated Jews! Besides, the Holocaust never happened. It's all propaganda!" Lacey shouted.

"Tell that to my uncle who was at Dachau as a Belgian POW. He survived the war by cleaning out the ovens and disposing of the corpses. You and your ilk disgust me. You know what else disgusts me? I talked to your grandmother, and I know for a fact that your grandfather fought in the war *against* the Nazis. You shame him, and you shame his memory."

Inmate Lacey added nothing else to the conversation. Instead, he sat perfectly still while looking down at the floor. After a few minutes, he looked up and in Scott's general direction and asked, "Are you finished?"

"Yeah, I'm done. Let me get you an escort back to your cell."

After Lacey was removed from the office, Adrian asked, "I thought you were Italian."

"My mother was born in Ghent, Belgium. Two of her elder brothers went back to Belgium during the war as partisans. One of them was captured by the Germans."

"Was your uncle Jewish?" he inquired.

"No, he was Catholic."

"How did you know about his grandfather?"

"It was a guess, but I think I was right judging by his reaction. If there is one thing that I hate, it's hypocrisy. Before we leave, we need to go see Rudy about Lacey's property."

Hidden within a labyrinth of archive boxes was the ad seg property officer Rudy Galvan, feverishly trying to stay ahead of the inflow of inmate property. "Rudy! I know you are in here. I can hear you shuffling," Scott called into the maze of boxes.

"Is that you, Dog? I'm over here," replied Rudy.

"Crap, Rudy, have you found the ark of the covenant yet? I need your valuable assistance once again," Scott implored.

"What is it this time?"

"Property for Inmate Lacey, in particular a baseball cap with the brim folded back."

"Yeah, I saw it, but his stuff is in the connex. Do you need it now?" he asked.

"It is of the utmost importance, my friend."

Scott dusted off the knees of his jumpsuit, retaped the box containing Inmate Lacey's property, placed the aforementioned baseball cap into a plastic bag, and exited the dusty cargo container that doubled as a storage unit commonly referred to as a connex. "I believe one would call this the proverbial nail in the coffin, Adrian, because you can tell at a glance this is the hat worn by the person of question in the photograph. Let's get back to the office, assemble this case, and get it over to the district attorney's office."

Chapter 20

Compelling Evidence

The evidence against Inmate McGregor wasn't overwhelming in any way but compelling nonetheless to support a charge of murder. He was seen by Officer Vargas shouting something to Inmate Higgins that had an upsetting effect on the young man, a Caucasian youth who was a member of the Crip street disruptive group. He and Inmate Lacey worked in the scullery during the time in question. Inmate McGregor and Inmate Lacey were acting suspiciously, were soaked to the bone, and smelled of bleach as they left their workstation. The bite mark found on the trapezius of Inmate Higgins was matched by a noted expert in forensic odontology to Inmate McGregor. Finally, a palm print was recovered from the table leg that was in front of the soffit for the missing leg. Inductive reasoning would suggest that to remove the leg used as the weapon, it was likely that McGregor placed his left hand on the front leg for support.

The motive for the murder was one of preserving racial purity among the neo-Nazi skinheads by removing what they perceived as a case of bad blood, a young man who brazenly flaunted disregard for ethnic separation. Inmate Lacey's DNA was found underneath the fingernails of Inmate Higgins. He had a scar on his hand, the origin of which he could not sufficiently explain. It was enough evidence for the district attorney's office to charge him for the murder as well. The

DA chose not to seek a gang enhancement against the pair because they didn't perceive the skinhead disruptive group as a legitimate gang, a decision Scott could not understand. The case went to jury trial complete with a number of court exhibits made by Adrian and Oswaldo. Scott also composed a victimology report that chronicled the life of Dana Higgins, growing up in and adapting to an integrated neighborhood and attending schools populated by an ethnic group that was diverse from what would be considered by his nemesis as pure and white.

For evidence to be allowed in trial, it must meet the following criteria: it must be legally obtained, it must be relative to the crime being charged, it must be properly collected and have a proper chain of custody, and it cannot be overpowering to play on the emotions of the judge or jury. Therefore, although the jury saw the photographs of the dishwasher, they were spared the very graphic photographs with the bludgeoned, deceased inmate stuffed inside. In spite of this, the jury reached a verdict of guilty on count one of homicide in the first degree. Both inmates were sentenced to life in prison without the possibility of parole.

When Scott last checked, Inmate McGregor was appealing his verdict on the grounds that he was wrongfully identified by the forensic odontology expert and that the expert did not use a scientific method as required under *Daubert*. He'd probably win, and Scott knew he would see him back in court. Nothing ever surprised Scott anymore.

The district attorney's office declined prosecution against Inmate Lacey for the attempted murder of Rob Finch. Presumably, it was because they were already charging him for the murder of Dana Higgins, so why waste money? Of course, the official decline cited insufficient evidence. Once again, Scott had been trumped by the system. It didn't matter. He knew he had found the guilty party, and for that, Inmate Lacey received a rules violation report wherein he was found guilty, lost 365 days of good-time credit, and was required to spend eighteen months in administrative segregation. Scott reminded Adrian and Oswaldo that the importance of that investigation wasn't merely finding the responsible party but also finding the evidence that exonerated Inmate Tanner and Inmate Keller. Scott got equal pleasure finding someone innocent of a charge as he did finding them guilty.

He made it a point to talk to Rob Finch and convince him that Jacob Tanner was not the stabber, although he did not tell him about Lacey. The stabbing of Inmate Birdsong remained a mystery to this day, yet another unsolved investigation that would remain on the books. Regardless of a thumbprint that Scott recovered from the silicone tube that matched the right thumb of Inmate Mayer and a lab report that matched the silicone in the tube to the one used to seal the Doritos bag, the district attorney declined prosecution. The DA's office even considered the ounce of methamphetamines found inside his mattress to be from a "common area" and declined prosecution. Once again, Scott had to be satisfied with an administrative penalty, the loss of ninety days' good-time credit and ninety days in the administrative segregation unit. Fortunately, Santa's custody level went up with the write-up, and he became somebody else's problem.

Jacob Tanner paroled to his parents' home. He served two years on parole and was granted a discharge by the governor's office. From what Scott understood, he had turned his life around. He was working in construction, had remained away from methamphetamine, and had stayed out of trouble. He was still too skinny for his own good, but Scott was, after all, an Italian and could be heard quite often make the call of "Vieni a tavola e mangia!"

Byron Sinclair White was convicted by a jury of his peers and was sentenced to twelve years in prison. The judge denied a *Romero* motion striking his previous strike, and his sentence carried at 85 percent, meaning he would not be eligible for parole for ten years. Floyd did a fantastic job of testifying. He even had the jury laughing on a few occasions, which was always good for the prosecution side. Barbara was spared the witness stand, but she sat faithfully in the courtroom every day until the trial was done. After the verdict, Barbara punched Scott in the right arm and said, "I knew you would do it."

Floyd asked the obvious question. "Does this mean I can get my money back?" Unfortunately, although the judge ordered restitution, it was unlikely the DeWitts would ever see a penny. Scott instructed him to write the money off as a bad debt on his taxes—after consulting with a good tax preparer, of course.

Scott lost Floyd a few years later just weeks before his ninety-third birthday. He was buried at the Punchbowl National Cemetery at Pearl Harbor. Barbara moved up to Benicia to live with her eldest daughter. Scott received a Christmas card every year, until her death three years later.

Scott recently learned that Byron White died in prison from an aneurism. He was only in his fifties. When Scott found this out, he had hoped Byron had the opportunity to see his mother before the Stuart police officers took him in custody. Somehow he doubted it. Scott hadn't had a home-baked cherry pie since Barbara left. Dr. Foster was greatly disappointed. Scott's insurance stopped paying for root canals, and the subject was never mentioned again.

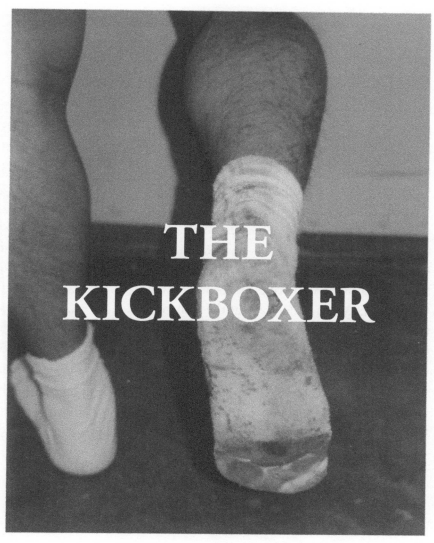

THE KICKBOXER

**And Other Lessons in the
Art of the Interview**

Contents

Chapter 1

The (Un)Happy Librarian

"Oh, Tyrus, I am glad you got here," Investigator Scott Doggett said, patting Sergeant Phillips on the back. "This is what we have so far. Oz and I are serving a search warrant on Rachel Rodriguez, the girlfriend of Inmate Hector Amador from the South Facility. Everything was going smoothly. She showed up this morning nice and early. Becky Romero and I went out to the visitor's processing center to greet her. We served her with the warrant, put her in handcuffs, and seated her in the back of my cruiser.

"I sent Adrian Kirby with Oz and his dog, Ruud, over to the visitor's parking lot to do a canine search of her vehicle. Much to their surprise, sitting in the driver's seat of the car was Amador's brother, Orlando, a mild-mannered librarian from Oxnard. He came out of the car, all right, but so too did a bag filled with pot, methamphetamines, and about a hundred ecstasy tablets. We've searched the girl, and she doesn't have anything on her. Right now, I have her in cuffs in the back of my cruiser with Adrian standing guard. Orlando is in the interview room, but all he says is that the dope was his for personal use."

"Sounds like you have things under control here. What do you need me for?" asked the bewildered sergeant.

"I need you to run interference for me," Scott responded.

"Interference?"

"Yes, Ty, interference. If you look over toward the oak tree in the corner of the yard, you will see Lieutenant Templeton standing in the shade with Warden Brown, and they are impatient as all hell. Warden Brown is not happy with the way I left old girl sitting in the back of my cruiser. I need you to keep them busy while I interview the brother."

"I'll do my best, Doggy."

Having given Tyrus his assignment, Scott returned to the interview and continued the questioning of Orlando. "Okay, Orlando, we are back on tape. Now as I said before, I just cannot believe what you are telling me is the truth. You were sitting in the car, thumbing marijuana and meth into balloons, and you maintain that the dope is for personal use?"

"Yes, sir, it's for me," replied the timid librarian.

"And the ecstasy tablets?" Scott asked.

"Mine too."

"That's a year's worth of ecstasy. You cannot expect me to believe you."

"I am telling the truth. The drugs are mine," he responded.

"Look, son, we have your brother and his girlfriend on tape making the arrangements to smuggle marijuana, meth, and E into the prison during the visit. We have surveillance of the supplier delivering the drugs to you at the library. And last but not least, we have you in the car packing the dope into balloons. Are you sure you want to stick with this lie?" Scott asked.

"I'm telling you the truth. The weed, ice, and E is mine, and it is for personal use," he insisted. This back-and-forth went on for the next twenty minutes. It resembled a prisoner of war interview where all Scott was getting was the kid's name, rank, and serial number.

Lieutenant Templeton stuck his head in the door and said, "Scott, can I see you for a minute?"

Scott went off tape for the second time and stepped outside. Fortunately, the videotape was still going. "Scott, the warden is not happy about you leaving the girl in the car for the past forty minutes. He wants you to finish up the questioning in there and get this thing moving. He wants you to arrest the male and release the female and to do it now."

Scott walked back into the interview room, started the tape again, and continued his questioning. "Look, son, you are a good kid, right? You have never been in trouble with the law in your life. You haven't even had so much as a speeding ticket. You have a good job at the library, and I am sure that everybody there thinks very highly of you. If you are using all these drugs yourself, you have a major drug problem, and I doubt highly you would be able to hold down a job at the library."

"I told you, sir, the drugs are mine. They are all mine. I use a lot of drugs."

"And what would possess you to bring all your drugs to the institution with you, not only that but to sit in the car and pack them into balloons as well?"

"I put them in balloons to keep them fresh."

"I'm not buying this for a minute, Orlando," Scott replied in frustration.

Just then, Lieutenant Templeton stepped into the room and loudly proclaimed, "Investigator Doggett, this interview is over."

Calmly, Scott held up one finger while continuing his gaze at the pudgy suspect. It was clear that Tyrus had failed him. It was time to step it up and put his plan in action. "Orlando," Scott said in a soft but firm voice, "you are lying through your teeth. In fact, I know that you are so full of bullshit that I bet you won't even write down on this piece of paper that everything you have told me is the truth." Scott spun a notepad toward him and dropped his pen on the desk in front of him.

"What do you mean?" he asked, curiously staring at the blank notepad.

"See, even you don't believe the stuff that has been coming out of your own mouth. You say that the dope belongs to you and that you had no intention of smuggling it into the institution to your brother, right?"

"Uh, yes," he replied.

"Then write on that piece of paper that everything you have told me is the absolute truth, just that. Write 'Everything I have told you is the absolute truth' and sign it, and then maybe, just maybe, I will believe you."

"You want me to write a confession?"

"Doggett!" exclaimed the red-faced lieutenant.

"See, you are a liar. You can't even bring yourself to write on that piece of paper that you told me the truth. I don't want you to write out a confession. I just want you to write down that everything you have told me is the truth." Scott leaned back in his chair.

Orlando picked up the pen and straightened the notepad. "You'll use this against me in court," he said. "What am I going to use against you? You already admitted that the stuff was yours. You possessed the drugs on state prison grounds. It is a felony, and you are going to jail. There is nothing I can do about that. It's a done deal. I am trying to give you the opportunity to tell the truth, and you clearly are not."

"Investigator Doggett, I want to speak to you right now!" fumed the lieutenant.

Scott held up his hand. "See, Orlando? Even my lieutenant doesn't believe you."

With that, Orlando picked up the pen and wrote these words: "Everything that I have told you is the absolute truth, Orlando Amador." "Is that what you wanted?" he asked in a snit.

Scott picked up the notepad, read it, turned it over, and placed it facedown on the desk. He dismissed him with "Get him out of here, Lieutenant."

Lieutenant Templeton escorted the nonrepentant Orlando from the room. As he reached the door, the lieutenant glanced at Scott with his molars gnashing. "We're going to talk about this later, Scott. You might as well look for another job right now." Scott shook his head and rubbed his forehead.

Scott asked Becky to get Rachel out of the car and to bring her in for a follow-up interview. A few minutes later, Becky brought the girl through the door, removed her handcuffs, and sat her in the chair next to Scott. Becky sat in the opposite corner. Lieutenant Templeton entered the room and stood in the doorway, blocking any egress with his arms folded—so much for the *Beheler* advisement.

Scott began his interview. "Rachel, we served you with a search warrant today. You were very cooperative, and the provisions of the warrant were satisfied. Fortunately, you did not have any drugs on your person, which is a very good thing. Unfortunately, there was a considerable quantity of drugs in Orlando's vehicle, the vehicle in which you were a passenger. At this time, although you are not under arrest right now, I do want to advise you of your rights pursuant to the *Miranda* decision."

Scott looked over at his lieutenant, who was still blocking the door. Scott furrowed his brow and clenched his back teeth. Lieutenant Templeton didn't understand the gesture, and the only reason Scott had to give the *Miranda* advisement was that the lieutenant was blocking the door, and there now was the perception of custody. "You have the right to remain silent. Anything you say can and will be used against you in a court of law. You have the right to an attorney and to have an attorney present during questioning. If you cannot afford an attorney, one will be provided to you free of charge. Do you understand these rights as I have explained them to you?"

Rachel nodded in the affirmative.

"I see you are nodding in the affirmative. Does that mean you understand your rights?"

"Yes," she said quietly.

"Okay, having these rights in mind, do you want to talk to me today?"

"I guess so," she replied. In the trade, they called that implied consent.

"All right, Orlando is a good kid, right? He's never been in trouble with the law ever in his life, right?"

"No, everybody loves him," she answered.

"And they love him at the library where he works, right?" Scott asked.

"Yes, they are very fond of him there," she agreed in a calm and quiet voice.

"Okay, he would never lie to me, correct?"

"Oh, no, he is very honest and so good to his mother," she responded.

"Right, so then you understand why he had to tell me the truth about the drugs. I don't want you to be mad at him for telling me the truth. In fact, not only did he tell me the truth in great detail about you and Hector but he also signed a document stating that everything he told me was the truth." With that, Scott turned over the notepad and showed her the writing. "That is his handwriting, isn't it?" Scott asked.

Tears began to well in Rachel's eyes, followed by the shoulder heaving, heavy sobs, and a flood of tears. "I told Hector he was a fool and that we would get caught, but he insisted. Orlando is such a good kid. He loves his brother and would do anything he asked of him. He doesn't even use drugs. He didn't know where to find them or anything," she confessed through the tears and sobs.

Scott looked over at his lieutenant and gave him a wink and a smile. His lieutenant just shook his head and walked out of the room, never again to question Scott's interview techniques. Rachel informed Scott that she was supposed to visit with her boyfriend on that day but that he had instructed her not to bring the drugs into the institution with her. Instead, she was to hide the bindles of drugs in the portable toilet in the visitor's parking area, where his bunkmate, whom she only knew as Trips and who was assigned to a work crew that cleaned the visitor's processing center and parking lot, would retrieve them on the following Monday.

Both Orlando and Rachel were charged with the violation of California Penal Code section 4573.6, possession of controlled substances on state prison grounds with the intent to smuggle and distribute, and they were transported to the county jail. Inmate Amador was charged with a violation of Penal Code sections 182 and 664/4573.6, conspiracy to possess and distribute controlled substances in a state prison. As Scott placed the handcuffed Orlando into the back of his caged vehicle, he overheard his lieutenant tell the warden, "I taught him everything he knows." Bullshit.

Chapter 2

Boredom Reigns Supreme

As Scott put the finishing touches on the transcripts from the Inmate Amador investigation, he sensed that he was being watched from behind. He spun his chair around and noticed his partner, Investigator Oswaldo Castaneda, sitting at his desk in the opposite corner of the office, with his chair facing Scott's direction. His feet were firmly planted on the floor, and his hands were on his knees. Upon his face was the blank, if not vapid, expression of a man without thought or, for that matter, apparent brain function. "Bored?" Scott asked.

"There's nothing to do," he replied.

"Go play with Ruud," Scott suggested.

"It's not time yet. I'll go to the kennel in about an hour."

"He's a dope dog. Go hide some dope for him to find."

"I did that this morning, on your car."

"Oz, I wish you wouldn't do that. That damned dog has scratched the entire area around the gas cap. Why couldn't you get a passive alert dog?"

"Passive alert dogs aren't as good."

"Well, I miss our Bella girl. She was a scratcher too, but she was delicate about it, and when she found a good alert, not only did she scratch but she took a crap too."

"She only did that once!" protested Oswaldo.

"Oz, she did that three times. I was there each time. I was just waiting for you to have to testify in court. 'And how does your dog alert?' 'She shits, Your Honor.'"

"Yeah," he replied with a chuckle.

"Why don't you read another motorcycle magazine?" Scott inquired.

"I don't have any new ones, but I do have a gun magazine," he responded while shuffling magazines on his desk.

"Where's Adrian?" Scott asked, hoping to get him involved in the entertainment of Oswaldo.

"He and Becky went to search a cell," replied the diverted Oswaldo.

"Another cell phone hunt?" Scott inquired.

"Yeah, some guy in Fox Wing, I think. Adrian got another tip."

"These flippin' cell phones are absolutely killing me. We're up to 414 we've taken from the inmates just for this year so far, and it's only September. Yet the legislature doesn't seem to have any problem with the inmate population being in possession of cellular telephones. They still refuse to pass any laws other than a two-bit misdemeanor prohibiting them in spite of my letter-writing efforts. It's killing me. Heck, we've even had an attempted escape planned on a cell phone, and lord knows they are running their dope operations with the damned things," Scott bloviated.

"Two to the chest, one to the head," muttered Oz.

"That's your solution to everything," Scott remarked.

"I need a good riot or something exciting to happen. Come on, Scotty, let's have a disturbance, a riot, a good crime scene, or a murder. That's it, another escape. That would be awesome."

"Oz, knock it off. You're going to jinx us. Here, it was nice and quiet, and I am finally getting caught up on my investigations, and here you go wishing for an escape just because you are bored. Go play with your dog."

"Got another one," announced young Adrian Kirby as he walked through the door. He walked directly to Scott and dropped a Samsung cellular telephone on his desk. "Can you see what you can get out of it?"

"Sure thing, Adrian," Scott responded as he began a forensic analysis of the telephone.

"Who'd you get it from?" asked Oswaldo.

"Inmate Hampton in Fox Wing," replied Adrian.

"These guys," remarked Oswaldo. "These guys" was Oz's latest catchphrase. It basically covered everything from "these guys are idiots" to "these fucking guys are driving me crazy" and "these guys just won't stop misbehaving." Sometimes it was just "that guy." That euphemism was generally reserved for guys in the prison whom Oswaldo keenly disliked.

"Anything good?" asked Adrian as he watched Scott fiddle with the cellular telephone.

"Lots of photographs of his erect penis," Scott replied.

"There's always a photograph of a dick." Oswaldo chortled.

"Yeah, most of the inmates are fond of photographing their willies," Scott said with a laugh. "Hang on, Adrian, I'm extracting the data now. It would appear that your inmate Hampton has been using the phone to resolve his dope debts. There are plenty of text messages regarding money being sent to different people. The amounts are consistent with marijuana. Did you find anything in his cell?"

"Nope," replied the young investigator as he plunked down onto his desk chair, adding, "Just the cell phone and some tobacco."

"Have him submit to a urine test. It will probably come back positive. Here's a text about a board hearing coming up. Maybe we can shake some information out of him in exchange for burying the drug results until after his hearing."

"Will do," responded Adrian.

Scott unplugged the cell phone from the Cellebrite data extractor computer. "Here ya go," he said as he tossed the phone back to Adrian. "Book it into evidence with the eighteen hundred other phones we have from the past four years, although for the life of me I don't know why. It's just a contraband beef. He'll lose thirty days' good-time credits, thanks to the idiots in the California legislature."

"Those guys," interjected Oswaldo. He resumed his boredom posture and watched Adrian as he typed up his rules violation report for the cell phone. Scott knew it was coming; he could see it in the blank expression on his face. "Hey, hey, Adrian, wouldn't an escape be great right now or a riot?"

"Damn it, Oz, knock it off!" Scott yelled.

The speaker in the office that connected the investigations unit with the central control room cracked to life. "Code 1, Echo Wing! Code 1, Echo Wing!" Simultaneously, the announcement was broadcast over the institutional radio system. The audible claxon alarm was noticeable in the background. Scott glared at Oswaldo.

"Charlie 2, this is Charlie 2-3. Request medical and code 1 responders to Echo Wing."

"Ten-four, Charlie 2-3. Code 1 responders are 10-17. Charlie 9, did you copy the last transmission?"

"Charlie 9 copies. Medical is 10-17. What is the nature of the emergency?"

"Charlie 9, this is Charlie 2-3. I have a man down, a cell fight with one in restraints to the holding cells. Charlie 4, clear the west corridor."

"Charlie 4, 10-4. Central Control, clear the west corridor."

"Central Control. Charlie 9 we're going to let the gurney through first."

"Are you happy now, Oz?" Scott asked.

"Charlie 9, this is Charlie 2-3. Notify medical the 10-15 is not breathing and is nonresponsive. We are starting CPR and rescue breathing."

"Come on, Scotty, I can sink my teeth into this one." Oswaldo rejoiced with an enormous grin.

"Adrian, take the keys to my cruiser and get the crime scene kit out of the trunk. Oz, grab the camera kits, and I'll get the bloodstain kit. On second thought, Oz, I'll take the camera kits. You go and put paper bags on the suspect's hands before they let him wash up. Oh, and, Oz, bag up his clothing. Get all of it!" Scott yelled as Oswaldo raced up the stairs with a stack of paper evidence bags and a roll of tape.

"Charlie 2, this is Charlie 2-3, I'm going to need CSI ASAP."

"CSI is en route. Secure the crime scene," Scott broadcast.

"Charlie 2 copies."

"Charlie 2-3, 10-4."

"Charlie 2-3, Central Control, the gurney is at your 10-20. We are closing the west corridor. You can move that 10-15."

"Charlie 2-3, 10-4. The 10-15 is 10-17 the holding cells."

"Central medical sergeant, RN Robinson."

"Central medical sergeant by."

"We need a doctor stat."

"Ten-four, RN Robinson. Dr. Abdullah is on his way."

"Oz!" Scott hollered up the stairwell. "Photograph the suspect before they take his cuffs off. I'll bring you a camera in a minute. If he has any blood evidence on his skin, collect swabs. Take Becky with you. Adrian, meet me in Echo Wing with the crime scene kit."

The electric gurney went whizzing past Scott as he entered the central corridor. Registered Nurse Robinson was driving the three-wheeled motorized, electric orange gurney back toward the infirmary while a nurse's assistant and Dr. Abdullah ran alongside. The patient didn't look good at all. Of what Scott could see, there was a lot of blood on his face and arms, and his eyes were swollen almost shut.

Lt. Randall "Pete" Petersen, Charlie 2, the watch commander, was standing near the control room window. "Hey, Pete, here we go again," Scott said as he closed the grille gate. "Who's Charlie 2-3?"

"It's Sergeant Hatch. He was just here a minute ago with the inmate at the holding cells. I think he went back down to the wing," replied the lieutenant.

Scott handed Oz a camera kit as he passed the holding cells. "Get some swabs, sterile water ampoules, and collars from Adrian when he comes past," Scott said as he pointed to bloodstains on the right leg of the suspect.

"What's your name?" Scott asked the handcuffed inmate.

"Vong, Thuwong Vong," he replied. "I hit my cellie. I had to. He was going to kill me. I did not want to fight, but I had no choice."

"All right, Vong, just follow the staff instructions, and we will come back and talk to you a little later," Scott said as he made note of the statement in his notebook.

He was met by Sergeant Bobby Hatch, affectionately called Ant Man at the institution because of his diminutive size but incredible strength. "What have you got, Ant Man?" Scott asked.

"Inmate Vong beat up his cellmate, Inmate Zhuang, in the cell—cell 346. He beat him good," he replied.

"No inmate movement. Are you on lockdown?" Scott inquired.

"We've been on lockdown for staff TB testing all week."

"Sergeant Hatch, telephone call for you," announced Officer Brian Dailey from the watch office.

"Go ahead, Ant Man," Scott said. "I'm waiting for Adrian to come up with the rest of the equipment."

Sergeant Hatch spoke for a moment on the telephone and then motioned Scott to step into the office. "He's dead," he said as he replaced the telephone receiver.

"Two inmates in a cell during a lockdown, and only one comes out alive, no mystery here. Bobby, can you go tell Pete that we need to notify the coroner's office and district attorney's office immediately? Do you have an officer on the cell door?"

"Yes, Dog, as soon as you said to secure the crime scene, I put Officer Banning on the door."

"Who found the body?" Scott asked.

"Rosie," replied the sergeant.

"Rosie Cortez?"

"No, the other one, Rosie Del Toro," corrected the Ant Man. "She's in the wing at one of the tables." He walked out the door to brief the watch commander. As he did so, he passed Adrian, who was struggling with the equipment boxes. Scott met him in the corridor outside the watch office.

"Third tier, Adrian, Echo Wing, cell 346. Relieve Officer Banning and stretch crime scene tape at the third-tier front stairwell. I'll be up there as soon as I make a telephone call." Scott picked up the telephone and called Tyrus, who was waiting at his desk for information.

"What's up, Doggy?" he said as he picked up the telephone.

"Apparently, an Inmate Vong—who is in the holding cell—has just killed his cellie, Inmate Zhuang. I need you to go down and photograph the decedent in the infirmary and stand by there until the coroner's investigator arrives."

"No, problem, Dog. I'll take the fellas down to the infirmary." By "fellas," Tyrus meant the two institutional gang investigators under his supervision.

"Thanks, Ty. Let me know the extent of the injuries."

Scott hung up the phone and walked the distance to Echo Wing. Upon his arrival, he noticed Adrian stretching crime scene tape across the railings of the first-tier staircase. Officer Banning was still standing near cell 346. "Third-tier stairwell, Adrian, and relieve Officer Banning first and get his entry/exit log if he has one. When you have done that, put out some sterile blankets in the area between 346 and 347. Drop the gear between 348 and 349. While you are doing that, I am going to go back to the office and get some Tyvek suits and a video camera."

"Becky is still at the office," interjected Adrian.

"I thought I told Oz to take her with him? No matter, I'll get her on the radio and have her bring that stuff up. In the meantime, let me put on some booties and take a peek in the cell." Scott sat down and started to stretch the blue crime scene booties over his size 11 boots when he noticed Chief Deputy Warden Eddie Caldwell walking through the front door with Capt. Geoff Sanderson. "Shit," Scott murmured to himself.

"Doggett, I don't want you in that crime scene until the coroner gets here," barked the chief.

"Sir, with all due respect, the district attorney's investigator wants a brief description of the crime scene. I'm going to take a peek inside and start a video before any changes or alterations have occurred in the cell.

Furthermore, I need to be certain that there is no perishable evidence or environmental conditions that may destroy or degrade the evidence."

"He's right," concurred the captain. Geoff and Scott used to work together before his meteoric rise through the ranks. Scott was the one who knocked an inmate off his chest when he was an officer during a dispute over the size of the piece of chocolate cake the inmate had received during chow. That episode went back almost eighteen years. Geoff was a good man and trusted Scott implicitly.

"Very well, but make it fast," ordered the chief with authority.

Scott met Adrian at the top of the stairs. "Damn, that was good," commented Adrian. "Did the DA investigator really want a brief description, or did you make that up?"

"Oh, did I say 'wants'? I meant to say 'will want.' My bad," Scott replied with a wink.

Central Facility cells measures six feet in width by eleven width in depth. Bunk beds lined either the north or south wall depending on the cell configuration, with one standing locker at the foot of the bunks near the cell door and another directly across from the head of the beds. There was a space of about three feet between the bunks and the adjacent locker. The toilet and sink assembly was either to the left or to the right of the cell door, again depending on the cell configuration. Needless to say, there wasn't much room.

In cell 346, the bunks were on the south wall, and the toilet was to the right of the cell door. Scott always told people that housing for the inmates in their facility was rather like two grown men living in a space the size of the bathroom in your parents' house. It smelled the same on occasion too.

Scott peered around the corner into the cell. Aside from the bloodstains on the floor and bunk and a few scattered pieces of paper, the cell looked fairly neat and well kept. Clothing and personal property was hanging or neatly stacked in the lockers, and the beds, although not made, were not messy by any means. There were no bloodstains on the cell door or ceiling. A 6" × 9" smudged bloodstain was present on the left interior doorjamb of the cell. Cast-off bloodstains were present on the eastside of the locker across from the bunk. Spatter was also present on a garbage receptacle that was against the locker, just below the cast-off bloodstains. Scott could see impact spatter on the lower bunk near the head of the bed. Blood drops were on the toilet seat and floor area in front and to the south of the toilet. Diluted bloodstains were visible in the sink basin and on the faucet handles. A piece of blood-soaked cardboard was against the west wall underneath the cell window, with a pool of blood forming on the floor around the cardboard.

Scott took one initial overall photograph of the crime scene and walked back downstairs to where the chief and captain were waiting. "Not much of a crime scene other than some good bloodstain evidence. Other than that, it's pretty clean. It's not your basic 'everything gets broken and is scattered over the cell' type of altercation."

"Okay, well, you're done in that cell for now," ordered the chief.

"I have the crime scene. It is secured, and we are standing by for the coroner's investigator, which is standard protocol," Scott assured him.

He shook his head as the chief and Captain Sanderson walked out the door, and he muttered under his breath, "I thought I was the certified senior crime scene analyst here."

Becky arrived a moment later with their bag containing the Tyvek suits and a video camera, which he used to get a preliminary video documentation of the cell. Scott stopped for a moment and talked with Officer Del Toro about what she observed, heard, and did in the crime scene. "Are you all right?" Scott asked.

"Oh yeah, Dog, I'm fine," she replied without hesitation.

"So, Del, tell me what happened."

"I was the only one in the hall when I heard a pounding on a door on the third tier. I went up there and yelled out for the inmate who was pounding to shout out which cell, and Vong hollered '346.' I went to that cell and looked in the window, but all I saw was Vong's face. He said through the door that he and his cellie had been in a fight. I couldn't open the door because I was alone, so I had to radio for Sergeant Hatch to come down to the wing. It took him about five minutes to get here, and I waited for him on the tier," she recalled.

"What was Vong doing?" Scott asked.

"He was standing at the door, but he kept looking back toward the rear of the cell. He didn't leave the door though. When Sergeant Hatch got here, we opened the door, and I had Vong step out. I noticed immediately he was bleeding from his mouth, and he had blood all over his right leg. As soon as Vong stepped out, he said he had to fight with his cellmate and that he didn't want to fight with him, but he had no choice. Sergeant Hatch put him in cuffs and put him on the wall while I went into the cell. Zhuang was still breathing, so I told Ant Man that we needed medical right away. Officer Barnes came over from Fox Wing, and we brought Mr. Zhuang out onto the tier while Ant Man took Vong downstairs. When we got Mr. Zhuang out onto the tier, Barnes noticed he wasn't breathing. That's when I yelled down to Ant Man that we were going to do CPR and that we needed medical ASAP. I guess you know the rest."

"Yeah, the rest I got, Del. Did Vong and Zhuang have any problems that you were aware of?" Scott asked.

"No, they seemed to get along very well. Vong was always in the cell or in the back of the hall reading his Bible, and Mr. Zhuang was just a kind old man, never gave any of us any trouble."

"I thought you were working in the culinary?" Scott asked.

"I was until the beginning of this month. I bid into this spot when Rosie Cortez went over to North." Scott thanked her for the information and reminded her to include everything that she had told him in her report.

Scott posted Adrian at the crime scene and went down to check on the progress of Oswaldo and Inmate Vong. He was busy collecting bloodstain specimen from the right shin area of the inmate. "Hey, Scotty, did you know Vong was a Thai kickboxer?" Oswaldo excitedly asked. He spent a summer doing cage fighting; it was a short-lived interest, although he did win a trophy.

"Nope, I hadn't heard," Scott replied.

"Many years ago before I come to America, I was champion in Bangkok when I was nineteen," added Inmate Vong as he stood in the holding cell.

"How old are you now?" Scott asked.

"I am thirty-nine years old," he answered.

"You look pretty good for being almost forty. I would have said you were still in your twenties," Scott remarked.

"I exercise every day. Watch this." While still standing in the telephone-booth-sized holding cell, Inmate Vong planted his right foot on the right side of the cage at face level without effort. It was a remarkable demonstration considering the cage was, as mentioned, about the size of a telephone booth.

"Holy crap!" Scott blurted.

"Yeah, yeah, he did that for me too," chimed Oswaldo.

"That's amazing," Scott said. "Mind if I take a photograph of that?"

"I do not mind," responded the agile Thai. Very quickly, Scott scooped up Oz's camera and took a photograph of Inmate Vong with his foot planted against the cage more than five feet above the ground.

"If I did that, it would take the Army Corps of Engineers to get my foot back down again, not to mention the month of traction," Scott commented as he put the camera back in its case.

A tall bespectacled gray-haired man looked around the corner of the holding cell room and announced, "I'm Dave Christiansen from the DA's office, investigation bureau."

"Pleased to meet you," Scott greeted. "I take it Alberto Gutierrez isn't coming?"

"Investigator Gutierrez is on vacation, so they sent me. I used to come out here a lot in the late '80s and early '90s. It hasn't changed much. In fact, I used to be with the Gabilan Police Department before I retired and went to work for the DA's office."

"You are welcome to our humble facility," Scott said, adding, "This is Mr. Vong."

"This is the deceased's cellmate?" asked Investigator Christiansen.

Inmate Vong bowed his head and said, "It is as I feared. My cellie is dead. It is most distressing."

"Yes, Vong, I'm sorry, but he didn't make it," Scott consoled.

"I must say a prayer for him, please." With that, Inmate Vong assumed a cross-legged position on the floor of the holding cell.

Oswaldo closed the door, placed the padlock on the latch, and diverted his attention to packaging the evidence swabs. "We'll come back and talk to you a little later, Mr. Vong," Scott said as he ushered Investigator Christiansen from the room.

"We hadn't told him yet," Scott said.

"Oh, sorry about that. I thought he knew."

"No matter, he probably already figured it out. Shall we take a look at the victim, Inmate Zhuang?" Scott inquired.

"Yes, yes, by all means and perhaps the cell too."

"Well, hopefully, the coroner's investigator will be here soon so that we can do it all at the same time," Scott responded.

"Who does the crime scene?" asked Investigator Christiansen.

"That would be me," Scott replied.

"Good, it's better that way. The evidence stays in one place for chain of custody, and I noticed the certified senior crime scene analyst pin on your pocket."

"Two-thousand-plus hours of formal training," Scott replied as they walked up the corridor to the central infirmary.

Scott was just about to ask the first-floor infirmary officer where they had taken the deceased inmate Zhuang when he saw Tyrus step out of emergency room no. 2. "Still waiting for the coroner guy," Tyrus said as they approached.

"Ty, this is Investigator Christiansen from the DA's office. He's filling in for Bert, who apparently picked the perfect time to go on vacation."

"Any idea who is coming out from the coroner's office?" asked Tyrus.

"No idea," Scott replied.

"Me either," responded the investigator. "I'm afraid I don't know any of the investigators at the coroner's office these days. I've been assigned to insurance fraud for the last five years."

"Still, an investigation is an investigation," Scott said encouragingly.

Inmate Zhuang was still lying in the orange Stokes litter with his right arm extended over the side. His eyes were swollen shut, and a clean fracture of the left maxilla with a corresponding missing tooth was visible behind the oral airway plastic mouthpiece. He appeared to be an Asian man in his sixties, short, and stocky with crew-cut white hair. He had deep tissue bruising on his right pectoral region, a red contusion on his right side in the area of his kidneys, a broken right ring finger, and defensive wounds to the inside of his right and left arms, as well as bruising on his left palm. A semicircular fracture of the skull was apparent on the right side of his head as if he was hit by something round or was thrown against an object of the same shape. "My money is on he was kicked to death," Scott commented.

"What was his first name?" asked Investigator Christiansen.

"Henry," replied Sergeant Phillips.

"What was he in for?" inquired the investigator as he recorded the information in his notebook.

"He stabbed a guy during an argument at a bar a few years ago. It was the first time he had been in trouble with the law, but it got him a fifteen-to-life sentence. The guy didn't die, but I guess it was a pretty brutal stabbing. He stabbed him in the chest and slashed his face, left a nasty scar. Booze and gambling were his downfall," detailed Tyrus.

"So he just started his prison sentence?" asked the investigator.

"Yeah, we got him five months ago. He's been in that cell for the last two months," replied Tyrus.

"Where was he before that?" inquired the investigator.

"He was in a reception cell for the first three months. He went from reception into Echo Wing. He spent a week in cell 139 and then was moved to cell 346 because he has a lower-bunk chrono, and there was already an inmate in the lower bunk in 139 with a medical condition."

"I believe I see our old friend Dan Johansen walking through the door right now," Scott interrupted.

The tall Salinas Valley native was standing in the entrance of the infirmary, talking to the door officer. The officer pointed in the direction of the assembled investigators. Dan nodded in recognition and walked down to where Scott was standing just outside the emergency room containing the body of Inmate Zhuang.

"Hey, buddy, we've got a brutal case for you this time," Scott said as he extended his hand. Dan grasped his hand and gave it a good shake. Scott wondered how seldom anyone shook the hand of an employee at the coroner's office. They had a "No food or drink in the autopsy suite" sign for a reason. "Do you know Investigator Christiansen from the district attorney's office?"

"I don't think I've had the pleasure," remarked Dan with a nod. Scott noticed they didn't shake hands.

"And of course, my partner, Ty Philips," Scott added. Tyrus shook his hand.

"So what happened? It looks like he got run over by a truck," observed Dan.

"I guess you could say that, but the truck was a professional Thai kickboxer," Scott answered.

"Kicked to death," added Tyrus.

"And the cellmate?"

"In the holding cell, Dan. He already made a statement of admission to the first unit responder and to myself and Oz."

"What did he say?"

"That he fought with his cellie. He didn't want to, but he had to."

"This guy looks like he's in his sixties. How old is the cellie?"

"Late thirties," Scott replied, "but in excellent shape."

"Anything interesting in the cell?"

"Some good bloodstain pattern evidence. We were just about to go down there if you're game."

"Lead the way. I've seen all I need to see here," responded the coroner's investigator.

They left the infirmary and strolled down the corridor, stopping briefly at the holding cells to check on the suspect and proceeding to Echo Wing. Adrian was dutifully posted by the cell door. Officer Banning remained close by. Rosie was still writing her report. There was still nothing much of interest in the cell aside from the bloodstain patterns. A few pieces of paper were scattered about the floor and top bunk. Shower shoes, a lunch bag, a blood-soaked roll of toilet paper, a plastic container with corn chips, and the bloodstained cardboard were the only items of note. Dan and Investigator Christiansen took overview photographs of the cell and then lost interest.

"So, gentlemen, that's it. I'll handle the crime scene with Adrian," Scott advised.

"Agreed," replied Dan, adding, "I'll collect up the body and get going."

"When's the autopsy?" Scott asked.

"Wednesday at nine. See you there," he said as he descended the stairs.

"I'd like to interview the cellmate," stated the DA's investigator.

"I can go with you," offered Tyrus.

"Let me know how it goes, Ty," Scott mentioned as he started to don one of the smelly Tyvek suits.

Chapter 3

The Crime Scene

"All right, Adrian, first things first. We need to photo- and video-document this cell before we do anything. Second thing to do is to talk to all the responding staff because we need to get an explanation for this blood transfer on the doorjamb."

"Why is that important?" asked the young investigator.

"Because the position of the bloodstain, had it occurred during the incident, would show that the door was in the open position. Therefore, that would suggest either additional suspects or staff complicity because they were on lockdown at the time. I'm banking on somebody brushing the body against the doorjamb when they took him out, but we need to make sure. Do me a favor. Before you put on your Tyvek suit, go downstairs and assemble all the first unit responders—Ant Man, Rosie, Barnes, and the medical personnel—and have them come up here to the third-tier landing just outside the crime scene tape. In the meantime," Scott said as he raised the Nikon D7100 digital camera, "I'm going to do the preliminary photographs."

Rosie was the first to stand just outside the crime scene perimeter. Scott asked her if she recalled brushing the decedent against the wall. She was certain she had not. Registered Nurse Robinson, who seemed terribly annoyed at having been summoned by a lowly crime scene investigator, bitterly complained and denied having touched the victim until he was on the gurney. *My bad*, Scott thought. He thought he already knew that, but he had to ask just the same. Sergeant Hatch said he was busy dealing with Inmate Vong and had not stepped into the cell or assisted with the removal of Inmate Zhuang. Officer Fredrick Barnes III, a senior officer with nearly thirty years of experience, was quite helpful but certain that he had not brushed the doorjamb with the victim. In fact, he ruled it out entirely as a possibility. Perplexed, Scott thanked Freddy for his help and stared at the blood transfer for a moment.

It wasn't until he saw Freddy walking down the stairs that he noticed the bloodstain on his uniform pants. "Oh, Freddy," Scott announced, "may I see you for a moment?" He turned around and ascended, stopping on the other side of the crime scene tape. "Turn around for a moment, my friend." Freddy turned away from Scott. Scott pulled a tape measure from his pocket and measured the stain; it was exactly six inches in length and twenty-eight inches from the floor to the bottom of the stain. "Now stay there for just a moment." He walked back to the cell and held the tape measure close to the transfer: five inches and three-quarters in length and twenty-six inches from the floor—close enough for him, allowing for a bend in a body that was carrying a heavy object.

"Thank you, Freddy. Oh, and if I might mention, you have a bloodstain on the back of your right thigh," Scott said as he stole a quick photograph of the back leg of Officer Barnes.

"I do?" responded the seasoned vet, adding, "I am sorry, Dog, I had no idea."

"Freddy, I'm not mad at you. I just needed to explain where the transfer came from. If I didn't, you can sure bet the defense attorney would point it out in trial. I'm perfectly happy now, but that blood probably soaked to your skin, so you might want to go down to the infirmary and make sure you don't have any open wounds in that area."

Fredrick Barnes III descended the stairs with the concerned expression of possible doom. Adrian passed him on his way up. "What's wrong with him?"

"Possible inmate blood contact. Poor fellow. It's a cop's worst fear next to being stabbed or shot. Hated to be the one to tell him. Still, I'm sure he'll be all right. Suit up, Adrian. We got our work cut out for us today."

"How do you want to do this?" he asked.

"Well, I want to document everything by diagram first. I already took my overview photographs and did the video. Then I want to drop the markers and photograph, map the bloodstains, collect swabs and whatever evidence might be in the cell. I don't think there will be any surprises in this one."

"What about the bloodstain by the door?"

"Accounted for on Officer Barnes's behind," Scott replied.

"How do you want to do this one?" asked Adrian.

"I am thinking the best thing to do is to designate a letter to each area that has a bloodletting event. We can start with the floor and give it the letter A, give the north wall the letter B, the west wall the letter C, the south wall the letter D, and the east wall the letter E," Scott responded as he stuck large vinyl letters in prominent places in each area.

"Now we can itemize each pattern as A-1, A-2, A-3, et cetera. I also want to place these disposable measuring tapes across the base and top of the wall and stand these freestanding tape measures in each corner. We'll move them as necessary," Scott said as the bloodstain pattern mapping got underway.

"After I photograph each distinctive pattern, I will apply these disposable scales along with the designated number next to the stains that I want to document and measure and from which I wish to collect specimen. Are you paying attention to what I am doing?" Scott asked Adrian.

"What about the bunk?"

"Good question," Scott replied. "The lower bunk is now area F, and the upper bunk is area G."

"But what about the toilet?" he asked.

"It's part of the wall with the door, so it is still area E."

"But aren't the bunks attached to the south wall? Shouldn't they be D something?"

"Adrian, since I believe this pattern on the lower bunk is of significance in the crime scene, I want to give it its own area of designation," Scott replied.

"But I still don't understand," he remarked with a raised right nostril and furrowed right eyebrow.

"You don't have to as long as I understand, but keep watching, and it will all be very clear to you shortly. Let's get area A taken care of first so that we can put some sterile blankets on the floor. We've got a cluster of ninety-degree drops right by the door, some of which have been wiped for obvious reasons—a few drops here by the toilet basin, a swipe over here by the bunk, a skeletonized drop smack dab in the middle of the floor, and clotted, pooled blood underneath the cell window," Scott detailed.

Once all the stains were documented and measured and the specimens collected, Scott unfolded several sterile blankets on the floor, stopping short of the pooled blood underneath the window. "Moving on to area B, not much here, just these three drops behind the toilet and a transfer on the towel rack. The three drops behind the toilet are pretty consistent. Let's just pick one for documentation . . . All right, width is 6 mm and length is 22.5 mm, which should give us an impact angle of about fifteen degrees."

"You didn't measure the entire stain," smirked Adrian.

"Not so fast there, smarty. You only want to measure the ellipse of the stain. It takes a bit of skill and experience to determine exactly where to measure. After that, it's second nature. Hand me three sterile cotton bunny swabs, three collars, and a sterile water ampoule so I can collect a specimen."

Adrian passed the required equipment, and the task was completed. "Why three?" he asked.

"One swab will be the control sample. The second swab will be the wet blood specimen. The third is what I call the defense sample. I use a dry swab to gather up what's left. If I can't get it on a swab, I will flake a scraping with a sterile scalpel into a sterile pharmaceutical fold. All right, that being done, let's move over to this garbage receptacle. I think we need to just collect it in its entirety."

"What's so important about the box?" asked Adrian from the doorway.

"Well, if you look at it from where you are at, you would almost think it was misting impact spatter, perhaps suggesting a firearm was used when, in fact, it's an expiration bloodstain," Scott replied.

"Which means?"

"Which means that our victim assumingly expirated the blood through his nose or mouth. Judging by the break in his maxilla and missing tooth, I would say this was caused by our victim," Scott answered.

"But why is it important?" he expressed.

"Because it means our victim was here at one point on the floor or very near it," Scott replied while carefully packaging the garbage bag and box in a clean butcher's paper and putting it into a large evidence box. "Moving on to the side of the lower locker, two dropped bloodstains about the same size, so we'll pick the larger of the two, which by my math is twenty-two degrees."

Adrian anticipated Scott's next request and handed him the required swabbing equipment. "You know, Adrian, judging by the top of the large locker, you'd never know that a serious battle occurred in here. Nothing is disturbed—television, deodorant sticks, cups, even this greeting card is still standing. Yet if you look here on the front of the small locker, you can see where the lower shelf is broken, and there is transfer on the sides and front of the shelf," Scott remarked.

"What's the worst crime scene you ever had to process?" asked the young investigator.

"South Facility, dorm no. 6, a riot between the whites and Southerners. Remind me to tell you about it sometime," Scott replied.

"I will," he replied.

"Okay, moving to the south wall. This is the wall with the cell window. No bloodletting events on the window itself. This blood-soaked piece of cardboard is very interesting. Look at this, Adrian. First, we can tell that the cardboard was in place against the wall when the bloodletting event occurred."

"How so?"

"Because if you look just above the cardboard, you can see blood against the wall that corresponds with the blood on the cardboard. And if you move the cardboard, you will see a line where there is no blood. This is a void. In other words, it is a lack or absence of blood in an otherwise continuous bloodstain pattern. Keep that in mind because it will show up again here in a minute."

"All right, but why is it important?"

"Well, Adrian, what is important is that this cardboard is against the wall where the victim was lying when staff came in. Very likely, the bloody top of his head was resting against it, resulting in the saturation of blood."

"Okay, and?"

"And if you notice these two cast-off drops, one on each side of the large bloodstain, what do you think is significant about them?" Scott asked.

"The one on the left goes up, and the one on the right goes down," he replied.

"Exactly, and why is that important?"

"No idea."

"It means that there was sufficient movement up and down to cause blood to be flung upward and then downward. In other words, it means that our victim was still being beaten while he was already helpless on the floor."

"Wow, you can tell that from just that?"

"Blood is a non-Newtonian viscoelastic fluid, which is more affected by viscosity and cohesion than surface tension. Because of this, it holds a rounded shape during flight. We are therefore able to make an analytical examination of the resultant stain distribution on a known target plane owing to their observable characteristics."

"Okay, Dog, you lost me completely."

"Too much too fast?" Scott asked.

"Yeah, maybe we can sit down later, and you can explain everything to me."

"Don't worry, Adrian, it took me 140 hours of formal training with Jan Johnson's Forensic Pieces, plus a week at Prof. Herb MacDonell's last Laboratory for Forensic Science, Institute on the Physical Significance of Bloodstain Evidence course in Corning, New York. Okay, so the cardboard gets booked into evidence," Scott said as he wrapped the cardboard in a clean butcher's paper.

"Moving on to the bottom bunk, we have three drops down here at the foot of the bed on the white sheet and a very interesting pattern up here at the head of the bed," Scott remarked while putting his measuring devices in place. "What do you make of this pattern up here at the head of the bunk?"

Adrian, by now, had ventured farther into the cell. "Looks like tiny splatters of blood," he replied.

"Spatter? Don't let me hear 'splatter,' please. Mud splatters, poop splatters, but blood spatters?" Scott declared.

"Okay, it looks like tiny spatter of blood."

"All right, perhaps to the untrained eye, it might look like that. But to me, it tells a very important story. If you notice, it is impact spatter consistent with blunt force trauma, radiating from a central point outward like a fan. The stains were distributed on the sheet from left to right or east to west. We can align the stains and determine the area of convergence. This is the common area to where the bloodstain was projected outward. As it happens, the area of convergence is to this part of the bed, where there is a rather large transfer of blood."

"Meaning what?"

"Meaning a bloodstained object pressed against a clean object, thus transferring the blood to the previously unstained target. Now taking a measurement of the bloodstains and determining the angle of impact and measuring the distance back to the area of convergence, we can determine the point of origin, the point in space from where the blood originated. But we have another clue right here," Scott said, pointing at an area between the transfer and the westmost spatter. "What do you see in this space?" He pointed to a clean area among the medium-velocity impact spatter.

"Nothing," replied Adrian.

"Exactly. It's another void pattern. Something interfered with the flight of the blood right in this area. What do you suppose it was?"

"You mean there was something on the bed?" he asked.

"Indeed, yes, there was. Any idea what it could have been?"

"You mean an object, like a club or something?" he inquired.

"What does the shape look like to you?" Scott asked.

"I don't know, maybe something curved, almost like one of those things you throw, and they come back to you. What are they called?"

"A boomerang?" Scott questioned.

"Yeah, like one of those. It's almost the same size too."

"The same size but highly unlikely. You are close, though, regarding the shape, but I'll lay you money it is the shape of our victim's right forearm."

"Yeah, yeah, I see it now!" exclaimed the student.

"So we measure the distance from the area of convergence to the base of each of these stains and do a little math, and we come up with a point of origin at about seven inches, which should put our victim on the ground in a seated or kneeling position. Immediately to the right of the bunk is the position on the floor where our victim was lying. What does this pattern suggest to you?"

"A beating?" asked the unsure pupil.

"More than that, Adrian, it suggests a coup de grâce blow. This was the final blow that sent poor Mr. Zhuang to the ground. He was kneeling or seated on the floor, his bloodstained body pressed against the mattress with his weight supported by his right arm and—bam— one last solid blow."

"You can tell all that by the splatter?" he asked with ignorance.

"Spatter!" Scott yelled as he set to work wrapping the bedsheet in butcher's paper, being careful to separate the head of the sheet from its foot with several layers of paper. "Okay, Adrian, it looks like the only thing left is the top bunk with the bloody T-shirt and crumpled letter and the east wall with the doorjamb and the toilet. That should be easy enough. Interestingly, there is no blood on the door itself, yet Inmate Vong pounded on the door several times. I guess that would explain the blood in the sink basin, around the faucet handles, and on the toilet seat. Now where is the towel he dried his hands on? Why, on the towel rack, of course. And look at this, hair fibers on the end cap of the towel rack here. We need to photograph that and collect them with sterile tweezers."

"What about the towel?" asked Adrian.

"Yup, that too but after we get that hair," Scott replied.

"What about doing the presumptive tests for the bloodstains?" he inquired.

"I collected an extra swab from each pattern. We'll do them back at the lab using the phenolphthalein and Hexagon OBTI tests," Scott responded. They collected their equipment and evidence bags.

"Make sure the window is closed and all electrical appliances and lights are off. We're going to boot the door just in case we need to come back in after the autopsy," Scott instructed. With that, Adrian set to work securing the cell. Scott handed him the boot device that allowed them to place a padlock over the Folger Adam locking mechanism.

"The cell is ours until further notice," Scott told Sergeant Hatch as he descended the stairs.

"So what made the South riot the worst crime scene?" asked young Adrian, reminding Scott of his promise to provide the details.

"Well, Adrian, two white neo-Nazi types got jumped by a couple of dozen angry Southerners. It scared one of them so bad that he soiled his boxers. They both had the right idea, though, and began flinging the feces at the Southerners, who smartly beat a retreat out of the dormitory."

"No way, like monkeys?" asked the shocked and somewhat disgusted investigator.

"Hey, I'm not blaming them. It was their weapon of convenience, so to speak. Well, when I got there, I could see reddish-brown speckles everywhere in the dorm. It was on the lockers, the bunks, and the ceiling. At first, I thought I had an incredible bloodletting event and that the whole area would need to be mapped. Of course, the closer I got, my olfactory senses told me it was splatter of a different kind. I still had to collect samples because some of it hit a few of the Southerners. It was, without a doubt, the nastiest crime scene I have ever processed. I also learned something that day—an inmate can be charged with a felony for gassing an officer with fecal matter, but there is nothing preventing them from flinging shit on one of their own. Nobody got prosecuted."

"Disgusting" was all Adrian said as they returned to the office.

Chapter 4

One Man's Interview

"Dog, Dog, that shit was off the hook!" exclaimed the excited sergeant Phillips.

"What, Tyrus, what was off the hook?"

"That was the weirdest interview I have ever sat in on. That guy, the DA guy, is way out there. Listen to this. First of all, he didn't do *Miranda* or anything. Vong was in cuffs, and we were in ad seg, and he didn't think it was necessary to read him his rights. Then Vong started going on about his cellie, uh, Zhuang, about how Zhuang was a hired assassin who was paid to kill him. While he was explaining all this, he stops and asks if it would be all right if he said a prayer for Mr. Zhuang. I said sure, but I thought he was just going to say a quick prayer or something, but instead, he sits on the floor with his legs crossed and starts doing this chanting and stuff. And it goes on for about five minutes with both of us just watching. Finally, he gets back up and sits in his chair. Then the DA guy—what's his name?"

"Dave Christiansen," Scott replied.

"Yeah, he starts talking to Vong about Thai kickboxing and about Thailand when he was stationed there in the army back in the 1980s. He told Vong that he was a big Thai kickboxing fan and that he was stationed in Bangkok and always went to the matches. Oh, and he said he watched Ultimate Fighting and cage fighting all the time. Dog, they talked for twenty, thirty minutes about that shit. And then out of nowhere, the DA guy closes his notebook, pats Vong on his forearm, and says, 'This looks like a case of self-defense to me.' I couldn't believe what I was hearing. So I interrupted, and I thought I better ask some questions about what happened. Vong starts to explain what happened. He said he was sitting on the top bunk, writing a letter to his mother or son or something."

"He was," Scott interrupted.

"Yeah, but he said he was watching TV and writing a letter when he was attacked by Inmate Zhuang. He said that he told Zhuang he didn't want to fight, and he kicked him down. He said that Zhuang kept getting back up and pulling at him and punching him in the mouth and legs, so he kicked him down again. That's when he jumped down from the bunk, and he said that Zhuang attacked him again."

"You wouldn't think that little old man had it in him," Scott said sarcastically.

"There's more. Right in the middle of my interviewing him, the DA guy turns on his digital camera and starts looking at the photos he took of Zhuang's injuries, and he starts asking Vong questions about the injuries. He asked him, 'How did he get this injury or that injury?' And Vong would think for a minute and say, 'It must have happened when I kicked him,' and stuff like that."

"What's wrong with that?"

"Dog, he was sitting at an angle, and Vong could see the screen, and if you ask me, I think he knew Vong could see them."

"You've got to be kidding me. An investigator actually showing the suspect a photograph of the victim's injuries. Even inadvertently, that's insane," Scott protested, adding, "The suspect can choreograph the entire event if he sees the injuries."

"Dog, that's exactly what he did. He asked him about that purple bruise on Zhuang's back, and Vong peeped at the screen and said that he kicked him in the back because Zhuang turned his back to him, thinking it was strong and tried to backkick him, but it didn't work, and Vong was able to kick him several times in the back. It was the craziest interview I have ever been on, and the DA guy kept saying it was self-defense through the entire interview. I swear, Dog, I thought he was going to ask Vong for an autograph. Once Vong did the prayer thing, I could tell that the DA guy was completely taken by him," proclaimed the befuddled sergeant.

"No matter, Ty, we'll just interview Vong later on if needs be. What was this about a hired assassin?"

"That's what Vong said. He said that his former cellmate, Inmate Vu-Yung, hired Zhuang to kill Vong and that Zhuang had no option but to follow through because he had already accepted the money."

"Isn't Vu-Yung Vietnamese?"

"I think so, yeah," replied Tyrus.

"Vong is Thai, and Zhuang is Chinese. It would have to be sanctioned by the Asian shot callers at central before anything like that could happen. Did he say why Vu-Yung hired Zhuang to kill him?" Scott asked.

"Yeah, because he snored" was Ty's short response.

"Well, it wouldn't be the first time we've had an inmate killed because he snored, but it would be the first time someone hired an assassin to do it. The thing I don't get is, why would Vu-Yung want Vong killed if he already moved out of the cell? Where is Vu-Yung now?" Scott inquired.

"He's still in the wing somewhere. I think he's on the second tier now in the back."

"Is Vong saying he snores so loud that he could be heard all the way down to the back of the second tier?"

"I couldn't say, Doggie."

"Well, Ty, we'll have to see what comes of it. We may not even have much input in this investigation. I'll do my incident report, crime scene report, and bloodstain pattern analysis, and we'll see where it goes from there. It should be a no-brainer—two inmates in a cell, and one turns up dead. The injuries to Vong are minor, and the injuries to Zhuang, including the defensive ones, are significant. It shouldn't take a brain surgeon to figure this one out."

"Anything good in the cell?" asked Tyrus.

"Yeah, we got some good bloodstain patterns and blood evidence but nothing in the way of weapons or the like. That cell tells a story though. A little bit of analysis, and we should have a complete picture of what happened in there. It's odd, but there was no blood evidence up high on the walls or on the ceiling, even though it was a pretty violent incident, and Zhuang was bleeding from the mouth and head."

"Well, Doggie, I can tell you one thing—it wasn't self-defense."

Chapter 5

One Month Later

"Doggett! Doggett!" bellowed the irritating sergeant Phillips from his office as Scott descended the staircase into the basement complex that contained the security and investigations unit. Scott ignored him as he generally did that early in the morning.

"Doggett! Doggett, you are late!" he shouted. Still, Scott ignored him while putting his frozen entrée into the freezer and his small bottle of Mountain Dew into the refrigerator. Mountain Dew was Scott's one vice. His doctor told him he must forgo his one daily pleasure, but Scott told him he would get his soda when he pried his Colt .45 1911A1 out of his dead right hand and his Dew out of the left. His doctor said it would be sooner than Scott thought.

"Doggett! You're late, Doggett!" Tyrus brayed. It was two minutes to the seven o'clock hour, and he knew he was not late.

"Doggett! Doggett! We arrive on time around here!" he continued shouting.

"Phillips, there are times when I wish your father had never whistled at your mother!" Scott yelled back as he stepped into his office. After the laughter died down in the institutional gang investigations office, Tyrus hurried into Scott's office.

"No, serious, Dog, I need to talk to you," he stated in an anxious tone.

"Why didn't you say so in the first place?" Scott asked as he snapped a new battery onto his Motorola radio.

"Look, I just got an email from Elisa Foyle, the court liaison. She got a decline from the DA's office on the Vong case."

"No way!" Scott exclaimed. "Shit, Ty, I didn't even know she sent the reports over. Did she say why?"

"I'll give you one guess."

"Self-defense," Scott answered with confidence.

"You guessed it. That ain't right, Dog."

"No, Tyrus, it isn't right. I didn't even have a chance to give them my opinion of the crime scene. I'll call Elisa right now."

"Hi, Dog," Elisa said into the telephone receiver.

"How'd you know it was me?" Scott asked.

"Who else would call me before seven thirty in the morning? Besides, I have a cheat phone now. I can see the extension of the person who is calling me. Did Ty tell you about Vong?"

Scott had known Elisa Foyle for more than fifteen years. He worked with her husband, Darryl, back in the early '90s in Alameda Hall at the North Facility. Elisa was a country girl, a vivacious blond, and quite capable of handling herself with the all-male inmate population. She did it, however, in a manner that was firm but polite. "Elisa, I didn't even know that you sent the reports over. Who did the decline?"

"Your friend Richard Rainwater."

"Playing it safe again. I'll give him a call. Maybe he can give it a second look or at least let me put in my two cents' worth."

DDA Richard Rainwater was an enigma. He's a Florida native who moved to Mississippi to attend Ole Miss. After graduating with a degree in law, for some reason even he can't explain, he moved to California and took a job with the district attorney's office. He was a gun aficionado. He believed in the death penalty and harsh punishment for criminals. He was short and had a Southern drawl, and Scott always had a mental picture of Richard with a mint julep, a string tie, and seersucker. In spite of all this, Richard was extremely picky about the cases he prosecuted, and he was more inclined to accept a lowball plea agreement than go to jury trial. It drove Scott crazy.

Scott actually put more years of work into one investigation than the suspect received as punishment. No, it was not a lie. Scott once put three years of hard work into a dope case before he made the bust. Richard took a plea agreement for two years at 50 percent; that was a one-year sentence.

"Richard, it's Dog. I just heard about the Vong case."

"It's a clear-cut case of self-defense, Dog. A man has a right to defend himself. The old man attacked him. He had no choice but to defend himself. It's not his fault that he was a better fighter than the old man. Ya roll the dice, and ya take your chances."

"Look, Richard, I don't want to say that your investigator didn't do a good job on this one, but I don't think he did a thorough job. Give me a chance to investigate this thing fully, and you can take another look at it. If it is still self-defense, then it is self-defense, but I think we owe it to the family of Inmate Zhuang to make sure every aspect of this homicide is covered."

"Well, it's your case. If you want to waste your time investigating it some more, you go right on ahead. But unless you come up with something remarkable, I doubt I'll change my mind."

"What if I said Mr. Zhuang's son graduated from Ole Miss?"

"Did he?"

"No, I wish he had, but I do think he's serving in the U.S. Marine Corps, stationed in the Philippines."

"Well, for you, Dog, I'll take another look—when you're done, that is."

If there was one thing Scott did know about DDA Richard Rainwater, it was that he was a patriot, loved his country, and loved the United States military. Scott was not a bad person for playing the military card, and for the record, Mr. Zhuang's son was a gunnery sergeant in the marine corps.

"Oz!" Scott yelled for the third time without a response. "Adrian, where the hell is Oz?"

"He's here somewhere. I saw him warming up his lunch a minute ago."

"He's probably enjoying his repast with the gang guys. Why can't he eat his lunch in here with us?"

"Guess he doesn't like the company," Adrian replied.

"Tyrus," Scott said into the telephone receiver.

"What do you want Doggett?"

"Is Oz over there?"

"Every day at this time, Doggie."

"When he is finished with his burger, tell him I need to talk to him, that is, if it is convenient for him."

"Oz," Tyrus was heard saying aside, "your uncle wants you."

"Very funny, Ty."

A few minutes later, Oswaldo walked through the door, asking, "What you got, Scotty?"

"Oz, the DA declined prosecution in the Vong case."

"The Vong case, which one is that?" he asked true to form as he chomped down the remaining onion rings.

"Oh, Oz, why can't you pay attention for a minute?" Scott said as he rubbed his forehead with his right hand. "It's the Zhuang homicide, the one in Echo Wing? Last month? None of this ring a bell? Oz, it's the guy who got kicked to death."

"Oh, yeah, yeah, yeah, yeah. They didn't prosecute?"

"No, Oz, they didn't, but they are giving us another chance. We have some work to do."

"Like?"

"Like interviewing the former cellmate, the housing unit staff, the other Asians in the hall, and finally Vong himself. We need to do all the stuff we should have done before it went to the DA's office."

"What are your plans?" asked Oswaldo.

"I intend to interview Vong with a Thai interpreter, and I plan on building a mock-up of the cell in miniature. I'm going to have Vong go over his version of what happened using a model of himself and his cellmate. I want to videotape his interview and the demonstration."

"When?"

"Day after tomorrow, Oz. Can you do the videotaping?"

"That's Saturday, isn't it?"

"And?"

"We'll have to get permission from the lieutenant."

"I'll take care of that, Oz. Are you in?"

"I wouldn't miss it, Scotty, but where are you going to find a Thai interpreter?"

"I'm thinking Sergeant Palagon would make a good translator. He was a major in the Thai army during the war."

"Which side?"

"I think the Thais were on our side. Does it really matter, Oz?" Scott replied. There was no reply as Oswaldo had already lost interest in the conversation and was making his way back to his cheeseburger.

"Saturday at nine!" Scott yelled as Oswaldo stepped back into the gang unit.

Chapter 6

The Interview

"You built that?" asked an amazed Oswaldo as he looked at the desktop model Scott made of the cell.

"Sure did. Looks pretty good, if I say so myself. The only problem is that I couldn't find any figures that were the right size. These are a little small."

"What are they?"

"They are artist's anatomical figurines. I painted one green and one orange. You can bend them. You can even bend the arms and legs and feet anyway you want. He can use these to show us what he says happened."

At nine o'clock precisely, Oswaldo and Scott were waiting in the administrative segregation unit captain's office for staff to escort Inmate Vong for the interview. Oswaldo familiarized himself with the video recorder while Scott briefed Sergeant Palagon on the format of the interview. Scott also confirmed that Sergeant Palagon was a state-certified Thai interpreter. Oh, and for the record, he was a captain in the Thai marines. He came to this country in 1979, achieved citizenship, applied for the department, and was accepted in 1992.

As Scott heard the sounds of chains jingling outside the door, he activated the digital recorder and cued Oswaldo to begin his videotape. The door opened, and two large escort officers entered with the fettered inmate Vong. One of the large escort officers pulled back a chair at the end of the table, turned it around, placed a meaty hand on Vong's shoulder, and applied sufficient pressure to achieve the desired response. Inmate Vong was seated. The two bulls exited the room, closing the door behind them without a word being spoken.

"Mr. Vong, I am Investigator Doggett. This is my partner, Investigator Castaneda, and this is Sergeant Palagon from the North Facility. I know that you speak English and that your English is very good, but I wanted to make sure that we had an interpreter present who could clarify anything that needed clarification. I want to interview you about what happened between you and your cellmate, Mr. Zhuang. Before I do that, however, I want to make sure that you are aware of your rights pursuant to the *Miranda* decision. Not only am I going to advise you of your rights in English but Sergeant Palagon will also advise you of your rights in Thai. Are you ready?"

"I am, sir," responded the meek inmate.

Scott advised him of his rights, pausing between lines to give Sergeant Palagon a chance to catch up. Inmate Vong acknowledged these rights and exchanged pleasantries with the sergeant in the Thai language. Inmate Vong suggested his English language skills were sufficient to understand Scott's questions but understood Sergeant Palagon would remain in the room just in case there was a word or two with which he was unfamiliar. "Mr. Vong, can you tell me in your own words exactly what happened on that day?"

"I will tell you what I can. I was on my bunk watching *The Price Is Right* and writing a letter to my son. He is a sergeant, like you," he said, looking over at Sergeant Palagon, "in the United States Army. I am so very proud of him, but we are not good friends like I would wish to be. I do not know what to write, and I make several attempts, but the words do not come. My cellie, Mr. Zhuang, is on the bottom bunk. I think he is reading. He stands up, and he say it is time and that he must kill me. I say he is crazy, and he should go back to reading his book, but he punch me in my leg, and he say it is time we fight because he want to kill me."

"How were you sitting on your bunk? Did you have your legs crossed? Were you facing the door or the window?" Scott asked.

"I had my legs crossed, and I was facing my TV, which is next to the door."

"Go on," Scott encouraged.

"He keep punching me in my leg and trying to pull me from the bed. He then stands on toilet and punches me in the mouth and grabs at my shirt like this," he said while leaning forward to where his restrained arm could reach his shirt collar. "I say no, and I hit him like this." He kicked with his restrained right foot.

"Now when you say 'hit,' do you mean kick?" Scott asked.

"Yes, in your language, it is a kick. In Thailand, it is a hit. I professional Thai kickboxer. I use language of my sport. I kick, as you say, and he fall to the ground. I heard a 'lump' sound. I think he has no air in his body, and he stay on the floor, but he get back up. I hit him—kick as you say—and he falls again. I move back to my pillow because I know he can reach me from the toilet, but he climbs on top of the locker across from me, and he hits me again."

"How did he hit you, and where?" Scott asked.

"He hit me in chest and leg. I hit, kick him again, but he does not fall. The locker was not good, and it moved, and he fell down. He hit his head on the . . . how you say?" He turned to Sergeant Palagon and said a few words in Thai.

"Towel bar," replied the sergeant.

"Yes, towel bar," answered Inmate Vong.

"How did he hit his head?" Scott asked.

"He hit the side of his head here." He pointed to the right side of his head. "I think he stay down but no. I did not want to fall from so high. I know I would be hurt. So I jump down, and I say, 'Okay, you want to fight, I fight.' I kick him, and he fall down. He get back up, and he turn his back to me because he know his back is strong. He think because he is kung fu master, he has strong back, and he can backkick me. But he is wrong. I kick him in the back one, two, three, four times, and he fall to the floor."

"Did you kick him again once he was on the floor?" Scott asked.

"Yes, yes, I kick him again in the leg because I think he will get back up, and he will kill me."

"What did you do after you kicked him again?"

"I pick up the letter, the papers from the letter that were on the floor, and I put them in the bag."

"The plastic bag by the toilet?" Scott asked.

"Yes, yes, by the door," he responded.

"What did you do next?"

"I wash. I wash my hands and my face."

"Did you take off your shirt?"

"Yes, I take off my shirt, and I put it on my bunk. Then I wash my face. I dry my face and my hands, and I knock on door. The lady replied to tell her who I was. I say Vong. She say, 'Where are you?' I say cell 346. After five, ten minutes, the sergeant come to the door with other officers. The lady look into the cell, and she say, 'What you do?' I say I hit my cellie because he want to fight. I do not want to fight, but he want to fight. I say how sorry I am."

"Why do you think your cellmate wanted to fight with you?" Scott inquired.

"He was paid to kill me, and they have already paid him, so he must fight with me. He is kung fu master. Vu-Yung hire him to kill me."

"Vu-Yung? Who is Vu-Yung?" Scott asked.

"My old cellmate, Vu-Yung. He is young man. He want me killed."

"So Inmate Vu-Yung is your former cellmate?"

"Yes, Vu-Yung, he young man."

"Why would Inmate Vu-Yung want to kill you, might I ask?"

"Because I snore. He say he kill me because I snore. He cannot sleep, and he tell me he will kill me. That is why he left. He get cell move to, uh, other side with Le. He make Mr. Zhuang move into my cell, and he pay him to kill me."

"How do you know this?" Scott asked.

"Mr. Zhuang tell me so."

"How long were you and Mr. Zhuang cellies?"

"Two, three months."

"Has he tried to kill you before?"

"He always say, 'We fight, we fight.' But I say, 'No, no fight.' I say, 'You go find other cell.' I tell Mr. Lee. I tell Mr. Lee he must do something. Mr. Zhuang very bad man. He not let me have any space in the cell. He not let me have a locker. He not let me be anywhere except on my bunk. He very mean man. He yell at me all the time. He say I snore too loud. I cannot help snore. I snore, he snore, people snore."

"Who is Mr. Lee?"

"He is Chinese. He is big man with the Chinese. I go to Mr. Lee. I say, 'Mr. Lee, you must find other place for Mr. Zhuang.' Mr. Lee say he cannot because Mr. Zhuang receive money from Mr. Vu-Yung to kill me, and there is nothing he can do."

"Did you go to the officers in your wing?" Scott asked.

"Yes, many, many times, and they say no. They say I must stay with Mr. Zhuang."

"Did you tell them it was an emergency and that your life was in danger?"

"No, I do not. I think they say no, so what good would it do? I do not want to kill. I like people. I kill once before in Thailand. I kill American serviceman. He challenge me to fight, and then he use knife. I did not want to kill him, but I had no choice. I like American servicemen."

"When was this?" Scott asked.

"Oh, maybe twenty years ago or more."

Changing the subject Scott asked, "Does Inmate Vu-Yung live with Mr. Lee now?"

"No, he with Mr. Le, L-E. He is Vietnamese."

"Where does Mr. Lee live?"

"He lives on first tier, in the back."

"Can you describe him?"

"Very tall old man. He has glasses and gray hair."

"Okay, Mr. Vong, I have a model of your cell. I also have two figures that you can use to represent yourself and Mr. Zhuang. The green figure will be Mr. Zhuang, and you will be the orange figure. Can you demonstrate to us how the fight occurred?"

"Yes, yes, I can do this," he replied, reaching for the figures.

"Uh, I think it's apparent that you are not going to be able to do this with your restraints on. I think it will be okay to take them off you. You won't do any kicking if I take off the handcuffs?"

"No, no, I do not kick you," he said with a laugh.

"Good because we are still videotaping this, and I would hate to have you kick my butt on camera," Scott said as he took off the restraints. He handed him the figurines, and Inmate Vong choreographed the events as best he could with the small mannequins while Oz videotaped his demonstration.

"I hear you are pretty agile for your age. Can you show me what you showed us when you were in the holding cell?" Scott asked.

"You mean with the wall?" he clarified.

"Yes, when you put your leg up on the wall."

"Oh, yes, very easy." With that, he placed his foot on the wall at shoulder height without hopping or jumping. It was very impressive.

"Incredible," Scott said. "Well, Mr. Vong, I want to thank you for your cooperation. I think I have everything that I need to complete this investigation."

"May I please," he said, returning to his seat, "may I please speak with the sergeant?"

"Be my guest," Scott said as he replaced his body chains and handcuffs.

Inmate Vong leaned toward Sergeant Palagon and began a dialogue in Thai. After a few minutes, he clasped his hands together with his extended fingers touching and lowered his forehead to tap his fingertips. Sergeant Palagon did the same. Scott called for the officers to escort Inmate Vong back to his cell. Once he had left the room, Sergeant Palagon informed Scott that Inmate Vong told him he did not want to kill Inmate Zhuang, only to stop him from trying to hurt him. He said that he had prayed every night since the incident for the soul of Mr. Zhuang and that he encouraged Sergeant Palagon to do the same. For the record, Scott asked Sergeant Palagon to be more specific about what Inmate Vong had told him, to which the sergeant replied that Vong stated, "I did not want to kill him, but I had no choice."

After concluding the interview and turning off the recorders, Scott asked Sergeant Palagon, "Well, do you believe him?"

"It's hard to say. There was something surreal about the way he said that to me," replied the sergeant.

"Odd how each time he kills someone, he says he had no choice," Scott remarked.

"I wonder if he really did kill one of our soldiers," inquired Oswaldo.

"It would take far too long to find out, and it isn't relevant to our investigation."

"So what do we do now?"

"We start asking questions of a lot of people, Oz, and the sooner, the better."

"Where do we start?" he asked.

"We start with Mr. Lee."

After making copies of the audio and video recordings, Scott booked the originals into evidence. He also processed the model and figures into evidence as well. Afterward, he sat down to write his report and transcribe the interview.

Chapter 7

Mr. Lee Et Al.

Oswaldo and Scott sat in the unit 2 sergeant's office, waiting for Inmate Lee to be brought down from his cell. Although the facility was no longer on the mandatory lockdown status that followed a suspicious death, there was limited inmate movement in Echo Wing. It was still unknown how the Asian inmate population was going to deal with the homicide of one of their own, even if it was by the hand of one of their own.

Normally, all Asian inmates banded together into a larger community regardless of their geographic ethnicity and historical animosities. There was always strength in numbers, and the Asian inmate population made up one of the smaller populations at California State Prison–Gabilan. Regardless of their lack of numbers, the Asian inmates were extremely resourceful and usually had no difficulty forming the alliances that they needed to fend off the other predatory gangs and groups. Of course, they were also creative in their ability to smuggle contraband into the institution.

Electronics were their gig—DVD players with the customary pornography, cellular telephones, bootleg CDs, and the occasional PlayStation. These were high-value contraband items in a prison and much appreciated by the other inmate populations. Therefore, the Asian inmates were generally left alone. That and most of the other groups of inmates labored under the false impression that all Asians knew kung fu or karate.

The door to the sergeant's office opened, and in walked Inmate Lee. He was slender and tall, about six foot one. He was a very distinguished-looking Chinese gentleman of about sixty. Inmate Lee was serving a life sentence for the murder-for-hire slaying of his business partner. He was not without his influence over the Asian inmate population, and because of his prowess as the number one electronic distributor in the Central Facility, he was well liked by all races and ideological persuasions. He was holding a bowl of Top Ramen noodles and a pair of chopsticks. "You wished to see me?" he asked.

"Yes, Mr. Lee, I did. Sorry to interrupt your lunch. I am Investigator Doggett, and this is my partner, Investigator Castaneda. We'd like to ask you a few questions about the unfortunate Mr. Zhuang."

"Oh yes, a very sad thing to happen. I had just spoken with him that very morning. He received a care package, and he gave me some canned fish and candy."

"What time was that?" Scott asked.

"It was after we returned from breakfast release and before we locked up for the first-watch status."

"So about 0900 hours?"

"Yes, more or less."

"How did he appear? Was he nervous or anxious about something?" Scott asked.

"No, he seemed very happy. He received the package the night before. We are both members of the Chinese Christian Church, and they sent him the package. We talked about the service we had last Sunday. Our pastor came from San Francisco and preached a sermon that was very good."

"Has he ever expressed any concern about his cellmate?"

"Yes, several times. He said that Mr. Vong was threatening to harm him, and he wanted a cell move."

"When was this?" Scott inquired.

"Several months ago, when he first come to E Wing. He did not know how to approach the officers because this was the first time he had been in prison. I took him to the officers and explained that Mr. Vong had threatened Mr. Zhuang. They asked if he was in fear for his life, but he said no. The officer said that Mr. Zhuang had a lower-bunk chrono because of his bad back and that he would have to find a cell with a bottom bunk."

"Was this the only time he went to the officers?"

"To my knowledge, yes."

"Do you remember which watch it was?"

Mr. Lee responded, "It was the third-watch officers."

"And did he say anything to you about a cell move any time after that?" asked Oswaldo.

"No, but he did say that if he asked again, the officers would only say no."

"Did he ever say anything about being afraid that Mr. Vong would kill him?" Scott asked.

"No, but he did say that Mr. Vong would snore very loud. And when he would tell Mr. Vong that he could not sleep because of his snoring, Mr. Vong would demonstrate his ability to kick very high."

"To your knowledge, did Mr. Zhuang have any special training in kung fu?"

"He said that he was trained in kung fu when he was a young man in the military."

"Did he say he was a master?" asked Oswaldo.

"No, but he would be wise to not say so if he was not."

"Mr. Lee," Scott began, "this may sound odd, but I have to ask. Have you heard anything about Mr. Vu-Yung paying money to Mr. Zhuang to kill Mr. Vong?"

A look of amazement came over Inmate Lee, and he dropped his chopsticks into the bowl. "That is a very funny proposition," he said before bursting into laughter.

"A very funny proposition indeed!" he exclaimed with a belly laugh.

"A little too far fetched?" Scott asked.

"Mr. Zhuang was a kind old man. He was good Christian man. He had a very bad back. Besides, how could Vu-Yung make such arrangements? Mr. Zhuang came from X Wing directly to this wing. No opportunity for Vu-Yung to go to X Wing and make such arrangements. Why would Vu-Yung make such arrangements?"

"Mr. Lee, that's what I'd like to know. Thank you for your help. If I have any more questions, do you mind if I come and talk with you?" Scott asked.

"You may call on me at any time," he responded as he stood and exited the room.

"What's next?" asked Oswaldo as they sat in the office recently vacated by Inmate Lee.

"We employ the Vernon Geberth method of homicide investigations. We canvass the area, and we talk. I want to talk to the two inmates who were on either side of cell 346."

"You want to know what they saw?"

"No, Oz, I want to know what they heard."

Scott summoned the housing unit officers and informed them that he wanted to talk to Inmate Enriquez in bunk 345 upper, Inmate Mendoza in bunk 345 lower, Inmate Smith in 347 upper, and Baker in 347 lower. Scott then told them that after he had interviewed those inmates, he wanted to talk to Inmate Vu-Yung and his cellmate, Inmate Le. After a few minutes, a small chubby Hispanic inmate was standing at the door. Oswaldo opened the door, and the inmate walked in. Scott motioned for him to sit in the chair at the side of the desk. The inmate held out his identification card, which Scott received. "Enriquez?"

"Si" was the response. Already, Scott knew he was in trouble, and Oswaldo diligently stepped in and began interviewing the inmate in the Spanish language.

They discovered that Inmate Enriquez stood on the tier with Inmate Zhuang and Inmate Vong just before the lockup. He confirmed Inmate Zhuang gave canteen items to Inmate Lee and learned that Inmate Zhuang also gave candy to Inmate Enriquez and his cellmate, Inmate Mendoza. He said although he could not converse with Inmate Zhuang, he found him to be a very amiable and kind old man. He said that after the lockup, he and his cellmate began preparing lunch. They were listening to music on the radio. Unfortunately, the radio was so loud that they did not hear any commotion in the adjoining cell and were only aware that something had happened when an officer tied crime scene tape to the exterior handle of their cell door.

Inmate Enriquez was excused, and Inmate Mendoza was interviewed in English in much the same manner. He provided the same information but also informed them that Inmate Zhuang did not seem happy to be in the cell with Inmate Vong. He said Inmate Vong snored excessively. He said that he and his cellmate could hear the snoring through the concrete wall, and they knew that Inmate Zhuang must have suffered. He did not know if Inmate Zhuang ever requested a cell move, but he did hear Inmate Vong yelling at Inmate Zhuang a few weeks earlier. He said Inmate Vong demanded that Inmate Zhuang find another cellmate. He rarely saw Inmate Zhuang and Inmate Vong together outside the cell. Inmate Zhuang preferred to sit with the Christian inmates in the dayroom, most of whom were Mexican nationals, and read his Bible.

Before leaving, Scott asked Inmate Mendoza if he ever saw Inmate Vong practicing kickboxing techniques. Inmate Mendoza said that he would often see Inmate Vong throwing kicks at the walls and doing different stretches in the cell. Scott asked him if he ever saw Inmate Zhuang practicing kung fu, to which Inmate Mendoza said that he never had and felt it was unlikely as Inmate Zhuang complained of terrible back pains.

Scott had known Inmate Curty-Bo Baker for almost two decades. He was his tier porter back in the days when Scott ran a housing unit, and they had a good rapport. He was always respectful toward Scott and always assisted him in resolving any problems that existed between his gang, the Crips, and the other factions in the housing unit. Now he was in his early fifties and had mellowed considerably from the turbulent youth that led to a gang-related shooting and a life behind prison walls. "Mr. Doggett," he said as he entered the room.

"Have a seat, Curty-Bo. I need to ask you some questions about the incident with your former neighbors. How have you been?"

"Oh, Mr. Doggett, I'm afraid we're all getting too old for all this."

"No argument from me. Any luck with the parole board?" Scott asked.

"They gave me a two-year denial this time. Oh, don't worry, that's actually a good thing. I haven't received anything less than a five-year denial in the past, so I'm thinking that's a good thing. I have my niece out there now. She's a councilwoman in the LA area, and she wants to sponsor me. You know, she was only nine when I got locked up. Now she's a councilwoman. Ain't that something?"

"Remarkable. I hope she can do something for you, Curty-Bo. If anyone around here deserves a break, it's you. Tell me about your neighbors."

"Mr. Zhuang?" he asked.

"Yes and the day it happened," Scott replied.

"Mr. Zhuang just seemed like a nice old man. He was always asking how I was doing, and any time he had any candy, he would give me some. I like Baby Ruths, and he always would have the little ones. Yeah, I was in the cell that day. I was fixin' lunch and talkin' to my cellie. I heard a sound like someone was draggin' a locker around on the tier above me, but then I heard a thump on the wall next door. Well, I didn't think much about it until I heard Miss Del call for help."

"Del Toro?" Scott clarified.

"Yes, Miss Del Toro. She was shoutin' for Sergeant Hatch to get the medical people down here. Sure is a shame that something like that would happen to that old man. He just got here too. First time down and all, just a shame." Inmate Baker confirmed that Inmate Vong could "snore up a tempest" but didn't know if there were any animosities between the two cellmates. Scott wished him well and luck with his parole hearing.

His cellmate, Inmate Smith, was a little less amicable. "I don't want to talk about it. I'm still under duress. Just you mentioning it makes it all come back to me, and I'm having flashbacks. I may have to sue the state because I can't sleep at nights." Scott asked Inmate Smith if he wanted to see a psychiatrist or get counseling from the medical department or perhaps even the chaplain. "I'd rather go out to the yard with my friends."

"Request denied. Get back to your cell."

Inmate Vu-Yung was a young man, about twenty-six years old, yet he had a K number, which meant he was sixteen or seventeen when he was sentenced to an adult institution. Scott didn't ask him what he did to deserve such a punishment, but the tattoos on his forearms said it all—Tiny Rascals. The Tiny Rascals were a notorious Vietnamese street disruptive group responsible for a lot of killings in Lemon Hill, Sacramento. Among their specialties were home invasion robberies, kidnappings for ransom, drug distribution, and murders. In spite of his notoriety and youthfulness, he carried himself well and appeared to be well-educated. "You wished to speak with me, sir?"

"Yes, Vu-Yung, I did. Have a seat. I'd like to talk to you about your former cellmate, Mr. Vong," Scott replied.

"I understand, although I don't know much about the fight he had. You see, Thuwong is from Thailand, and my people are from Vietnam. We did not have very much in common, so I moved to the back of the hall with my friend. I really didn't know anything about what happened until the counselors conducted their interviews."

"Would it be fair to say Mr. Vong was a . . . well, a difficult person to live with?" Scott inquired.

"Oh, no, to the contrary, he was a very good cellie. We would cook our food, the food of our people, in the cell, and he was a very good cook. He kept to himself mostly, but he was a good cellie."

"What about his snoring?"

"It didn't really bother me. I just had to make sure that I got to sleep first."

"Vu-Yung, what is your first name?" Scott asked, trying to build a rapport.

"Manny," he replied.

"Manny? That's not very Vietnamese," Scott remarked.

"It is really Mi, but my friends call me Manny, although I am not sure why."

"All right, well, Mi, let me tell you what I have heard, and you can tell me if it is correct. I've heard that you and your former cellie did not get along very well at all and that you guys argued all the time. In fact, you argued about his snoring so much that you went to the housing unit staff and begged them for a cell move."

"I wanted a cell move because my friend, Le, was losing his cellie, and he wanted me to move in."

"Vu-Yung, the housing unit officers made an entry in their logbook. Why would they do that if it wasn't true?"

"I do not know, sir. Oh, Thuwong snored, but it was not a problem. As for the arguing, all cellies argue."

"What if I were to tell you that Mr. Vong said you hired Mr. Zhuang to kill him and that you paid him a considerable amount of money for his efforts? Is Vong lying too?"

"I would say that someone has been watching too much television. May I ask you something?"

"Yes, Mi, you may ask anything you want to ask," Scott responded.

"Why are you doing this?" he asked.

"Doing what exactly?" Scott asked in turn.

"Why are you investigating this?"

"Should I not be investigating a homicide?" he continued.

"Mr. Vong is a good man. He has been through a lot. He doesn't need to be investigated for this. He has a family out there, a son he is very proud of and a daughter. Mr. Zhuang was just an old man who probably would not have lived very long anyway."

"Mi, I am a homicide investigator. It is my duty to investigate this matter. I have an obligation not only to the people of the state of California but also to Mr. Zhuang and his bereaved family."

"I just think you are wasting your time," he said smugly.

Scott dismissed him and decided it would be a waste of time interviewing Inmate Le. Instead, he wanted to talk to the regular housing unit officers in Echo Wing. They were lucky in that Officer Del Toro was working that day. Del had been working at the Central Facility for the past twelve years. She was an experienced officer and knew how to deal with the inmates. Scott waited for her to finish the close B custody count and asked her if she had a few minutes to talk with him and Oswaldo. "I don't want to take up too much of your time, Del, but I would like to ask you a few more questions about Inmate Zhuang and Inmate Vong," Scott said as he followed her into the E Wing office.

"Dog, I'm a little busy," she said as she called in her count to the central control sergeant.

"I just wanted to ask if Inmate Zhuang ever asked for a cell move."

"Yes, within a few days after he got here from X Wing," she replied without hesitation.

"What did you tell him?" Scott asked.

"I asked him if it was an emergency, and he said no, so I told him that he couldn't move because he had a bottom bunk chrono, and he was close B custody. I told him he'd have to find a suitable cell, which would be nearly impossible because we just don't have that many Asian cells," she replied.

"Okay, Del, don't take offense, but I have to ask this next question. What would you have done if he told you he needed a cell move because his life depended on it?"

"I would have sent his ass back to X Wing," she said without batting an eye. It was the correct answer. Scott didn't push his luck with additional questions, and Oswaldo and Scott went back to the office.

Scott caught Sergeant Hatch later in the day on the telephone. He had not spoken with either Inmate Vong or Inmate Zhuang regarding a cell move but also would have made reasonable accommodations if it were a matter of life and death. The staff was well trained in such matters.

"What's next?" asked Oswaldo, who had already tired of this investigation and was ready to move on to something else.

"What's next is to try to contact the relatives of Inmate Zhuang and see if he had any formal training in the martial arts," Scott replied.

"How are you going to do that?" he asked.

"I am going to send a letter to their family attorney. He sent a letter a few weeks ago demanding we not destroy any evidence. It's pretty standard practice any time we have an in-custody suspicious death. The lawyers sense the blood in the water and just want to remind us that there might be legal action forthcoming. Aunt California has deep pockets," Scott said as he began typing an official letter to the attorney of the Zhuang clan. He also asked the attorney to check with the family if, by chance, any large sums of money were deposited into any bank accounts associated with their father.

Chapter 8

The Response

Two weeks had passed, and Oswaldo and Scott put the wraps on yet another drug operation with the successful service of a search warrant in the city of Bakersfield. It was a clever operation, to say the least. An inmate at the Central Facility had convinced the interfaith chaplain that there was a particular soft drink from Mexico that was manufactured with holy water from the Guadalupe shrine and that the Hispanic inmates at the facility would benefit from this water. The inmate's brother would be only too happy to drive down to Mexico and bring back the beatified beverage, which he would deliver to the chaplain. The chaplain would, in turn, bring it into the institution one six-pack at a time. Unbeknownst to the chaplain, one of every six cans of soft drink was loaded with about two ounces of black tar heroin. It was an ingenious operation. The brother would buy whatever cheap brand of soft drink he could find, cleverly remove the top of one of the cans, and empty out the contents. He would then add the heroin, reseal it, and paste on a new label. Once the loaded can was attached to a ring with the other five, it was almost impossible to tell which one held the product.

The entire operation was discovered in the garage of the Bakersfield residence during the service of the search warrant along with six ounces of black tar heroin and four ounces of marijuana. They elected not to have criminal charges filed against the chaplain. Scott did not think it was his intent to smuggle drugs into a state prison. He was just another product of the highly manipulative nature of the inmate population. He was, however, terminated from state service for overfamiliarity and would need to find a flock somewhere other than in prison.

Scott had forgotten he had sent the letter to the attorney of the Zhuang family and was apprehensive about receiving a letter from a law firm. "What am I being sued for this time?" Scott asked as Oswaldo passed out the mail. "Ah, it's from the Zhuang family attorney. None of the children were aware of any specialized training their father might have had in martial arts."

"So Vong is lying?" asked Oswaldo.

"Not necessarily, Oz. It just might mean that Zhuang might have just talked up a good story, one that might have precipitated his death."

"I don't follow," announced the bewildered Oswaldo.

"Well, if you were an old man first time in prison and you didn't want anyone messing with you, it is not out of the realm of logic that you might just let slip that you are a kung fu master."

"But I studied Brazilian jujitsu," replied Scott's partner.

"No, Oz, not you, Inmate Zhuang."

"Oh, I get it now. That would work until you came upon someone who really was a kung fu master," he wisely articulated.

"My point exactly, Oz. There's more. The family is unaware of any external bank accounts held by their father and believes the only money he had was in trust at our facility. He, of course, is requesting to be notified immediately should our investigation determine that there is, in fact, a bank account outside the institution. Hmm, he must be in need of a retainer. Do we have Inmate Zhuang's property?" Scott asked.

"Yeah, yeah, yeah, it's boxed up in the storage room," said the attentive Oswaldo.

"Okay, little buddy, while I am going through the property, I want you to go over to the trust account office and get a statement of the monies that were held at the institution for Inmate Zhuang."

All that was possessed by Inmate Henry Zhuang at Gabilan State Prison fit into one archive box; its contents included a plastic bowl, plastic spoon, comb, plastic tumbler, one small English/Chinese Bible, toothbrush and toothpaste, a photograph of his son in marine dress blues, a dated photograph of his daughter, a photograph with him standing between two Asian ministers from the church taken three months before his death, one letter from one of the ministers, one letter from his son postmarked from the Philippines originally sent to the county jail, and a few canned food items—what remained of the care package. Scott read the letters and thumbed through the Bible for any clues that might have been hidden in the binding or between the pages; there was nothing to assist the investigation to be found. Scott placed the three photographs together on the scanner and printed an 8" × 10" copy, which he retained in the investigative file as a reminder of why he would push this case to a conclusion.

Oswaldo returned from the trust account office with the final statement for Inmate Zhuang—$54.12. The records reflected that he received fifty dollars of that sum the day after his death. It was a gift from the church.

"Well, Oz, I think we've done all that we can do in this case. We've interviewed every one of whom I can think. We've explored the hired assassin theory as much as possible. I just don't know what else to do. The problem is we only have two eyewitnesses to what exactly happened in that cell, and one of them is dead. At least this time, we have Inmate Vong on tape."

"Are you going to take it up to the DA's office?"

"Yes, Oz, I'll take it up as soon as I finish my report. I just can't think of anything else to do in this case. We have an old man who was brutally kicked to death and a suspect who has a small cut to his inner lip, a cut he may have made himself when he jumped down from the upper bunk. In our favor, there are three bloodstain patterns that don't match with his story of the fight. The impact spatter on the lower bunk, the castoff on the cardboard, and the expectorated blood on the garbage box suggest that Mr. Zhuang was on the ground at least twice during the incident. Vong conveniently left that out of his narrative."

Scott sat down and began typing his report. He started with the incident and crime scene and included the bloodstain pattern analysis, interviews, and victimology report. He made the report as impartial and unbiased as possible, injecting no personal opinions or conclusions. He stated only the facts and left it to the reader to be the judge. In all, the report was twenty-nine pages in length, single spaced. Scott felt it was far superior to the page and a half, double-spaced report submitted by the DA investigator. Lieutenant Templeton signed off on the report, even though he didn't actually read it, and Scott was ready to meet with Deputy District Attorney Rainwater once again.

Chapter 9

The Verdict

"No, Dog, I'm not filin' it, and that's my final word on the matter," declared Richard Rainwater with his trademark Southern grin.

He continued, "Self-defense is self-defense. There is nothing in your report that changes my mind, especially since I have a senior district attorney's office investigator who is going to testify that it was pure and simple a case of self-defense."

"Rich, don't you think the injuries alone are disproportionate to self-defense?" Scott pleaded.

"Just means he picked the wrong guy to fight. That's all, Dog."

"All right, what if you don't charge him with murder, but what about manslaughter? Surely, it meets the definition of manslaughter—Penal Code section 192(a), manslaughter, voluntary, upon a sudden quarrel or heat of passion. Come on, Rich, it fits."

"One-nine-seven, justifiable homicide, when committed in defense or habitation, property, or person against one who manifestly intends to do any violence to any person therein. That fits," argued the attorney.

"But, Richard, we only have his word that it was self-defense, and some of what he says is not supported by the bloodstain evidence in the cell."

"So he left out a few details. When you are fightin' for your life, you tend to leave out a few of the details. Besides, bloodstain experts are a dime a dozen. He can get one to say that your analysis is wrong. I'm not filin'," he said with a sense of finality.

"All right, Richard, I can appreciate your point of view, but I'm taking this one to the attorney general's office. It's nothing personal, but I just think that we need to have another set of eyes look at it."

"You do what you gotta do, Dog, but I don't think they are going to be of much help to you."

"Maybe not, Rich, but I have to try," Scott said as he shook his hand and walked out of the office with an enormous feeling of failure.

"I just didn't do enough, Ty. I failed this one miserably. What do you think? Do you think it was self-defense?" Scott asked his former partner in criminal investigations.

"No, Dog, I don't think it was self-defense at all. I mean, I see his point though. He has an investigator who is going to testify that it was self-defense. Even if the DA doesn't call him, you can bet the defense will," interjected Sergeant Phillips.

"Yeah, that, and they probably don't want it to get out that their investigator inadvertently showed the suspect a photograph of the guy he killed," Scott replied.

"I do agree with you, though, Dog, that they should at least look at this as manslaughter if nothing else."

"Thanks, Ty. That's why I want to take it to the attorney general's office. Unfortunately, I have to prove misconduct on the part of the DA's office before they will even look at it."

"Just how are you going to do that?" he asked.

"*State of California v. Inmate Cooper,*" Scott replied.

"Cooper? Why does that name sound familiar?"

"It should sound familiar, Tyrus. It was your case—well, yours and Alex Rowland's," Scott responded.

"Right, I remember. Cooper killed that kid . . . uh, what's his name? Jones, Johnson?"

"Rodgers, Ian Rodgers. Knocked him out with two punches and then strangled him in the cell. Claimed it was self-defense, but they charged him with murder second. He was found guilty by a jury. It's practically an identical case. Do you remember who the prosecutor was?" Scott inquired.

"Richard Rainwater, I think, but that case was different, Dog."

"How so?"

"He lured that guy in the cell and then killed him. Rodgers was his cousin too. It had something to do with bad blood on the streets."

"Yes, Tyrus, but there was a weapon found in the cell, and Cooper said he only lured the kid into his cell to talk to him about whatever the family issue was, but the kid sprung on him with the weapon. Whatever the case, I remember that an argument could have been made for self-defense. I'm going to ask Elisa to look up every homicide case that has been prosecuted here in the last ten years and see how many of them could have been argued self-defense. I'm also going to call up to our sister prison on the hill and ask them to do the same thing. Unfortunately, I don't think that is going to be enough. I really need to take another look at this entire investigation, but I want to do it in an unbiased and neutral way."

"And just how are you going to do that, Dog?"

"The only thing I can think of, Ty, is to take a serious look at Vong's interview and then do a complete crime scene reconstruction using Poser 6 and Punch Pro software."

"Poser what?" asked the naive sergeant.

"Three-D computer software that allows us to recreate the crime scene complete with the cell and its furnishings and figures that I can pose in any position I want practically."

"Well, good luck with that," expressed Tyrus Phillips as he walked out of Scott's office.

Chapter 10

Reconstructing the Crime Scene

"Alright, Oz, first things first. I need your help," Scott asked as he grabbed him by the collar to get his attention.

"What's up?"

"I need you and Becky to come with me to E Wing for a little video documentation. You are about the same height as Inmate Zhuang, and Becky is the same height as Inmate Vong. I want to see how easy it would be for you to hit her while she is up on the top rack, and I want to get it on videotape. But, Oz, if it's plausible, it's plausible. I don't want you pretending that it can't be done if it can be done. You got it?"

"Squared away, Scotty."

"Okay, you and Becky meet me at cell 346 in about fifteen minutes."

After clearing two confused inmates out of the cell, Scott instructed Becky to climb up onto the top bunk, face the door, and cross her legs meditation-style. Scott then told Oswaldo to put one foot on the toilet seat and the other on the lower bunk. He put his right foot on the toilet seat and his left foot on the lower bunk, but in this position, he could not reach Becky for a good punch. Scott instructed him to switch feet and put his right foot farther down on the bunk. He did so and discovered that he could, in fact, hit Becky in the left leg and arm, but it was at the extreme of his reach.

Scott immediately noticed two things: (1) Becky could easily scoot farther up on the bunk and be completely out of Oz's reach, and (2) Vong's cut lip was on the right side of his mouth. To get a cut on his lip while he was on the top bunk from a blow by Inmate Zhuang, Vong would have had to turn his face completely and unnaturally to the left. It was clear that he did not receive that injury in the manner he described in the interview. "Okay, although it is plausible that Inmate Zhuang hit Inmate Vong while standing on the toilet, it is unlikely, and Vong certainly did not receive his one and only injury in the manner he suggested," Scott explained to his actors.

"There's something else that also doesn't match up, Oz. The forensic pathologist said the heavy bruising and liver injury might have occurred during the fall onto the toilet but only if it was the pendulum effect. Well, if that was the case, both of Inmate Zhuang's feet would have to have been on the lower bunk. He would have had to hold on with one hand and punch with the other, not to mention the form that the medical department filled out on the day of the incident listed bruises on the right leg of Inmate Vong. There were no bruises on his left leg. The left leg is the leg that Zhuang would have been hitting. There's something else, but I need to get back to the office and look at the crime scene photos."

They hurried back to the office, and Scott pulled out the big file that contained all the crime scene photographs. He was looking for one photograph in particular; it was the very first photograph that he took. "Here it is and just as I suspected. Take a look at this, little buddy, and tell me if you notice something," Scott said as he passed the photograph to Oz.

"Anything in particular?" he asked in turn.

"Where did Vong say he was when he got attacked the second time by Inmate Zhuang?"

"He was at the head of the bunk."

"Correct. And where did he say that Inmate Zhuang was standing when he was attacked the second time?" Scott queried further.

"He was . . . uh . . . uh, he was . . . he was standing on the locker!"

"Absolutely correct. And what happened when Zhuang was standing on the locker?" Scott asked.

"He fell," replied his partner.

"Why?"

"Because the locker wobbled, and he lost his balance, something like that" was his response.

"Look at the locker in this photograph. There are a lot of small items on the top of the locker like deodorant sticks and bottles of soy sauce and hot sauce, a standing greeting card, and even a TV that was sitting precariously on top of four toilet paper rolls. Do any of these items looked like they were disturbed?"

"No, Scotty, nothing is moved or disturbed at all. He wasn't on top of this locker. There is no way."

"The bottom shelf is broken, but look at the blood transfer all around the bottom shelf. This happened by a body falling against it, not from standing on it. All right, Oz, let's go a little further out in the interview. What did Vong say happened to Zhuang when he fell off the locker?"

"He hit his head on the towel bar."

"Exactly, but if we look at this photograph of the semicircular injuries in his scalp, we see that they are on his right-side way above his ear. Let's say that he is standing on the locker and punching at Vong. The locker moves, and Zhuang falls toward the towel bar. It wouldn't be his right side that would hit the bar. It would be his left side. Even if he managed to twist on his way down, the towel bar is so close to the locker that he would almost have to twist and drop straight down, which is not very likely. Do you agree?"

"I don't know, Scotty. I'd have to see it, but it does seem unlikely."

"You're going to see it, Oz, in computer-assisted 3D. Give me about an hour, and I will visually reconstruct this scene using computer software and then put it all in a PowerPoint presentation. I'm also going to include the bit about his kicking Zhuang in the back when there was no evidence of bruising on the back, only lividity, and the expectorated blood on the garbage box and the bloodstain evidence on the lower bunk. I think we figured this one out, Ozzie. I only wish I had thought of this before I submitted it to the DA's office."

With that, Scott set to work creating the 3D images and PowerPoint presentation. Elisa came through on the previous homicide investigations submitted to the DA's office for prosecution. She found two additional cases that were submitted, filed, and successfully prosecuted, even though the argument could have been made for self-defense. The court liaison officer at the California State Prison–Monterey Bay found five examples. Scott assembled an investigative file for the attorney general's office; copied the PowerPoint presentation, interviews, and photographs to a CD; and obtained a letter signed by the warden on official state letterhead requesting that they review the investigation. Scott put everything together and mailed it off to the attorney general's office with his fingers crossed.

Three days later, he got a telephone call from Deputy Attorney General Karen Ballard. She had received the investigative parcel and would review it in good order. She promised to call Scott within the next few weeks with her decision. Two months had passed without a word.

Chapter 11

Meanwhile, Back at the Ranch

"Charlie 9, Charlie Wing officer."

"Charlie 9."

"Charlie 9, I need a gurney and medical to Charlie Wing."

"Ten-four, Charlie Wing. What is the nature of your emergency?"

"Well, it looks like I have a stabbing."

"Holy shit, Ty, did you hear that radio traffic?" Scott exclaimed as he bolted for the camera kit.

"Where is it, Doggy?" he shouted back.

"Charlie Wing!"

"Get down! Get down! Get down! Charlie 2, this is Charlie 3-3! I need medical and CSI stat!"

"Ten-four, Charlie 3-3. Break. Any CSI unit, we need immediate response to Charlie Wing."

"Ten-four, Charlie 2, we are en route!" Scott barked into the microphone as they ran up the stairs from the basement offices of the security and investigations unit. At least they didn't have to run very far. Charlie Wing was the third housing unit to the left as you passed through the control room sally port.

Tyrus and Scott entered the corridor at the same time and were on the heels of the motorized gurney driven by the medical department personnel. It came to a skidding halt directly in front of the Charlie

Wing door, and Scott saw Correctional Officer Benjamin Schwartz escort a black inmate out of the wing and place him on the gurney. He was holding a white towel against the right side of the inmate's head. The white towel was quickly turning red. "Ty, go with the victim to the infirmary and take pictures. Let me know the extent of the injuries," Scott requested.

"Sure thing, Doggy," replied Sergeant Phillips as he did an about-face and started for the infirmary knowing, at some point, the gurney would pass him by. "Schwartz, did any inmate go in or out before or immediately after the incident?" Scott asked the harried officer.

"No, nobody went out. The front door was locked. We did have inbound movement about five minutes before it happened, but nobody went out," he detailed as he looked at the blood on his hands. Scott looked in the hall and noted about thirty inmates lying on the ground. Responding officers were moving about in a fever pitch, trying to secure the area.

"That means our attacker is still inside," Scott remarked as he patted him on the shoulder. Scott entered the hall and passed the security gate into the chaos. Three inmates were sitting in the shower area to his left. Two were in various stages of undress. The third was wrapped with a towel. Scott looked to his right and saw two inmates—one an elderly white inmate, the other a slender black inmate with a salt-and-pepper beard—sitting near the restroom. The front staircase was directly in front of him. The black inmate was staring intently at Scott, but when Scott finally made direct eye contact with him, he quickly looked away.

Scott took a quick look up to the second and third tiers. Three Hispanic inmates were sitting on the ground in front of the second-tier shower area. One white inmate was sitting near the front of the third-tier staircase. Stepping a little farther into the hall, Scott could see two more inmates—one white, one Hispanic—sitting in the back of the third tier.

The first tier was another story. At least thirty inmates were lying on the concrete floor while ten officers swarmed about them, looking for additional injuries, weapons, and bloodstains. A lieutenant was directing officers to drop rubber gloves near blood drops to keep people from stepping in them. Scott looked over at the trail they were marking and quickly determined it was the blood drip trail left by the victim as he made his way to the front office. "Good, that'll keep them busy while I find the real crime scene," Scott said quietly to himself as he followed the trail of blood to the third steel table from the back of the hall, where he found four arching projected arterial spurt patterns.

Just then, Oswaldo appeared, carrying one of the crime scene kits. "Perfect, Oz, here is our crime scene. Tape off this area," Scott said while pointing at the table and immediate area.

Oswaldo looked back toward the rubber glove trail leading to the office and asked, "What about all that?"

"Secondary. We'll document it, but with all this movement, I don't think we stand a chance of preserving it." As Scott said that, another wave of about twelve responding officers rushed in through the door. "Tie off the tape from the door handle of cell 139 across to cell 115. That'll give us the entire back of the hall, the back staircase, and about five of these tables. I don't want anyone in this area."

Correctional Lt. Emilio Fernando approached the tape barrier. "Dog, what have we got?" he asked.

"Well, Lieutenant, just give me a minute to look over these bloodstain patterns, and I will have a little better idea," he replied. Scott summoned Oswaldo over to where he was standing. "Okay, Oz, we have a nice projected gush or spurt right here by table number 3. It is to the right of the east attached stool. Our victim was seated on this stool. He gets stabbed and stands up. The blood begins to drop right here on the table, the stool, and the floor. He either cups his hand over the injury or grabs a towel or one of these blankets and presses it for a moment against the wound, resulting in these drops on the left side of the stool. I'm inclined to say it was his hand because he couldn't stop the blood from spurting across the table. Whatever it was, it was overwhelmed with the blood. That's why we have drops of blood around the projected blood.

"Now if you notice, we have one arching pattern going in a semicircle from west to east, a second from north to south, a third over here going south to east, and another going east to west. This, I gather, is our victim looking around him for the attacker. Finally, right here is where he puts it into gear and starts moving at a brisk pace toward the front office. Now let's see what is on the other side of the table."

Oswaldo and Scott gingerly stepped around the bloodstain patterns and made their way over to the west side of the table, where they found only two small blood drops. "Two drops do not a pattern make, Oz," Scott said as he examined the remaining area with his forensic flashlight. "We'll document them. Do me a favor and get Sergeant Phillips on the radio. See if you can get the victim's name and a synopsis of the injury." Oswaldo stepped to the back of the hall and spoke quietly into his radio.

Scott continued his examination of the floors, walls, tier ceilings, and staircase, with negative results. He then studied the tables. The first table was bare. The second held various craft projects like paper picture frames and greeting cards. The third table was where the victim sat. Pinochle cards and a scoring sheet were still on the table. They had just dealt the hand. "They," Scott murmured to himself.

Oz rejoined him. "His name is Inmate Sutherland, Vincent Sutherland. Here is his CDC number," he said as he passed Scott a piece of paper with his undecipherable writing.

"Is that an E 132?" Scott asked.

"Yeah, yeah, yeah, sorry, I was standing while I was writing. According to the medical people, he was stabbed three times. Two were superficial, but one went through his right earlobe and did some real damage. They are calling in Life Flight to take him to San Jose."

"Is he going to make it?" Scott asked.

"It doesn't look like it," replied Oswaldo.

Scott walked over to where Lieutenant Fernando was waiting. "You're looking for a red ink pen," Scott stated.

He turned to Sergeant Jesus Beltran and gave him instructions to search the inmates for a red ink pen. Before Sergeant Beltran could react, Oswaldo declared, "Hey, that guy's holding a pen." They all looked at Oswaldo, who was pointing toward a bald-headed black inmate who was sitting against the wall between cell 115 and cell 114. The inmate appeared to be in a state of shock. Scott walked over to the inmate and held out his hand. The inmate gently placed the pen into Scott's outstretched hand; it was a red ink pen, and there was what looked like blood on the barrel. Sergeant Beltran motioned for the inmate to stand up. When he complied, Sergeant Beltran placed him in handcuffs and turned him to face the wall.

"That is remarkable!" exclaimed Lieutenant Fernando. "How could you tell that you were looking for a red pen from the patterns of the blood?"

"You know, Fernando, I'd like to say that it's all about skill and training. But in reality, it had nothing to do with the bloodstain patterns. They were keeping score at the table with a red ink pen, and there wasn't one in the crime scene. I'm not ready to say that's your weapon or that's your suspect, but at least we have a place to start. If nothing else, we now have a witness." Scott walked over to the inmate and asked, "Where's your ID?"

"It's in my cell," he responded.

"And where is your cell?" Scott inquired.

"One-one-five," he replied.

Scott sent Oswaldo into the cell since it was inside the crime scene. He retrieved the identification card. "Peabody?" Scott asked as Oswaldo passed him the card.

"Yes, sir."

"You seem to be in shock. How are you doing?" Scott asked.

"Yes, sir, just a little."

"Okay, Peabody, what I want you to do is to kick off your shoes. You have just a little bit of blood on the top of your right shoe, and I need to collect it. Then I want you to go with this sergeant. He's going to have medical take a look at you," Scott instructed.

"I knew you were going to find me when you saw that blood drop on the floor. That's where I was sitting."

"I'll come by and talk to you in a little bit, Peabody, when you are feeling a little better." With that, Sergeant Beltran escorted the stocking-footed inmate out of the wing.

"That was easy," remarked Oswaldo.

"Not so easy as you might think, Oz. We still have two other witnesses that need to be found."

"How do you know?"

"They were playing four-hand pinochle. See the cards and the score sheet?"

"Oh, yeah, yeah, yeah, and I think I see one of them right now."

"Get 'em, Sniper," Scott encouraged.

With that, Oswaldo made a direct path to another inmate who was sitting against the west wall near cell 109. From a distance of about twenty-four feet, Oswaldo spotted the smallest drop of blood on the inmate's left shoulder and another on his left shoe. "How did you manage that?" Scott asked Oswaldo in amazement.

"I didn't see the blood, but I saw him trying to wipe it off," he replied.

"Nicely done, Eagle Eyes," Scott commended before turning to the inmate and saying, "I'll need your shoes, shirt, and name."

"Moore" was all he said while handing Scott his identification card.

"Well, Mr. Moore, we will talk to you in a little bit. For now, please stand up, remove your shoes and shirt, and hand them to my partner." Inmate Moore complied with Scott's request and then presented himself for handcuffing.

"Two down and one to go. He's around here somewhere. We need a scribe," Scott said as he looked around for an officer with nothing else to do. Now he spotted Correctional Officer Carl Humphreys, a pudgy fellow with the face of a cherub. "Humphreys, I need you to help us out." He became attentive. "I need you to take this notepad, draw a quick diagram of the interior of this building, and then write down the names of every inmate in the place where you found them on every tier. When you get their names, make sure you see a photo ID and be sure to check it before you write down the name. Can you do this?"

"Sure," he said as he took up the pad and extracted a pen from the pocket of his jumpsuit.

"Watch him for a bit, Oz, and make sure he's doing it right. I'm going to start photographing the crime scene. Then I want you to stand

by here while I run back to the office and grab my bloodstain kit."
Oswaldo acknowledged his instructions. After taking the preliminary
overview photographs of the crime scene and ensuring that Oswaldo
was standing guard, Scott went back to the office to get his equipment.

On his way back, he ran into Tyrus. He had accompanied the
gurney to the helipad and stayed there until Inmate Sutherland was
loaded onto the helicopter. "It doesn't look good, Dog," he said as he
held the control room sally port gate for Scott and his heavy burden.
"He's lost a lot of blood. The blade of the weapon went through his right
earlobe and into that area behind the ear. You should see it, Dog. It was
like a raw piece of meat protruding from behind his ear, like they dug
in the blade and then pulled it out at an angle. I'm going to find one of
my guys and drive up to San Jose to the trauma center where they are
taking him."

"What kind of weapon are we looking for?" Scott asked.

"Looks like an ice-pick-type blade," he surmised.

"Did he say who stabbed him?"

"He didn't know."

"I want photographs, Ty, good ones," Scott said as he left him at
the gate.

When Scott got back to the crime scene, he found Oswaldo dutifully
standing guard. "We're looking for an ice-pick-type weapon according
to Ty. We'll need to check all the garbage cans on all three tiers. Of
course, he could have pushed it under any of these doors if he had an
accomplice."

"Which way do you think he went, Scotty?"

"Well, Oz, I'm kinda thinking that he wouldn't go back toward
the front of the hall on the first tier, not with the victim going in that
direction. My money is going to be on him going up these back stairs
and cutting across either the second or third tier. He might still be up
there, although I really doubt that."

"Why's that?"

"Well, Oz, I only see a few Hispanics and two white guys up on
the tiers. If it was one of them, I can assure you that the other black

inmates in this hall would be just sitting there. We'd have a riot like nobody's business."

"You think it was a black?" asked Oswaldo.

"I'd put money on it. Do me a favor and go up to the holding cells. Don't talk to Moore just yet but see if Peabody will tell you at least the race of the suspect. Remember, Oz, only interview him as a witness right now and be careful. He's in a holding cell, which means there is custody and questioning. *Miranda* applies. Tell him you are interviewing him as a witness only and you just want to know if other races were involved. If he makes any incriminating statements, stop the interview and administer *Miranda*." Oswaldo acknowledged his instructions and left the housing unit.

Two Southern Hispanic inmates remained lying in the back of the housing unit, which was technically still in his crime scene. One watched with great interest as Scott dropped his markers and completed his photo documentation and diagramming. Once the bloodstain work began, the inmate started making the usual comments about the television program *CSI*. "Hey, *CSI: Las Vegas*! Who are you? Who, who, who, who? You gonna bring out the lights and stuff?"

"That and more." Scott smirked.

"You got all that fancy forensic stuff, I bet," he continued.

"Yeah, and I know how to use it unlike that guy on *CSI*, and I'm certified, which is more than I can say for him too."

The talkative inmate took note that his comrade was not overpleased that he had started a conversation with Scott. He closed with the usual "Right, right, right" and went back to minding his own business.

While Scott was swabbing the bloodstains and conducting presumptive tests, Oswaldo reappeared and whispered into his ear, "He was black and went up the back stairs." Oswaldo then proceeded up the rear stairwell to the second tier, where he inspected the contents of the garbage can that was immediately off the landing. He looked at Scott and shook his head in the negative. Like a bloodhound, he shone his flashlight on the floors, wall, and tier ceiling along the entire west side of the second tier, returning on the east side. Again, he looked at Scott and shook his head in the negative before ascending the stairwell to the third tier. He repeated his actions on the third tier and once again suggested a negative result for his search. Then he was off to the shower areas on all three tiers. After that, he inspected the garbage cans in the front of the second and third tiers. No luck there either.

He returned to the crime scene dejected and said, "I bet he pushed it under one of the cells."

"Very likely, little buddy, very likely indeed," Scott said as he packaged the blood specimen swabs. "Not much left for us to do in the crime scene, Oz. Why don't you organize some of the troops and get these inmates stripped out and checked for bloody garments?"

"We can do it in the dayroom," he replied with his new task in hand.

"Make sure you take charge, Oz. I want it done right."

Oswaldo returned after about ten minutes holding a state-issued blue chambray shirt. "Inmate Haney," he stated as he approached. "Blood on the right cuff." He selected the appropriate-sized paper evidence bag.

"And that makes three, four counting the victim. Let's do a phenolphthalein and Hexagon OBTI presumptive test on that before you bag it," Scott suggested. The tests produced positive results for suspected human blood. "Where's the inmate?"

"On his way to a holding cell," Oswaldo replied. He returned to the dayroom and completed the search of the inmates without any additional blood evidence having been discovered. The inmates were locked in their cells, and Scott took some photographs of the empty housing unit. They then gathered their equipment and evidence and exited the cell block, stopping first to get the report from Officer Humphreys detailing the position of all the inmates.

They returned to the investigations unit, booked their evidence, downloaded the digital images, polished the diagram, and wrote their reports. The three inmates who were at the table with Inmate Sutherland were sent to the administrative segregation unit for their own protection. After that, they left for the day as it was past eight at night.

On his way home, Scott got a call from Sergeant Phillips, who was still at the hospital. Inmate Sutherland had survived but barely. He flatlined once on board the helicopter, but the crew was able to revive him and get him stabilized before landing. The doctors did major surgery to find and close the severed tributary of the right external carotid artery. Although the doctors would not let Tyrus into the operating room to take photographs, one of the doctors took the camera in and snapped a few photographs before and after the surgery; cooperation between medical and law enforcement was very rare and probably owing to Ty's amiable and convincing demeanor.

It was then when Tyrus offered his challenge. "Dog, I'm giving you forty-eight hours to solve this one." It was in reference to one of his favorite television crime shows. In response, Scott suggested they start their interviews in the morning.

Chapter 12

The First Forty-Eight

The next morning, a Saturday, found Tyrus and Scott driving up to the San Jose trauma center. Tyrus had received a telephone call late the night before from a doctor who said that he believed Inmate Sutherland would be well enough to answer questions in the morning. It was about an hour and fifteen minutes' drive north from the prison. Finding the patient's room at a hospital foreign to both Tyrus and Scott took nearly as long.

They found Inmate Sutherland in the trauma center being guarded by two large officers from the San Jose Police Department. Apparently, there had been a mix-up, and the prison hospital guarding team hadn't yet arrived. With their apologies to the officers, Tyrus and Scott entered the room. Sutherland was propped up in his bed. Tubes and hoses were in his arms, nose, and mouth. He had a large bandage against the right side of his neck. He opened his eyes slowly. "Sutherland, I'm Sergeant Phillips, and this is Investigator Doggett. We are assigned to your investigation. I know that you had some pretty major surgery, but I'm hoping you can help shed some light on what happened to you. Did you see the guy who stabbed you?"

After spitting up a mouthful of blood, Inmate Sutherland mustered enough strength to reply, "No, just that he went up the back stairs. He tried to kill me. He did kill me. Doctor said I died, but they brought me back."

"Did you have any enemies who would want to do something like this to you?" Scott asked.

"Me? No, no, I get along with everybody. I get along with all races."

"Do you think this was a racial issue?" asked Tyrus.

"No, no, he was black," replied Sutherland.

"How do you know?" pressed Tyrus. "Well, I saw the back of his head as he went up the stairs. He was black. Besides, there was no way another race was going to come up behind me like that without someone at the table getting involved."

"What about the guys at your table?" Scott asked.

"You mean, was they involved?"

"That and who exactly were they?" he clarified.

"It wasn't none of them. Deacon was on my left."

"Deacon?"

"Yeah, Deacon Peabody. He's like my best friend really. We play cards in that same spot every day, have done for almost ten years. He's a good dude. Then Moore was on my right. That young kid was across from me."

"What's his name?" asked Tyrus.

"The young one? I don't know. We just call him youngster. He hasn't been in the hall very long. He lives down there in 128. It wasn't him because he was across from me. I know it wasn't him because I had just dealt the cards, and I was watching him put his cards in order when this body just kinda leaned on top of me. I felt him hit me in the side of the head. I thought he just hit me, so I got up and turned to see where he went. That's when I saw him go up the stairs, real casual like. Then I felt this warm feeling and noticed the blood on my hand. I grabbed a T-shirt that was on the table, but it wasn't enough. When I saw the shirt wasn't stopping the blood, I just moved as fast as I could up to the front."

"Okay, let me see if I have this straight," Scott said, flipping his notebook to a clean page. He drew an octagon to represent the table with four corresponding circles to represent the stools. He showed a directional arrow pointing toward the top of the page and told him the arrow pointed toward the front door. "Where were you sitting exactly?" Inmate Sutherland pointed to the circle that was to the right of the arrow, showing the east stool.

"Now where was Peabody?" Sutherland pointed to the circle opposite the direction of the arrow, showing the south stool.

"Where was Moore?" Scott asked.

He pointed to the circle next to the arrow, showing the north stool.

"And Haney, I mean the youngster, he was sitting at the west stool?"

"Yes, sir."

"So you don't know why anyone would do this to you?" inquired Tyrus.

"No, no idea at all," he replied.

"Do you have any debts?" Scott asked.

"I don't use no drugs," he fired back.

"I didn't ask you if you used drugs. I asked if you had any debts."

"Maybe fifteen or twenty dollars for tobacco, but I was going to give him canteen today."

"Who do you buy your tobacco from?" asked Tyrus.

"Uh, they call him Jay-Jay. I don't know his real name. It's only twenty dollars. He wouldn't hit me for no twenty dollars. He wants my business too bad."

"Have you and Jay-Jay ever argued?" Scott asked.

"Yeah, once or twice. He sells things—you know, extra clothing, old radios, junk mostly. If you want say a sweatshirt sold, you give it to Jay-Jay and tell him you want five dollars for it. He sells it for eight and keeps the rest."

"Very enterprising," Scott remarked, adding, "What did you argue about?"

"Oh, an old TV that my old cellie left behind, but it wasn't nothing. It was just an old black-and-white TV with knobs. It wasn't worth more than fifteen, twenty dollars. He was okay about it. It was just a misunderstanding."

"Back to the guy you saw go up the back stairs, do you remember how he was dressed?" asked Tyrus.

"Yeah, all blues," replied Inmate Sutherland.

"CDC jacket?"

"Yeah, all blues—pants, jacket, boots."

"All right, Sutherland, I think you've told us enough for now. If you think of anything else, let us know when you get back to the prison. Can you think of anything else, Dog?"

"No, but we will come back and talk to you and bring some photographs of the guys who were in the hall. Maybe it will jog your memory."

"Yeah, whatever you guys want. I want to get this guy. He tried to kill me."

"At one point, he succeeded," replied Scott as he stepped out of the hospital room.

"The clock is ticking, Doggy," reminded Tyrus as they drove back to the institution.

"I hope you aren't counting drive time. And I hope you didn't have any plans for this afternoon, Ty, because we are going to do some more interviewing when we get back."

"The guys at the table?" he asked.

"The guys at the table and every inmate that was out during the incident," Scott replied.

"That's going to take a while, Dog."

"I've only got forty-eight hours, Ty, remember? Do me a favor. When we get back to the institution, print me a photo collage of all the black inmates that were on the list we got from Humphreys."

The conversation for the remainder of the drive back to the institution revolved around Ty's children and their most recent machinations involving leaving the freezer door open on the refrigerator for a day and how much it was going to cost to replace the kitchen floor—a floor he had only just installed. Upon their return, Tyrus printed a photo collage and 8" × 10" portraits of the sixteen black inmates who were in Charlie Wing during the incident. Armed with these photographs, they proceeded to the administrative segregation unit to interview the witnesses.

The first inmate they requested to be escorted to the captain's office was Inmate Peabody. They both had the feeling he would be the most inclined to assist them with their inquiries. Now the door opened, and two escort officers guided the restrained inmate into the room and seated him in the chair at the end of the conference table. Once seated, the officers left the room, closing the door behind them. Inmate Peabody was a tall well-built black inmate of about fifty. He was bald but had a large and bushy mustache. Although he was serving a life sentence for second-degree murder, he seemed meek. He sat in the chair opposite them, staring at the table in front of him. He did not make eye contact with either of the investigators, which made both of them initially very suspicious, so much so that Scott advised him of his rights pursuant to the *Miranda* decision but stressed that they were seeking his help as a witness and not as a suspect.

It wasn't until he began to speak that Scott asked him if he wore glasses. The reply was in the affirmative, but he hadn't yet received them from the administrative segregation property officer. He was extremely nearsighted and thus the need to stare at the table before him. To him, Tyrus and Scott were very blurry. Scott pulled his chair a little closer to the table and opened the conversation. "We stopped by to see Vincent this morning. He's recovering. He wanted us to be sure that you were okay. He thinks very highly of you. In fact, he called you his best friend."

Inmate Peabody seemed humbled by the remarks. To add severity to the purpose of their tête-à-tête, Tyrus stated, "He was almost killed. They had to cut his neck open to get to the artery that was cut. He's got a big scar across his neck."

"In fact, he was killed for a moment or two, but they brought him back to life in the helicopter," Scott added.

"I want to help you, guys, but there's a problem. You see, I don't wear my glasses when I play cards so that I can see them. My glasses were on the table. I could see the guy, but I couldn't get a real good look at him. He was tall, about five eleven or six, slender, and he had a salt-and-pepper beard. But other than that, I couldn't tell you who it was. I saw him come walking up to the table. He leaned over Vincent like he was telling him something and then walked away up the back stairs. I saw Vincent jump up and look at the guy, and then I saw all the blood come squirting out—well, red stuff, blurry red stuff. I just jumped out of the way of the blood because I knew that you would lock up anyone that had blood on them. I must have got the blood on me when I got up. I don't know why I picked up the pen or why I still had the pen in my hand. I just felt like holding something. I was trying to see where he went after he went up the stairs."

"You looked like you were in shock when I approached you," Scott remarked.

"I was. I was torn between running after the guy and running with Vincent up to the office. I didn't know what to do because I didn't have my glasses on. I was just standing there in shock until the youngster grabbed me and pulled me over to the wall."

"Which one is the youngster?" asked Tyrus.

"Oh, I don't know his name. We all just call him youngster. He just got here from North Facility. He was our fourth at the table. He lives on the first tier, somewhere near 127 or 128."

"Well, I just happen to have some photographs with me. Maybe you can identify some of these guys for us," asked Tyrus.

"Can you see them all right?" Scott inquired.

"Yes, I think so if I can hold them close to my face." Tyrus opted for the larger photographs and started putting them on the table. Inmate Peabody examined each of the photographs with his face just inches from each photograph. "Well, that one is me, and this one is Vincent. This one is Dennis."

"Dennis?" asked Tyrus.

"Moore. You got him in here too. He's two cells down from me. He was opposite me at the table. This one is the youngster," he said, pointing at a photograph of Inmate Haney.

"This is the guy!" he exclaimed.

Tyrus and Scott leaned forward to see who he had identified. Tyrus checked his cheat sheet that corresponded to the number on the photograph; it was Inmate Ellis. "How can you be sure?" Scott asked.

"Because I saw him in the hall, and it was him. See, he has a salt-and-pepper beard, and he is tall and slender. I know that's him," he replied.

"Okay, let's just set that one aside for now. Keep looking through the photographs," encouraged Tyrus.

"All right, well, this one is Larry, my cellie, Larry Jackson."

"Yeah, I know Jackson. In fact, I stepped over him to get to the crime scene," Scott said.

"Yeah, and this is Jay-Jay," he said, pointing to a photograph of Inmate Norris. "I didn't see him in the hall."

"What do you know about Jay-Jay?" inquired Tyrus.

"Oh, he sells stuff. He sells TVs and radios and the like, sweatpants and sweatshirts, books and magazines. He sells just about anything."

"Does he sell dope?" Scott asked.

"No, no drugs."

"What about cell phones and tobacco?" asked Tyrus.

"Yeah, sometimes he does, if he can get his hands on any."

"Do you know where he gets his tobacco?" Scott asked.

"He has some connection in the culinary," he replied.

"Staff or inmate?"

"I think it's an inmate. I don't think he deals directly with staff. He's too shy."

"Have you ever seen him argue with Vincent?"

"No, never."

"Anything about a television set?" asked Tyrus.

"No, never," he replied with some certainty.

"Okay, let's go back to this one," Scott said while pointing to the photograph of Inmate Ellis. "What do you know about him?"

"He's been in the hall for a long time. He plays cards with my cellie, Larry. He and Vincent don't get along. They argue all the time. He's always mad at Vincent because when they play chess together, Vincent usually wins, and then he rubs it in Marcus's—that's his name, Marcus Ellis. He rubs it in his face."

"And you're sure it was him that stabbed Vincent?" asked Tyrus.

"Yeah, I would lay my life on it," replied the now tearful witness.

"All right, Deacon, I think that's it for now. If you think of anything, I want you to send us a note. The property officer here is a good friend of mine. Just ask for the property officer, and when he comes up on the tier, just tell him you need to talk to Dog. He'll know what you mean. Rest assured that we are going to get to the bottom of this thing and get you out of here."

"Thank you, sir, I appreciate it. I have a board hearing coming up in October. I hope you can get me out of here by then. It won't look too good me being in here. What is your name again?"

"Doggett, Investigator Doggett, and this is my partner, Sergeant Phillips." With that, they called for the escort officers to take him back to his cell. They asked them to bring Inmate Moore on their way back.

"Moore, what's your first name?" inquired Tyrus.

"Dennis," replied the middle-aged, dark-skinned, short, and round inmate.

"All right, Dennis," Scott said, "we're here to talk to you as a witness of the stabbing of Inmate Sutherland. We believe you are a witness. However, I do want you to know that you do not have to answer any questions or talk to us at all. If you do not want to talk to us, we'll have you escorted back to your cell. Is that all right with you?"

"Yeah, that's fine, but I don't know how much help I can give you. I just got my cards dealt to me, and I arranged them in my hand. I reached over to my right to get my coffee cup off the ground, and the next thing I know, the youngster is pulling my arm. I was like, 'What the hell are you doing?' He was pulling so hard I almost fell off the stool. Then I saw Vincent standing up, and there was blood coming from his neck."

"So you didn't see the guy who did it?" asked Tyrus.

"No, my back was to the front of the hall. If he came up from behind me, I didn't see him."

"Did you see where he went?"

"No, I didn't see any of it."

"Did you see someone going up the back staircase?" Scott asked.

"No, I didn't see anyone going up the back. I was gettin' my ass pulled by the young one."

"Who was that?"

"Who, the youngster?" he responded.

"Yeah, what's his name?"

"I don't know his name. Heck, I don't think anyone knows his name," he said with a laugh.

"I want you to take a look at some photographs and tell me if any of these inmates were in the hall," instructed Sergeant Phillips.

Inmate Moore scanned the collage and pointed to the photographs of Inmate Jackson and Inmate Ellis. "They was in the hall. They was somewhere behind me playing cards. I could hear them arguing. They was loud too," he said, pushing the collage away.

Tyrus pushed it back and pointed at the photograph of Inmate Norris. "What about him?" he asked.

"Jay-Jay? Jay-Jay wasn't in the hall. He was probably still at work or out on the yard selling his stuff."

"Look, Moore, we'd really like to get this investigation solved. Is there anything else at all you can think of to tell us?" asked Tyrus.

"Nah, I was looking at the ground when it happened. The only thing I saw was youngster pulling at my sleeve and Vincent bleeding all over the place."

Sensing that they weren't going to get any more information from Inmate Moore, Scott pushed his chair back and stood up. "Let me get you a ride back to your cell. We'd like to get this investigation solved so that we can get you and Peabody back to the main line. If you think of anything else, get at us."

Scott found Officer Martin standing outside, waiting to escort Inmate Moore back to his cell. "Who's next?" he asked.

"Inmate Haney," Scott replied.

"Who?" he asked with a confused look.

"Inmate Haney?" Scott repeated, this time as a question.

"I'll check, but I don't think we have a Haney in here," he responded as he took Inmate Moore by the arm and led him away.

A few minutes later, Officer Martin stuck his head in the interview room and confirmed there was no Inmate Haney housed in ad seg. "Thanks," said Tyrus, and they both exited the administrative segregation unit. "Where to next, Doggy?"

"Charlie Wing, Tyrus. The clock is still ticking."

Chapter 13

Charlie Wing

Charlie Wing tier officer William Skinner was standing in the office when Tyrus and Scott knocked on the door. Charlie Wing was on lockdown, and there was no inmate movement. The door officer flipped the Folger Adam lock and allowed them to enter. "Skinner, I hope you don't mind, but we have to interview some of your bad boys. Mind if we use your dayroom?" Scott asked.

"No, not at all. How many were you thinking of interviewing?" asked the officer, who sensed he was going to have to do some escorting duty.

"Oh, about thirty or so, but we want to do the blacks first."

"Shit" was the reply. "Well," he added, "it will get us out of running a shower program."

"Hey, is Inmate Haney still in this wing?" asked Tyrus.

"Yeah, first tier in the back," replied Officer Skinner.

"I wonder why they didn't lock him up," inquired Tyrus.

"We were wondering that too. They said they were going to lock him up with the other two, but the paperwork never came down."

"An oversight, I'd imagine. Give us a few minutes and bring Haney down to us," Scott instructed.

Tyrus and Scott chose a table at the back of the dayroom, which was a long rectangular room that jutted off the housing unit. Originally designed as a room where the inmates could watch TV and play cards, the dayroom was now generally used as an overflow housing unit. When needed, bunk beds were brought from the maintenance department and an additional twenty-eight to thirty-four inmates can be housed in a makeshift dormitory for emergency purposes, such as a late transportation bus or an emergency at one of the other facilities requiring the evacuation or transfer of inmates. It was empty, aside from a desk in the back of the room and a partition that they dragged into place to prevent people from seeing who was being interviewed.

Scott had just set out his digital voice recorder when he heard the shuffle of feet and noticed the approach of a young, tall, and fit black inmate. He looked as though he had just awakened from a nap. "Did we wake you?" Scott asked.

"Yeah," he said with a broad smile. "There isn't much else to do. I don't have a TV."

"Haney?" asked Tyrus as he reached out for the inmate's identification card.

"Yes, sir," he replied.

"Have a seat, son," Scott said as he pushed the chair out. "We have some questions to ask of you regarding what happened to Vince Sutherland. I want you to know that we are talking to you as a witness and not as a suspect. Do you understand?"

"Yes, sir, but why do you want to talk to me?"

"Haney, we know that you were at the table when Vincent was stabbed. There is no reason to deny it," Scott said.

"No, sir, it was me at the table. I was there. Are you going to lock me up?"

"We have no desire to lock you up at this time, providing there is no reason to lock you up. However, with that said, there is someone still in this hall who is capable of murder, and you are a witness to his actions. Is there any reason why I should be worried about your safety?" Scott asked.

"I didn't see him," replied the shy inmate.

"Haney, what's your first name?" asked Tyrus.

"Charles, but everybody calls me Chuck."

"Actually, everybody calls you youngster," replied Tyrus. "You were at the table in the best seat to witness what happened. In fact, not only did you see Sutherland get stabbed, you also had enough presence of mind to try to pull Inmate Sutherland and Inmate Moore out of the way."

"No, I was pulling him away from the blood, but I guess he still got some on him. I don't know how I didn't get any more blood on me than that little drop. It was sprayin' out his neck. I've never seen anything like that before. This is my first time down."

"How long have you been down?" asked Tyrus.

"About eight months. They sent me over to North in the gym dorm—I mean Fairfield Dorm, but when they closed it down, they sent me over here. I only got here last Friday."

"Welcome to prison," Scott said dryly. "When do you get out?"

"In three years. I robbed a guy, and they said I used a weapon, but it was a plastic pipe that wouldn't have hurt nobody."

"Your victim didn't know that," replied Tyrus.

"No, it was a stupid thing, the first time I ever been in trouble. I don't even know why I did it, except to impress this girl, I guess."

"How old are you?" Scott asked.

"Nineteen, twenty next month. I'm going back to Georgia when I get out, Atlanta. Gonna live with my grandmother."

"On that note, Chuck, I'm thinking I want to make sure you actually do get back to your grandmother. I'm thinking you want to help us find the guy who stabbed your friend so that we can keep him from stabbing you too. What did you see?" Scott asked.

"I didn't see much. I could see this guy come walking from the front of the hall. He walked straight over to Vince, bent over him, and punched him in the ear a couple of times. When I saw the blood, I jumped back from the table, and I guess I must have reached out and pulled the other guy with me. Later, I saw Deacon just standing there like he was in shock, and I pulled him back to the wall, and we sat down, but I tried to move farther down so you wouldn't think I was involved. That's what they tell you to do because they said if you don't get away fast, you will go to the Hole."

"Can you describe the guy?" asked Tyrus.

"Sort of tall, I guess, not as tall as me but tall, five nine or five ten, skinny, older cat. I didn't see his face, really, just his beard. It was salt and pepper in it and his hair too."

"Where did he go after he stabbed Vincent?" asked Tyrus.

"He just casual like walked up the back stairs. I didn't see where he went after that, just up the stairs."

"How was he dressed?" Scott asked.

"All blues," he replied.

"Was he wearing a jacket?"

"Yes, sir."

"Did you see anything in his hand?"

"No, sir."

"Haney, I want you take a look at these photographs and tell me if you see the guy," instructed Tyrus.

Inmate Haney studied the photographs. He stopped for a minute at the photograph of Inmate Ellis and then went on. "No, sir, I don't see him. I don't know what he looks like. I wish I could help you, but I didn't see his face."

"Okay, Chuck, I'm going to let you go back to your cell now. As long as you guys are on lockdown, I am not going to put you in ad seg providing we catch this guy before you come off lockdown. However, if for any reason we—or you for that matter—think that your life is in danger, you will be going to the Hole," Scott remarked. Inmate Haney thanked them for trying to find the attacker, told them he would send a note if he remembered anything else, and left the dayroom. Tyrus and Scott asked Officer Skinner to bring Inmate Ellis for the next interview.

Before long, Inmate Ellis walked up to where Tyrus and Scott were sitting. "You wanted to see me, Chief?" asked the tall thin older black man. The first thing they noticed was the silver and gray beard and the white hairs among the black on his head.

"Yes, Ellis," Scott replied, "we did want to talk to you. You were in the hall when Inmate Sutherland was stabbed. In fact, you were just a few tables over. We were wondering if you saw anything."

"I was playing cards with Larry . . . uh, Larry Jackson, and I had just stood up to stretch when I heard Sutherland holler out something, and then he went walking past me, holding his neck, toward the front office. I saw the blood, and I got out the way," replied Inmate Ellis in a slow and methodic manner, his eyes focused on an imaginary spot on the desktop.

"Did you see anyone walk past you on his way over to where Sutherland was sitting?" asked Tyrus.

"No, can't say that I noticed. You see, Larry and I were in a bit of a disagreement over the last hand of cards. He cheats. I don't know why I play with him. He cheats like nobody's business."

"Do you ever play cards with Sutherland?" asked Tyrus.

"No, play chess with Sutherland. He cheats too. They all cheat, sore losers too."

"Can you take a look at some photographs and tell us if they were in the hall?" Scott asked. He looked up from his imaginary spot. Tyrus pushed the collage over to Inmate Ellis, who studied them intently.

"That's Curly . . . uh, Curtis Payne. He just stepped into the shower before it all happened. He's my cellie. And this one here is Jay-Jay. He was standing in the front of the hall when Sutherland went past. Of course, this one is Larry Jackson. And Deacon Peabody and Dennis Moore, you got them last two locked up. Here's the youngster they been playing cards with. The rest I don't remember if they was or wasn't in the hall." They thanked Inmate Ellis for his time and information and allowed him to return to his cell.

Before the next inmate was brought up for interview, Tyrus and Scott took a moment to gather their thoughts. "What do you think, Dog?" asked his partner.

"I'm thinking we have two matching descriptions of our assailant. Peabody clearly remembered a thin black inmate with the salt-and-pepper beard as did Haney. Peabody was adamant it was Ellis, but Haney wasn't sure. He stopped for a minute at the photograph, only to tell us that he was playing cards with Larry Jackson. Let's take another look at the photographs of the black inmates that were in the hall during the incident. How many of them have beards?"

"Six, I think—Ellis, Payne, Norris, Haney, and Richmond," replied Tyrus, adding, "I guess that's only five."

"How many of them look old enough to have a salt-and-pepper beard?"

"Only Ellis and Payne have beards. Both Haney and Richmond are in their early twenties. All right then, for now, our suspects are the two cellmates, Inmate Ellis and Inmate Payne, and Jay-Jay Norris until something else comes along."

"Norris was way up at the front of the hall when we came in," reminded Scott.

"Who do you want to interview next, Dog?"

"I'm thinking we interview Payne and Jay-Jay and then break for some food. I'll buy."

"All right, I'll tell Will to send in Payne first," Tyrus responded.

Inmate Payne was in his early fifties and about five foot nine but not what anyone would call skinny by any means, muscular perhaps but not skinny. He did have the requisite salt-and-pepper beard but gray hair that was tied in short braids. "I walked in just a few minutes before dude came up to the office," he said when questioned. "I came in from work and wanted to jump in the shower before it got crowded. I had just taken off my clothes, and I said to the guy who was already in the shower, I said, 'Look at that guy go past. Who does he think he is, Usain Bolt?' I didn't think anything about it, and I got into the shower. Man, I just got soaped up when the alarm went off. I thought it was just another false alarm, and I continued lathering up, but that's when the officer stuck his head in and yelled at us to get out of the shower. Man, I didn't even get to rinse all the way."

When asked to look at the photographs, he said, "Well, I didn't really see anyone in the hall other than Butler and my cellie. He was playing cards with Larry. Oh, and Jay-Jay was up by the front stairs." Tyrus and Scott dismissed him, and he went back to his cell. Jay-Jay was up next.

In short order, a medium-build black inmate was standing before them. Jay-Jay Norris was of average height and appeared to be in his early forties. Much to their surprise, he had a tight black beard that was speckled with white hairs. The photograph of Jay-Jay Norris in the collage was clean shaven. Scott wondered what his hair looked like, but he was wearing a blue knit cap, and Scott didn't want it to appear obvious that he was curious. "You all wanted to see me?" he said as he took the back of the empty chair.

"Yes, Norris, we did. I noticed that you were in the hall on the day Inmate Sutherland got stabbed. I'm wondering if you saw anything," Scott asked.

"Well, I had just come in from my job. I didn't even see him in the office, but they said he was in there when I walked past. All I know was that I was going in to piss, and the officer said that I couldn't."

"Hey, don't I know you from the North Facility?" asked Tyrus.

"Yeah, I was over there about three years ago, Sarge. Were you over there?"

"Nah, but you sure do look familiar. Do me a favor and take off your hat for a second," Ty requested.

Good one, Ty, Scott thought to himself. *You're heading in the same direction as me.*

Inmate Norris complied, revealing a head of short gray and black hair. "No, I guess it wasn't you. The dude I remember was bald," said Ty, playing his cards close to his chest.

"So you were coming in from work?" Scott asked.

"Yeah, a minute or two before the alarm. I was up in the front near the stairs and the bathroom."

"What were you wearing?" asked Tyrus.

"I had on my boxer shorts. I was going to piss and then get into the shower. I'd already taken off my work clothes."

"Where do you work?" asked Tyrus.

"I'm the janitor in the library," he replied.

"Aren't you the guy that sells stuff out on the central yard?" Scott inquired.

"I do my thing," he responded.

"How well did you know Sutherland?"

"I knew him, but we wasn't what you would call close. I mean, I am cordial with him, but we are from different parts on the streets. He is from the Bay Area, and I am from LA. But yeah, I know him. Is he going to be all right?"

"It was close, but he will survive."

"Man, that's something. To think that there is someone in here who is capable of that. You just never know."

"And he's still out there somewhere," added Tyrus.

"Yeah, I'm going to stay in my cell for a while."

"You said you were going to step into the shower?" Scott asked.

"Yes, sir."

"Do you remember who was in the shower area?"

"Well, I saw Reggie and Curly in there," he replied.

"Who is Reggie?" asked Tyrus.

"Oh, I don't know his last name. I think it's Booker or something like that, and Curly is . . . uh, Page."

"Butler and Payne maybe?"

"Yeah, Payne, that's it. He stuck his head out and said something about Jesse Owens. 'Who does he think he is, Jesse Owens?' or something like that."

"Do you know who he was talking about?"

"Not really."

"Did you see anyone come down from the second or third tier when you were standing by the stairs?"

"Yeah, a white and a Mexican came down the stairs when the police told them to come down. The white guy stood next to me, older cat."

"Can you think of anything else, Ty?" Scott asked.

"Yeah, Dog, just one more thing. They call you Jay-Jay, but it says here that your name is Richard. Why is that?"

"They been calling me Jay-Jay since I was little. Ain't nobody ever called me Richard much except my mom when I was bad."

"Called you Richard a lot, did she?" Scott amused.

"Yeah, I guess you could say that," he replied with a laugh.

"All right, Norris, you can go back to your cell. Let us know if you think of anything that can help our investigation." With that, Jay-Jay put his beanie cap back on, stood up, and walked out the door.

Once he was out of earshot, Tyrus asked, "What do you think, Dog?"

"The jury is out, Tyrus. It would seem that he has an alibi if he just came in from work."

"Do you want to interview anyone else?"

"Actually, Ty, I am starved, and there is something that I want to do before we interview anybody else," Scott replied.

"Such as?"

"Such as a trip to the records department and a review of our three current suspects' previous criminal history."

"Okay, Doggy, but you're buying lunch."

"Hot dogs it is, Tyrus, but there is just one thing I noticed regarding Jay-Jay."

"What's that?"

"His cell was directly behind where Vincent Sutherland was sitting."

Chapter 14

Records Search and a Late Lunch

"I've got Ellis's central file right here, Tyrus. Have you found Jay-Jay's yet?"

"No. I can never figure out this filing system. It seems backward to me."

"Everything is backward to you, Ty. Hang on, I'll come over and help you. Bottom to top and right to left, you're right, this doesn't make any sense at all. Geez, it's right here in front of you. Now we just need to find Moore's."

"I've already got it, Dog. Do you want to take them back to the office?"

"Nope, I'm thinking of just going through them right here."

"What are you looking for?"

"We're looking at any past violent criminal behavior, disciplinary reports involving weapons or assaults, and anything in the confidential section that might shed some light on the behavioral characteristics of our suspects. Furthermore, I'd like to take a look at Sutherland's central file to see if there is any perversion, lewd and lascivious behavior, or documentation that would label him as an informant, but I'm sure the unit has his file."

Inmate Ellis had the thickest file, while Moore and Norris had surprisingly thin files. Scott chose to scour the thick file and let Tyrus handle the others. "Nothing in Norris's file," remarked Tyrus. "He's in for petty stuff and dope, career criminal, robbery second but no violence. He gets out in about five years."

"Well, it's a different story for our friend Mr. Ellis, Tyrus. It goes back about a decade or more, but he's got plenty of violence in his jacket. Of course, he's in here for a murder, and that murder was involving a knife fight of all things. Starting in 1986, he has one, two, three write-ups for possessing weapon stock. The last one was seven years ago. He's got a PC 4502 for possessing an inmate-manufactured weapon for which he received seven years on top of his murder conviction. He's got two beefs for being disrespectful to staff, one with violence, and a staff assault that bought him another three years concurrent to his PC 4502. He also stabbed a guy at Folsom State Prison back in 1993. I don't see a disposition on that, but he was found guilty on the disciplinary report. It would appear that our Mr. Ellis is a prime suspect for a man handy with a blade."

"Moore doesn't have much in his file either. He's been down sixteen years for a forcible rape and sodomy with a foreign object, but there is nothing with a weapon in it, not even the rape. He actually even has a date to get out soon, less than a year."

"Well, Tyrus, by criminal history, our prime suspect would have to be Inmate Ellis. Let's go track down Sutherland's central file."

"Dog, I'm hungry."

"Forty-eight hours, Ty, you set the pace."

"Lunch first. After all, it's after two."

"File first and then lunch. Besides, I know where it is, and it should be closer than you think."

Tyrus flipped the Folger Adam key in the locking mechanism to close the heavy door of the records department and turned around to find Lt. Norma Vega standing next to him, holding a large central file. Scott greeted her with his usual "Abby Normal!" in homage to *Young Frankenstein*. "What up, Dog?" she replied.

Norma had been the warden's secretary until Tyrus and Scott persuaded her to take the correctional officer examination, which she passed to enter the academy. Three years later, she was promoted to correctional sergeant; and three years after that, she was promoted once again to correctional lieutenant. Norma climbed the ranks with amazing speed while Tyrus and Scott languished. "Here's the C file you were looking for, but I want it back in fifteen minutes."

"You can have it back in two minutes. We just need to see what he's about," Scott replied.

"I already looked through it. He's in for a pretty chickenshit murder, ran a guy over with his car whom he thought was having an affair with one of his girls."

"Pimp?" asked Tyrus.

"Most likely the case. Not much in the way of disciplinary actions other than not going to his job assignment and a fistfight back at San Quentin."

"Anything in his confidential section, Norma?" Scott inquired.

"Nope, just something with the fight and having a drug debt, but that was ten years ago at San Quentin."

"Interesting. I wonder if he has a drug debt now. When he gets back, why don't you ask him if he'll submit to a urine test? If he doesn't, we'll know," Scott recommended.

"And if he does? What will we use for probable cause?" she asked in turn.

"Well, tell him you'll send someone with a bottle later or you've changed your mind. Besides, I'm sure they've pumped him up with so many painkillers at the hospital that he'd be smart enough to point that out if he were a dopehead. Either way, we'll have our answer."

"Okay, Dog, just for you. Do you still need the C file?"

"No, thank you, Norma. But big whiny Tyrus is hungry, and I must feed him, burp him, and put him down for his nap."

"One hot dog with cheese, onion, and tomatoes and one hot dog with cheese and onions, no tomatoes, please," Scott ordered.

"Would you like fries?"

"No, thank you. I think it will be chips today and two sodas, bottles. You know, I never eat hot dogs unless I am here. You guys have the best dogs anywhere."

"Thank you. I'll tell Raymond, the owner. It will be just a few minutes."

Scott walked over to where Tyrus had staked out a small table overlooking the California State Prison at Monterey Bay parking lot. "No tomatoes. I remembered."

"So what do you want to do next, Dog?"

"Well, as I said, there are only three guys that really match the descriptions that we got from Sutherland and Haney. We have to go on the premise that one of them is our suspect."

"Yeah, Dog, but which one?"

"Occam's razor, Ty. When a problem presents itself with more than one plausible solution, you always go with the simplest one. I think we need to interview the rest of the inmates that were in the hall. Let's see if we can get someone else to give us more details of the suspect. Also, if we can get alibis for where some of our suspects were at the moment that Sutherland was stabbed, maybe we can do this by a process of elimination."

"Uh, it's going to take some time to do all these interviews. Are you sure you want to do it today?"

"You set the clock, Ty. Besides, it won't take too long. There were just over thirty witnesses. We've already talked to about a half dozen. The majority of them are only going to be there long enough to say, 'I didn't see nothing,' and leave."

"Your hot dogs, gentlemen," said Raymond as he proudly presented the best franks in the county.

Chapter 15

Finishing up the Wing

By the time they got back to Charlie Wing, Officer Skinner had been relieved by the third-watch shift, and Officer Carl Meeks was now at the helm. Scott showed him a copy of the list of inmates detailed to be in the hall by Officer Humphreys on the day of the stabbing. They asked him if he would escort first the remaining black inmates, then the Hispanic inmates, and finally the whites. He snatched the list from Scott's hand, grunted, and asked, "What about our shower program? You'll have to get this cleared with my sergeant."

"Meeks," Scott said as he put his hand on his shoulder, "I don't work for your sergeant. I work for the warden. This is a priority. You don't want me to report back to the warden that there was a problem, do you? Besides, this isn't going to take much time at all. You know how things are around here. Nobody sees anything, and nobody says anything. Relax, buddy, we'll be out of your hair before you know it, and you can go back to running your showers, okay?"

"Do you mind if I notify my sergeant?"

"By all means, Carl. I wouldn't want you to get in trouble, but this is more important than your showers."

Within minutes Sergeant Monica Meléndez was standing in front of Scott in the dayroom. "What's this all about, Dog?"

"Interviewing witnesses in the Sutherland investigation," Scott casually replied.

"Got it," she answered, aware of the orders of the warden. She waved over the reluctant Carl and instructed him to forgo his shower program and assist them with their investigation. He stormed off with his rookie partner in tow.

"Lazy ass," Tyrus said quietly.

"Yeah, he was lazy from the minute he got here. There's no work ethic these days, Ty," Scott replied.

The first inmate to come through the door was Larry Jackson, the cellmate of Inmate Peabody. Short and round and walking with a cane, Larry Jackson was one of the more popular inmates in Charlie Wing. Tyrus and Scott both knew him for a long time mostly because anytime an inmate needed a character witness during a jury trial, they would haul out Larry. He usually didn't help much, but they liked his Caribbean accent, and he didn't mind the quick trip away from the prison for a day.

"Walking a little slower these days, Larry. How are you doing?" Scott asked.

"Oh, Inspector Doggett, I didn't know it was you that wanted to see me," Larry said in his island accent.

"Larry, we go through this every time. It's investigator, not inspector, although I do like the sound of inspector. Inspector Doggett—I must admit it does have a certain ring to it."

"You must forgive me, but I grew up in the Bahamas, and they still have constables and inspectors there. It's a force of habit, I'm afraid."

"It's not a problem, Larry, but I called you down here because you were in the hall when Vincent Sutherland was stabbed."

"Oh yes, I was," he replied without adding the traditional "man" to denote the end of the sentence.

"Yes, I stepped over you to get to the crime scene. You were sitting in a good spot, only two tables away at the most. Can you tell me what you were doing and maybe what you saw?"

"Well, I can tell you that my cellie didn't have nothing to do with it. He is a good man, a nonviolent man. He has his parole board hearing next month and wouldn't do anything to jeopardize dat."

"He told us it was coming up," interjected Tyrus, adding, "That's why we would like to get some help to get him back to the main line."

"I was playing cards, man."

"With whom were you playing cards?" Scott asked.

"Marcus."

"Marcus Ellis?"

"Yes, we play cards every day at that time. I'd play with my cellie, but they are too aggressive with their pinochle and too loud for my likes."

"All right, Larry, I have two very important questions for you: where was Marcus at the moment Vince got stabbed, and which way were you facing?"

"Marcus was at the table. He was facing me. He stood up just as Vincent ran past. I was facing toward the side where Vincent was sitting. I saw the man walk past us going in the direction of Vincent. I saw him lean over Vincent, hit him in the neck with his right hand, and casually walk up the back staircase. He went to the second tier, and I watched him walk all the way down to the front staircase and descend just before Vincent ran into the office."

"Really? He got all the way down the tier and down the stairs that fast?" Tyrus asked in disbelief.

"Yes, he was most deliberate in his progression," replied the native of the Bahamas.

"Was he running?" asked the still disbelieving sergeant.

"No, he was walking as if not to draw attention to himself."

"But you saw him all the same?" Scott asked.

"I see everything. I've been in this housing unit for eighteen years, more time than anyone, I would say."

"What was he wearing?"

"Blue jacket, pants, and shirt," he responded.

"And you saw him come from the direction of the front door?"

"Yes, from the front door. He stopped for a moment at the showers and then proceeded directly to that table with Sutterlan', man. I didn't see nothing in his hand that looked like a weapon though. I thought he had just hit him in the side of his head with his fist. It wasn't until I saw the blood that I knew he had been stabbed. There was so much blood that I knew it didn't come from a punch, and I knew he hit something vital."

"All right, Larry, now for the big one—who was it?"

"I didn't get a good look at him. Sorry, but I cannot help you with dat."

Scott put his head in his hand and pushed up his right eyelid with his right little finger. "Black, white, or Mexican?" he asked in annoyance.

"Black."

"Let me guess, medium build, medium height, and salt-and-pepper hair?"

"Correct."

"Wait a minute, you mean to tell me that you saw all this, and you didn't look at his face or know who the guy was? You've been eighteen years in this place, and you don't know everyone in here by sight?" shouted Tyrus.

"I didn't say dat, Sergeant. I just said I could not help you," he said softly.

"But you want us to help your cellie!" shouted Tyrus back.

"Because my cellie is innocent, sir."

Tyrus pushed himself back into his chair with his hands on the armrest. "Oh, come on," he groused.

"It's all right, Larry, I understand," Scott interrupted. "You never know, he might need a character witness someday."

"Thank you, Inspector Doggett. May I go now?"

"Just one more thing, Larry, do you know Curly Payne?"

"Yes, I do. He is a good man too."

"Do you know where he was during the stabbing?"

"Indeed I do. He was in the shower."

"One more thing, do you recognize this man?" Scott inquired as he pushed the 8" × 10" of Jay-Jay toward him.

"Everyone knows Jay-Jay, man."

"And where was he when the deed was done?"

"I can tell you where he was when you came through the door, by the front staircase."

"Just one more thing, Larry, did you ever see Jay-Jay and Vincent arguing?"

"Did I? Who didn't? They had a big argument right in the middle of the yard just the other day."

"Do you remember what the argument was about?"

"It was over a cheap television that belonged to his former cellmate."

Scott offered him his hand. As he shook the inmate's hand, he said, "I hope someday you make it back to that island of yours, Larry."

Larry shook Scott's hand gently and limped out of the room supported by his cane. As he opened the door, he said, "In my mind's eye every day, Inspector."

"I'm not buying it, Dog," grumbled Tyrus.

"Neither am I, but I can't force him to tell us. At any rate, he alibied out two of our suspects, and he is a credible alibi as far as I am concerned. Besides, he told us who did it."

"Who?"

"Patience, old friend."

They went through the next ten inmates very quickly; they didn't see anything. One Southern Hispanic inmate went so far as to tell them that he would rather be shot by a firing squad than to provide any information to the Goons. Scott told him he was being dramatic. He told them they were putting his life unnecessarily in danger by dragging him out of his cell and talking to him because now he might be considered a snitch. Scott and Tyrus thought about keeping him in the room for another twenty minutes or so to make it look like he really was providing information, but they decided they just didn't need the drama, and he was excused. They did give him a collective "boo-hoo" as he went out the door. It was all part of the game.

The next inmate to come through the door was a Southerner. Scott noticed it was the same talkative fellow from the crime scene. Prison politics would suggest he wouldn't be inclined to talk to them as exemplified by the previously ejected inmate. This fellow was jovial and very communicative. "Hey, how's it going? I figured it was only a matter of time before you guys got to me."

"You know, I meant to get to you earlier, but I've been a little busy. What exactly is your name?" Scott inquired.

"Herman Santos. I was standing right there when it happened. I was right next to him."

"What did you see?" Scott asked.

"This *vato* comes up from the front, walking all stealthy and stuff. I thought he was just going to his cell or something because he wasn't running or anything, just walking like he was coming home from work. He walks right up to dude with the dreads, and—pow!—he hits him right in the neck. I saw the weapon. It was small and very shiny. He had it in his hand like this, between the fingers."

"Did you get a good look at him?" asked Tyrus.

"Nah, nah, I was watching that weapon though. I just stood back to get out of his way. He was like you though"—he pointed at Tyrus—"not real dark skinned, maybe about your height too but not your build, skinnier, much skinnier."

"No more hot dogs for you, tubby," Scott remarked.

"Beard and mustache or clean shaven?" Tyrus asked, shoving off Scott's comment.

"Kind of short beard with gray in it," replied the witness.

"Which way did he go after he stabbed him?"

"Up the stairs to the second tier. I tried to tell you that day, but my homeys—you know, they were getting upset that I was talking to you. I can't help it. I talk to everybody. I laugh too. This place is a joke, all hard. They think it's a hard prison. They don't know. I know hard joints. I been in the Bay."

"You were in Pelican Bay?" asked Tyrus.

"Yeah, four years."

"And you transferred down here?"

"Nah, I'm on a violation. I only gots two more months."

"Santos, did you see what he did with the weapon?" Scott asked.

"No. I thought he would have put it in the garbage can in the back, but he didn't. I saw you guys looking for it there though. Maybe he shot it under one of the doors. It was kinda small. It would have pushed under a door, but I didn't see him stop to bend over or anything."

"Which side did he go down?" Scott asked. "The . . . what is that? The . . . uh, the west side? The side with the yard." It was the west side.

They showed him the photographs, but he didn't recognize anyone or know where they were in the wing. Scott told him he was one of the most helpful witnesses they had and that he needed to get back to his cell before his homeys noticed him being in the room too long. The remainder of the Southern Hispanic inmates who were out on the first tier during the incident were far less helpful than Inmate Santos. In fact, they were quite hostile to the idea.

It was time to interview the white guys who were in the area, which wasn't much of a task; there were only two. Inmate Julius Meredith, a seventy-two-year-old embezzler from Milpitas. He didn't see much in the way of the assault, but he was standing next to Jay-Jay in front of the hall. Unfortunately, he didn't see him coming down the stairs.

Inmate Jason Trimble, on the other hand, was a little more helpful. Although he was affiliated with the Southerner Hispanic street disruptive group, he was listed as a white inmate. All of about twenty-two or twenty-three years old, he looked scared when he walked into the room. He sat down and looked carefully at both of the investigators and then looked directly at the floor. "Are you nervous, Jason?" Scott asked.

"Am I in trouble, sir?"

"Should you be?" Scott countered.

"It's just that any time you guys are around, somebody is in trouble."

Scott chuckled. "No, Jason, it's quite the opposite. We're interviewing all the guys who were in the hall but not in their cells on the day that Inmate Sutherland was stabbed. We're looking for witnesses right now, not suspects. I'm thinking you were a witness because, from what I can see on the list, you were right between the front stairs and the table where it happened. So what did you see?"

"Okay, yeah, yeah, okay, I saw it all," he said with rapid succession. "I saw dude get stuck in the side of the head. I saw him get up, look around for who stuck him, and then come walking this way toward the front office."

"Did you see where the stabber went?" Scott asked.

"Yeah, okay, he went up the back stairs and came along the second tier almost parallel to the guy who got stuck. I think he wanted to keep an eye on him, where he was going. I saw him shove something into a piece of paper that was in his hand, and then he came down the front stairs. I don't know where he went when he came down the stairs because that's when the officers were yelling at us to get down."

"Jason, do you think you could identify the guy if you saw his picture?"

"Oh, I don't know. I can try, but you know, I'd never be able to testify in court or nothing like that."

"Just look at these three photographs and tell me if you saw these guys in the hall on that day."

"This guy was sitting at the table next to me. When the guy went past, the guy who was bleeding, he jumped up from the table. He was playing cards with Larry. They are always at that table."

"Ellis," Scott said over his hand to Tyrus.

"This guy was in the shower. I remember because he had to get his shower bag, and he almost ran me over getting up the front stairs. He went to his cell and ran back down with his shower bag and jumped into the shower. He was definitely in the shower when it happened."

"That takes care of Payne. What about the other guy?"

"I don't recognize him."

"Naturally."

"Can I ask you something?" Jason inquired.

"Sure."

"What happened to the guy? Did he die?"

"No, Jason, he lived. It was a close thing though. The blade pierced the carotid artery."

"I thought for sure he would have died. It's the first time I've ever seen anything like that. Will I have to testify in court?"

"I doubt it. You've been very helpful. Go on back to your cell now before your cellie gets curious about where you've been and who you've been talking to."

Chapter 16

The Summary Report

"Well, Tyrus, my forty-eight hours are up, and that should just about do it," Scott said as he closed up his notebook. "Let's go talk to Capt. Pat Crosby."

"Wait, Doggy, we're not finished yet. We should start interviewing all the inmates in Charlie Wing, even the ones that were in their cells. Maybe somebody saw something out the door. We should also look through those cells on the second tier west for the weapon. We don't have a positive ID on the suspect yet," protested his partner.

"No, Ty, we're done. We've done all we can do. I don't know if you noticed, but the unit 3 lieutenant and sergeant have started their interviews while we were in the dayroom. Soon the only thing we are going to get out of the potential witnesses is what the lieutenant and sergeant will tell them. Our lieutenant announced in the morning briefing that our prime suspect was Jay-Jay, and our witness pool will now be tainted. Larry Jackson, Herman Santos, and Jason Trimble told us all we needed to know on Saturday. We have four independent eyewitness descriptions of a medium-height medium-build middle-aged black man with a tight beard consisting of gray and black hair as our suspect. We have three inmates who were present in the room at the time of the stabbing that match that description. We have provided more than one competent and independent eyewitness alibis for two of them.

We cannot provide an alibi for the third, Jay-Jay Norris. Therefore, by a process of elimination, Jay-Jay Norris is our prime suspect. I say we provide this information to the captain and tell him that we need to lock up Jay-Jay in ad seg for his own protection. At least we'll be able to get him off the main line, and we can release Moore and Peabody, and we won't have to worry about Haney getting stabbed."

"But what about a motive, Dog? Jay-Jay didn't have a motive."

"There was an argument over a television set."

"It was a twenty-dollar TV. That's no motive to kill somebody, especially since Norris doesn't have any violence in his file."

"Ty, let's just put this thing to bed now. The facility unit lieutenant is handling it from now on, and I have a feeling they are going to have their own opinion about what happened. Come on, let's go talk to Pat and get Jay-Jay locked up."

They provided a summary of their investigation to Capt. Patrick Crosby, and he agreed to lock up Inmate Norris. He asked Scott if he thought they had enough information to forward the investigation to the district attorney's office for prosecution. Scott informed him that he thought they had enough to send it up, but he was doubtful that the DA would pick up the case because they lacked empirical evidence of any kind. However, Scott did think there was sufficient information for a guilty finding on a rules violation report and that perhaps they could move him to a maximum security facility. Scott promised to provide the captain with a summary report, and he promised Scott both Inmate Peabody and Inmate Moore would be released from the administrative segregation unit, but it would probably take two weeks to get them through the committee hearing and the placement order set up to return them to their cells.

Before they got back to the office, they heard the radio transmission. Inmate Norris was being escorted to the central corridor holding cells for placement in ad seg. A search of his cell produced a variety of televisions, radios, tobacco, and cellular telephones for sale. Scott couldn't fault him for his entrepreneurial skills.

Within an hour, Scott had formulated his notes into a collective report. He summarized the incident, crime scene investigation, injuries sustained, interviews conducted, victimology, and suspect evaluations and added a conclusion regarding the motivation, ability to commit the crime, and the lack of an alibi for the one suspect of three described by the eyewitnesses. He walked into Ty's office and set the folder down in front of him. "Read it and sign it," Scott said.

"Sign what?"

"Sign the investigation summary report. I put your name on there too."

"I noticed your name was first."

"Doggett comes before Phillips alphabetically."

"Investigative sergeant comes before investigative officer alphabetically."

"No, it doesn't. Just sign it, you pompous ass."

A little over a week had passed, and Scott had gone on to other investigations. They had given a full accounting of the Sutherland affair to the warden, and the matter was mostly relegated to an administrative action when Tyrus came into Scott's office with information that they had not heard the last of from Inmate Norris. "Hey, Dog, Norris wants to talk to us. I got a note from him this morning in the mail."

"Oh, Ty, he's just going to tell us some story about how he didn't do it. Are you sure you want to waste our time with it?"

"We've gone this far. What time do you want to go up there?"

"Let's go up there this afternoon, after lunch. I'm not going to give him *Miranda*."

"Don't you have to? I mean, he's in custody."

"Custody and questioning initiated by law enforcement, Tyrus. He wants to talk to us. I'm just going to go up there and tell him he wanted to talk to us, and now is his opportunity. As long as we don't ask any questions, we don't have to give him *Miranda*. If he implicates himself, I'll let him to say his piece, give him the *Miranda* advisement, and then we will question him."

Later that afternoon, Tyrus and Scott were once again in the administrative segregation unit captain's office. It was the best office to use because, technically, ad seg no longer had a captain, so the room was always available. It also had a conference table, which meant Tyrus and Scott could sit opposite each other with the interviewee at the foot of the table.

Scott started the digital voice recorder that was next to his hat. "I wouldn't make no bones about that," said Tyrus quickly while pointing to the diminutive recorder.

"It's in the open, Ty. He'll see it."

Inmate Norris was brought in full restraints into the room by two burly escort officers and seated in the chair next to the two investigators. The two officers then backed out of the room, and Norris sat looking at them. "You wanted to see us, Jay-Jay?" Scott opened.

"Yes, sir, I did," he sheepishly replied.

"Well, I have your note saying you wanted to talk to us. This is your forum. Say what you want to say," Scott said as he leaned back in the chair and placed his clasped hands on his chest, confident he phrased that opening not to appear as a question.

"Well, you see, I been thinking since I been here. I know I want to just take this one, but there's something I need from you." He looked at both of the investigators for a response. They were both resolute in only listening at this point. Scott turned his head slightly and raised his right eyebrow. This was sufficient encouragement for Jay-Jay to continue.

"You see, well, it's like this. They took my TV. I'm in here without a TV, and I'm going crazy. All I do is stare at the walls and the ceiling, and I feel them closing in on me. I'll tell you what you want to know, but I need a TV. Can you do that for me?"

"It is not an unreasonable request," Scott remarked.

"And you have to let these other guys you got in here out. They didn't do anything. They are good men, and they don't need to be in here for something what I done."

"So are you saying you want to tell us that you did it?" asked Tyrus.

"Yeah, yeah, I want to tell you guys what happened, but I need a TV. Can you get me a TV?"

"Well, like he said, it isn't a . . . uh, an . . . what did you say?"

"I said it was not an unreasonable request. We understand that it is difficult to be in an administrative segregation cell without the means of keeping oneself entertained," Scott replied.

Jay-Jay blurted, "I hit him in the neck. I hoped I didn't kill him, but I wanted to hurt him bad."

"Uh, Jay-Jay," Scott said as he leaned forward, "I would really, really like to explore this with you, but let me ask you something. Are you willing to confess?" Scott inquired.

"Yeah, yeah, I will tell you everything."

"This is remarkable, Jay-Jay. In all the years that I—that we have been doing this and the hundreds of investigations and interviews that we have conducted, I can count on one hand the number of inmates who wanted to confess. As I said, I would really like to talk to you about this, but I want you to first be aware of your rights as guaranteed by the Constitution. Is that okay?"

"Yes, sir," he quietly responded.

"Jay-Jay, you have the right to remain silent. Anything that you say can and will be used against you in a court of law. You have the right to an attorney and to have an attorney present during questioning. If you cannot afford an attorney, an attorney will be appointed to you free of charge. Do you understand these rights as I have explained them to you, and with these rights in mind, do you wish to continue this interview without a lawyer present?"

Inmate Norris planted both feet firmly on the floor and with a slight grin said, "Yes, sir, I do." To Scott, it appeared that a burden was being lifted from Jay-Jay's shoulders.

"All right, Jay-Jay, let's start at the beginning. What exactly did you do?" Scott asked.

"I hit him in the neck."

"Can you be a little more detailed? Let's start with the day of the incident. What happened when you came in from work?"

"I came in from work. I knew he was going to be down there. In fact, I heard him playing cards and laughing. He was laughing, and that's what did it for me. I knew at that moment that I wanted to hit him. So I came in through the door to C Wing and went around the front stairs to the showers. That's where I hid the shank earlier that morning."

"You put a shank in the shower area? Where?"

"Behind that big pipe that is right there as you walk in. I put a piece of tape on it, and I put it down low so nobody would see it."

"And you put it there in the morning? Did you know then that you wanted to stab him?"

"Yeah, I thought about it all night. That's when I decided to make a weapon. I didn't have anything metal in the cell to make a shank with, but I knew one of the windows in my cell was broken. I kept working at it until I got a piece out of the frame. It was like a small triangle. I wrapped tape around the base and put it in my hand, between my fingers. The sharp end came through like this. I tried it out on my pillow, and it worked really good. I thought I would cut myself, so I put a piece of sock in my palm and it worked.

"So I walked down to where he was sitting, just like I was going to my cell. I got up on him, and I punched him with the glass. My heart was pumping so loud I couldn't hear anything but the beating of my own heart. My ears couldn't hear anything but the pounding. I didn't even look at him. I knew I had to get out of there before I got caught. I went up the back stairs and came around the side across from him on the second tier. I was watching him because I couldn't believe he wasn't looking at me, and I wanted to see where he went. I came down the front stairs just before he passed. There was an old white man standing there and I said, 'Did you see what just happened?' He said no, he was in the bathroom. I told him that I just came in the door and saw a dude walking past, and it looked like he was bleeding. The old guy said that we probably should sit down, and I did."

"Jay-Jay, I'm having a problem visualizing the weapon. Can you draw us a picture of it?" Tyrus asked.

"Oh, I'm no good at drawin', but I can try." With that, Scott handed him a piece of note paper and a pen. He took the pen in his right hand and straightened the paper with his left.

"Can you reach, or do you want me to take off the handcuff on that side?"

"It's a little hard to reach," he replied.

"How about if I just remove the padlock from the chain that holds the cuff to your waist chain?"

"That might work." It did.

He drew a triangle with a small rectangle at the base. He then drew a circle around the base and said, "This is where I wrapped it with the tape and put the sock over it here."

"And that's about the size of it?" Scott asked.

"Yeah, just about, maybe about three inches long." Scott took the paper from him and tucked it into his notebook. Now he knew Jay-Jay was right-handed, and Scott had an evidentiary drawing of the weapon provided by the suspect himself.

"What did you do with the weapon?" asked Tyrus.

"I put it in my mask, and I threw it away."

"You had a mask?"

"From work, one of those masks that you put on your face when you are cleaning—you know . . . uh, what do they call those things?"

"N95 dust masks," Scott replied.

"Yeah, one of them. While I was walking on the tier, I had the mask in my back pocket. I thought, 'Oh, I need to get rid of this before I go down the stairs, or they will have me.' So I pulled out the mask, and I had it in my left hand, and I tucked the blade and the cloth from the sock into the mask. And when I came down the stairs, I dropped it into the big dumpster in the front. I saw one of you all looking in there. I thought, 'Sure, he was going to find it.'"

"Well, he was probably looking for a metal weapon and not a piece of glass tucked into a mask," Scott remarked.

"Why are you telling us all this?" queried Tyrus.

"Well, you know, I was thinking about it since you put me in here. I was thinking I might as well fess up to it and tell the truth. My mama always told me that I should tell the truth when I did something wrong. I didn't want nothing to happen to the other guys you have in here. They never done nothing wrong to me, and my beef wasn't with them." Jay-Jay looked down at the floor for a minute and then at the heel of his left shoe, the side Scott was sitting on. "I might as well just stay here in prison. I mean, I got a lot of time left on my sentence."

"When do you get out?" Scott asked.

"Five years."

"Five years? That's just around the corner."

"But I got no place to go when I get out. I always lived with my mom, and now she's gone. My auntie is gone. My grams is gone. My daddy died in prison. I might as well die in prison too. I mean, I don't got no wife or children. Hell, I don't even know how to talk to a woman anymore. Don't get me wrong, I like women. I really do, but I wouldn't know what to say to one. I had a friend at Mule Creek who tried to hook me up with a girl. She came to visit, and I just sat there." He gave an odd, almost childish laugh and continued, "I didn't have nothing to say to her. I mean, what am I going to talk about, prison? I've been in prison all my life, all my life. I'm forty-two years old, and I got no friends. My cellie I got now, Simms, he's been a good friend. He tried to tell me the TV wasn't enough to get worked up over."

"Is that what this was all about, the television set?" asked Tyrus.

"Yes, sir. I couldn't let it go. It just kept eating at me. He lied to me. Selling stuff is my thing, man. That's all I do. I don't make no enemies. I just do my own thing."

"His cellie sold it to you before he left?" Tyrus confirmed.

"Yes, sir, he sold it to me for $20 cash money. He said I could pick it up on the morning after he left, and his cellie, Sutherland, would give it to me. Well, when I went to get it, that worm told me that his cellie took it with him. I told him he better get my money back, but he said it wasn't his problem. Well, when he went out to breakfast that morning, I went into his cell, and I found the TV under his bunk covered with a towel. I should have taken it then, but I didn't. I wanted to confront him about it. I waited until I saw him out on the yard later that afternoon, and I confronted him. I told him he was lying and he needed to give me my TV now. He said that was an old TV he used for parts, but I know it wasn't. We got into an argument, and it was about to go into shoves when one of the towers alerted the yard officer. He came over and asked us if there was a problem, and we just said we were arguing over a football game.

"After that, my cellie came over and tried to get it straight. He told me to leave it alone because it just wasn't that important. I should have listened to him. He's a lot smarter than I am, but I couldn't let it alone. I kept thinking if I don't do something, then everyone will just take my shit. They'll just walk right up to me and say, 'Jay-Jay, I want that shirt,' or 'I want that radio,' and they will just take them. I knew I had to send a message that you couldn't take my stuff without paying for it. He was a lot bigger than me, and I knew if it came to a fair fight, he would win. So I knew I had to hit him when he was vulnerable, and I had to hit him in a way that he couldn't retaliate against me. I didn't want to kill him. Really, I didn't."

"But you knew that was a possibility?" Scott asked.

"Oh, yeah, well, you know, you hit someone in the side of the head, he just might die. I knew that, and I didn't care. Well, I guess that's about it then, huh?"

"Yeah, I'm thinking that's enough."

"So do I get my TV?"

"Yeah, we'll get you a TV. It won't be legit, but we'll get you one. We'll square it with your sergeant here, but remember, if you do anything wrong or you get transferred, you could lose it. Let me ask you something. Would you have confessed if we said no to the TV?"

"Yes, I wanted to get it off my chest, but I thought it wouldn't hurt to ask for one. You know something? I do feel a lot better. I feel relieved and peaceful." He did look at peace with his decision to admit his guilt and accept the consequences of his actions. It was a truly unique moment in correctional history.

The two brawny escort officers took their charge back to his cell. Scott turned off the digital recorder and put it back in its pouch. "Say what you will, Ty. I kinda like the fellow. He may be somebody who would stick a sharpened piece of glass in your neck, but you have to admire his determination."

"Yeah, Dog, but what did you think of that bit about the women?"

"You mean the childlike laugh?"

"Yeah, that was weird."

"Probably just breached an uncomfortable subject with him. He might have been a little embarrassed too. One thing for sure, we had nothing on him for a good prosecution until he went and opened his mouth."

"I don't think he knew that, Dog."

"Oh shit, I just turned in that report. We need to get it back and make an adjustment. We should also take a camera kit down to the wing and photograph his cell, the window, and the front dumpster."

"Note to self: next time, check the dumpster myself," muttered Tyrus in retrospection.

They returned to the office, procured a digital evidence camera, and walked down to Charlie Wing. They found and photographed the small window frame with the missing triangular-shaped piece of glass. They also took more photographs of the hall, including the shower area with the large drainpipe, the second-tier west side, and the front dumpster.

Officer Schwartz was standing in the middle of the sally port, watching their activity. Scott walked up to him and said, "It's all over. He confessed."

"Who confessed? Peabody?"

"No, Jay-Jay . . . uh, Inmate Norris confessed. He told us everything. We don't have the weapon, but it will be all right. He described it for us and even drew us a picture."

"Wow!" exclaimed the officer. "What was it over?"

"A $20 broken television set. Life has no great value these days, especially in prison. By the way, did you ever find an old black-and-white television set with knobs in Sutherland's cell?"

"Sure did. It's in the hot room. I think it belonged to his ex-cellie."

"I'm sure you don't mind if we book that into evidence." No objection was heard, and Tyrus, the old television, and Scott returned to the office.

"I just wanted you to know that your forty-eight hours were already up, Doggy."

"We had him in custody before the forty-eight hours was up. Besides, Ty, that's the part you don't see on your precious television show, the editing."

"Whatever, Dog, I said forty-eight hours."

"You know, Ty, when I grow up, I want to be just like you, only good looking."

Chapter 17

The Epilogue

Scott personally delivered the Sutherland attempted homicide investigation to the district attorney's office. They were reluctant, at first, to file any charges against Inmate Norris owing to a lack of physical evidence. Scott requested and was granted a conference with DDA Richard Rainwater and his supervisor. He sat down with them and explained their investigation and the steps they went through to isolate their suspect. Scott explained the interviews and the confession, and he showed them a copy of the picture of the weapon provided by Inmate Norris. "If you file it, he will plea," Scott said as he finished his presentation.

It took several weeks for them to finally come to a decision—they would file. Inmate Norris pleaded guilty during the arrangement and asked for the sentence to be determined on the same day. The judge decided to give Inmate Norris a fortnight to think about his guilty plea and set a calendar call two weeks hence on a Wednesday. The result was the same, and after a probation office report and a mental evaluation of Inmate Norris were submitted, he was sentenced to sixteen years in prison at 85 percent, plus a strike.

Personally, Scott thought Jay-Jay was hoping for more time than he got. He likely realized he might get kicked out of prison when he was sixty years of age and would have no support outside the gray walls.

Who knows? He might kill another inmate when he was in his late fifties just to remain in prison. Scott wouldn't have to worry; three more years was all he planned on giving to the prison. Let the next man process that crime scene.

Over a year had passed since the Zhuang homicide went back to the DA's office for reconsideration. Karen Ballard had moved on to some other position in the attorney general's office and had lost all avid interest in the matter. She did write a letter to the district attorney with a recommendation to reconsider their decision and file charges. The decision remained the same, however; the district attorney declined to prosecute Inmate Vong. Scott had done all that he could, but sometimes it just wasn't enough. It's funny how some cases you work until your eyeballs bleed using every available forensic science, and the suspect eludes punishment. Other cases simply come together through clever interview techniques, and the conviction is assured.

But when it came to interviewing techniques, Scott's father always said, "You catch more snails with a good beer than with balsamic vinegar." And he did too.

The trick is to get them talking first. If they lawyer up during *Miranda*, your chances of getting a confession are greatly reduced, not impossible but greatly reduced. Once the suspect is talking, just look for the discrepancies. Sometimes they can be very subtle and easily overlooked.

The other thing of importance is to always be a nice guy and genuine. Scott had been told by more than one offender that he was the nicest guy they ever got arrested by. Scott wasn't sure how to take that. One thing Scott knew—if you tell a suspect you didn't care what he did in the past and the only thing that mattered was what he did in the present and the future, you had to be sincere and genuinely mean it. An inmate especially can see through a phony. Some criminals think they are clever and can win in an interview. Some of them owe their skill to experience. Some of them, on the other hand, lie through their teeth. Here's a good example.

On one particular day, institutional gang investigator Mark McShane was returning to the institution from a conference. As he exited the freeway and drove over the overpass leading to the prison gatehouse, he spotted a tattoo-adorned young Hispanic male wearing blue jeans and a white T-shirt frantically trying to wave down cars coming off the freeway. Well, any time you have any male wearing blue jeans and waving their arms over their heads in an effort to catch a ride in front of a prison, you'd think of only one thing—escape.

Mark keyed his radio microphone and broadcast a quick "Any mobile security and investigation unit, I need immediate backup at the freeway overpass." Tyrus and Scott were downstairs in their basement office and were anything but mobile, but when one of their own broadcast they needed help, help came fast. Not knowing the circumstances, they ran at full speed up the stairs, out the door, down the path, through the entrance building sally port, and across the parking lot to Scott's faithful Crown Vic cruiser. It was called a "cold start" when you fired up a Crown Vic early in the morning and slam it into gear. Fortunately, you couldn't hear the pinging of the engine rods over the sound of the siren for the one-third-mile sprint to the freeway overpass. Now, of course, in hindsight, they might have made a stop at the armory and collected up their firearms first, but Tyrus and Scott were of the Andy Taylor mentality and tended to enter dangerous situations underarmed.

Scott spotted Mark standing next to his cruiser, talking to the young male. They were the first unit to respond but certainly not the last as units started emerging from every direction. While Tyrus was being briefed by Mark, Scott backed the young man over to the sidewalk on the overpass and had him take a seat. "What's your name, son?" Scott asked.

"Anthony Ramos, sir. I'm sorry for all this mess. I caught a ride to work, and they dropped me off here. I was just trying to find someone to take me the rest of the way to work."

"Do you have any identification?"

"No, sir, I left my wallet in my wife's car. I'd call her and tell her to bring it back, but I left my cell phone in her car too."

"Okay, where did you say you worked again?"

"I do landscaping in Soledad, sir."

"But you're flagging down cars going north. Soledad is south of here."

"No, sir, I was coming from Soledad. We have a job in Gonzales today."

"Well, you could have walked to the city of Gonzales. It's not that far away. Here, Anthony, take this piece of paper and write down your name, California driver's license number, date of birth, and social security number," Scott instructed while handing him a notebook and pen.

"I don't remember my social security number, sir . . . or my driver's license."

"Okay, son, then write down your date of birth and your address, and I will see if I can find out your license number that way," Scott encouraged. He took the paper and scribbled out some details.

"Says you live in Salinas?" Scott asked as he looked at the notebook.

"Yes, sir," he replied.

"Well, Anthony, Salinas is north of here also. Are you sure you weren't trying to get back to Salinas?"

"No, sir, I am working a job in Gonzales, and I live in Soledad."

"Okay, Soledad now, not Salinas. What's the name of your boss and I will give him a call?"

"It's John, uh, Higgins, but I don't know his phone number," he stammered.

"Let me ask you something, Anthony. Are you on probation or parole?"

"Probation."

"What is the name of your probation officer?"

"I'm on, uh . . . what's it called? Uh, informal probation. I don't have a PO."

"Okay, Anthony, you wait here, and I will get right back to you. As soon as I get you identified, we can get you back on your way. Now don't go anywhere because, as you can see, we have you surrounded," Scott warned.

"I won't, sir, I promise."

"Oh, and your birthday is October 27?" Scott asked as he looked at the paper.

"Yes, sir, October 12."

"The twelfth?"

"Yes, sir, it's the twelfth."

Scott walked over to where Tyrus was talking to Mark. "I already called the watch commander, and we are doing an emergency lockdown and count," said Tyrus as Scott approached. "He has no identification and says he is on probation. I'll try and call teletype, but it's a little early. They don't come in until eight. Not sure how much luck I will get. I've already got two different dates of birth."

"You know, Dog, I don't feel good about this guy. Let's put him in cuffs." Tyrus turned and signaled to Investigator McShane and made the telltale "cuff him" sign of one hand miming a handcuff onto the other wrist. Before Scott could blink, McShane had yanked the kid off the curb, had slapped him in handcuffs, and was frisking him for weapons.

"What do you want me to do with him?" asked Mark.

"Um, put him in the back of my cruiser for now, McShane. The door isn't locked," Scott responded as he tried to call the teletype operator. "No luck, Ty. She's not in yet."

"I know. I just saw her drive by. Hey, I'm going to have a talk with this young man." Scott saw Tyrus bend over the rear window of his Crown Vic and converse with their young interloper.

"Hey, Dog, did he say his birth date was October 17?"

"That's three!" Scott yelled back.

After a few minutes, Tyrus walked back over to Scott. "I think he's on parole, but he says he was discharged a few years ago and was only on nonsupervised probation right now."

"Does he remember his old CDCR number?" Scott asked.

"No."

"Bullshit, Ty, that's something you never forget. Let me have another talk with him, and in the meantime, you call county probation and see if you can get some information from them. Here's his name and all three dates of birth." Scott transferred the information to another sheet of paper.

"Do we have probable cause to detain him?" asked Tyrus.

"At this point, absolutely yes. He has provided misleading information to a peace officer, and we think we may have an escapee on our hands." Scott walked back over to the car, climbed in the front seat, and drove the car back onto state prison property. He got out of the car, opened the back door, and knelt down close to their detainee. "Anthony, are you by any chance gang affiliated?" he inquired.

"I was when I was younger. Are you going to arrest me?"

"Well, you say you are an ex-felon, right?"

"Yes, sir, but that was like ten years ago that I got out."

"No matter, just for your information, being an ex-felon on state prison grounds without the permission of the warden is a violation of Penal Code section 4571, a felony. Now that's just for your information. You actually were not on state prison grounds. Do you see that yellow line that we just drove over?"

"Yes, sir."

"You were on the other side. I brought you over here. That doesn't count. So no, you are not going to be arrested. As long as your identification can be verified and we figure out that we don't have an escaped inmate, you can go. Which gang were you affiliated with?"

"Varrio Soledad Locos," he replied.

"Well, that would explain the 'VSL' tattooed to the side of your head. Sit tight, Anthony. I will be right back." Scott closed the door and pulled out his outdated state-issued cellular telephone. "Lisa, are you logged on yet?" Scott asked their teletype operator.

"I saw you out there, Dog, and I am logging on now."

"Okay, write this down in the meantime: Anthony Ramos, DOB October 12, 17, or 27. Take your pick. No driver's license or social security number. He lives in Salinas, Soledad, or Gonzales. Take your pick. Five foot five or six inches, maybe 170 pounds, brown eyes, black hair with 'VSL' on the left side of his head. Call me back if you get anything."

"You're not giving me much to work with here, Dog," she griped.

"Yell at him, not at me. Call me back."

Scott hung up the phone and was walking back to where Tyrus was standing when he heard "sir!" come from the small opening in the top of the rear window of his cruiser. "Yes, Anthony?" Scott asked.

"Sir, I want to tell you something. My birthday is actually October 12, and my name isn't Anthony. It's Andrew."

"Andrew Ramos?"

"Yes, sir, Andrew Ramos, and I think I have a traffic warrant. That's why I gave you my brother's name."

"Okay, Andrew, hang tight," Scott said as he redialed Lisa to give her the updated information. Scott continued to where Tyrus was standing and talking on the phone. "Try Andrew Ramos with the October 12 birthday."

Tyrus moved his head away from the receiver. "I'm not getting anywhere, Dog, with probation. I'm going to check with parole and see if we can get the old CDCR number." Lisa called Scott back; she still had no luck, but she was still working on the information for Andrew Ramos.

Tyrus was leaning against the trunk of Mark's car as he talked to the Salinas Parole Unit. He waved Scott over with his left hand. "Dog, Andrew Ramos is on parole and is supposed to be living at a halfway house in Salinas. Hang on, the agent is going to call the halfway house and see what time he left. Let's go over and ask him if that's where he lives."

They walked back to Scott's car, and Scott opened the door. Anthony—rather, Andrew turned in their direction. "Are you still living at the halfway house in Salinas?" Ty asked.

"Yes, sir, I do" was the reply.

"What time did you leave there this morning?"

"I left at six thirty. Please don't tell my parole agent I am down here. I'm not supposed to be in this area, but it's the only place I could get work."

"I see. Okay, thank you. I'll call you right back," said Tyrus as he disconnected his call. "Dog, come over here for a minute." He backpedaled from the cruiser.

Scott closed the door and complied. From that moment on, Scott was determined to leave the door closed. Once they were a fair distance from the car, Tyrus said, "Dog, he's still at the halfway house. The agent called them, and the guy at the counter said, 'Andrew Ramos, he's standing right here in front of me.' I heard him on the line. The agent seems to think this guy is one of Andrew's brothers, either Anthony or Albert."

"Well, let's give him one more chance to tell the truth," Scott said as he walked back to the car with Tyrus.

"Okay, Not-the-Andrew," Scott said through the cracked window, "last chance to tell us your real name before we take you to jail. It's not Andrew. He's still at the halfway house. So what's the *nom du jour*?"

"It is Anthony, sir. I am sorry," he replied.

"Anthony, what is your middle name?" asked Tyrus from the open door on the other side of the car.

"I don't have one. Tony, it's Tony," he unconvincingly responded.

"Aw," remarked Tyrus as he backed away from the car and slammed his hand against the door.

"Smart kid. Tony is short for Anthony. I'm done with you. You're going to jail," Scott stated as he backed away from the car.

"But, sir! But, sir!" he protested.

"You know what, Ty, let's just call the local police over, have him taken to their station jail, and we can run him through Live Scan over there. In the meantime, we arrest him for a 148, providing false identification to a peace officer and interfering with our investigation. It's a misdo, but it'll hold him until our count clears."

Scott placed the call to the dispatch operator, and it took about twenty minutes before a much newer Crown Victoria pulled up. A very tall and large police officer exited the vehicle. Scott remembered seeing a lot of stars on his collar. At the time, Scott had no idea it was the chief of police. As soon as their mystery guest saw the chief, he elected to be forthcoming and almost tell the truth. In fact, the chief asked the kid if he was indeed on active parole, to which the kid adamantly replied, "No."

Tyrus, who had received a callback from the parole unit, was certain that they were talking to Albert Manuel Ramos, a wanted parolee at large. Lisa called Scott also and told him that Albert was not only wanted on a no-bail felony warrant but also wanted in Nevada for murder, a double homicide in fact. The chief was pissed when he found out that the kid lied. He opened the back door of Scott's Vic and yanked the offender out of the back seat. The handcuffs were switched, and he was introduced to the back seat of the shinier newer Ford. Scott got a call from the chief a few hours later; the fingerprints confirmed their catch.

Again, sometimes a big fish washes up onshore right in front of your house or, in this case, prison. If the story smells fishy, trust me, it is.

ESCAPE?

Contents

CSP-Gabilan

South Facility - Minimum

Chapter 1

Compacted

"I'm telling you, Ty, it would be sweet if there really was a body in there," Scott said as they drove the short distance from their office to the vehicle sally port providing access to the Central Facility.

"It's probably just red Jell-O, Dog, from the culinary. Let's get this over with and go get something to eat," Tyrus replied.

"Can't you think of anything other than food?"

"Not when I'm hungry."

"Well, I brought the phenolphthalein kit, and I threw in a couple of Hexagon OBTI kits in case the phenolphthalein is positive for blood. We'll be able to tell if it's from a human or a little critter with the OBTI. But, Tyrus, can you imagine if it really was a body crushed in the back of a garbage truck? That would be my all-time favorite crime scene ever."

"You're a sick man, Dog," replied the concerned sergeant.

As they pulled up across from the California State Prison (CSP)–Gabilan Firehouse, Scott looked over into the sally port and observed the dull white 1987 International Harvester garbage truck parked inside. Old Mr. Graves was standing near the driver's door, holding an unlit cigarette near his lips. He had grown old driving that truck, and both shared a pungent odor, the result of hauling thousands of tons of inmate-generated trash for the past three decades. As the outer perimeter gate of the sally port opened, Scott could see a red liquid dripping from the huge container over the left rear tire. "You gonna get this thing out of my sally port, Dog?" inquired Officer Donny Ferguson, adding, "I've got a mess of transportation vans coming out. It's Friday, and it's court day."

"No worries, Fergie, it's probably just fruit punch," Scott encouraged.

"It don't smell like fruit punch," he replied as he stepped into his small guardhouse.

"All I smell is garbage truck, Fergie. Good morning, Mr. Graves. What sort of trouble are you in this morning?"

"I made my first pickup from the minimum yard, Mr. Doggett. I was on my way into central to make the morning run. Mr. Ferguson saw the red stuff dripping, and I guess he called you all."

"You're not going to light that thing, are you, Mr. Graves?" asked Tyrus, pointing at the cigarette, aware there was a ban on smoking on state prison grounds and that Mr. Graves existed with the aid of an oxygen tube that linked his nostrils to a small steel bottle attached to his hip.

"We wouldn't want you blowing up," Scott added.

"No, no, Sergeant Phillips, I can't smoke no more. I just hold it. My doctor said I can't smoke no more."

"When are they going to let you retire?" Scott inquired.

"They said maybe in May, but I'm not sure I want to. You know, I would lose my medical insurance, and I just don't want to rely on Medicare. Maybe I'll just keep working."

"I know one thing for sure—on the day you retire, we are getting rid of this old bucket of bolts."

"She's been good to me, Mr. Doggett. I've known this old girl almost as long as I've known my wife, Rose, and she's been just as good."

"Well, Mr. Graves, I think you should probably keep that to yourself," Scott said, refraining from the obvious comparative jokes. "But if you ask me, I think on the last day you work, you should just drive this old truck to the landfill and park it as homage to the tons of trash you've hauled."

"Why don't you drive the new one we just bought?" asked Tyrus.

"Sergeant Phillips, they paid over $250,000 for that garbage truck. That's more than I paid for my house. It just wouldn't be right. Imagine paying that much money for a garbage truck. I'll keep driving my old girl here until they tell me to stop."

"Okay, Mr. Graves, let's take a look at this red fluid. It's probably nothing, but we need to make sure," Scott said as he pulled the presumptive kits out of his cargo pocket. He extracted a small cotton-tipped swab and dabbed it on a large drop he found on the rear tire sidewall.

"Okay, first the alcohol, then the phenolphthalein, and finally the hydrogen peroxide," he called out in order of the bottles and applications.

Suddenly, before their eyes, the small cotton swab turned bright pink. "Well, that's not good," Scott commented, adding, "We seem to have a positive reaction for blood."

"What?" ejaculated both Tyrus and Mr. Graves at the same time. Fergie also leaned out of his small guard shack.

"Don't get excited," Scott encouraged. "I'll do the OBTI to see if it's an animal, not to mention there might be all kinds of contaminants in here." The Hexagon OBTI immunochromatographic rapid test resembles a pregnancy test kit. It has one small bottle that contains the liquid transport medium and a test strip in a plastic housing that is capable of detecting even minute quantities of hemoglobin.

"I've seen all this on *CSI*. Is that luminol?" inquired Mr. Graves.

"Mr. Graves," Scott lectured, "luminol has been around since the 1930s and must be applied in complete darkness. We're a little more high-tech these days. This is a presumptive test kit that will tell us if this red fluid is human blood or perhaps one of the primates, a ferret or skunk."

"With this smell, we'd never know if it was a skunk." Tyrus chortled.

"Well, how does that one work?" asked the old truck driver.

"First, I swab a little bit of the fluid with this small Q-tip. I then break off just the cotton part into the bottle like this, being careful, of course, not to touch the tip. Okay, now I put the cap back on and shake it vigorously for about thirty seconds, break off the tip of the bottle, and put a drop or two right here in this small well. The mixture will travel up the strip to the test zone, where it is captured by a second immobilized antibody directed against the human hemoglobin, forming a blue test line. The unreacted agents migrate farther up the strip and are bound by a second line by immobilized antibodies that—crap— show a positive result."

Scott was met again by a collective "what?"

"Gentlemen, it is a positive result for human blood. Either that or you have managed to crush a ferret, monkey, or skunk."

"What do we do now?" asked Tyrus excitedly.

"First things first, Ty. We need a camera kit. Second, tell Fergie to have them reactivate the North Facility vehicle sally port. We are going to be here awhile. Third, we need an emergency lockdown and count for the entire institution. Fourth, I need my crime scene kit. Fifth, we have to open the truck in a methodical manner. And sixth, you ain't eating anything anytime soon."

"Should we do an emergency count not knowing exactly what's in there?"

"It couldn't hurt, Ty. It'll take them an hour to set up the count and get all the inmates back in their cells and bunks. At least we'll be able to figure out if any of the inmates are missing, and we might just notify all supervisors to do a head count on all the employees as well."

"I better call the watch commander and our lieutenant."

"This is a contained crime scene, Ty. I don't want a lot of people out here. Too bad Oz is in training. He'd love this."

"Mr. Doggett, do you really mean to say someone is in there?" asked a shocked Mr. Graves.

"It looks that way, Mr. Graves," Scott replied, placing his hand on the old man's shoulder.

"You mean, I might have crushed someone in there?" His eyes went wide, and he stumbled a few steps back and fell to the concrete.

"Ty!" Scott shouted. "Ty! I need you now!" His partner was on the telephone in the guard shack.

Scott immediately knelt and placed his fingertips to the old man's neck. "Crap, no pulse," Scott said to himself as he rolled Mr. Graves flat on his back and checked his oxygen bottle to see if it was turned open. He opened it all the way, took out his CPR mask, and figured out he could insert the tube sufficiently into the mask to allow oxygen to flow into his open mouth. He then began the chest compressions.

The officer in the adjacent tower observed his actions and immediately called a medical code over the institutional radio system. Fergie and Tyrus eventually appeared at Scott's side. Tyrus knelt down next to Mr. Grave's head and checked the mask to make sure the seal was tight and that there was a sufficient flow of oxygen. Fergie tapped Scott on the shoulder and said, "Medical is coming from central with a ton of responding officers."

"Fergie," Scott said while panting heavily, "I don't want anyone other than the medical personnel in here. It's a crime scene. Make it happen, buddy."

Officer Ferguson looked up at the tower and motioned with his hands to open the inner perimeter gate only a few feet. He then walked toward the opening while waving his hands over his head and suggesting he would allow only the medical staff to enter. This caused quite a commotion as the watch commander had run down the corridor with the responding staff and was anxious to get into the sally port. The fire department personnel had also responded and were standing outside the outer perimeter gate, demanding to be let into the sally port; but since both gates could not be opened at the same time, they too were at an impasse.

Scott finally had to stand up and yell at the tower to close the inner perimeter gate and open the outer perimeter gate as he was in greater need of the firemen than an angry watch commander. "Marcus, take over. I'm spent," Scott said to Fire Chief Marcus Brewer as the emergency responders surrounded them.

Scott walked over to where Fergie was standing near the closed gate. "Fergie, can you please go write down the names of all the emergency responders who got in before we closed the inner gate?" He acknowledged his instructions and walked off toward his shack to get a piece of paper.

Lt. Randall Petersen, the watch commander, was standing just outside the closed gate with his arms crossed. "What the hell is going on in there?" he demanded.

"Randall, here's what we have so far. I have what appears to be blood, human blood, dripping from the back of this garbage truck. Mr. Graves, having had the sudden realization he might have just crushed someone, apparently has had a heart attack. This is a crime scene, and although I have an incredibly contaminated garbage truck as my main piece of evidence, I do not want to have an incredibly contaminated crime scene."

"Shouldn't you open the truck and see if there is someone in there that he isn't just hurt and needs immediate medical attention?" grumbled the anxious lieutenant.

"Randy, do you see that big puddle of red stuff under the truck? The adult human male holds about a gallon and a half of blood in the body or a twelve-pack of beer's worth. Not counting the amount that dripped all the way from the South Facility to here, I'm guessing that's at least a gallon and maybe a little more. If there is someone in there, he's gone by way of exsanguination. I need to clear the truck methodically. This cannot be a perfunctory examination of the contents of that vehicle."

"Let me in, Dog."

"No, Randy, I can't."

"What if it's an order?"

"I still can't."

"You've got balls, I will give you that. Then I'm going to park my butt right here until you open that damned thing."

"He's stable, Dog," said a heavily breathing Sergeant Phillips. "The fire department is putting him on the gurney and will wheel him out to their ambulance and meet the outside ambulance near the gatehouse. The chief thought that was clever what you did with the oxygen bottle."

"I figured I would let his little bottle do all the breathing. This is going to be one hell of a report, Ty. As soon as all the medical people are out, let's get back to the crime scene."

Officer Ferguson appeared with the piece of paper bearing the names of the responding emergency personnel. "Twenty-two years I've been at this sally port. Twenty-two years, and I've never had an escape. I've never had anything so much as a catfight. Ninety days from retirement, and this has to happen. Chief Brewer said Mr. Graves should be okay. You know he's seventy? Seventy years old, and he's still working here, still driving this truck. Maybe now they'll give him a medical retirement. He can keep his medical insurance that way, and he will be covered by workmen's comp."

"Fergie, can you operate this truck?" Scott asked.

"Sure can. I'm the one who compacts it before it leaves the sally port."

"Can you uncompact it too?"

"It's the same lever but in reverse."

"Okay, when the time comes, I'm counting on you to gently raise that crusher."

A quick trip to the old Crown Vic produced the necessary crime scene kit, crime scene tape, and digital camera to begin the gentle process of documenting the event and collecting the evidence. Scott began taking photographs of the garbage truck in the sally port from across the parking lot, facing north, northeast, and northwest and then from the east and west sides. He crossed through the sally port, entered the prison, and took the same photographs facing south, southeast, and southwest. He then repeated the same steps while standing inside the sally port. He placed the camera on a piece of cardboard on the ground, opened the f-stops to f-16, and set the focus at infinity minus one. He set the timer on the camera and held it steady until it released the shutter. This effectively captured the underside of the garbage truck and the blood-soaked concrete. He walked to the front of the truck and took a photograph documenting the license plate and vehicle number. He then positioned himself directly behind the beast and started taking a series of photographs cataloging every inch of debris that swirled in the giant pool of blood that slopped out from under the great crusher.

He looked over his shoulder and took note of the great many spectators who had assembled on the prison side of the sally port gate. "Ty, before we open this thing, I really don't mind the staff members standing there, watching, but I'd really rather not see the three inmates that are mixed in among them. Let's get them out of here just in case it's a staff member stuck under this thing."

With that, Sergeant Phillips walked over to the gate and addressed the watch commander regarding the issue. Everyone was so intent on seeing what was concealed within the stomach of the beast that they didn't even notice that an officer from the North Facility who had been escorting three inmates to a medical appointment at the Central Facility had joined the queue of spectators complete with his charges. For this indiscretion, he received a severe scolding and reprimand from the acrimonious watch commander.

Satisfied that no inmates were present as spectators, Scott gave the signal for Officer Ferguson to very slowly raise the crusher. Slowly, the giant jaw opened. "Better stand to the side," prudently suggested Fergie. As they did so, a farrago of blood and juiced garbage spattered the ground where they just recently stood.

"Stop!" Scott shouted. As the crusher groaned to a stop, plastic bags filled with rubbish, flattened cardboard boxes, and muck rolled down from the top.

Visible between the bags was a left forearm complete with wristwatch and a badly mangled left leg adorned with a distinctive Prison Industries Authority brown inmate work boot on the foot. A gasp went over the assembled crowd. "Merciful god," murmured the normally affable sally port officer as he turned away in disgust. Scott looked up briefly at the tower officer who had, without a doubt, the best viewing perch. He was peering inside the cavernous belly with his binoculars.

"Dead?" asked Tyrus.

"Without a doubt," Scott replied as he retracted his ungloved hand from the victim's wrist.

"Lime green jumpsuit, Dog. He was a worker somewhere on the outside work crew."

"Yeah, well, that should make it easy. Have them call in all the work crews, if they already haven't. The farm gate will know who is missing when they have one extra identification card."

"Yeah, I'll get Randy to do it," Tyrus said as he walked over to confer with the watch commander.

"Tell him I will start making the contacts," Scott added.

"Do you need me anymore?" asked Officer Ferguson.

"You might want to start on your report. I'll have quite a task with this one, and we aren't even going to start until the coroner's and district attorney's office investigators get here."

"I think I'll go get a cup of coffee at the firehouse. I can check on the status of Mr. Graves while I'm there. Twenty-two years and not a single incident," Fergie muttered as he wandered off.

"Seven-fifteen," Scott said under his breath as he dialed the county communications center.

Chapter 2

The Guts of the Beast

"How many pounds of pressure do you think that thing produces?" asked Tyrus as he looked up at the raised crushing mechanism that was still dripping blood.

"Shouldn't that be force, Tyrus? At any rate, maybe thirty tons of force if it was full, I would imagine. Our incident time will probably be 0715 hours."

"Shouldn't it be 0810 hours, the time we were called?"

"Probably, but if you look at his wristwatch, you will notice that it is a dial watch, and it stopped at 0715 exactly. I'm no Sherlock Holmes, but I'm going to guess that is the time of death."

"Who's coming out from the DA's office?"

"Our little round friend Alberto Gutierrez," Scott replied.

"And from the coroner's office?"

"Andy Dykman, coroner's investigator savant by his own admission."

"Dick-man?"

"Dike-man, it's Dutch. He was the one who was out there when the bus got hit by the train near the freeway just south of here."

"Oh, yeah, tall white guy with horn-rimmed glasses and a buzz cut."

"What were you expecting, a pince-nez?"

"A what?"

"Never mind. Bert should be here in a few minutes. He was on his way to the south county when he got the call. Speak of the devil, and in he walks. That's his car now, if I am not much mistaken. I want full Tyvek suits on this one, Ty. We are going to have to sort through every bag of garbage."

"Why?"

"Clues, dear friend, clues. There should be fingerprints and DNA on those bags," Scott remarked.

"So we are booking all those smelly bags into evidence? I mean, come on, Dog, the stench is unbearable as it is!" exclaimed the perturbed sergeant.

"Actually, Ty, what I intend to do is dust the bags for prints using disposable powder and brushes, and I will record whatever prints we find using photography and gel lifts. If it looks like we cannot lift the print, we will take a sterile scalpel and cut that section out of the bag, label it accordingly, and preserve the removed section. As far as the DNA, I intend to swab the twisted portion of the bags where someone might have touched them. We are going to label each bag and photograph it and then dispose of it properly. If necessary, I will cut off the top portion of the bag and book that into evidence.

"One thing I want you to do, Tyrus, is to call over to the garage and have them bring up the new garbage truck and park it outside the sally port because we are definitely going to need to transfer the better part of this trash from one truck to the other. Oh, and we are definitely going to need a boatload of those hazardous material bags from the firehouse. We are going to uncover this body just like a buried body case. Every layer of sediment must be inspected for the smallest clue. Oh, and, Ty, call Lieutenant Templeton and let him know what we have. He's been blowing up my phone and is probably quite pissed I haven't answered."

"Oh my god, Doggie, what have you done this time?" exclaimed the diminutive and rotund district attorney investigator as he rolled out of his car.

"Alberto! I have something special for you this time. Have you had breakfast? If not, I think I see some scraps from the kitchen in this soup."

"Uh, no thanks, I'm fine. I thought you said you had an in-custody death?"

"I do."

"Don't tell me he's in there."

"Okay, I won't tell you, but he is. Wanna see?"

"I wouldn't miss this for the world," replied the investigator, teeming with anticipation.

Scott instructed the tower officer to open the outer perimeter gate a few feet. He then instructed him to open it a few feet more and ushered Alberto through the gap while handing him a double extralarge Tyvek suit. "It's a bit splashy, Bert." He squirmed into the suit and followed Scott to the back of the truck.

"How the heck did he get in there? You're sure he's dead?"

"Legs don't generally bend in that direction, Bert," Scott replied.

Alberto raised his camera and took a few photographs. "Are we going to fish him out of there, Doggie?"

"Just as soon as Andy Dykman gets here," Scott replied.

"Ah, the big Dick-man is coming."

"That's Dike-man, Bert. It's Dutch."

"Whatever. Do we know who he is yet?" he said, pointing into the truck.

"Not yet but soon, I suspect. Wow, look at that fancy new white Dodge Charger pulling up. I've never seen so many lights on a slick top before. That thing has red and blues on the back of the side mirrors, grille, bumper, dash, and up by the rearview mirror."

"That would be the new ride for the coroner's office and His Highness Detective Dick-man," advised Bert.

"Hey, Dog!" hailed Tyrus from the guard shack while motioning Scott over with his free hand. The other hand was on the telephone receiver. "It's Roger Pippington from the farm gate. They are missing an inmate, Inmate Richard Weller. He works at the recycling plant. He's a white boy, early twenties with an Alpha-Boy number. He went out this morning at about 0650 hours."

"Twenty minutes later, he was dead," Scott remarked as he copied the information Tyrus was writing on a notepad.

"Thanks, Roger," said Tyrus as he replaced the receiver. "Recycling is doing a thorough search for the missing inmate, but I'm sure that's him in there. Lieutenant Templeton is handling the staff roll call and emergency count. It's still necessary for the headquarters that we do it. Who's that standing at the gate?"

"That would be Detective Dykman of the coroner's office," Scott replied.

"Nice wheels."

"So I am told." Scott motioned for the tower officer to open the gate. Alberto had joined them and was also copying the identifying information.

"Hi, guys. Detective Dick-man from the coroner's office," he said while extending his hand to Scott.

"I thought it was Dike-man," Scott asked as he gave his hand a hearty clamp.

"It is, but nobody ever pronounces it right. So what's with the garbage truck?"

"That's where you will find your body," Scott replied.

"Cool. Can I see it?"

"By all means," Scott replied as he led him to the back of the truck.

"This is bad but not as bad as that bus crash I worked over here on the freeway. There were bodies hanging out the windows and underneath the bus," he reminisced.

"Oh, here we go," said Alberto quietly behind Scott, who looked over his shoulder and saw Alberto rolling his eyes and shaking his head. "His Highness will now speak."

"Be nice, Bert," Scott said.

"What a dick, man," Bert proclaimed as he walked away. Scott chose to follow him, leaving poor Tyrus to listen to the dissertation of how Detective Dykman single-handedly performed the functions of a coroner's investigator in a multifatality, multipassenger vehicle accident.

Officer Ferguson was waiting to get back into the sally port. Scott gave the nod, and the outer perimeter gate tugged open. "Chief Brewer said it doesn't look good for Mr. Graves. Poor soul. He was stable for a minute but then took a turn for the worse. Chief also said Mr. Graves stopped by the firehouse for coffee at about 0700, and he looked fine. I guess I better get started on my report. I might need your help, Dog."

"Alas, ask for Mr. Graves tomorrow, and you shall find him a grave man."

"What?"

"Nothing, Fergie, just let me know when you are done with the basics of your report, and I'll help you with the rest." Scott motioned for the tower officer to leave the gate open for a moment while he nudged Alberto to follow him through. Scott stood for a moment, looking at the trail of reddish-brown liquid that dripped from the truck as it passed into the sally port.

"What are you looking at, Doggie?"

"Well, Bert, it's this way. Mr. Graves said the last run he made was from the minimum security facility. The road to that facility is to your left, but the trail of blood the truck left behind appears to be coming from the right."

"What's over there?"

"Recycling is over there, and that's where the young man worked."

"What do they do in there?" asked Alberto.

"All the garbage from inside the four facilities is delivered to the recycling plant, where the inmate workers sort through, looking for recyclable goods that can be sold for money that goes back to the operation of the prison. It's also a hub for most of the contraband that is smuggled into each facility. Dope, cell phones, and tobacco are dropped off on prison grounds and then picked up by the garbage crew. The truck delivers the contraband-laden trash to recycling, and the inmate workers sort it, package it for smuggling, and then pass it back to the garbage crew, who in turn spread it to awaiting inmates at the North, Central, East, and minimum facilities."

"Well, Doggie, they are enterprising, if nothing else."

"No argument, Bert, but I think I better get a camera and start taking some photographs before we lose this trail to vehicle and foot traffic." Scott went back into the sally port and explained to Tyrus his intentions and that there would be a slight delay in recovering the body, but it could not be helped because of the perishable nature of the evidence.

Within a few minutes, a line of evidence markers snaked its way over toward the firehouse and sharply to the west for a few yards and again to the south toward the recycling plant. Scott decided he had two options for getting a good overview photograph. He could ascend either the sally port tower or the double-duty lookout perch and house drying tower on top of the firehouse. He chose the tower and had his photographs in good order. The trail of blood stopped at the vehicle gate leading into the recycling plant. Two inmates assigned to the receiving warehouse were meandering about in the area between the warehouse and the recycling plant, as well as a few at the firehouse.

Interviews of the recycling plant officers would have to wait until later as they still had a body in the back of the truck and an impatient coroner's detective. "Let's get back to the sally port, Bert, and begin the unpleasant task," Scott said as he reversed his steps. Tyrus was grateful of their return as he had spent the last twenty minutes being harangued with the tales of derring-do by the boastful detective.

"Ready to get started?" Scott asked as he laid out sheets of plastic along the left side of the truck.

"How do you want to do this?" asked Detective Dykman.

"One bag at a time, labeled, photographed, and documented." With a clean Sharpie marking pen, Scott began making notations on the odiferous garbage bags as they photographed and then gingerly removed them from around the decedent. "Bag SD no. 1, upper left of head; bag SD no. 2, immediately on top of head; bag SD no. 3, resting behind the head," Scott called out as he made his notations, and Tyrus recorded the details in a notebook.

Bag by bag, they cleared out the end portion of the truck until they had uncovered the badly mangled body. Each bag was marked and lined up next to the truck. "Well, the neck is snapped to begin with," commented the all-knowing agent of the coroner's office.

"Yes, and I would imagine there is trauma to the chest, brain, and skull with epidural hematomas as well as severe contusions of the torso and mechanical asphyxia or maybe positional asphyxia or smothering, not to mention the many skeletal fractures," Scott replied as he studied the lifeless form.

"Young" was the only thing Alberto said as he took a photograph of the young blond-haired, blue-eyed man.

"Yeah, and he was in pretty good shape too. I can't imagine it would have been an easy task to get him in the truck, let alone hold him down while working the levers of the crusher," added Tyrus.

"What, I'd say about 5'10" and 165 pounds?" Scott observed.

"That would be my guess," replied his partner.

"My guess would be that he was probably knocked out or killed just before being dumped into the truck. Is that left leg even attached?" Scott asked.

"Barely," replied Andy as he wiggled the tibia.

"So you don't think this was an escape attempt?" inquired Alberto.

"Well, I'm not going to rule it out, but he was already outside the minimum security yard. It would seem to me he would have had a lot of alternatives at his disposal. All he needed was somebody to drive up next to his jobsite and jump in. They'd be halfway to the freeway before we even got to our cars."

"But the chase would be on. Maybe he thought the truck was heading straight out to the dump?" asked Tyrus.

"They crush it again right before they leave the prison," remarked Officer Ferguson as he spied into the container.

"Back to your shack, Fergie. You're in my crime scene."

"Oh, Dog, I just wanted to ask what you were going to do with Mr. Graves's lunch box. It's in the cab of the truck."

"I hadn't thought of that. I guess I'll go through it when we are done and hold it until his wife can come by. I'm sure an old lunch box is the least of their concern right now. Anyway, Fergie, have the garage supervisor see what else belongs to Mr. Graves over there, and I will come by and pick it up from him later."

"Righto," said Fergie as he withdrew back into his shack.

Scott returned his attention to the assembled investigative staff. "Are we ready to extract the decedent?" asked Andy.

"I am if you are. Have you got a body bag?" Scott inquired.

"I can have one in a jiffy."

"I just thought of something. The neck is definitely broken, and there is a gash on the side of his head. It looks like the crusher got him pretty good on the leg and somewhat on the torso, but I don't think it made this gash."

"Why is that?"

"Well, Andy, the crusher would have come down fairly slow and consistent. The gash runs from about an inch from the top of the left ear back toward the mastoid process. This looks more like a sharp blow than a slow press, if you know what I mean."

"Do you think he got hit on the head by the thing and then just fell in?"

"Not if he was the operator. Try as he could, I doubt he could fall in and still maintain a grip on the levers. No, he had help. I'm going to take a few more photographs while you go get the body bag."

Within a few minutes, a new white coroner's office body bag was stretched out behind the garbage truck. Tyrus and Scott both reached into the belly of the beast and slid the young man forward into the trough. From there, the four investigators were able to scoop him out and place him on top of the bag. The smell of garbage and dead body was pervasive. They made sure there were no shanks protruding from any part of the body and then zipped the bag shut.

The mortician arrived and parked just outside the sally port. A gurney was wheeled in, and Tyrus and Scott grabbed the body-filled bag and set it, probably less gently than decent decorum required, onto it. "Do I need a body receipt?" asked the veteran sally port officer.

"Hold up a minute!" Scott shouted at the departing body collector. He unzipped the bag, felt inside for the solitary right hip pocket on the lime green jumpsuit, and extracted a small plastic card. Scott pulled it out, looked at it, and confirmed by the photograph on the inmate identification card that the young man was very likely Inmate Weller.

"We'll know after I compare the fingerprints, but this is our inmate," he said as he showed the card to Officer Ferguson. "In the meantime, have the control sergeant fill out a body receipt with his name, and I'll get the mortician to sign for it."

Within a half hour, the proper paperwork had been completed and signed. Officer Ferguson was satisfied, and the decedent left the prison. "The autopsy will be in the morning at nine o'clock," announced Detective Dykman as he climbed out of his Tyvek suit and into his fancy unmarked patrol car.

"I'll be there," responded Investigator Gutierrez as he too shed the paperlike white jumpsuit.

"Us too," replied Tyrus. It wasn't time yet for the two prison investigators to take off their coveralls as there was still much work to be done. Each bag was dusted for prints using sterile powder and brushes. Developed prints were photographed and lifted where possible, cut and preserved when not. The twisted part of each bag was removed using sterile scalpels and placed into paper bags for DNA analysis, if needed. After several hours with the unbearable stench that one would get with the basic garbage truck filling their nostrils, they were done.

Officer Ferguson, who didn't appear disturbed by the odor, was awaiting his instructions. "Can you drive this thing out of here, Fergie?" Scott asked.

"You betcha. What about the lunch box, Dog?"

"Damn, Ferg, I forgot. Pass it down here."

"His jacket is in here too." His voice dropped off sharply.

"Problem?" Scott asked.

"There's something in the pocket, and I don't want to have anything to do with it," he said as he jumped out of the cab and quickly stepped away from the truck with his hands raised as if to denote he didn't touch anything.

"Let me see, Fergie," Scott said as he stepped up on the running board.

"What is it?" inquired Tyrus.

"Well, Ty, it feels very much like—and it looks very much like—and it is very much a gun."

Chapter 3

The Secret Lives of Walter Graves

"It appears to be an antique Harrington & Richardson top-break .38 Smith & Wesson that has seen its day about a half century ago. Look at all the rust, Tyrus. This thing is half chrome and half rust."

"Is it loaded, Dog?"

"Five .38-caliber Smith & Wesson cartridges, better known as .38 short or .38/200 if you were in Britain during the war and wanted a severally underpowered pistol."

"He is so fired."

"If he lives, Tyrus, if he lives, not to mention prosecuted. Now why do you think a seventy-year-old black man from Tallahassee, Florida, who has worked for this prison for over thirty years would need with a gun?"

"Yeah, and how long has he been carrying it?"

"Two questions I hope we get the chance to ask him."

"What else is in there?"

"Nothing else in the jacket, but there is an old lunch box in here. Let's see, Tyrus. One sandwich, bologna, and American cheese—yuck, one apple, a bottle of water and a disposable camera."

"Come again?"

"A disposable camera."

"Film or digital?"

"Thirty-five millimeter and all frames used. Too bad we still don't have the old photo lab."

"Are you thinking what I am thinking, Dog?"

"That we need to search this entire truck?"

"Smelly as it is but yes."

As Scott began a thorough inspection of the cab area and engine compartment of the truck, Tyrus decided to be the intrepid explorer and began the search of trash compartment, fuel tanks, and undercarriage. "Found something!" he shouted from the back of the truck. Fergie and Scott were all ears and eyes.

"What have you got?" Scott hollered while lowering the bonnet of the engine compartment.

"Magnets, two great, big magnets stuck on the underside of the lip behind the handrail where the inmate stands on the back."

"Clever little monkeys," Scott mused.

"What? I don't get it," remarked the confused sally port officer while scratching his head.

"Well, Fergie," Scott said as he inspected the magnets, "my guess is that the inmates affix contraband by a corresponding magnet onto these magnets and then as the truck is driven through the sally port, the inmate riding on the back is able to smuggle the contraband inside the prison without detection by the unaware sally port officer and then pass it off to other inmates inside."

"Shit, Dog, these trucks go into all four facilities several times a day," stated the bewildered officer Ferguson.

"Exactly, Fergie, and where else do they go?"

"They go to the dump."

"They go to recycling," corrected Tyrus.

"And recycling was where our crushed inmate worked," Scott added.

"And recycling should be our next stop when we are finished here," suggested Tyrus. They finished their search of the foul-smelling behemoth and instructed Officer Ferguson to park it in a gated area on the outskirts of the prison. It would have to sit there fermenting for a few days or at least until after the autopsy. They cleaned up the mess in the sally port, hosed down the blood, and put all the items of collected evidence in the trunk of Scott's Crown Vic.

Tyrus and Scott then walked the forty yards or so to the recycling plant, where they were met by Correctional Officers Duane Parkinson and Ronnie Richmond. "Dog, dude!" greeted the country-bred red-faced officer Parkinson with an accent somewhere between a hick and a surfer.

"Duane, dude! How the heck are you, old friend?" Scott replied in kind.

"Oh, you know, Dog, I'm just out here with the rest of the trash, just me and Ronnie, like the hillbilly Sanford and son. What's up, Sergeant Phil?"

"Pretty good, Park," returned Tyrus, adding, "So you got any inmates out here?"

"Nope, just me and Ronnie. Ronnie took them back to the farm gate with the warehouse workers. We've been searching this mess."

"Find anything yet?"

"About thirty pounds of tobacco."

"One pound is 456 grams. So you have, what, 13,680 grams at two dollars a gram prison value. That's over $27,000. That's a good haul," Scott remarked.

"Where was it?" inquired Tyrus.

"Ron found it over there in the baled cardboard bins."

"And which inmates work over there?"

"Well, one of them is Inmate Martinez. They call him Spider, and another one is Inmate Gottfried."

"Wait, Gottfried? They call him Smooth?" Scott interrupted.

"Yeah, Dog, that's him, big pain in the ass," replied Officer Parkinson.

"Who's he?" asked Tyrus.

"You remember, Ty, we caught him over at the sewage treatment plant shoving a cell phone *and* charger up his ass? When we made him squat and cough, I said I expected to hear the sound of a vacuum cleaner when he spread his butt cheeks. Not only did he have a capacious rectal cavity but he also has a metal hip joint, so he doesn't have to go through the metal detector when he goes back into the minimum yard. I cannot believe he still has a job outside the fence!" Scott fumed.

"Wait a minute, Park, you said you have Martinez and Gottfried. That's a Mexican and a black. You should have a white on your crew too. Who is he?" asked Tyrus.

"Well, Sergeant Phillips, somebody said he was in the back of the garbage truck this morning."

"Weller?"

"Yup."

"Did any of your workers come out this morning, Duane?" Scott asked.

"Nope. Ron and I don't get here until eight, and then we go over to the farm gate and pick them up with the bus, but the bus had a low tire, and we were getting it checked out at the garage. We were still over there when Graves took the garbage truck into the sally port."

"So you guys don't get here until eight? Does anyone else have a key to this area?" Scott inquired.

"The outside patrol sergeant, the fire chief, and the garbage truck driver."

"How many inmates are assigned out here?"

"Not too many now, Dog, just the three. We used to have twenty-two assigned out here, and I only had work for maybe five at best. Ron and I couldn't keep our eyes on all of them. I finally told the warden he had to do something. We're supposed to have six, but right now, there's just the three. How's old man Graves? I heard they took him out of here in an ambulance."

"Not good, Park, not good at all," responded Tyrus.

"That's too bad. That old man has been out here forever, at least ten years before I got out here. He's been driving that truck for as long as I can remember. I think he started at the warehouse back in the '80s."

"What do you know about him, Duane?"

"Well, Dog, he's married to Rose. She used to work out here too, at the warehouse, but she retired about five years ago. Every now and then, she brings him lunch. They have two kids, a son and a daughter. I think the boy went to college, but something happened to him. The daughter is married to a correctional officer at CSP–Los Angeles and lives down there. They have grandkids. One of them just turned eighteen and is going into the navy or marines. I think old man Graves was in the army and retired from them as a sergeant with the quartermaster's office."

"Ever hear of any financial problems?" asked Tyrus.

"That old skinflint? I couldn't imagine he would have much debt. He bought his house in Pacific Grove back in the seventies."

"Did you ever hear him talk about being threatened?"

"No, Dog, everyone liked the old man and felt sorry for him because of his medical problems. I mean, come on, Dog, he should have retired years ago."

"Is there anyone else we could talk to who would know about him out here?"

"Yeah, Ty, you should talk to Alf Garza, the other driver. They are . . . uh . . . or were pretty close."

"Thanks, Duane, dude. Let us know if you find anything else in here. Oh, by the way, did you happen to notice any bloodstains or pools in here?"

"No, but I'll keep my eyes open for ya, Dog."

They left the two trash hounds to finish their search of the mounds and mounds of cardboards, plastics, e-waste, metals, and rubbish and walked back to the car. "What's next?" asked Scott's appetite-suppressed partner.

"Well, Ty, we need to get this evidence booked, and then I'm thinking we need to go take a look at Mr. Graves's personnel file and Inmate Weller's central file."

"And then talk to Alf?"

"And then we talk to Alf."

"You may view his personnel file in here," said Personnel Manager Susan Hawkins as she opened the door to a conference room. "I suppose I will have to talk to Rose and help her with the financial arrangements.

She was, of course, the beneficiary of his life insurance and retirement plan. They said he slipped into a coma and then just stopped breathing."

"Grief struck, Sue. It was a real tragedy. The sudden realization that he was the agent whereby the young man died, however accidental, was too much for his heart," Scott consoled.

"Do they really think it was an escape attempt?" she asked.

"Well, Sue, we have yet to rule it out."

Tyrus and Scott sorted through all the documents in the personnel file of the late Walter Graves. He had no disciplinary action against him in his nearly thirty-three years of state service. His military DD 214 reflected an honorable retirement after twenty years with the United States Army, Quartermaster's Office, reaching the rank of detachment sergeant. Sadly, the last piece of paper they turned was his request for retirement. The sum of one man's entire career fit in a legal-size file folder. They made a routine note of any addresses and telephone numbers they found in the file, handed it back to Sue, and departed.

They drove over to the minimum security facility and walked to the office of the watch commander. There they were greeted with a hug and a cheek kiss by Lt. Amara Bennetti. They had both known Amara for many years and were like part of her large and extended Italian family. "Any chance I can go to the autopsy?" she asked as she handed Scott the central file of Inmate Weller.

"Tomorrow morning at nine at the coroner's office, Amara. I'll make the notification," Scott replied.

"Really? Cool. Where is the coroner's office exactly?"

"It's on the corner. The coroner's office is on the cor-o-ner of the sheriff's office. Get it? You can't miss it. Drive past the jail toward the sheriff's administrative building, but instead of turning into the parking lot, just go straight, and you will see it on the northwest corner of the building. Park in the front where you see my Crown Vic."

"I'll be there. Did you know he was local boy?"

"How local?"

"Pacific Grove."

"That's about forty-five miles from here."

"Did he still have family there?" inquired Tyrus.

"I made notification of death to his father, who still lived in Pacific Grove. He's listed as the next of kin on the form. He also listed a brother and sister. The sister lives in Seaside, and the brother lives in Marina."

"What's he in for?" Scott asked.

"He was in for a lewd and lascivious with a girl under the age of fourteen. They were dating at the time, but he was nineteen, and she was thirteen when he was first arrested and charged. He was given probation and required to stay away from her. He was arrested again when she was fourteen, and he was twenty. That time, they gave him nine years for violating the restraining order imposed by the judge. He could have gotten a lot more because they originally charged him with kidnapping. He was scheduled to get out next year. I guess the girl is twenty-one now, and they were planning on getting married. She applied to visit him, but the request was denied because she was the victim in the controlling case."

"And is she local too, Amara?" Scott asked.

"Pacific Grove again," she responded.

"And his property?" asked Tyrus.

"Still in the dorm, I hope. They dragged his locker into the dorm 6 office and put a padlock on it."

"Amara, I do wish you guys wouldn't disturb the inmate's property before we have a chance to go through it. This is either an escape or a homicide investigation. Now we have a chain of custody issue to deal with."

"Sorry, Scott, that's the way they do it here. I figured you'd want this," she said as she handed him a small address book.

"Sweet. Is she in here?"

"Veronica Mendez, under L for 'love.'"

"Oh, barf."

"Do you think I should call her? I'd hate for her to see it on the news."

"Amara, I think that would be a good idea. Make it all romantic, and she will be just fine. Tell her he died professing his love for her."

"Yuck, Scott," she replied with a laugh.

"Tyrus and I will go over and go through his property now. What dorm was he in?"

"Dorm 6, bunk 54, low. Robert Rallis is the officer in there today. He's waiting for you." With a hug and a kiss, they left Amara's office and walked across the yard of the minimum security facility, also known as the South Facility.

They walked past the handball court, the basketball court, the tennis court, and finally the golf putting green before crossing the running track and entering dorm 6. They were greeted by Officer Rallis, who showed them the area of Inmate Weller's bunk. Scott asked him to check the outgoing mail for any correspondence that might have been posted by Inmate Weller the night before. He retrieved one letter addressed to Veronica Weller in Pacific Grove, California. Scott placed the letter in his cargo pocket and began searching the contents of the boxes from underneath the bunk while Tyrus searched the bunk area with Officer Rallis.

After this, Scott searched the locker in the dorm 6 office. He searched every garment pocket and hem and collected every letter or scrap of paper and anything bearing an address or telephone number. While inspecting the unopened bags of Top Ramen, Scott felt something solid. Scott attempted to snap the brick of noodles in half but encountered resistance. Inspecting the seams, he noticed what looked like a bead of silicone. He opened the packaged oriental noodle soup mix and discovered that a hard sponge had been substituted for the noodles. Fragments of noodles had been glued to the outside of the sponge and a cardstock cover that slid into a channel grooved into the upper wall of a hollowed-out depression. Sliding this cardstock out of the recess revealed a small Samsung cellular telephone and charger. "As I expected," Scott muttered to himself.

Scott closed the door of the locker, placed the padlock back onto the hasp, and tilted it backward toward the desk of Officer Rallis. "Also as expected," Scott muttered as he removed an envelope taped to the underside of the locker. He looked inside the envelope and discovered several "buy/owe" sheets, commonly carried by drug dealers to track debts, and two handwritten notes. One was from his girlfriend, and the other was signed "Spider." Once finished, Scott placed all the items of contraband and interest into a small plastic bag and joined Tyrus at the bunk area.

"Jackpot" was all he said as Scott walked up.

"What did you find?"

"Tobacco, rolling papers, cigarette lighters, and what looks like a baggy of weed."

"Where'd you find it?"

"Stitched into the mattress. I could smell the weed. Did you get anything?"

"Cell phone, buy/owe sheets, and a couple of letters taped under the locker."

"Can you get into the phone?"

"No, Tyrus, it's locked. We'll have to use the extractor."

"Anything good in the notes, Doggy?"

"Both are contemporary to each other. One is from his girlfriend, Veronica. And the other is from Spider, Inmate Martinez, I am assuming. And both reference a meeting with G."

Tyrus took the two notes out of the envelope and inspected them. "This one signed 'Spider' just says, 'Twelve for 600.' What do you suppose that means?"

"I'm guessing twelve cell phones for $50 each. Inside, they would get maybe $300 each. Not a bad profit margin, Ty."

"This one says she gave the note to G. I wonder what was on that note. How did he get a note from his girlfriend?"

"Well, it looks like it was taped to something. Ty, maybe one of the twelve phones. Let's go talk to Roger Pippington at the farm gate while we are here."

"And then Alf?"

"And then Alf, but I want to know which inmates were out and how Weller got on Walter Graves's truck."

A quick drive to the farm gate revealed that Inmate Martinez and Inmate Gottfried had been processed for their work assignments at 0815 hours but were brought back forty minutes later. The two inmates who went out that morning at 0745 hours worked at the sewage treatment plant, and that was on the other side of the institution. The three warehouse workers and four garage workers went out at 0710 hours.

Mr. Graves picked up Inmate Weller because he said he needed a hand clearing out some recycling material from his garbage truck before he could make his morning run. Officer Pippington called the watch commander, who authorized the release of the inmate to Mr. Graves. All protocols were followed. Mr. Graves picked up Inmate Weller at 0650 hours.

Chapter 4

What's It All About, Alfie?

"Alfredo, how are you doing?" Scott asked as he reached out and placed his hand on the corpulent shoulder of the large man.

"I'm still a bit in shock over all this, Mr. Doggett. Wally was my friend. We were like . . . oh, what's the name of those comedians?"

"Abbott and Costello?" asked Tyrus.

"No, no, the big guy and the little guy."

"Mutt and Jeff?"

"Who?"

"Laurel and Hardy," Scott suggested.

"Yeah, them because Wally was such a little guy, and I'm, well, you know. I'm over three hundred pounds and all. We just were buddies, you know. I could always make him laugh, you know."

"How long have you two worked together?" asked Tyrus.

"Oh, maybe about six years, you know. Wally was talking about retiring, you know. Wow, I really need to go talk to Rose."

"Alf, when was the last time you talked to Mr. Graves?"

"I saw him yesterday afternoon before we went home, you know," replied the gentle giant while rubbing his nose.

"Did he seem worried or concerned about anything?"

"No, Mr. Doggett, he and Rose were babysitting one of their grandchildren last night, and he seemed real happy about it, you know."

"Did he ever talk about needing protection from anyone?" inquired Tyrus.

"Protection? With me around? I don't think so. Besides, Wally was the nicest man around. I don't know why anyone would want to harm an old man who did his breathing through a bottle."

"Did you ever know him to carry a gun?" Tyrus persisted.

"What? A gun? No way. He said he had enough of them in the army, you know."

"Did he ever talk about any financial problems he was having?" Scott asked.

"No, not Wally. He was in pretty good shape. He paid off his house years ago. I wish I could pay off mine. He's got a real nice house over in Pacific Grove. It's a long drive, but he doesn't mind, you know."

"What about medical bills?" asked Tyrus.

"Yeah, he had some of those, but who doesn't? I mean, it wasn't too bad, you know. The insurance was picking up just about everything."

"Alf, why do you think he picked up Inmate Weller this morning?" Scott pressed.

"Weller was about the only good worker out there. The rest of them are all scrubs, you know. Mr. Pippington said that Wally needed to offload some recycle from his truck before he could make his run. We do that all the time. Sometimes I will get Martinez to help me before the recycling crew gets there, you know."

The investigators thanked Alf for his time, gave him a pat on the back as there was no really good way of getting your arms all the way around him for a hug, and walked back to the car. "Something just isn't right about all this, Ty," Scott said.

"What are you thinking, Dog, you know?"

"I'm thinking something just doesn't add up here. If he had to pick up Weller to help him unload some recycling from the truck, why then was there still cardboard in it?"

"Oh yeah, there was cardboard in there. It came out when we raised the crusher, you know."

"Yes, Ty, I do know, and that's enough of those you-knows, if you know, you know. It rained last night, didn't it?"

"Yeah, just a little."

"Let's go take a look over there where the garbage truck was parked at recycling."

Just as they were walking from the garage over to the recycling plant, Scott heard Alf call out his name. Scott turned in his direction and waited for the huffing and puffing man to catch up. "Mr. Doggett," he said as he placed his hands on his knees and grabbed for a deep breath, "there is just one thing I think you ought to know, you know. Wally was having money problems. I know you are going to find out, you know, but his medical bills were out of control. The medical bills were too high, and it looked like they was going to lien his house, you know. I think he was doing something with the inmates."

"Something like?" Scott pressed.

"Tobacco" was his reply. They thanked him for the corrected information. Tyrus advised him that he did the right thing by telling the truth and that they would have found out eventually.

They resumed their walk to the recycling plant. "Man, Ty, I wish we had a way to get elevated over this area."

"What about the fire truck?"

"Sure, if we had an aerial ladder or a boom, but I think being on the ground is actually better. I think we can climb on top of that storage container over by the warehouse to get a good overview photograph. Okay, look at these tire tracks over here where the blood is next to the recycling plant vehicle gate. Notice the pattern of the tread?"

"Yes?"

"It's pretty well worn. Now look over here on the side of the fence that is facing the warehouse. There's another set of tire marks here, and the tread is much deeper and newer. Would you not agree?"

"Yes, but maybe it was a truck here for the warehouse."

"I don't think so. To get here, the truck would have to go through the staff parking lot and around the back of the warehouse, where all these storage containers are parked in a row running along the back and around toward the loading bay. It would have to be a staff member who knew there was this little access road here that ended up right next to recycling. And why would a warehouse truck be here? These cargo containers haven't been opened in years."

"What are you thinking?"

"I'm thinking, Tyrus, that we should get a camera kit, my tripod, and all the casting mix that we can find."

For nearly two hours, they photographed the tread marks with the digital camera suspended underneath Scott's favorite Giottos tripod and using an off-camera shutter release. They used a wireless flash to obliquely light the peaks and valleys of the tread marks from different angles. They photographed without scales and then with scales for comparative purposes. They mixed bowl after bowl of the casting material, poured it into the framed impressions and waited for them to set and dry.

They asked the tower officer if he saw any vehicles at the recycling plant early in the morning. He believed he saw Mr. Graves's garbage truck over there earlier in the morning but couldn't be sure because he was busy working the gates. Once they were back in the car, Tyrus remarked, "You know, Dog, just because these tread marks are here doesn't really prove that the vehicle that left them is connected in any way to the crime."

"You are correct, it is circumstantial at best. However, we would be remiss not to document and collect the evidence and look who has been watching us."

"Alf?" he replied.

"Yes, my friend, Alf has been watching us since we started."

"That seems natural to me. Mr. Graves was his little buddy."

"I wonder, Tyrus. I just wonder."

Chapter 5

An Escape by Any Other Name

"I don't care! I am submitting this one to the headquarters unit as an escape attempt, and that's that! I don't care about no gun! I don't care about no camera! I don't care about any tobacco! I'm done with it! The old man is dead! Exactly who do you want to prosecute?" The bellowing rang in Scott's ears as Lt. John Templeton shouted Tyrus out of his office. Scott was sitting in the chair just outside the supervisor's door. Tyrus faced the bull walrus alone—brave man. He closed the door and looked at Scott, rolled his eyes, and motioned for Scott to follow him.

They didn't stop at his office or Scott's but went up the stairs, out the door, out to the parking lot, and into Scott's Crown Victoria and accelerated toward Raymond's Snack Bar. "Tyrus," Scott opined, "sometimes I feel like I am standing on the bow of a sinking ship with the sole consolation it is going down stern first."

"What do you want to do, Dog?"

"Keep working the case, and if necessary, we will go to the facility captain or the associate warden."

"Yeah, I guess having an uncooperative supervisor never stopped us before. Why should it mean anything now? What happened at Weller's autopsy this morning?"

"Well, first of all, Amara was a champ. She didn't pass out or anything. I gave her the standard warning, though, that if she did pass out, I would photograph her on the floor, enlarge the print, and post it all over the prison. She was right in there, with Dr. Hansen asking him all kinds of questions while he dissected the body and organs. Anyway, the body was pretty mangled, but he seems to think it was mostly postmortem. The vertical laceration that ran along the temporal muscle to the temporal ridge just above the left ear and down to behind the ear corresponded with a cranial fracture that definitely would have left him unconscious if nothing else. Couple that with traumatic asphyxia from being crushed in a garbage truck, and the manner of death is definitely homicide."

"So he got hit in the head with something?"

"Like a bar or a pipe, definitely something solid and long enough to leave a two-and-a-half-inch laceration. It wasn't the crusher. That moves too slowly. This was a hard, sharp blow. Oh, and it was slightly angled as if Weller was bending over when he got cracked. Let's swing by and take another look at that garbage truck. I'm hoping we didn't miss a blood-spattered lead pipe."

"Yeah, but can we go to the snack bar before we look at that truck? I'm likely to lose my appetite again."

"Not a problem, Tyrus."

"What's next, Doggy?"

"Well, Tyrus, I think we are going to need to go talk to the kid's parents and girlfriend, although I don't know how with the lieutenant being in one of his moods."

"I think that's where I can help. The gang conference is at the end of the week. I'm pretty sure I can talk him into going since it's in Palm Springs this month. They have good golf courses, and he never misses a chance to go golfing on the state's money. Of course, it will mean that I will have to go with him."

"Tyrus, it wouldn't be the same without you here, but at least Oswaldo should be back from his sniper school training by then. I think we might just stop by and talk to Rose while we're out there. In all this, Tyrus, what is the common denominator?"

"Pacific Grove."

"Indeed, the sleepy coastal town of PG—for the newlywed and nearly dead."

After lunch at Raymond's Snack Bar, they drove out to the back forty to the gated maintenance yard, where they stowed the odorous International Harvester Jabberwocky. Scott didn't waste too much time inspecting its guts and hide mostly owing to the swarm of flies that had assembled, but he came up with nothing that they had missed. "Any splatter?" asked Tyrus.

"It's spatter, and no, I don't see any cast-off spatter."

"How can that be?" he asked.

"Well, either he didn't get hit near the truck or, more likely, the first blow generally doesn't produce a bloodletting event that deposits blood on the weapon. Think about it. You swing the object once, and it causes the injury. Well, if you're done swinging, there might not be any transfer of blood to the object. If you must continue to swing, whether it's in a backward or forward motion, the blood that is deposited on the object will take flight. If the first impact was deep enough to transfer blood onto the surface of the object, there might be dropped blood falling from it if you hold it still, and there might be castoff if you start flinging it about for whatever reason. But castoff produced by blunt force trauma is normally generated by the subsequent blows. That's why you never definitely say how many blows were inflicted. If you have two distinct cast-off patterns and you can tell the direction of travel by the shape of the drops as they impacted the target, one backward and one forward motion, then you can say with some certainty that there were two or more blows inflicted. I've lost you completely, haven't I?"

"I should have gotten a Philly cheesesteak sandwich instead of those tacos."

"You know they aren't as good as they are in Philly. Let's get out of here. The stench is unbearable. What's this in my pocket? Oh, I completely forgot about the letter Rallis pulled out of the mail. It's still in my pocket."

"The letter Weller wrote to his girlfriend?"

"Yeah, let's get back in the car and upwind of this fetor, and I'll read it."

Babe,

I hope that you are in the best of health and God's graces are upon you. As I write this missive, I am overjoyed that we shall soon be together. I love you, Veronica, and always have and will love you forever. I want to marry you as soon as I get out, and then we can go away, far away. We have enough money saved now that we can finally go to Utah and leave California for good. I don't know what to do about my parole agent. I know he won't want me to marry you until after I am done. That's why we have to go because I cannot live another day without you. Your parents will understand, and I don't care about my parents anymore. I don't have a family. You are my only family. Don't worry about what that old man says. What we are doing isn't wrong. We are doing this for us, and that's all that matters. He can't stop us. I won't let him stop us. The next time he calls you, tell him that it is none of his business and to just leave us alone. I understand what you are saying, and I know that you are scared. If you want me to stop, I will, but we need as much money as we can possibly get to start our lives over in Salt Lake City. I love you, Veronica, forever.

Your loving husband,
Ricky

"Curious and more curious, Tyrus. What do you make of it?" Scott asked as he folded the letter and placed it back in the envelope.

"Well, he's a dope dealer at the least. I'd like to know who is 'the old man,' and why is he calling her?" he queried.

"Perhaps she will have an answer for us when we go talk to her at the end of the week, providing you lure our boss to Palm Springs."

"Consider it done, Doggy. Oh, and Bert called me this morning and said the gun isn't registered to anyone. It's a curio or something like that."

"Then I will have something to ask Rose too," Scott replied.

"Did you take the camera to get the pictures developed?"

"I did, last night. I hope there isn't anything obscene on there. I had to take it to the pharmacy. I'll pick up the prints tomorrow after work."

"What about the cell phone?"

"Weller's?"

"Yeah, the one you found in his locker."

"I'm going to get a telephone subscriber and call detail warrant and then have the phone itself analyzed for data by the headquarters. They can use their Cellebrite extractor. Theirs is better at unlocking phones than ours. That way, we can get the text messages and photographs off the phone too."

"Don't you need a warrant to get into the phone, Dog?"

"No, Tyrus, an inmate has no expectation of privacy, particularly on a contraband cell phone. But also, neither do the dead."

The following morning found Oswaldo and Scott standing in front of the large dry-erase board in their office. "Here's how the case stands thus far, Oz," Scott said as he put the chisel-tipped dry-erase marker to work listing the details. "First, Inmate Weller is picked up at the South Facility farm gate at 0650 hours by Mr. Graves, who says he has to offload cardboard at the recycling plant before making his run into the Central Facility. He drives the garbage truck over to the recycling plant but either does not offload the cardboard or doesn't offload all the cardboard as there is still plenty of cardboard in the back of the truck as it enters the vehicle sally port to the Central Facility. At some point at or near the recycling plant, Inmate Weller's head is met with a heavy object, and he ends up inside the trash compartment of the truck and gets compacted. Cause of death is blunt force trauma and traumatic asphyxia. Manner of death is homicide. The body is discovered in the sally port, recovered, and the evidence is processed. Oh, and Mr. Graves has a massive heart attack and dies."

"He what?" Oswaldo asked.

"He dies."

"Wait, Mr. Graves is dead? That little old guy who drives the garbage truck? The one with the oxygen bottle?" Oswaldo inquired with short rapid bursts.

"Yes, Oz, haven't you been paying attention? Back to the scenario, an antique but functional and fully loaded revolver and disposable camera are found in the cabin of the truck. Thirty pounds of tobacco are found in his work area."

"Mr. Graves's work area?" interrupted Oswaldo again.

"The tobacco was found in Inmate Weller's work area in the cardboard baling area of the recycling plant. That is where he works with Inmate Spider Martinez and Inmate Smooth Gottfried, the human walk-in rectal pantry. A search of the locker and bunk area assigned to Inmate Weller produces a cell phone and charger, several buy/owe sheets, two notes, tobacco, and marijuana. A letter authored by Inmate Weller to his girlfriend, Veronica Mendez, alludes to some suspicious activity and some warnings from an old man. Alfredo Garza informs us that Mr. Graves is doing something 'dirty' with the inmates. Also, two different sets of truck tire impressions are found at the recycling plant. An item of interest but could be purely coincidental is that Mr. Graves and the parents and girlfriend of the decedent all live in Pacific Grove."

"PG road trip?"

"Pacific Grove, Oz, God's vacation spot on the West Coast, if he could afford it. We leave this afternoon. Remind me to stop at the pharmacy on the way back and pick up the photographs. Any questions so far?"

"Yeah, what kind of gun was it, Scotty?"

"Harrington & Richardson top-break .38 Smith & Wesson with a two-inch barrel, chrome with ivory grips."

"Sweet!"

At 1300 hours, Scott merged the aging Crown Victoria onto the Monterey–Salinas Highway 68 and applied the throttle. "Man, this car pings," remarked Oswaldo.

"Cheap gas, Oz. This old girl will get up and go when it needs to. You sure couldn't ask for a nicer day, sunny and mild."

Twenty minutes later, they swung around the Holman Highway and dropped into the southern part of Pacific Grove. As they descended, the sunny and mild day turned quickly into cold, wet fog. With the help of Oz's iPhone, they found the listed address of the widow Rose Graves and knocked on the front door. Rose answered and welcomed them inside the modest bungalow that she shared with her late husband. "Mr. Doggett, Chief Brewer said you were the first one to do the CPR on Walter. I know you tried, and I want to thank you ever so much for that."

"It was quite a shock, Rose, and I am sincerely sorry for your loss," Scott replied while taking her hand into his. They hugged for a moment, and then the aged woman asked if she could sit down because of the strain on her knees. "Rose, is there anything that we can do for you? We are all family, and all you have to do is ask."

"Oh, Scott, everything is fine. Sue Hawkins has been an absolute joy. She comes by almost every day, and we have all the pension and life insurance in order. He wasn't the best man in the world, but he left me very well provided for. Lord, how that man could annoy me."

"I have a few questions for you, Rose, and I hope it isn't too early. If it is, please tell me, and we can do this some other time."

"I know you have a job to do. I guess this has to do with the unfortunate young man that was in the truck?"

"Yes, unfortunately, it is looking more like a homicide investigation, and Walter was very likely one of the last people who saw him alive. Did he ever mention the name Richard Weller before?"

"No, I can't say that he ever did. Was that his name?"

"Yes, a young man from this area. His parents actually live just a few blocks away."

"Oh my, those poor folks, they must be grieving."

"I'm sure of it. His girlfriend also lives fairly close by. Her name is Veronica Mendez."

"Was that the young boy who was seeing that underage girl a few years ago? I remember reading that in the papers. No, although Pacific

Grove is such a small town, I never met them myself. Maybe I saw them at the grocery or the shops. Do you have a picture?"

"No, sorry, I don't, but it is no matter if he never mentioned them."

"Oh, but I would like to tell them how sorry I am for their loss. Do you think you can let me know where they live?"

"Sure, I don't think that is a problem. Rose, I know Walter wasn't in the best of health. Were the medical costs covered by his insurance?"

"Oh yes, mostly, I mean. Those doctors are so expensive, and the insurance doesn't cover everything, but he had the insurance from the prison, and his retirement from the army had an insurance plan. So we were managing well enough. I haven't been too healthy myself, what with my diabetes and my knees. Oh, they hurt me something terrible. I don't get around as much as I used to. I haven't been able to tend to the garden or the flowers in months. The lawn needs mowing too. I suppose I'll have to hire a gardener."

"Rose, this might be a personal question, but did Walter have any large sums of money in a bank account that you could not account for?"

"Oh my, Scott, you don't think my Walter would be doing anything dishonest, do you? My Walter wasn't the best man, but he was a good churchgoing man, honest as the day is long."

"I just have to ask, Rose. It's a routine question."

"Oh, no, we have our savings, and it sure isn't much, but I know every dollar that went in there."

"Did he seem worried about anything at work?"

"He never mentioned anything to me."

"One last question, if you don't mind. Did Walter own a gun?"

"A gun? You mean like a revolver?"

"A small silver Harrington & Richardson revolver to be exact."

"That old thing? What would you need to know about that? He's had that old gun for years. He said he got it from his uncle. It's in the drawer over there on the table in the hallway. I hate the damned thing."

"Do you mind if I look for it?"

"No, no, Scott, if you don't mind. I'd rather not get up just yet."

Scott got up and walked over to the small end table that sat at the entrance to the hallway. He pulled open the one drawer, and as anticipated, there was no gun. "It's not here, Rose, which is what I expected. We found the gun in his jacket pocket in the truck he was driving."

"That old fool! What on earth was he doing with that in there?"

"That's what I am trying to find out, Rose."

After a few minutes of chatting about family and plans, Rose offered them a glass of lemonade and limped into the kitchen. Scott followed her closely and pushed open the butler's door to the small room. As she poured the beverage into two glasses, Scott heard the sound of a lawn mower in the front yard. It was Oz. "You old softy, now you smell like grass clippings."

"I know, Scotty, but it wasn't much of a lawn, and it did need cutting. When do you think the funeral will be? I'd like to go."

"We both will go, Oz."

"Where to next, the parents?" he asked.

"No, little buddy, I'm thinking the girlfriend. Get out your miracle phone and type in this address," Scott said as he passed him the paper with the girlfriend's Pacific Grove address.

Ten minutes and a few winding streets later, they were in front of a luxurious two-story house that overlooked the old Pacific Grove lighthouse, municipal golf course, and the Pacific Ocean. They parked the car and walked up the path to the solid oak front door. The mailbox was engraved "Dr. & Mrs. Gerald S. Mendez, MD." A distinguished Hispanic man in his late fifties opened the door. "Dr. Mendez?" Scott asked as he handed the gentleman his business card. "We have a few questions to ask your daughter. Is she home?"

"Yes, she is, but she is in mourning. May I ask you what this is about?" he inquired.

"My partner and I are conducting a homicide investigation regarding her late boyfriend, Inmate Richard Weller."

"So he was murdered? They told us he was trying to escape. Please come in, Investigators."

"Wow, what a house," declared Oswaldo as he stepped into the foyer and looked up at the tall ceilings and the second-floor balcony.

"I am a surgeon and my wife, Carolyn, is a copyright and trademark attorney," he said as if by habit.

"I am sure you would therefore like to have your wife present when we ask our questions," Scott offered.

"If you do not mind," he replied.

"No, not at all. Your daughter is not a suspect or in any trouble so far as we know, but if it would put you at ease . . ."

They were led into a large room that looked like an old college library and took their seats at a round table. After a few minutes, they were joined by the mother, a tall woman with graying hair and fashionable glasses, and a red-eyed young girl. "He was murdered?" said Veronica as she sat at the table.

"Unfortunately, it would appear as such," Scott said in reply.

"They told me he was trying to escape. Did he get shot by the tower guards?" she asked, fighting back tears.

"No, I'm sorry, but it was a bit more traumatic than that. We are not releasing the details at this time, but the death was not a matter of course in the usual manner you would expect during an escape attempt. He wrote a letter to you the night before he died. I have a copy for you. You must understand that the original letter is part of the investigation, and I cannot release it to you. When our investigation is concluded and any court proceedings are adjudicated, you may petition for the return of the original letter from the district attorney's office," Scott said as he passed the folded letter to the young girl.

She read it intently, began to cry, and pressed her face to her mother's bosom. After a few awkward moments where Oswaldo and Scott basically just stared at each other and the contents of the room, Veronica composed herself sufficiently to continue the interview. "Veronica," Scott continued, "we found a cell phone in Richard's property, and we know he has been calling you and sending you text messages."

Veronica's mouth dropped open. "Is my daughter in any trouble?" interjected the mother.

"No, Mrs. Mendez, she is not in any trouble as far as I am concerned. Section 4570 of the Penal Code, the unlawful communication with an inmate, is a misdemeanor, and I am not interested in arresting your daughter for a misdemeanor. I need her help with a homicide. One of the messages left by your daughter said she met with someone with the initial G. Veronica, can you tell me who G. is?"

"I don't know anyone with that initial. I don't know. He would ask me to do all kinds of things. I don't remember anything like that."

"Are you familiar with an inmate at the prison by the name of Martinez? They call him Spider."

"That was one of his friends, someone he worked with at his job."

"What about an inmate they call Smooth?"

"He works with him too."

"Were they involved in any activity at the prison that was, uh, questionable?"

"What do you mean?"

"Smuggling."

"Do you mean like drugs and stuff?"

"Drugs, tobacco, and cell phones."

"No, nothing like that."

"Veronica, we have documents and text messages stating a lot of money was collected from the associates or family members of inmates at our prison and sent to you. In fact, the letter I just gave you alludes to a large sum of money being collected."

"He had some money sent to me," she said sheepishly.

"How much?" asked Mrs. Mendez.

"Not much, Mom, just a little really," protested Veronica.

"I said how much?" demanded her mother.

"It's about $30,000" was her reply.

Her mother grew ashen white. "Gerald!" she shouted with a shrill.

Within a few seconds, Dr. Mendez appeared at the table. "Whatever is the trouble, my dear?" he said, comforting his wife.

Carolyn Mendez informed her husband of the details of their conversation. He did not look happy with his daughter. "You must tell this man everything you know, and I mean everything," he instructed with stern regard.

"But, Daddy, it is nothing. He would have people send checks and money orders to my post office box, and sometimes I would have to pick up money at the Western Union downtown. He told me to put the money in my bank account until he got out, and then we were going to go away where we could be in love together without anyone to disapprove of our love."

"Oh, my dear child, what have you done? What have you been doing? You foolish girl, what have you done?"

"Nothing, Daddy, I have done nothing!" she protested.

"Ever since that boy has come into our lives, it has been nothing but misery. He abused you when you were a child. He kidnapped you when you were a teenager. Now this!" His anger was apparent.

"You had him thrown in prison! Haven't you done enough?" Veronica shouted as she stood and stamped her foot.

"Dr. Mendez, if I might, perhaps I can be of help," Scott said in an attempt to gain control of the interview. "There are many things that good girls do when they are in love. Inmates are very good at manipulation and at convincing otherwise good people to do things they know are wrong. There is nothing more convincing than love. Veronica, I know you are a good person. I also know you loved Richard dearly and would do anything for him, especially if it meant you would live happily together for the rest of your lives. Unfortunately, what has happened may have cut short that happiness and led to his death. You are not responsible for that, but I need to know who was, and I need for you to help me."

"Spider and him had something that they were doing. I don't know what it was, and he never told me. I only collected the money. That's all I did." She sobbed.

"Sir, we will turn the money over to you," said the father as he held his wife's hands. "But I think we must have the proper representation for my daughter. If you do not mind, I think we must consult legal counsel."

"I understand. Of course, I will ask you to meet me at the bank, and we will have a hold placed on the account by the district attorney's office until we can straighten this matter out. I do have just one more question, if that is all right," Scott said as he rose from the table.

"Yes?" he inquired.

"A note was found in the property of Inmate Weller that was written by your daughter. It looked as though it had been smuggled into the institution. In the note, it said she met with a person identified only as G. It is imperative that I know who this person was and why it was that she met with him." Dr. Mendez looked at his daughter.

"It was an old man, an old black man. I was to give him a message from Richard. It was something from him, and it was about Spider. It was a small note that was wrapped up in plastic. He gave it to someone during a visit, a girl, and she brought it to me. I never read it. I just met with the old man and handed him the paper."

"Veronica, can you describe this old man?" Scott asked.

"He had an oxygen bottle and tubes that went to his nose."

Before leaving, Scott placed a telephone call to the district attorney's office and spoke with DDA Richard Rainwater. Scott advised him of the situation and handed the phone to Dr. Mendez. They came to an agreement to have the money remain in the account untouched until a determination could be made in the matter. Scott thanked the parents for their assistance and asked them to contact him should their daughter provide any additional information that would be helpful to the investigation.

As they entered the highway and emerged from the fog into a brilliantly sunny day, Oswaldo asked, "I thought you said that phone was locked, but you said he had been calling her."

"I did say it was locked, Oz. I was bluffing, and she fell for it."

"Oh, why didn't you Mirandize her?"

"I didn't read her the *Miranda* warning because we were in their home. There is never a need for *Miranda* when you are sitting in someone's library or living room because there is no custody. It's the same as when you question someone over the telephone. *Miranda* is only necessary when there is questioning and custody combined. They could have asked me to leave, or if you are on the phone, they could always hang up. Also, her mother was present and is an attorney. *Miranda* does not apply if the person you are interviewing has their attorney sitting next to them. When they informed me they wanted a criminal defense attorney, that's the same thing as telling me it was time to leave. Besides, at this point, I don't know if she has done anything other than collect the money. I sure do wish I knew one thing though."

"What's that?" asked Oswaldo.

"I wish I knew what was in that note she gave to old man Graves. That note was about Spider, and I'm thinking it must have been important."

"Don't forget, Scotty, to pick up the photographs on the way back."

Chapter 6

Smooth Spiders

"And so, Tyrus, that's the gist of the trip to Pacific Grove . . . No, we didn't talk to the kid's parents, just the girlfriend and her parents . . . Sure did, I have the photographs right here. They look like they were taken at the little park that is in Pacific Grove at some kind of function, like a barbecue, not that I can tell, just a lot of people . . . Yes, some are from work. Well, Rose is in some of the photographs with Mr. Graves, smoking a fat cigar with his oxygen tank hose drooped under his chin. Alfredo is there in a big Hawaiian print shirt. You can't miss him . . . Sure thing, you can look at them when you get back to the office on Monday . . . No, I have no plans for the weekend. Hold on, Ty, my desk phone is ringing . . . Okay, I'll call you back. You guys have a nice flight. Don't forget to help the lieutenant with his golf clubs."

Scott popped the handset of his desk phone into his left hand. "Investigator Doggett."

"Investigator, this is Stan Forman, the plant supervisor at the Salinas Waste Management Facility."

"How can I help you, Steve?"

"It's Stan, and I think we found something that you guys or someone might be interested in seeing. I already called the county sheriff's office, and they said I should call you too."

"What exactly did you find? Please say it isn't one of our inmates."

"Well, as you know, you guys have your own place to dump things out here, and our skip loader was moving the trash around, and he uncovered something."

"Was it an arm, a head, or a leg?"

"It's a bloodstained pipe."

"I'll be right there."

Oswaldo and Scott raced to the dump, which was about forty minutes east of the prison. A deputy from the sheriff's office beat them there and was waiting at the gate. They were met by a garbage-encrusted skip loader tractor, and the deputy and Scott were instructed to follow a rubbish-strewn dirt highway to the farthest northeast corner of the dump. There, they were met by the plant supervisor and the operator of a second even dirtier skip loader. "That's it right there," announced Foreman Forman as he pointed to a metal pipe that protruded from a pile of recently deposited trash. A smudge of blood was clearly visible on one end. "It must have come in on one of your trucks. I don't know if it's important, but I thought I had better make the contacts."

"Didn't you guys have a dead body in a truck a few days ago?" asked the young deputy.

"Yes, but it didn't come from that truck because it is isolated at our corporation yard. However, I think I might know where it did come from. Stan, I noticed you have surveillance cameras. For the life of me, I don't know why."

"We sure do, and your truck would be recorded coming back here, complete with the license plate and the driver. We're required to have the cameras in case someone dumps some toxic waste."

"Oz, can you photograph the crime scene, collect the pipe as evidence, and get a statement from the skip loader operator? I'm going to go with Stan to look at the video surveillance tapes."

It was clearly the prison's quarter-million-dollar new garbage truck recorded driving through the front gate and down the road toward the designated dump site, and it was clearly Alfredo Garza driving. It was also undeniable that it could only have been that truck that made the deposit the day after the unfortunate circumstance. Scott collected a copy of the videotape and drove back to where he had left Oswaldo with the crime scene kits. "Well?" he asked.

"Our truck and our driver," Scott responded.

"Which one?" he inquired.

"Alf was driving, and it was the day after the incident."

"The pipe's still in the pile. It looks like a handle from a mop bucket. It's been photographed. The driver of the tractor said he got down to remove a big piece of plastic that got caught in his wheel well and was rubbing against the tire. He said he pulled loose the plastic and tossed it back onto the pile. That's when he looked down and saw the pipe sticking out. He said he didn't know why he was interested in the pipe, but something told him to take a closer look."

"It's a good thing that he did. Was there much blood?" Scott asked.

"The stain is really, really small, maybe a quarter inch by a half inch right at the tip. Oh, and it was partially wrapped in a newspaper that has the date of the day when the kid got killed."

"We'll collect a swab back at the lab and send it in for DNA sampling and analysis. I'll call Detective Dykman and see if we can get a sample of the blood they drew at the autopsy."

"Well, Scotty, there's a problem. This deputy guy says it's his jurisdiction, and he's insisting he needs to take the evidence."

"Wonderful. Let me call Andy now. Maybe I can get him to come out, and we can deal with this together. In the meantime, go tell Deputy Do-Right that I don't want anything touched until we get the chain of custody figured out."

After an hour and a half of standing idly among the mounds of debris growing ever more pungent with the afternoon sun and the valley heat, the impeccable detective Dykman arrived in his fancy unmarked vehicle. Immediately, he took control of the scene and insisted on taking possession of all items of evidence. Scott was able to persuade him to let him collect a swab of the blood from the pipe, and Andy agreed to take the swab and the sample of blood that was collected from the decedent at autopsy to the department of justice forensic laboratory. The deputy was appeased and left after being dispatched to a domestic violence call.

Andy handed the evidence bag containing the pipe to Scott, who in turn handed it to Oswaldo. Andy then drove to the nearest car wash.

Oswaldo and Scott drove back to the prison. During the drive, Scott reminded Oswaldo that just because it was their new garbage truck and Alfredo driving it did not mean that he was connected to any criminal activity. It would not be out of the ordinary for someone to pitch a weapon used in the commission of a crime into a dumpster, garbage can, or the back of a garbage truck.

"Well, Tyrus, how was your trip?" Scott asked the recently returned gang investigator.

"Doggie, I can tell you that the gang conference, classes, and updates were pretty good. Our lieutenant can tell you that the golf courses were great. How are you doing on the investigation? Anything good?"

"You know about the interviews in PG and the discovery of the pipe at the dump. Other than that, we have nothing new. I'm thinking about pulling Spider and Smooth in for an interview. Of course, I wouldn't dream of interviewing them without you there."

"I haven't seen the photographs yet," he reminded Scott, who produced the twenty-four photographs for his inspection. "Yeah, Dog, it looks like a barbecue or something. There's all kinds of our noncustody staff members there."

"I'm thinking it was a retirement party for someone because you can just barely see the banner, and it says congratulations to someone in there. Here's the photograph of Alfredo Garza in his Hawaiian print shirt."

"That is a big loud shirt. He's got a bottle in one hand and a shot glass of tequila in the other."

"Yes, he's a two-fisted drinker, a man after my own liver."

"You don't drink tequila, Dog."

"I hardly ever even get a beer these days. Man, a beer does sound good. Do you recognize anyone else in those photographs?"

"Isn't that what's-her-name over at the warehouse?"

"Indeed, yes, Tyrus, you have successfully pointed out the widow Graves who retired from the warehouse a good number of years ago. That's Rose."

"No, Dog, the other girl. Look at the one that's next to her, that one," he said, pointing to one of the figures, "the one in the pink top."

"Is that Patty?"

"Yeah, that's her name, Patty . . . uh, uh, Patty . . . oh, Dog, come on, you know her. She used to work the package room at South."

"That's Patty Shepard?"

"That's it!"

"Man, she looks a lot different with her hair down. If that's the case, we can very easily put a date on this event. Let me call over there." A telephone call to the warehouse revealed the event was indeed a retirement party for one of the warehouse workers that took place three months before their incident. "So, Ty, it looks like the photos have nothing to do with the case. I'll hang on to them for a bit and then turn them over to Rose."

"At least keep the negatives," he suggested.

They drove over to the minimum security facility and asked that Inmate Martinez and Inmate Gottfried be located and escorted to the watch commander's office, which they had commandeered to conduct their interviews. Inmate Gottfried was the first to be escorted to the makeshift interview room. "Gottfried, or should I call you Smooth?" Scott asked as the large-framed man assumed the wooden chair across from the investigators.

"You know who I am, and I know who you are. I don't care which you use. What's this about?" he asked with an air of annoyance.

"We would like to talk to you about Richard Weller and some of the . . . uh, things that have been going on out at the recycling center," Scott explained.

"There ain't nothing going on out there," he huffed.

"Actually, Smooth, there is plenty going on out there," countered Sergeant Phillips. "And you are in the thick of it."

"At least thirty pounds of tobacco worth," Scott interjected.

"What's that got to do with me?" he queried.

Scott turned to Tyrus. "Let me ask you something. Would you smoke something that has been in someone's ass?"

"Maybe if it was mentholated."

"More like 'rectalated,'" Scott jibed.

"Well, after all, it is a natural humidor," replied Tyrus.

"And no one's rectum has the capacity of our friend, Smooth. We've seen it in action. How much did you have shoved up there that day out at the sewage treatment plant?"

"Look, Doggett, that was back then. I don't do that no more."

"Two cell phones, one charger, and two thumb-sized plugs of tobacco—I believe that was the inventory once it all came out. What I'd like to know is how in the world did you get a job outside the gate?"

"I paroled but came back on a violation. There wasn't nothing in my file about that time you guys caught me, and I got a job on the garbage truck, but I couldn't do all that lifting no more, so they moved me over to recycling. That was then. I don't do nothing no more, and neither do nobody else out there."

"When do you get out?" asked Tyrus.

"Got six more months."

"Would you like to make those six months or maybe you'd like to add another six to that?"

"How you going to do that, Sarge?"

"I'm going to charge you with that tobacco. I can do it too. You have priors, and it was in your area."

"You can't put that on me. It ain't mine, and that's the truth. Oh sure, I used to do all that, but that was in the past. I'm behaving myself these days," he protested.

"Then whose is it?" Scott asked.

"I'm also not in here for tellin'," he answered.

"All right, tell me this. You had to notice what was going on out there. I mean, come on, this is your gig. Nobody is better at the keistering game than you. You are the master smuggler. You tell me that you were not involved. I believe you. So if it wasn't you, then who was it? What kind of deal did Spider and Weller have going on?"

"I ain't in here for tellin'," he proclaimed.

"Weller is dead, Smooth, murdered," interjected Tyrus.

"Murdered? They said he fell in the truck."

"Murdered, and that means someone is getting charged with murder."

"Sergeant Phillips, I didn't murder no one. I wouldn't murder that boy. I liked that boy. We all did. He weren't that bad, real nice boy. They said it was an accident. Are you lyin' to me?"

"Murdered," Scott confirmed.

"You all need to talk to Spider about that. They wanted me to be part of their game, but I wouldn't do it."

"What game exactly? There's no turning back. You've gone this far."

"I ain't—"

"In here for telling, yes, I know. Smooth, I am not going to put your name in any report. I am not going to even make any mention of our discussion, but I need to know what direction to go in. This young man, the one whom you liked very much, was hit in the head, knocked unconscious, and then crushed by a garbage truck. There are grieving parents. There is a grieving young lady who loved him dearly. I need to find the person responsible for this terrible crime. You have the key, and you have an obligation to that young man to point me in the right direction."

"Mr. Doggett, when you put it like that, I guess you are right. Him and Spider were moving all the tobacco, cell phones, and marijuana that was coming into this place. You name it—real alcohol, blunts, even them little PlayStation games, oh, and DVD players and porn too. They was moving everything and making good money at it too."

"How were they doing it?" Tyrus asked.

"Oh no, Sarge, I done told you enough. I ain't going to tell you no more. You guys are investigators. Investigate it yourselves."

"Was it old man Graves?" Scott quizzed.

"No, but he knew. He would tell Rick that he needed to stop, or he would go tell the warden. He would tell him that what he was doing was wrong and that he would get his girlfriend in a lot of trouble, arrested even."

"And how did that make Weller feel?"

"It was on his mind something fierce. He would tell me he didn't want to do it anymore, but Spider wouldn't let him stop. I've said enough. I want to leave. I've been in here too long, and I can see Spider coming up the path." The investigators dismissed him with a promise to interview him again. It was not a promise he wanted to hear.

As he passed Inmate Martinez, Scott heard him say, "I didn't tell them nothing, and you better not tell them nothing either, or I will break your neck."

"Well, Ty, we can't come at Martinez hard, or he will know Smooth talked."

"I agree with you, Dog, but we have to make him think that we do know something."

"Dying declaration?"

"You mean old man Graves?"

"It's worth a try, Tyrus."

"I'm game."

Inmate Martinez was ushered into the room, and it was clearly visible why they called him Spider. He had long spindly legs and arms, but he was not tall or lanky. He was, in fact, somewhat short and pudgy. His anonym was well given; he looked just like a fat spider. His head was clean shaven, and his eyebrows were very light, which made his dark eyes stand out. To add to the illusion, Inmate Martinez had a spiderweb tattooed on the top of his head and down his neck. Woven within the web were the years he had been incarcerated starting with "'09." Tattoos on his arms showed he was a gang member.

"Sit down, Martinez," instructed Tyrus, pointing to the wooden chair.

"Have you got your identification card?" he asked robotically. Inmate Martinez surrendered his identification card, and Tyrus slowly examined it, examined the arachnid inmate, copied the information, and handed it back.

Scott opened the interview with "Inmate Martinez, the reason we called you in here was to talk to you about Inmate Richard Weller and some information that has come to light regarding the recycling plant."

"How can I help you?" replied the creepy young man. "Are you aware that Inmate Weller was murdered?"

"No, I was told that he was accidentally killed while trying to escape. I heard that the old man who drives the garbage truck is dead also."

"Partially correct. Weller was murdered, and Mr. Graves expired from natural causes. Although we were not able to talk to Weller, for obvious reasons, we were able to talk to Mr. Graves just before he died. He made a declaration, and it was about you and what you have been doing."

"What I have been doing? No. What Weller was doing maybe."

"How so?"

"Everyone knows that he was the man to go to for everything. Everyone knows that. What he and that old man were doing is on them. I have done nothing, and I know nothing."

"And the thirty pounds of tobacco at your work site?"

"It belonged to Weller."

"Why would Mr. Graves say it belonged to you?"

"He is mistaken."

"Was."

"He was mistaken."

Just then, Tyrus—who had been looking at his cell phone—interrupted with "Dog, we gotta go." He ordered Inmate Martinez out of the room.

"What the hell, Ty?"

"Rose is in the hospital. She's been beaten."

Tyrus and Scott made a hasty trip to the office of their surly supervisor, begged for permission to drive to the Community Hospital of the Monterey Peninsula, drew weapons, and were heading toward the freeway when Scott noticed a familiar face in a brand-new pickup truck exit the freeway and turn toward the prison. It was Alfredo.

Chapter 7

Also Sprach Teufel

Inmate Reginald Cooper stepped out onto the busy Central Facility Yard. He scanned the eleven hundred inmates milling about the yard and settled on the northeast corner telephone bank and the bleachers behind the baseball diamond. His course set, he began walking in that direction. Reggie Cooper was of mixed race, and although not a full-fledged member of the Southern street disruptive group, he had an allegiance to the Mexican Mafia after a kindness they did for his grandmother after the imprisonment of his grandfather in the 1970s. It was rumored his grandfather had befriended a high-ranking capo and put himself between the capo and an inmate-manufactured stabbing weapon, commonly called a shank, on the San Quentin exercise yard. In return for the "kindness" shown to his grandmother over the years by the gang, Reggie had repaid them with a number of "hits" on the yard or in his cell.

In spite of his young age, as he was only twenty-six, Reggie was on his third cellmate. Calamity had befallen two of his cellmates in the form of sudden and mysterious death. For this reason, the other inmates at the prison bequeathed him with the sobriquet "Reaper." Reggie was clever. He had dispatched his first cellmate, a chronic asthmatic, by replacing his inhaler with one that was empty. The boy was only nineteen. He died reaching for an empty inhaler. It was rumored he

441

was in debt to the gang for refusing to pay a pecuniary penalty for an unsavory arrest that appeared on his court-provided minute order. Reggie was never charged; he wasn't even investigated.

His second cellmate was found hanging from a ligature tied to the vent screen in the corner of the cell. A note begging his mother for forgiveness and blaming the evil "guards" for causing the untimely death was found pinned to his shirt. Scott investigated this death. He was disturbed by one observation: the noose was tied to the left. The inmate was left handed. Scott could not convince the medical examiner that it would be unlikely a left-handed person would tie a noose to the left side. The cause of death was determined to be suicide, and Scott reluctantly left it at that.

"You wanted to see me, Diablo?" Reggie said to a husky Hispanic inmate of about thirty-six who was sitting on the bleachers, flanked by two muscled, sunglass-adorned bodyguards.

"Reaper!" exclaimed Inmate Humberto Serrano, alias Diablo, as he extended a ring-encumbered hand. The two exchanged handshakes, and each looked the other directly in the eyes.

"I have a need of your talent," Diablo expressed. "Your luck has been good. Two favors you have done for me, and these amateur cops, *putos*, have pinned nothing on you."

"Am I due for number 3?" inquired Reggie.

"Yes, but this one may not be so easy. We have a . . . well, shall we say misguided youth. It has come to my attention there will soon be an impostor in our ranks. There is a young man who managed a lenient sentence for information that put two of our soldados in the Bay for a very long time. I am told that *rata* is on his way here from Pleasant Valley State Prison. I wish his stay here to be brief and unpleasant, if you know what I mean."

"Clearly," replied the grimmest of reapers.

"You have a cellie now. A young Blood?"

"Clarence, a good kid. He is related by blood, son of a great-aunt."

"Please encourage him to house elsewhere, perhaps with another Blood. You can reunite with him later. Leave us to be sure this *excremento* will be housed with you. The X Wing inmate clerk is in our employment."

"Consider it done, Diablo," replied the assassin.

"Compensation for your trouble?" asked the shot caller.

"A pleasure" was the only reply.

"Young Blood, you have to find another cellie and quick," remarked Reggie to his kin.

"But why?"

"Best you don't know. Don't fret, you'll be back. That's on my mama. Something has come up, and I need your rack."

"Where will I go and how?" asked the crestfallen youth.

"It's all in the works. You're going up to 315 in two days. Healy is losing his bunkie, and you will be moving up there. The unit clerk already has the paperwork ready and signed by the lieutenant. Pack your things." The young cousin of Reggie dutifully packed all his belongings into a large plastic garbage bag and awaited the tier officer to unlock the door for his move.

"DeSantos! Abel Kilo, last two twenty-four!" shouted the receiving and release officer. Still tired from the transportation bus ride from Pleasant Valley State Prison, the twenty-year-old Hispanic inmate stared into space while sitting in the large caged holding cell. "DeSantos, Armando! Abel Kilo, last two twenty-four!"

"That's me!" exclaimed the young man, having been nudged by the inmate seated next to him.

"Well get over here, youngster," responded the senior officer. Inmate Armando DeSantos, a first-term inmate who had been offered a safe stay at a sensitive needs yard but who insisted he was still "good with the homeys" and was therefore transferred to the general population of CSP–Gabilan, stood and opened the unlocked chain-link gate and walked to the counter that separated the uniformed officer from the newly arrived inmate.

"Sir, DeSantos," murmured the weary inmate.

"Your ID card, son, give me your ID card," replied the officer who was two years away from retirement ten years ago. The green state-issued identification card was duly passed and scrutinized by the officer. "You've been medically cleared, and classification is complete. Your property is inventoried. Grab a fish roll and line up at the line to the right of the door. After you get a new photograph taken, you will be escorted to X Wing in a few minutes. The bathrooms are to the left. Don't lose your place. You are going to X, cell 112."

"Sir, how long will I be in reception, and when can I get visits?"

"Generally, two weeks for your counselor to complete classification. But according to the computer, you must be done already. You'll be going to Charlie Wing, cell 216, in less than a week. Visits for X Wing are behind glass every Saturday and Sunday, 1200 hours to 1500 hours. Your visitors must be approved and call for reservations. Stand over there, son. Next! Ramos! Bravo Charlie fifty-five!"

Inmate DeSantos dutifully assumed his place in line near the door leading to the central corridor. He placed his fish roll, which consisted of a dark gray wool blanket, white sheets, boxer shorts, socks, and a T-shirt on the floor; asked the inmate in front of him to hold his place in line; and slipped into the bathroom. While sitting on the exposed commode, he studied the tattoos on his forearms and hands—the bluish-gray tattoos on each anterior forearm, signifying his proud membership in the gang; three dots on the back of his right hand at the knuckle of his middle finger; and "only God can judge me" along the knuckles of his left hand. He was proud of the accomplishments of his twenty-two years and even more proud that he sired a son who would follow in his footsteps.

While awaiting trial for his participation in the gang-related assassination of a gang dropout, he was visited by a seasoned investigator from the Los Angeles County District Attorney's Office who extended a proffer of a lenient sentence for his cooperation against his coconspirators. The investigator plied him with thoughts of seeing his male offspring before his fortieth birthday in exchange for testimony against the others being charged with the same offense. After gaining the cooperation of the reluctant hector, the investigator engaged Armando in a discussion regarding the future of his offspring. "You do want more for your son, don't you? You want a life of education, career, and accomplishment removed from the gang life?" asked the enforcement arm of the Los Angeles district attorney.

"My son will be my shadow," replied the stalwart street tough.

"This isn't what a father should want for his son!" barked the investigator. "What would you think if your son was shot by some punk from another gang?"

"I would be proud and think my son died as a hero," replied Armando.

"You piece of shit!" exclaimed the red-faced investigator. "I will see your son is put in foster care before I ever see him raised by you!"

The hand of a cautious deputy district attorney reached out and lightly tapped the investigator's arm. "There, there, let us not be too hasty. Perhaps maturity and absence will temper his opinion on gang life."

DeSantos thought of all this as he gazed at his tattoos and reached for the single-ply state-issued toilet paper. "Fuck them," he quietly said to himself. "For life."

Chapter 8

A Sheep to the Slaughter

"Hey, man, I'm Reggie. Go ahead and take the bottom rack. I prefer being on the top bunk. Your locker is the one by the door." The two inmates shook hands, and Inmate DeSantos began unpacking his meager belongings from the plastic bag he hastily filled as he was evicted from his X Wing single cell.

"I haven't had a bunkie since county," replied the fish inmate as he arranged his belongings in the locker and spread a thread-worn sheet across the heirloom mattress, a veritable cornucopia of DNA.

"You might want to wrap your mattress in plastic, man, before you put that sheet on," suggested Reggie. "That thing is twice as old as you. What do they call you, and where you from?"

"Armando, Mando, and LA."

"What part?"

"East Twenty-First and Adair."

"King Taco!"

"You know it?"

"Man, do I know it! Best damned carnitas tacos in the world."

"I heard that, bro. I mix *suadero* and *buche*, bro. Damn, I wish I had some now. Where you from, bro?"

"Maywood, Riverside, and East Sixty-First. Who do you roll with?" probed Reggie.

"Sur. You?"

"I'm my own man, coz. What are you in for?"

"Putting in work on a DO," replied Armando. "You?"

"One eighty-seven times two. Cool pic. Your boy?"

"Yes, he's my son. He's two years old and a real killa. Here's one with little man holding Daddy's 9 mm. You?" asked Armando.

"No, man, I been down since I was sixteen. I got life twice. No kids for me. Not that I want 'em. Hey, not that I don't trust you, but I don't, not yet, man. You got your papers?"

"Minute order and abstract of judgment right there, bro. It's legit."

Reggie studied both documents, intently matching the information with that provided by Diablo. He had the right target. In a way, he was sad. He liked the kid, but he took great pleasure in taking life. He knew he couldn't act too fast. He needed to plan, to lure his victim into a trap. He needed to find that one thing that would make this chore easy. "Two TVs?" asked Armando, astonished at the breach of prison policy.

"One's for you. It's a floater, man. Don't get it taken by the bulls. You like the drank?" Reggie asked.

"The real stuff or that toilet shit?"

"I got both, man, and some smoke."

"Shit, yeah, I can go for that."

"Tonight, man, after the last count. Don't do that shit during the day or the COs will get you, especially CO Edwards. He's got a nose for it, man. Oh, and about the cell, motherfucka better keep this pad clean. Don't make me tell you what to pick up and when. My floor is shiny, and I like to keep them that way. I even get some floor polish from the foyer work crew. Cost me smoke every week, but I get the stuff they use in the warden's office." Armando shook Reggie's hand for the second time and promised to be a good cellie.

Weeks passed with the routine daytime activities found in the controlled environment of the prison system, nights filled with contraband St-Rémy VSOP, toilet booze made from potato peels and sugar smuggled from the culinary, and pin joints—a lot of pin joints. Reggie began to develop the one thing missing from his entire life: the bond of friendship with another man. Reggie spent the previous years of his confinement doing his best to ignore the other male locked in the small compartment that was home, an intimate space the size of a walk-in closet with one shared, open commode and no privacy.

Nature had to be well timed in the prison setting, best when your cellie was on the yard or at an assignment. Otherwise, one simply held his nose or pressed it against the small opening in the cell window or relied on tightly rolled strips of toilet paper, often doused with cologne, set alight as an attempt to mask one offensive odor with another. Most cells and inmate property had a distinctive odor, which the officers called "inmate funk." It was a combination of body odor, flatulence, rotting food from last month's men's advisory committee chicken sale, and soap. The smell of soap was the result of hand-washing clothing in the commode/sink combination and a failure to fully rinse the garments, thereby producing a film that adhered to everything.

Scott knew where the soap came from. Two decades before, he spent a month as the North Facility culinary officer. Every time he replaced the powdered soap in the lavatory dispensers for the mandatory postbusiness handwashing, it would disappear in its entirety within minutes, whisked away by inmate magpies to be used for in-cell laundry. This funk was not present in cell CW-216. It was clean and pleasantly decorated with wall art purloined from the best magazines pinched from the library, and it smelled, well, like the warden's office.

Reggie was never short of foodstuffs, candies, and sodas from the yard canteen or quarterly care packages sent by ranking members of a notorious prison gang. As prison life went, Armando was living more comfortably than when with his mother, uncle, sisters, brothers, girlfriend, and assorted toddlers—one his own—in the two-bedroom apartment on East Twenty-First Street. Reggie was keenly aware of his instructions, "brief and unpleasant." But Reggie knew he had two problems to overcome: Armando was 5'11" and 210 pounds, and Reggie was 5'7" and 135 pounds, and he really liked Armando, like a brother.

It was a rainy day on the Central Facility Yard. The two men, each adorned with clear plastic garbage bags with holes for the head and arms pulled over yellow slickers, stood in the center of the yard. The larger man was flanked by his two bodyguards. "Three months, my friend, and the *gusano* has lived well, like a capo even. He eats the food we provide you for your skills. This does not make me happy. I answer to people higher than the warden of this *pinta*."

"In good time, Diablo. I promise you will be happy with the results," assured Reggie.

"Do it soon, Reaper, very soon." The two men shook hands, and Reggie began walking back toward the yard gate, aware that the eyes of the tower and yard gate officers were on him.

Tower no. 2 officer Roy Hubbard put down his binoculars, picked up the telephone, and called Scott. "Reggie Cooper, CW-216, he's up to something, Dog. I bet my tower on it. Get 'em, Dog. Go get 'em." It was a voice mail message, for at the moment, Scott and Tyrus were sitting in the intensive care unit, waiting to see Rose.

Chapter 9

Writing with Light

"You may go in, Officers, but please only a few minutes and be very quiet—and no cell phones," sternly said the intensive care unit nurse as she addressed Scott and Tyrus. Tyrus quickly pushed his cell phone back into his breast pocket and removed his hat. They followed the swift-walking nurse to the last room in the unit.

Rose Graves was awake but clearly in pain and discomfort. "Don't say it, Sergeant Phillips. I am not in the mood," groused the elderly woman with one hand raised and the other adjusting the oxygen tubes lying on her upper lip.

"I wasn't, I promise, but you know we're here for you," replied Tyrus, not exactly sure what he was not supposed to say.

"How did this happen, Rose?" asked Scott, aware of the time limitations on their visit.

"I was in the garden, deadheading the marigolds, and the lights went out. The mailman found me lying there on top of the flower bed. The police said someone came up behind me and hit me in the back of the head with a small shovel Walter kept by the potting shed. Have you talked to the nice officer from Pacific Grove?"

"Just before we came in, Rose," replied Scott, adding, "He said your house has been ransacked, but nothing appeared to be stolen."

"He wanted to know about our investigation, but I think we'll keep that close for now," added Tyrus.

"Rose, do you mind if we stop by your bungalow and see if there is anything we can do to tidy it up a bit for you?" asked Scott. Tyrus looked at Scott with that telltale "you're up to something" squint in his right eye.

"The key is under the mat at the porch door. Can you please bring me back my makeup bag and cell phone? They say I will be here a few days, and I want to look my best for these handsome doctors. It's on the dresser in my bedroom. Thank you, sweetheart. You come back now. Bye-bye," Rose said as she shooed them with her right hand. It was obvious her strength was gone, and she wanted sleep.

Tyrus and Scott stepped out of the room and pulled the curtain closed. "Are we really going to go clean her house, Dog?" whispered Tyrus.

"Indeed, we are. It's the Christian thing to do, Ty, and it will give us a chance to see what the shovel-wielding brute was looking for."

Just then, Ty's attention was drawn to a young officer in a blue uniform who was standing by the nurse's station and motioning him to parlay. "Be right back, Dog."

Pacific Grove police officer Jeff Gold was an affable young man, tall with a broad smile. "I talked to the neighbors, and they said there were two cars in the neighborhood they didn't recognize when Mrs. Rose was hit, but they didn't have much more information than a black sedan like a Honda and a fancy white pickup truck with dealer plates. There's a small store on the corner of their street. I'm hoping they have cameras. I will let you know." Tyrus shook his hand, thanked him for the information, and handed him his business card, pointing to the email address for any video the officer might obtain.

Scott joined Tyrus at the nurse's station, greeted the young officer, and shook his hand. "Food, Ty? It's on me. I'm hungry."

"Papa Chano's on Alvarado?"

"Sounds good to me. We'll make a loop through Monterey over to Pacific Grove and then hit the Holman Highway back to the prison," responded Scott as he checked the status of his billfold.

"Regular al pastor burrito and an ice tea with lemon," said Scott to the young man behind the counter.

"Make that two," added Tyrus in his usual unimaginative manner. "I'll get the chips and pico de gallo, Ty. Grab that table over there."

"Green salsa, Dog," Ty said as he lowered himself at the table.

"What's going on with this, Dog? No one meant Mr. Graves harm, but Rose is lucky she isn't dead."

"Not to mention she was lucky the postman found her when he did," added Scott. "The officer said the gate was open, and the postman saw her legs. Thirty years walking the streets of PG delivering the mail, and he's probably seen his share of old biddies expiring in their gardens."

"Hey, Dog, didn't I see an old black Honda Civic sedan at the house where Weller's girlfriend lived?"

"Dark blue, but I think you are correct, something to check on before we leave the peninsula."

"Holy cow, Ty, a tornado went through this place!" exclaimed Scott as he opened the back porch door with the under-the-mat key.

"Whoever did this must have thought he killed Rose because he sure did take his time in here. Every drawer is opened and dumped."

"We never made a mess like this when we serve a warrant, Ty."

"Or search a cell for that matter," added the sergeant.

"This was deliberate and thorough. Do you think it was more than one person?"

"Yeah, most likely, Dog. Damn, they even tossed the family photo albums. Here's Mr. Graves and Rose on their wedding. Jeez, would you look at that bow tie, ruffled shirt, and wool-felt fedora. Nineteen-seventies?"

"No doubt, Ty, or late 1960s. Why did we ever dress like that? Box of photographs dumped here and a few more boxes in the hall closet. Why go through the photographs? This makes no sense."

Scott and Tyrus made quick work ransacking in reverse, and the house was restored to order in no time. While tidying the spare room, obviously preserved after the departure of a beloved dependent, Scott made a discovery while inspecting an old tin box he picked up from the floor. "Found it! Here, Ty, take a whiff of this."

"Doggie, that's corrections lesson 1. 'Hey, CO, smell this.' You don't."

"No, really, smell this and tell me what you think," Scott encouraged as he handed the box across to Ty.

"Damn! Vinegar? No, worse than vinegar."

"Like an old goat maybe?" Scott suggested.

"Yeah, I guess, if you go around sniffing old goats."

"Chivas, Ty, black tar heroin, and there must have been quite a bit in there if the smell is still there. Close it up, put it in a plastic bag, and we'll take it back with us. Oz can run K-9 Ruud past it. If he alerts, that's likely what was in there."

They finished their task and exited as they entered. Scott replaced the key under the mat. Tyrus carried two clear plastic bags, one containing the tin can and the other the makeup bag and cell phone requested by Rose. "Dog, look at this. The cell phone just lit up, and there is a text on the screen. It's from Alfredo."

"How long ago, and what does it say?"

"Last night at eleven and 'Tomorrow at nine.'"

"Interesting, Ty, and do you know what else is interesting? Pacific Grove didn't collect the shovel as evidence. It's sitting right there by the flower bed."

"Are we taking it, Dog? What am I saying? Of course, we are taking it." Scott smiled.

They stopped by the Mendez family residence and rolled to a stop two houses down. "See, Ty, it is dark blue."

"Dog, that car hasn't been driven in months. Look at the dirt piled up against the tires."

"Agreed, Ty, let's get out of here before we are noticed." They pulled away from the curb and made a three-point turn so as not to cross the front of the residence.

On the drive back to the hospital, Scott and Tyrus talked mostly about football. Scott preferred talking football over basketball. He did not like talking about Ty's Detroit Lions, but he had to admit he liked their new quarterback. After a lull in the conversation, Scott looked over at his partner and said, "My father always said the same thing to me every time he thumbed through a photo album from family events. He'd look at me and say, 'Your presence in family gatherings is conspicuous only by your absence.' Do you know what he meant by that?"

"You do work a lot, Dog. Lord knows how many birthdays and holidays you've missed."

"No, Tyrus, I was there, but I am not in the photographs. I was always behind the camera. Who do you think was taking the photographs at the picnic?"

"Mr. Graves?" asked Tyrus.

"He's in most of them himself as is Rose, Alfredo, Patty, and everyone else from the warehouse. Perhaps Rose can answer that question for us."

"I'm sorry, Officers, Mrs. Graves is asleep. She is not to be disturbed. The doctor has prescribed a sedative. She'll be asleep for hours. I will put her makeup bag on the nightstand with her phone," stated the intensive care unit head nurse apologetically.

"If you will include this note, I would be much obliged," said Scott as he quickly scribbled a note on the back of his business card."

"Certainly, gentlemen. Good day," replied the taciturn lady with the lamp. She looked at the back of the card as she closed the ICU doors—"Rose, who took the photographs at the picnic?"

Scott pulled the Crown Vic to the outpatient pickup area and waited for Sergeant Phillips to come out of the hospital. He said he needed to use the restroom and separated from Scott with the promise to meet him out front. In reality, Tyrus stopped by the gift shop and had a nice bouquet of flowers sent up to Rose's room. He didn't want Scott to see his moment of generosity. Scott was convinced that Tyrus was the quintessential parsimonious keeper of the dole, more likely to cut the marigolds from Rose's garden than to actually pay for overpriced flora at a gift shop. "Took you long enough, Tyrus. You might as well get that prostrate checked out while we're here."

"Just drive, Dog."

"Oh, Ty, remind me to call Hubbard in tower no. 2 when we get back. He left a voice mail on my desk phone. Do you know anything about an Inmate Cooper in Charlie Wing?"

"Never heard of him. What's up with him?"

"Apparently, Hub wants me to 'go get him.' That usually means dope."

Scott eased the creaking Crown Vic onto Highway 1 northbound and gave it gas. The Enforcer engine responded in kind, and they were at freeway speed in seconds. "So, Doggie, let me tell you about our running game." Scott rolled his eyes.

Chapter 10

What, Will These Hands Ne'er Be Clean?

"No, man, I mean it. Reg, you are my best friend, bro, like . . . like we was brothers, bro, homeys. I wish I knew you when I was out," slurred the inebriate Armando as he passed the VSOP up to Reggie on the upper bunk.

Reggie took a long pull from the bottle, rolled over, and slid an inmate-manufactured stabbing weapon from out of his makeshift pillow. He checked it for sharpness by scraping it along his arm hair. It was sharp—razor sharp. He tied the handle of the shank to the drawstring of his sweat shorts and tucked it inside.

Armando took a drag on a small thin marijuana cigarette and blew the smoke out of the small opening in the cell window. "Reggie, I mean, bro, I've never had a friend like you, never. I love you like a brother, bro. Man, I am faded." He took the second and final drag off the diminutive cigarette and pitched the butt out the window. "I would die for you, bro. Bro, I'm telling you, bro, you need to marry my sister. She would be into you, bro. You watch, bro. You can send her a visiting application, and she'll come visit you with me and my girl. She's pretty too, bro."

"You all right, man," was the only thing Reggie could muster.

"No, really, bro, my sister is hecka pretty."

"What would your sister want with a double lifer, man? I don't even get the boneyard. She needs someone out there she can touch." He took another slug of brandy, hid the bottle underneath his pillow, and intently watched the arrow-slit window in the cell door. He looked at his watch. It was eleven thirty at night.

Within five minutes, a flashlight lit the cell. Reggie raised his right hand and waived at the first-watch officer doing his tier security check. The beam of light fell on Reggie's forehead, paused for a moment, and dropped down onto Inmate DeSantos, who suddenly had an attack of the giggles. The light then moved away, and Reggie heard the jingling of the officer's keys fade away down the tier. "You are an idiot, man." Reggie chortled. "Do you want to get us caught?"

More giggles came from the bottom bunk. "I'm zooted, man. I can't help it, but you really should date my sister."

Reggie put his hands to his face and took a deep breath, which he let out slowly with a barely audible "Fuck." He let himself down from the upper bunk and came to a standing position near the foot of the bunk beds. "I gotta piss, man. Turn to the wall," Reggie directed his still giggling bunkmate.

"Afraid I'll look?" Armando giggled as he rolled to his side and faced the cell wall.

Reggie relieved himself, washed his hands, and turned to face Armando. "Get up, man," he calmly said.

"What?"

"Get up, man."

"Why?"

"Just get up, man."

Inmate DeSantos slowly rose from his bunk, steadied himself with difficulty, and faced Reggie. "You better not hug me, bro."

"Reggie grabbed the bunk rail with his left hand, twisted his body slightly, and threw his entire 145 pounds into a right cross, which landed on Armando's left cheek. Armando's head smacked the side of the upper bunk hard. He blacked out and fell headfirst into the cell's small metal writing desk.

Reggie froze for a moment. His cellmate's fall was louder than he anticipated. He focused on the sound of the jingling of the officer's keys and the thump-thump-thump of boots on the tier. It was from the third tier; he had time. He hoisted Armando's limp body off the floor and dropped him facedown on the lower bunk. He stopped and listened intently. The sound of the keys was distinctly descending the front staircase. Reggie dropped his shorts, untied the handle of the shank, and stuffed it into a stack of toilet paper rolls, and sat on the commode. He could hear the officer frantically checking each cell in the direction where his seasoned ears heard the commotion.

Faster than expected, the officer's flashlight illuminated the partially lit cell. Reggie put his left hand up to shield his eyes and looked toward the door window. He could see the face of an officer against the solid glass. "I'm shitting, man!" Reggie shouted, motioning the officer to be quiet with his right hand and pointing to the still inmate DeSantos. "My cellie's asleep, man."

"Did you hear a crash?" was the muffled question through the glass.

"A what? A crash?"

"A crash" was the muted reply.

"First tier, man. It came from the first tier." The flashlight beam retreated, and the tier pounded with boots thumping as the officer ran, taking two steps at a time down the front staircase. He heard additional voices on the tier just below him. The officer was joined by another officer from the adjacent wing. A third voice was heard. *It must be the corridor officer*, Reggie thought.

He flushed the toilet to give his quick-thinking credibility, climbed up to the top bunk, and pretended to be asleep. He heard the clinking of the keys of the officers as they searched cell to cell, with their flashlights beaming through the arrow-slit windows of each cell door, intent to find the source of the crash. The prison was on first-watch status. The cell doors were locked, and the security bar was set in the deadlock position. Although the officers had keys for the doors, they were not allowed to carry the bar key; it was safe in the control room.

They were on his tier. His heart pounded in his ears. *Shit*, he thought as his head felt the bottom of the hip-flask-shaped brandy bottle jutting from under his pillow.

"They're just doors away," he murmured to himself. "Gotta risk it." He slowly slid his left hand up to his pillow and pushed the bottle farther beneath.

Just at that very moment, four things happened: the cell was filled with the brightest flashlight beam he had ever seen, his hand was still under the pillow, he noticed a bloodstain on the left corner of the writing desk, and Armando was coming to with a moan. It was then Reggie noticed something: his right hand was swollen and throbbing with pain. He raised himself slightly, turning toward the window; placed his barroom-brawl-fractured right hand over his face to shield his eyes from the blinding light; and yelled, "Damn, man! I said it was on the first tier! Son of a bitch! The first tier!"

The light abated, and Reggie heard a muted alert. "Hey, Bill, let's do the first tier again."

With that, Reggie turned out the dim cell bunk light, leaving the cell bathed in the eerie combination of hard shadows and faint streaks of yellowish light coming through the cell window from the yard and fence lights. Out of the cell door window, Reggie only saw blackness. He listened for a moment. The officers had abandoned their search. Armando was moaning louder now. Reggie had to do something fast. Maybe if he rolled him onto his back, the moaning would stop.

Reggie pushed Armando over by the left shoulder. He hesitated for a moment; his hands were on Armando's bare deltoid muscles. Even through the pulsing of his enlarged right hand, Reggie felt the flesh of his cellmate, his friend—flesh that was warm and soft. It was the first time Reggie touched the flesh of a victim who was still alive. He found it disturbing. "Damn, man," Reggie muttered.

Armando stopped moaning, but his right eye opened slightly and attempted to focus on the face of Reggie. "No, fuck that, no," Reggie said as he shook his head from side to side for clarity. He let go of Armando's shoulders, stood up, pulled off his own white T-shirt, and threw it onto the top bunk. He reached into the stack of toilet paper rolls and retrieved the shank with his right hand. He drew the privacy screen sheet at the foot of the bottom bunk across, hoping it would block the view if a curious officer continued his search for the crashlike sound, and positioned himself to the right side of the lower mattress. He leaned over Armando's body and drove the blade of the shank into Armando's right side and stomach while holding his left hand over the mouth of the semiconscious inmate. A huff of air and a "hu-umph" sound from Armando's lungs came through the gaps in Reggie's fingers as he drove the shank in a third time. A tear dropped from Armando's left eye, rolled down his cheek and around his ear, and was wicked into the dingy white bedsheet.

Unknown to Reggie, the blood had made the handle of the shank slippery, and it fell to the ground. Reggie drove his empty right fist two more times into Armando's stomach before he realized the shank was on the floor. "This won't work," he calmly said as he reached down and picked up the stabbing weapon with his left hand.

Now both of Armando's eyes were open, staring at Reggie's face, trying to focus, trying to understand. Reggie was in a silent rage. He drove the blade of the knife nineteen times into the right chest of his former homey. Each time, he felt the blade sink deep through skin, muscle, bone, and organ. Each time, blood would take flight. Reggie's strength was nearly spent. His eyes welled with water. He mustered only enough strength to push the knife three more times into the right side of Armando's stomach. He stood emotionless and dropped the blood-saturated weapon onto the cell floor.

Armando's mouth was open. His eyes had rolled back and upward, fixed and empty. Reggie looked at his swollen hand and attempted to straighten up from his crouched position without thought; his balance was off, and he stumbled, fell, and struck forehead first with force into the concrete cell wall, producing a large contusion on his right brow. He dropped to his knees and intently searched the shiny floor of the cell for blood drops. *Nothing? How can that be?* he thought.

He looked at Armando's lifeless body. "There should be more blood," he breathed. "Why don't I see more blood? Is he still alive? No way can he still be alive." He lowered his ear close to Armando's mouth, his ear touching Armando's thin mustache—nothing, no sound, no air, nothing but almost no blood. How can this be?

For once, Reggie was not in control of himself or the situation. His thinking was confused and clouded. *It's the pain*, he thought.

"Cold water for the swelling," he concluded. Unthinking, he turned the cell light on, leaned against his mattress, grabbed a pair of state-issued blue denim pants, and pulled them over his sweat shorts. He then opened the cold-water faucet and began washing his hands over and over again.

It was at that time Officer Thurgood, who was collecting the outgoing inmate letters from the tier, peered into cell 216. Calmly, Officer Thurgood initiated a soft alarm using his radio in a hushed voice. "Control, code 1, Charlie 216. Send a supervisor, medical, and the bar key. I have a man down." After this, the officer watched Reggie repeatedly scrub his hands, mesmerized by the flow of red water from his hands.

Chapter 11

A Matter of Self-Defense

Officer Thurgood inserted the large Folger Adam key into the tumbler and waited instructions from Lt. Chris Freiburg to open the door. Sergeant Mateo Gonzales looked through the cell door window, now smeared with soap by Reggie's still lathered left hand. Reggie stood motionless in the center of the cell, his eyes transfixed on a solitary droplet of blood on his normally spotless floor. Officer Rice stood by the bar-raising mechanism with his hand on the large lever.

"My cellie's dead! That's the matter with my cellie! He's dead, man!" shouted Reggie when asked the obvious question by Sergeant Gonzales.

Medical personnel had finally arrived and were assembled on the first tier of Charlie Wing, still darkened by the absence of the main cellblock lights. The yellow-blue tinge of the tier lights produced a tenebrous effect reminiscent of a tourist grotto. No sense waking the 294 other inmates in the wing. "Cooper, it's Lieutenant Freiburg. I want you to turn around and face the cell window. When I open the door, I want you to slowly back out with your hands behind your back." Lieutenant Freiburg gave the signal for Officer Rice to drop the bar lever into the key position and looked above the door, watching as the giant metal bar slid to the right, freeing the door from its encumbrance. "Now," instructed the lieutenant.

Officer Thurgood turned the key sharply to the right and pulled open the cell door by the highly polished brass handle. Inmate Cooper slowly backed toward the awaiting officers, his hands clasped behind his back. Upon reaching the door, Officer Thurgood drew out a pair of handcuffs and clicked them over the wrists of the offender. "My hand! Watch my hand!" warned Reggie. He was pulled from the cell and placed against the wall that separated cell 216 from cell 217, where he was subjected to a cursory pat search for weapons.

"It was self-defense, man," was all he said as he was led, half-walking and half-hopping, down the tier to the staircase.

Medical department personnel waited patiently at the bottom of the staircase for Inmate Cooper and Officer Thurgood to pass by and then scrambled to the second-tier landing. Sergeant Gonzales and Lieutenant Freiburg stepped into the cell, each grabbed a corner of the foot of the bottom mattress, and yanked it onto the floor complete with the lifeless inmate DeSantos. They then dragged the mattress out of the cell and down to the awaiting assortment of nurses.

Officer Rice joined them, dropping to his knees, and immediately initiated chest compressions. "Stop! Stop!" commanded the lieutenant, adding, "We got to plug up these holes first. You're just squirting blood out each time you do that." Reluctantly, the registered nurse on scene agreed and began collecting extralarge sterile gauze pads from her medical kit and passing them to Officer Rice. Another nurse stood by with the ever-present but seldom used oxygen bottle. Officer Rice, with his limited training, packed the wounds with the gauze and returned to his chest compressions, stopping occasionally to give two rescue breaths. After forty-minutes, the outside ambulance company arrived on scene. Inmate DeSantos was declared deceased seven minutes later by the ambulance crew.

The small screen of a smuggled cell phone illuminated in the Adam Wing cell by a short inbound text message. Diablo glanced first at the cell door and then celeritously at the small screen, which had been cupped by his hand to limit the glow. "Cops stopped CPR. He is dead." The mystery text messenger had a good view of the activities of staff from his third-tier cell in Charlie Wing. Satisfied with his special missive to Diablo, he dropped onto his bottom bunk mattress and went to sleep. Inmate Serrano was indeed pleased. He quickly dispatched a text to his superior: "DeSantos está muerto. El segador tuvo éxito."

It was nearly three o'clock in the morning when Scott and Oswaldo arrived at Charlie Wing with their equipment. They first had to walk to the central infirmary to take initial photographs of the deceased inmate DeSantos. An apologetic Lieutenant Freiburg insisted he had to move the body because he did not want to "disturb the other inmates in Charlie Wing" by leaving the departed inmate on the tier "for all eyes to see." Scott had accepted the predictable movement of dead inmate bodies but knew Andy Dykman would not share his blissful surrender to the inevitable.

Tyrus and Investigative Officer Adrian Kirby were at the central corridor holding cells, making their observations of Inmate Cooper and advising him they would be conducting an interview shortly. Oswaldo stretched crime scene tape across the front and back staircase landings of the second tier, effectively making the entire tier a crime scene. He hadn't thought to keep the stairs themselves open to the third tier, and adjustments had to be made.

"Start your photographs, Oz," instructed Scott as he snapped the speedlight onto the Nikon camera body and handed it to Oswaldo. "Overviews, evidence establishing, and close-ups, Oz. And we'll need the tripod for bloodstain patterns."

Scott zipped up the Tyvek suit he donned over his uniform and utility belt. He covered his mouth with an N95 mask, pulled the hood over his head, and stretched a pair of cotton gloves over his hands, followed by one layer of nitrile gloves; he would pull a second pair over the first to maintain a constant skin barrier. After the habitual ritual of personal protective equipment, he stepped into the cell, being cautious not to touch or disturb anything. Oswaldo handed him the camera, and Scott satisfied the initial photography sequence within the cell.

He stepped out and provided Oswaldo with a briefing. "Again, Oz, they dragged the mattress through our crime scene. There is a swipe pattern on the floor from the pooled blood that soaked the mattress.

There is blood on the sink, soap bar, and towel on the towel bar. There are also two cast-off blood drops on the left-hand side of the sink. Aside from that, we have one altered drop on the floor, transfer beneath a blood-soaked inmate-manufactured stabbing weapon just under the writing desk, and impact spatter against the bottom bunk left wall. There is one blood transfer on the right front corner of the writing desk and a transfer on the upper-bunk mattress. Radio Sergeant Phillips and make sure they collect all the clothing of Inmate Cooper before they do anything else. It's a pretty straightforward crime scene to process— blood swabs, the weapon, bloodstain mapping, and diagramming. We'll be done in two, maybe three hours. Coroner's investigator Dykman won't be here until 0600 hours."

Oswaldo acknowledged his instructions, adding, "Adrian just came down. He and Sergeant Phillips are going to interview the cellmate in the unit lieutenant's office. Oh, and, Scottie, Adrian says the cellie has small blood spots on his chest."

"Impact spatter, Oz, take the DNA kit and your camera to the holding cells. Photograph the cellmate, Inmate Cooper, if the address and name on this magazine is correct and swab those bloodstains. And, Oz, do me a favor and tell Ty this is the inmate Hubbard warned us about."

Oswaldo grabbed the blue DNA collection kit and disappeared through the grille gate and the wing door, only to reappear a moment later to retrieve the forgotten camera and flash. "Heart of gold," Scott softly said as he watched Oswaldo disappear once again. He then went back to presumptive testing of the suspected bloodstains.

"Inmate Cooper, what is your first name?" asked Sergeant Phillips as he started his interview.

"Reginald Patrick Cooper" was the reply.

"Do they call you Reggie?"

"Yeah, Reggie" was the second brief reply.

"All right, Reggie, I hope you don't mind me calling you Reggie. I'd like to talk to you about what happened to your cellie and why you told Officer Thurgood it was self-defense, but I'm going to be up front with you, man, and let you know you have a right to remain silent. Anything you say can be used against you in court. You have a right to an attorney to be with you during questioning, and if you cannot afford an attorney, one will be appointed to you at no charge. Do you understand these rights?"

"Yeah. Am I under arrest for this?"

"No, man. You told Officer Thurgood you were defending yourself, but I have to tell you what your rights are. Feel me?"

"Yeah, yeah, I gotcha, man."

"Tell me what happened tonight. Officer Edwards said you guys were buddies. What happened?"

"Man, I don't know, man. He must have got hold of some bad weed. I was off my rack, taking a piss. I told him to, you know, face the wall. I do that with all my cellies. You know, man? He says something like he ain't no fag, and the next thing I know, he's swinging at me with that sticker. I knocked it out of his hand, and he punched me in the head."

"I see you have a bruise on your right eyebrow. So let me get this straight. You were at the toilet, and he gets off his bunk, and he's holding a shank."

"Yeah, man, that's right."

"Okay, and you are facing him now, so your back is to the cell door, right?"

"Yeah, yeah."

"And he's between you and the back of the cell?"

"Yeah, yeah, with that knife."

"Which hand was the shank in?" asked Tyrus.

"Uh, his right hand."

"And you knock the shank out of his right hand?"

"Yeah."

"How?"

"I hit him, man."

"Where?"

"In the jaw, man, in the jaw."

"And he dropped the shank?"

"Well, yeah, he hit his head on the side of the top bunk."

"Okay, Reggie, and then he hit you in the head?"

"Yeah, yeah."

"With which hand?"

"What?"

"With which hand did he punch you?"

"The right one, I guess."

"I see," replied the skilled interviewer. "Reggie, how did your cellie get stabbed so many times?"

"We were wrestling on the bottom bunk for the piece. I got it, and I just started stabbing him, man. I had to stab him, or he was going to stab me."

Tyrus leaned back in his chair and studied the young inmate before him. After a few minutes of silence, Tyrus leaned forward and said, "Got any questions for me?" Adrian turned to Sergeant Phillips in half belief that he wasn't going to ask more questions of the inmate who brutally stabbed his cellmate.

"Yeah. Will I get to go back to my rack?"

"No, Reggie, no, you certainly will not. You're going to the Hole, man. It's routine when your cellie is killed. This interview is over." Tyrus stood and motioned Reggie to do the same. He told him to turn around and instructed Adrian to put the handcuffs back on Inmate Cooper.

He then told Adrian to escort Inmate Cooper to the central infirmary to get his hand x-rayed. He pulled Adrian aside and said, "Make sure you walk him past the examination room where they got his cellie stretched out. Make sure he gets a good look. Oh, and get that bump on his eyebrow—his right eyebrow—checked out as well. And before you ask, he would have been punched on the left eyebrow by a right-handed man, but maybe he got that while they was wrestling. I'm going down to see Dog."

Tyrus exited the unit office and started walking westbound down the corridor to Charlie Wing. As he walked, he heard the eastbound crash gate open just wide enough for Adrian and his charge to pass through on their way to the central infirmary.

Chapter 12

The Blood Speaks

"No, Ty, I don't want to know what his cellie said. I want you to see what the blood is telling me first," Scott replied when Tyrus started to tell him about the interview. "I'm done here, but I'll go over it for you. First, you will notice there is an absence of blood on the right side of the cell, except for the one small blood transfer on the front right corner of the writing desk, suggesting that a bloodletting source came in contact with the desk. I'm betting on that blood belonging to our victim, Inmate DeSantos, perhaps before he hit the floor. Officer Thurgood said he heard a crash about a half hour before but couldn't find the source. There is a corresponding transfer stain on the floor to the right of the desk. There is an absence of blood on the wall with the cell window, an absence of blood on the ceiling, and an absence of blood on the south wall aside from the cast-off drops on the other side of the sink, likely from Inmate Cooper when he turned on the faucet.

"If you notice on the floor, there is a swipe pattern, the result of having a blood-soaked mattress dragged out the door. Near the side of the lower bunk is a solitary altered blood drop of ninety degrees. Before drying, an object moved through the stain, thus producing this perimeter stain with a wipe through the drop, suggesting movement of the object through the blood in the direction of the door." Tyrus studied the stains, attempting to see the significance.

Scott continued, "Here is the money shot, Ty. Look at the interior-facing side of this privacy sheet. Originally, it was drawn across the bottom of the bunk, thus blocking the view from the cell door window."

"Now how do you know that, Dog?"

"The bloodstain tells me it was, Tyrus. Observe. On the right side of the sheet, left if you are looking at it, is an area that is clean. Yet on the periphery of the clean spot, or void, is a continuous pattern of small blood drops consistent with impact spatter. There is a corresponding absence of blood, again a void, on the left lower corner—right if you are looking at it—of the bottom bunk sheet. Yes, we brought the mattress back in for the bloodstain pattern analysis. This is the position of our stabber, facing the victim who is lying supine on the bottom bunk. The void is created by the body of the suspect, ergo the impact spatter on his chest.

"Now here is something interesting. All the impact spatter is on the left wall of the cell, or south wall, but only in the area of the bottom bunk. This impact spatter is from the impact of the shank into the bloodletting event. Cast-off spatter is mixed in with the impact spatter. If we string out the patterns to a centralized area, or area of convergence, there are two—one approximately where the victim's stomach would be and one here where the chest would have been. Once I do the math back at the office, I will have the point of origin, which I believe will correspond with the position of the bloodletting sources on the right side and stomach and chest.

"Look at the sheet just here. This is where the left side and stomach of the victim likely was. Notice there is no impact spatter or castoff in this area. The shank was not thrust in, drawn out rapidly, and thrust in again. Instead, it was pushed in, perhaps two or three times. For whatever reason, the suspect transitioned the weapon from his right hand to his left hand. I'm rather thinking his right hand was incapacitated."

"Fracture of the last two knuckles of his right hand, Dog."

"Ah, a brawler's fracture, as I suspected."

"What's this on the wall, Dog?"

"Oh, that, supernano black fingerprint powder. I thought there was a handprint there, but it is something else. I don't know what, though, almost like thread or hairs."

"I know exactly what that is, Dog. It's an eyebrow, and I know how it got there too," confidently expressed Tyrus. "What about this stain on the top bunk frame?"

"Now that is a bloodstained palm print, Ty. Either the suspect grabbed the lip of the bunk bed to pull himself out of the lower bunk or he put his hand here to grab something on his bunk."

"Bottle of St-Rémy brandy maybe?" said the eagle-eyed Lions fan.

"Well spotted, Ty, perhaps just the thing. How do you suppose he got that in here?"

"Maybe that's what Hubbard was trying to tell us."

"I'll talk to Roy when he comes in at six. Oz is going to finish up here, Ty. Let's go down to the infirmary and have a look at the late inmate DeSantos."

As they walked up the corridor to the central infirmary, they met Adrian, coming from the other direction. "Where is Cooper?" asked Tyrus, surprised to see Adrian without the inmate whom he entrusted to the young investigator.

"They're transporting him to an outside hospital. His hand is broken in two places."

"Did he get to see his dead cellmate?"

"He wouldn't look at him. I even stopped in front of the window and pulled him up to it. He looked away."

"Shall we?" urged Scott as he pointed to the infirmary door. Adrian proceeded to the cell to see the bloody scene for himself. "We can't do much until Andy gets here, but I'm sure he won't mind if we look. How many stab wounds in the chest do you see, Tyrus?"

"Seventeen, eighteen, maybe twenty in the chest alone, Dog. Two, maybe three in the right side and stomach and two, maybe three on the left side and stomach. He has one heck of a bruise on his left cheek and jaw and a cut over his right eye. What do you see, Dog?"

"Two things stand out to me, Tyrus. There are absolutely no defensive injuries, and most significantly, look at the impact spatter on the back of his right hand. Inmate DeSantos was completely incapacitated during the stabbing. He never even raised a hand."

"Could there have been a struggle or wrestling match over the weapon?" inquired Tyrus.

"Not at all. Look at his left hand, no blood on the palm, no blood on the fingers. He didn't move his hands, either of them, during the stabbing."

"So Inmate DeSantos is punched hard on the left side of his face. His head hits the side of the metal bunk, opening the cut over his right eyebrow, and then he falls into the desk, which is heard by Officer Thurgood. Cooper picks up the knocked-out cellie and dumps him on the lower bunk."

"And then stabs him, Tyrus, over and over again. Looks like a clear case of murder to me."

"Motive?"

"Who knows with these guys, Tyrus? Who knows?"

Adrian returned to the infirmary and interrupted the concentration of Investigator Doggett as he collected blood specimen from the back hand of the deceased. "You guys got to see what Oz found in the cell."

"What did you guys find in the cell?" came a question from behind Adrian.

"Andy, you are just in time," remarked Scott, adding, "Adrian, go back and tell Oz we will be there shortly. Andy, let us tell you what we have thus far." He gently pushed Adrian from the doorway and allowed Detective Dykman past. The two investigators and one detective scrutinized the decedent, collected his clothing, swabbed the back of his hands, and documented the condition of the body thoroughly with photography. They came to an agreement about the wounds and the time of the autopsy later on that day.

As they walked out of the infirmary to introduce Andy to the crime scene, Tyrus spotted Inmate Cooper sitting alone in a locked holding cell. "Wait a minute, Dog, there's something I want to do." He disappeared into an examination room and emerged with a bottle of sterile water and two packets of sterile gauze. Scott watched him say something to Inmate Cooper, who nodded in the affirmative. Tyrus motioned the infirmary officer to unlock the holding cell. Tyrus donned gloves, dripped a few drops of the water onto a sterile gauze pad, and swabbed the left forehead of Inmate Cooper. He repeated the steps with another sterile gauze pad for the right side. He carefully sealed each gauze pad back into the respective sterile envelope from which they were wrapped. He put them into a brown paper sack and instructed the officer to lock the gate.

He rejoined Scott and Andy, asking, "If someone punches you in the face, they should transfer their DNA to your face, right?"

"In theory, Tyrus, according to Edmond Locard," responded Scott.

"Well, he don't know that, Dog, and now he has something to think about."

"Maybe it's time you told us what he said in the interview as we walk, Tyrus."

Sergeant Phillips explained in detail the statements of Inmate Cooper as the three men walked down the corridor to Charlie Wing. Scott and Tyrus discussed the significance of the bloodstain pattern analysis as a means of discounting 90 percent of Reggie's defense. The only thing they could not agree on was the possibility that Inmate DeSantos ever possessed the shank. Scott theorized the DNA of both inmates would be present on the handle owing to the amount of blood that transferred to the handle during the stabbing assault; therefore, there would be no way of knowing. Detective Dykman was quick to point out that not knowing this element of the crime might reduce the charge from murder to manslaughter. This did not sit well with Tyrus, who was dead set but lacked any evidence that Inmate DeSantos never had the weapon.

As they walked into the Charlie Wing foyer and through the sally port, Scott looked up to the second tier and saw Oswaldo standing with his foot on the lower rail and a hip flask bottle of brandy in his right hand. "I'm a firm believer in day drinking, Oz, but even I have my limits," said Scott as he ascended the front staircase.

"Scottie, there are eight more bottles of these and a big bag of weed taped underneath Cooper's locker. This one was inside the locker behind a false back of the top cubbyhole," replied Oswaldo as he dropped the half-filled bottle into a brown paper sack. "And there was one under the top bunk pillow."

"That's a big bag of weed," remarked Andy as he studied the gallon-sized plastic bag, adding, "He didn't get this through visiting. How come nobody smelled this much dope when they were searching?"

"Two reasons, Andy. The cell is spotless, and most cops don't do a good job searching immaculate cells for fear of getting them messy. And it was vacuum sealed until Oz accidentally cut this corner of the bag, extracting it from the tape," surmised Scott.

Detective Dykman took a few photographs of the cell; collected a bottle of prescribed Tazarotene, an acne medication, from the locker of Inmate DeSantos; and departed the wing, reminding Scott the autopsy would be at 1300 hours. Scott and Oswaldo collected up their equipment and evidence and hauled it to the first tier. Scott instructed Adrian to boot-lock the door and place evidence tape on the gaps, which would alert them if the door was tampered. Scott wanted to maintain custody of the cell in case anything unusual was discovered during the autopsy necessitating a return to the scene of the crime. Once accomplished, they picked up the cases of crime scene equipment and bags of evidence and made their way up the corridor to the sally port. "My life as a beast of burden," remarked Scott as he passed Lieutenant Freiburg, who was holding the sally port gate open for the weary investigators.

Chapter 13

Scott's Eye in the Sky

Officer Roy Hubbard had spent twenty-two of his twenty-five-year career with his feet high off the ground, bouncing from tower to tower. He settled on tower no. 2 in the southeast corner of the Central Yard not because it had the best days off but because he had the best view of the areas the gangs selected to assemble. He also got to monitor the inmate yard telephones used by most of the drug smugglers who couldn't afford the exaggerated price of a smuggled cellular telephone. Therefore, he was a constant source of information for Scott and a trusted friend. Roy would end each conversation with "Get 'em, Dog," and most often, Scott would. Roy also had an uncanny knack for knowing when Scott had only just returned to his desk.

"Doggett," Scott said into the telephone receiver before settling into his chair.

"What's up, Roy? Once again, you caught me before I even sat down." Oswaldo spun his chair around and listened to Scott's half of the conversation.

"Dog, I hear you got Cooper. I told you he was up to something. I saw him rooting in the dirt over by the bleachers just yesterday. I keep telling them worthless yard officers to use the metal detectors over there, but that jackass lieutenant told them to leave that patch of dirt alone because the inmates were growing onions there. Onions, my ass, Dog!

They are growing shanks. Is this any way to run a yard? You gotta do something about this, Dog. Go talk to the warden or something. I heard the kid got stabbed twenty times and you caught Cooper in the act."

"Good morning to you too, Hub. I did not catch him. It was Thurgood in Charlie Wing who caught him. What was the message about the other day?"

"Yeah, Dog, I heard you went to visit Rose Graves in the hospital. I saw you when you guys got back."

"Damn, Roy, you can see all the way to the Monterey Peninsula from that tower of yours?"

"Not quite but close. Alfredo told me. He went to see her too but after you left. And that's another thing you have to talk to the warden about. I've told you about that garbage truck being on the yard when inmates are out now that Mr. Graves is gone. Alfredo is driving that damn truck right onto the yard with inmates on the yard, Dog! Is this any way to run a yard? You tell me, Dog."

"I'll take care of it, Roy, but what was the message from the other day?"

"It was raining hard, Dog, and there weren't but thirty inmates on the yard all day. There was Cooper standing in the middle of the yard talking to Diablo."

"Who?"

"Serrano, the Southern shot caller. He's got keys to the entire Central Facility, Dog."

"I've never heard of him. Maybe the gang guys know who he is. No idea what they were talking about, I imagine."

"Whatever it was, Dog, Serrano looked mad, and Cooper looked like he didn't have a friend in the world. I'm telling you something, Dog, Serrano wanted him to do something. You and I both know his cellie didn't hang himself."

"Cooper! That's right, Roy, I forgot all about that. Let me ask you something, Roy. Did you see Cooper digging in the dirt before or after the conversation with Serrano?"

"The day after, Dog. I'm sure that dirt was nice and soft after the rain."

"Did you document that in your logbook?"

"You know I did, Dog."

"Thanks, Roy. Think of me when you get your subpoena."

Scott hung up and relayed the information to Oswaldo, followed by instructions. "Oz, before you book the shank into evidence, I want to inspect it in the laboratory. After that, I want you to swing by tower 2 and get Hubbard's logbook and book it into evidence. Take a new one with you. Take a camera and go up into the tower and take a picture of the bleacher area from that of Hubbard's perspective. Set the camera lens at 38 mm and figure out where he was standing. Zoom in if he used his binoculars. Also, find out how he knew for certain it was Cooper digging in the dirt. Now let's take a look at that shank."

Scott and Oswaldo entered the small laboratory Scott had made out of the old photography lab after they switched to digital imagery. The room still smelled of the photography chemicals, but it was just the perfect size for a microlaboratory. The enlarger had been replaced by a copy stand, and this was where Scott began his examination of the weapon with evidentiary photography.

After the weapon was photographically documented, Scott conducted a series of presumptive tests of the red liquid absorbed into the cloth and tape handle. Satisfied it was presumptive positive with blood consistent with the human species, Scott cut bits of cloth with a sterile scalpel, wrapped the cuttings in a sterile gauze, and placed them into separate sterile envelopes. He collected DNA-typing swabs from the blade. After this, he began meticulously deconstructing the handle until he found what he was looking for—fresh, wet dirt. "What's that, Scotty?" asked Oswaldo.

"That's the difference between manslaughter and murder" was Scott's reply as he photographed his findings and scraped the dirt into a pharmaceutical fold. "Oz, while you are up in the tower, I want you to take a photograph of me collecting a small jar of the dirt in that onion patch by the bleachers. The time stamps will prove I collected the dirt after I conducted my forensic examination of the shank. You can never be too careful, little buddy."

"Hey, Dog!" Tyrus yelled from his office as he heard the familiar clanking of Scott's boots and keys on the stairs up to the door of the investigations unit.

"Damn, it, Phillips! Why do you always wait until I'm at the top of the stairs before you call my name?"

"Come back down here. You're going to want to hear this. I got Duane Parkinson on the phone."

"What have you got, Tyrus?" Scott said as he reached the bottom of the stairs.

"Park has been watching Spider Martinez, and he's acting way suspicious. Park wants to hit his work area and see if Martinez is hiding anything out there. He wants to know if we can join him."

"You bet we can join him. Just tell him to give me about an hour to get to the yard and collect a jar of dirt. Oz should be done with his chores too. We can get Oz to pick up his dog, and we can let his nose do the hard work for us."

"Cool, Dog. Oh, and Rose sent me a text message. She said it was a friend of Alfredo who was taking the photographs at the BBQ, a female friend."

"Can she be a little more specific?"

"I'll ask, Dog, but it may be a little later. They are releasing her from the hospital today."

Chapter 14

Spider's Web

"Okay, Adrian, I want you to come in through the back gate of recycling and block the gate with your car. Oz is going to come down the service road between the warehouse and recycling and block that area in case anyone goes over the fence or throws anything over. Tyrus and his gang investigators are going to approach from the firehouse side, and I am going to go straight up the front gate. I want this thing timed just right, so nobody move until we are all in position. Duane Parkinson and Ron Richmond will come out of their office as soon as they see my car. Martinez is in the cardboard box bailing machine area. Gottfried is in the connex next to the cardboard storage area. Once we have the inmates secured, Oz is going to run his dog through the area first. Be sure to turn off any fans and machinery that is running and close the doors so the odor settles. Okay, as soon as you are all in position, key your mic once. Four mics, and we all go."

One click, two clicks, three clicks, four clicks counted Scott before keying his microphone and uttering one word. "Go!"

Adrian's slick-top Crown Victoria appeared through a cloud of dust and skidded to a stop at the rear vehicle gate. Oswaldo pulled up to the fence line between the warehouse and recycling plant and jumped onto the hood of the car to give him a better view over, or nearly over, the fence. Scott drove his faithful Crown Victoria straight up the driveway and through the front gate with his overhead lights activated for effect. Tyrus and his investigators stepped through a pedestrian gate adjacent to the firehouse.

As planned, Officers Parkinson and Richmond stepped out of their *Sanford and Son* office. Inmate Gottfried stepped out of the connex with his hands raised, saying, "No trouble. No, sir, no trouble from me." Inmate Martinez attempted to run into the inmate restroom, but Adrian was fleet footed and grabbed the door before the spindly Spider could get it closed. Anticipating a brawl, Adrian yanked Martinez out of the small bathroom and "aided him to the ground" as his report would later read. A third inmate, unknown to the investigators, was sitting on a broken office chair, watching and laughing.

The older white inmate looked up at Sergeant Phillips as he approached and said, "I'm sixty-four years old, Sarge. I ain't going to give you no trouble. What took you guys so long? I been out here two days, and I coulda told you what these guys were up to out here. Serves them damned right. Best job in the world out here, and they go and blow it off for what? Money? Bragging rights? Big shots on the yard?" With that, Tyrus patted him on the shoulder, told him to put his hands behind his back, handcuffed him, and gave him a quick pat down. The unclothed body search would come later.

Oswaldo brought his K-9 vehicle around and parked it next to Scott's car. Ruud hopped out and began his ritual by first relieving himself and running around a bit with his tail wagging. And then without prompting, he went to work.

Tyrus and Adrian took Inmate Martinez, Inmate Gottfried, and the newly assigned inmate Morton into the large sorting area; selected a mostly clean space; and conducted unclothed body searches. They started with Inmate Gottfried and provided the following instructions. "Disrobe completely. Now stand facing me and hold out your hands, palms up first and then palms down. Lift your testicles. Pull back your foreskin. Lift your arms over your head. Bend forward and run your fingers through your hair. Face me, open your mother, and stick out your tongue. Push down on your lower jaw. Keep your mouth open and raise your tongue. Now run your fingers between your teeth and gums. Flare your nostrils. Show me the back of your right ear and your left. Turn around and lift your right foot, your other right foot. Wiggle your toes. And now your left foot, wiggle your toes.

"Okay, here is where you have to pay attention. Face away from me. Take three deep squat coughs. Cough hard each time, or you will do it again. After you squat and cough three times, bend at your waist and keep your legs straight. Bend only at the waist. Spread your butt cheeks apart and cough three more times." Adrian always wondered why they performed this task in this order. If it were up to him, he'd have them lift their private parts after they put their fingers in their mouths, but that was the way it was taught to him, and that was the order he had it memorized. While Adrian was giving the instructions, Tyrus was meticulously inspecting every hem of each item of clothing removed by the inmate being searched before handing the inmate his boxer shorts, T-shirt, and socks once Adrian was satisfied with the search.

Scott stood watching Oswaldo work with Ruud, but he noticed Officer Parkinson escort Inmate Gottfried from the sorting area to his office, shortly later followed by Officer Richmond escorting Inmate Morton to the same place. After a few minutes, Scott observed Tyrus and Adrian escorting Inmate Martinez from the same area. Inmate Martinez was in restraints and was dressed in his lime-green jumpsuit emblazoned with black "CDCR-Prisoner" lettering down both pant legs and across the back. "Where's he going?" asked Scott.

"Contraband watch," remarked Tyrus as they walked past.

Adrian looked back at Scott and said, "It's like a refrigerator up in there. I swear a little light came on when he spread his butt cheeks."

Oswaldo and Ruud were everywhere—inside bins and on top of machinery, storage areas, connex cargo containers, ledges, portable toilets, sheds, and stacks of bailed cardboard. Finally, both Oswaldo and Ruud approached Scott. Ruud assumed his usual ball-chewing prone position next to Oz's legs, and Oswaldo pointed at the portable toilet. "That's the only place he *didn't* alert," he said before breaking out into a hearty laugh. "Oh, and, Scotty, there's a big plastic bag that has a lot of black tar heroin residue on top of the cardboard bailing machine. I didn't even have to look for it."

"Thank you, little buddy. You go put Ruud back in the kennel. We've got some searching to do, but first, I am going to make a phone call."

"Who you gonna call?"

"Lieutenant Templeton. I'm going to ask him to call the warden and get as many officers as he possibly can out here. There's easily a half acre of area here to search. We need reinforcements." Scott stepped into the recycling plant staff office affectionately called Sanford and Son's and placed his telephone call.

Officer Richmond was preparing to return Inmates Gottfried and Morton back to the South Facility farm gate in the big brown bus. As the bus drove away, Duane turned to Scott and said, "Morton was my informant. He gave me a list where to search. You probably don't need as many officers out here as you may think."

"True, Duane, but this place can have a thorough search, and it will protect the identity of your informant. However, we'll just make sure we search the areas on the list."

Oswaldo pulled out of the front gate and started to drive to the kennel when he had remembered something he needed to tell Scott. He slammed on the brakes and jumped out of the car. "Scotty! Scotty! I remember now. I needed to show you something," he explained in his usual three-round staccato burst.

"Slow down, Oz. What did you find?"

"It's over here. I noticed it when I jumped off the hood of the car. Do you remember when we were over here making the castings of the tire treads left by the garbage truck and the treads next to it?"

"How could I forget, Oz? The castings are still in our office."

"Yeah, yeah, but they are back," Oswaldo said excitedly.

"The garbage truck tread impressions?" Scott inquired for clarification.

"No, Scotty, the other tires. Come and look." The two investigators studied the newly deposited tire tread impressions and agreed they had been recently created by a vehicle, most likely a pickup truck, after the recent rains, and that vehicle had been parked on the fence line between the cargo containers used by the warehouse for storage and the steel building that housed the cardboard sorting and bailing area.

"Well spotted, Oz. Take Ruud to his kennel, bring back everything we need to photograph, and collect these new impressions.

Chapter 15

A Veritable Cornucopia of Contraband

"How many officers do we have searching, Dog?" asked Tyrus as he returned to the recycling plant.

"Twenty-five officers. They were in training at the in-service training building. We have them for an hour. They've already found three gallons of tobacco and twelve cell phones packaged up and ready to go. Oh, and you need to look at the trolley they use to move the cardboard carts in and out of the facilities. Each cart has a false bottom, Ty, exceptionally well done too. You'd never know it. Where's Adrian?"

"Contraband watch on Spider. Man, Dog, the warden almost didn't let me put him on potty watch. He didn't want to pay any overtime, so I told him we would only do one bowel movement instead of the usual three."

"Yeah, Ty, I'm okay with that. He shoved it up there. He didn't swallow it. Oz is over there, casting those new tire treads. Are you ready to get dirty? I saved the list for us."

"Dog, these cardboard carts are towed over to the culinary back dock of each facility. The inmates assigned to the culinary throw the cardboard from the canned goods into the carts every morning and night, and Duane or Ron pick them up the following morning. They can move contraband into North, Central, and South Facilities from here. How did you find it?"

Scott pointed at the list provided by Inmate Morton and said, "It's number 1. At first, I didn't find anything until I started banging on the undercarriage with my baton. You can hear the hollow space. They used rivets to hold the aluminum plate covering the hole in place. To look at it, you'd think the plate was engineered into the design. The rivets are just for show. You can pull them out with your fingers. The plate itself is attached with Velcro."

"So they weren't smuggling shit in the garbage truck?"

"Tyrus, I think they used the trolley to get big stuff into the prison and the garbage truck to get in small items. What is Duane carrying over to us?"

"Looks like a box, and he's smiling."

Officer Parkinson placed the box on the fender of the trolley, producing a clinking noise from within. "Thirsty, Dog? Jose Cuervo and St-Rémy brandy. There's got to be thirty bottles in here."

"Where'd you find that?" asked Tyrus.

"Those bastards dug a hole over there in the corner, covered it with plywood, and then put a pallet with old batteries from the garage on top of it."

Just then, they heard a heart-stopping hue and cry. "Gun! Gun!"

Scott and Tyrus strained their heads to see where the alert had come. It was the same corner recently abandoned by Officer Parkinson. "Did someone say gun?" asked the bewildered sergeant.

"Don't touch it!" yelled Scott.

Scott, Tyrus, and Officers Parkinson and Richmond clustered around Officer Mitchell Dwyer, who held a soft leather pouch. "Where'd you find that?" asked Tyrus.

"One of the car batteries on this pallet is fake. It seemed lighter than the others. I picked it up, thinking it was going to be as heavy as the others. It wasn't, and I dropped it. The top of the battery came off, and this fell out. I haven't looked in the bag, but I can tell from its shape it is a small handgun," reported the officer.

"That's it! I'm bidding out of here! It's safer inside the prison than out here!" exclaimed Ron Richmond.

"Ty, call our lieutenant. Tell him what we have. And tell him I'd like Gottfried and Morton transferred to ad seg. Mitch, let me relieve you of your find. I need to process it for evidence," Scott instructed, gingerly accepting the leather pouch from Officer Dwyer. He carried the pouch over to his Crown Vic, spread a clean waxed butcher's paper on the trunk lid, and carefully extracted the pistol from its comfortable poke, placing it on top of the paper.

"What kind is it?" asked Sergeant Phillips while holding his cell phone to his ear.

"Glock, Model 43, 9 mm Luger, loaded with one in the pipe," replied Scott as he began photographic documentation of the gun, followed by the collection of DNA swabs from the grips, trigger, fore strap, backstrap, and magazine and safety levers. "There's an extra magazine in the pouch too. I'm saving that for latent prints back at the lab."

Tyrus relayed the information to Lieutenant Templeton, who raced from his office and up the stairs to the office of the warden. Tyrus called over his two institutional gang investigations officers, who were busy searching. The three jumped into the newest Crown Victoria in the investigations fleet, generally called the gang mobile, and took off to the South Facility to collect the two inmates.

"Nice gun, Scotty. Whose is it?" asked Oswaldo while picking dried bits of dental stone casting material from his arm hair.

"I'm not sure at this point to which inmate this gun belonged," replied Scott as he strapped the small pistol into a firearm evidence box.

"Inmate!"

"Yes, Oz, inmate. And, Oz, if you look over your right shoulder, you will see the approach of the warden, chief deputy warden, two associate wardens, and an assortment of captains and lieutenants. Please take my camera over to them and show them the photographs I took of the gun and fake battery on the little screen. I have no intention of opening this box up for a show-and-tell for the brass."

Warden Brown walked past Scott, surveyed the recycling plant facility and yard, and summoned Officer Parkinson and Officer Richmond to his side. The pointing and shouting began. "I want this gone. That has to go. Break that up. Search that over there. Clean this area over here. All those electronics need to go. Get rid of all these lean-tos the inmate workers built. I want that out of here today, and search this place for a month if you have to." The warden and his entourage stormed past Scott without a word and disappeared in the direction of the Central Facility.

Scott looked at Oswaldo and said, "Well, that was painless, except for Duane and Ron, I'm sure."

Later that afternoon, Scott and Tyrus found themselves in the warden's office, sitting at the end of the long conference table that filled the room. Warden Brown hung up his desk phone and addressed them. "The headquarters is sending someone from the office of correctional safety out tomorrow morning. I want a complete list of everything you found—now!"

Tyrus passed an inventory sheet to the red-faced executive bearing the following:

12 pounds of Bugler brand tobacco
16 cellular telephones
32 cell phone batteries
16 cell phone chargers
5.5 pounds of marijuana
3 Nintendo Switch game systems
24 hip flasks of St-Rémy VSOP brandy
16 750 ml bottles of Jose Cuervo Especial tequila
28 grams of methamphetamines
4.5 grams of black tar heroin
20 hypodermic syringes
1 Glock Model 43, 9 mm Luger, with magazine containing 6 cartridges
1 Glock Model 43 magazine containing 6 cartridges
1 9 mm Luger cartridge from chamber of Glock pistol
1 car battery, altered and used for concealment

Warden Brown looked up from the list and initiated what was commonly referred to as an ass kicking. "I cannot begin to tell you what an embarrassment this is to me and this department! How did you let this happen? You, Doggett, you are supposed to be this impressive narcotic-interdiction investigator. I can tell you, I'm not impressed! You, Sergeant Phillips, you are supposed to be in charge of gang investigations. When I was running the IGI at Avenal, I had informants, lots of informants. Where are your informants? Huh? I ask you?"

Scott stared at the top of the table, trying to control his blood pressure. *Take a five-second draw of breath, hold it for five seconds, and release it for five seconds. Repeat.* Tyrus looked at the warden but knew it was pointless to say anything—pointless to explain the information came from an informant, Inmate Morton. The warden is always right and should never be corrected ever, period. The belittling of the investigators continued for fifteen minutes until Lieutenant Templeton rapped at the door, opened it, and let himself in.

"Boss, I thought you'd like to know. Inmate Martinez produced a bowel movement, which included an amazing array of contraband. Investigator Kirby is sorting through it now."

"Sir," interrupted Scott, "may I be excused to assist Investigator Kirby with processing the evidence?"

"You may," responded the still fuming warden. Scott rose, looked at Tyrus, and rolled his eyes as his back was toward the warden. Tyrus noticed but kept his eyes forward, a trick he learned in the army. Lieutenant Templeton pulled up a chair and began outlining his "plan of action," which included an all-out search of the South Facility dormitories.

Ten minutes later, Tyrus and Lieutenant Templeton descended the stairs and approached Scott and Adrian, both adorned with N95 masks and double-layered nitrile gloves. A stick of incense was burning on the evidence processing table, and two fans were positioned in a manner to draw air from the stairwell and push it out the open window. "Jeez, that stinks!" Tyrus balked.

"It's been in an ass," remarked Adrian, pointing out the obvious.

"Are you all right, Scott?" asked the lieutenant.

"What's left of my ass is missing, but other than that, I'm fine. It's not the first time he's yelled at me, and I'm sure it won't be the last."

"The headquarters is breathing down his neck and wants answers not only for this but also with Inmate Weller," interjected the lieutenant, adding, "What do we have so far?"

"Twenty-five grams of black tar heroin bundled for distribution. Each latex glove finger has fourteen match-head-sized tabs of heroin wrapped in plastic. That's about $10,000 prison value on the heroin alone. Over here, we have six grams of marijuana and eight grams of methamphetamines. Here's a plug of tobacco, and he had this." Scott held up a feces-encrusted object.

"What's that?" asked Ty.

"One Remington brand 9 mm Luger hollow-point cartridge."

"In his ass?" asked the lieutenant, realizing it was rhetorical.

"Shit, Dog, does that mean we have another gun inside the prison?" asked Tyrus, also realizing his question likely did not need an answer.

"Shit," remarked Lieutenant Templeton as he turned around and lumbered back up the stairs.

"Lockdown" Scott uttered.

"More ass chewing," murmured Tyrus.

Chapter 16

Where a Beetle Black Could Keep

Scott, Oswaldo, and Adrian entered the office they shared, each dragging a large plastic garbage bag filled with contraband. One by one, they each lowered themselves into their chairs and began rummaging through the collection of smuggled goods seized from the inmate population. In short order, Sergeant Phillips appeared in the open doorway. "How goes the searching?" asked Tyrus of the weary trio.

"The usual, a catalog of pornography, seven cell phones and accessories, about a pound of tobacco, some weed, oh, and Oz's friend there," replied Scott.

Tyrus looked over at Oswaldo, who was holding up a foot-long dildo wrapped in silk women's panties. "Please don't tell me you found that in—"

"No," interrupted Oswaldo. "It was in a footlocker."

"How did the meeting go with the headquarters brass?" inquired Scott.

"You should have been there, Dog. Lieutenant Templeton was in control. He told them the information leading to the discovery at the recycling plant was a lengthy investigation between us and Duane and Ron, and the information we got from our informant, Morton, was what led to the raid. You should have seen the warden. He was fuming, and before he could blurt out anything like, 'You never told me that,' the HQ guys congratulated us and said we deserved a commendation. Warden said we were 'his best detectives' just like that," Tyrus said, rolling his eyes. "We took them over to the armory and showed them the gun. I hope you don't mind I took it out of the weapon evidence locker and opened it, Dog."

"You can explain it to the judge when he looks at the chain of custody, Ty," replied Scott.

"Lieutenant and I are going up to ad seg to interview Martinez, Gottfried, and Morton," said Tyrus as he turned away from the door. Lieutenant Templeton was ready to leave the unit for the administrative segregation unit.

"*Miranda*!" Scott advised as he turned to answer his ringing desk phone. "Doggett."

"Dog, that son-of-a-bitch garbage truck is back on my yard!"

"Roy, it's a lockdown. Nobody should be on your yard."

"Just the slugs in the canteen, but they are from Wimpy Mouse Town. It's the principle of the thing. I don't want that truck on my yard ever."

"Right now, Hub, Wimpy Mouse Town—also known as the minimum support facility—is the cause of all our headaches."

"You need to search that canteen, Dog. I bet you'll find god knows what in there."

"If I was an inmate, I'd hide my junk in a tower."

"Yeah, Dog, you can start with tower 3, that lazy-ass dump truck of a cop over there. Dog, he's asleep. I can see the bottom of his boots from here."

"Roy, I know about your house slippers."

"House slippers because of my plantar fasciitis. But don't ask me why I ain't got any pants on," Roy laughingly responded.

"Who was driving the truck, Hub?"

"Alfredo, and he had two farm gate inmates with him. I thought they were on lockdown, Dog?"

"We just finished searching dorm 6. The two inmates on the truck are probably from dorm 6. Roy, I'll talk to Alfredo today."

"I heard you got a dildo," Roy added before bursting into laughter again and hanging up.

"Nothing gets past that guy," Scott said as he hung up the phone and began the task of sorting through the bags of illicit treasure.

"Wimpy Mouse Town?" asked Adrian.

"That's what Hubbard calls the South Facility. Ten minutes, and we'll go back to Wimpy Mouse Town. Oz, on the way, we will stop by the garage and have a word with Alfredo and his boss, Mr. Prado. What are you looking at, little buddy?"

"See this bubble in the tire impression casting I made? It's almost perfectly round. I thought it was a dimple, but it's too big, and it's on the block of the tire and not the shoulder," replied Oswaldo, using his knowledge of and fascination for tires fostered by a love of motorcycle racing.

"You are correct, Oz, that's a defect in the tire, and you know what?" Scott remarked as he produced the casting made on the day of the Weller homicide. "It's on this one too. I thought it was an air bubble also, but look, it's in the exact same place. That is what we call an individualized characteristic. Good catch, Oz."

Scott and Adrian jumped into Dog's faithful Crown Vic and started their next foray of searching at the South Facility, but first, they had a stop to make—at the garage to talk to Alfredo and his boss. Oswaldo drove in the opposite direction just long enough to pick up Ruud, who was basking in the sun in his specially built kennel behind tower no. 2 on the outside of the security perimeter. Ruud was standard topic number 4 for Roy Hubbard during his daily telephone calls to Scott. The number 1 topic was dirty inmates, number 2 was dirty cops, number3 was lazy cops, and number 4 was the nonstop barking every time a feral cat sat outside the kennel, taunting Ruud. He was convinced that the cats did it on purpose so he can't hear the inmate conversations on the yard telephones, feral prison cats being agents of the inmate population.

Scott parked in front of a garage vehicle bay and exited the Vic, while Adrian dutifully remained inside. "Can I help you, boss?" asked an inmate worker from the South Facility, his lime-green jumpsuit nearly blackened by the grease and grime of a mechanic.

"Looking for Mr. Prado. Is he in?"

"Sure is, boss. He's over in the toolroom."

"Thanks. What dorm are you in?"

"Six. You guys tore us up this morning. They just let us all out for work about thirty minutes ago. Get anything good?"

"Yeah, you could say that."

"Wait until you hit dorm 3. They've been squirreling shit over there for a few days. The cop they got over there has been hiding things for them. You might want to open everything he has a personal lock on. I'm just saying."

"Thanks for the tip," Scott said as he turned his attention to other inmates at the garage who might be in earshot.

"They feel the same. We got a personal grudge against that lame-ass bitch officer, no offense."

"None taken. We're doing dorm 5 next, but we'll get to him soon," Scott remarked as he stepped away in the direction of the toolroom. Of course, they would change their plans and raid dorm 3, but the garage had yet to be searched, and he wasn't certain if a pirated cell phone was concealed among the grease rags.

Benjamin Prado was a good man. He started working at the prison when he was nineteen. It was forty years ago when his father gave him three choices on his eighteenth birthday: go to college and he would pay for it, go into the army, or go work at the prison. Ben chose the prison but had no idea what skill he could bring. His father had an answer for that too. "I'll send you to locksmith school. If there's one thing a prison will always need, it is a locksmith." Ben spent more than twenty years as the locksmith before being promoted to the position of stationary engineer for eleven years, also a good position to have at a prison. Finally, he was persuaded to take another promotional exam and became a manager, and that was how he ended up in the garage for the past eight years.

"Good morning, Ben," Scott greeted as he walked through the door.

"Is it still morning, Scott? I wouldn't know. I only got half my work crew out, and transportation needs two vans on line quick. Fortunately, one's got a sticky lock." He paused, looked directly at Scott, and said with a grin, "I can do that one."

"Yes, you can, and I bet you are looking forward to it. Ben, Alfredo was back on the Central Yard again with the truck. You know the captain said he absolutely does not want that truck out there anymore."

"I had a feeling that's what you came over for. Mr. Hubbard already reddened my ear about it. Central is locked down, and there are no yard workers. He needed to pick up the cans on the yard and at the canteen, so he took his two inmate workers onto the yard with him."

"Yeah, Ben, I understand but no more. Where is he?"

"He said he was going to his truck to make a phone call on his cell phone. It's parked over there by the motor pool."

"That shiny new white one?" asked Scott.

"Yup, bought it about a month ago, but he hasn't been driving it much. He says it gets bad gas mileage. And he doesn't want to get it dirty, but he drove it the other day when it rained hard. Paid nearly $70,000 for that truck—for a truck. What are these guys thinking paying that much? I'll stick to my Honda. Forty miles to the gallon, Scott."

"Ben, did he have that truck the day Mr. Graves died?"

"Sure did, Scott."

"Yeah, I thought I saw it over there."

"How's Rose?"

"She's out of the hospital and back in her garden. She's a tough old girl."

"I sent her flowers."

"She could use a friend, Ben. Let me ask you, were you at the retirement party in Pacific Grove with Rose, Patty, and Alfredo?"

"At the park? Yes, I think we were all there."

"Let me ask you this then, who was taking the pictures?" asked Scott.

"Some young girl, very pretty. She came with Alf."

As Scott crossed the pavement toward the motor pool, Oswaldo drove up and rolled down his window. "He's sitting in his truck behind the motor pool, Oz. Park your car behind in-service training and break Ruud over on the grassy area next to the recycling plant. It's all coming together now, Oz, and I have a plan." Oswaldo did as he was instructed, and before Scott reached the shiny new pickup truck, Ruud was rolling in freshly mown green grass, relieving himself at will and desire and chasing his favorite ball.

"Good morning, Mr. Doggett," hastily called out Alfredo, hanging up on his telephone conversation before Scott got into earshot.

"Good morning, Alf. First things first. Captain wants you to stay off the Central Yard, period. Second, sweet truck. I saw it the other day when you came off the freeway. I bet this baby gets three gallons to the mile. Ram 2500?"

"Special edition, Power Wagon, limited, 410 horsepower, 17,000 pounds towing, but you are close. It gets about 10 mpg."

"Yikes. I wish I could afford a midlife crisis," replied Scott as he circled the impressive vehicle, paying close attention to the tires.

"Mr. Doggett, the watch commander gave me permission to go onto the yard, you know."

"I know, Alf, but he didn't check with the captain first. Just don't go out there anymore, even on lockdowns. The cats and seagulls can feast for a week."

"All right, Mr. D., I promise. I better get back before Mr. Ben starts hollering. We're short staffed, and I'm expected to help get a transportation van on line. I keep telling him I'm a driver, not a grease monkey, you know." Scott shook Alf's hand, and the two men separated. Alf walked toward the garage, and Scott walked toward Oswaldo and his frolicking canine.

Once Alfredo was sufficiently inside the garage, Scott turned to Oswaldo and said, "Take Ruud and have him do an air sniff around that new pickup. Oh, and, Oz, it's the left rear tire. You can barely see it because it's almost on the bottom, but you'll see a 6 mm circle of rubber missing from tread block. Oh, and, Oz, we're hitting dorm 3 instead of dorm 5."

Scott stood back and watched the Dutch shepherd circle the truck, sniffing every inch of paint, rubber, and metal. Finally, he returned to the right rear passenger door of the club cab and sat down, his eyes moving back and forth between Oswaldo and the door and his nose periodically touching the bottom gap between the door and the frame. A rolled terry cloth towel, taped at both ends, flung past his ears, and he bolted like a cheetah after the illusive prey. Once he had the towel firmly clenched in his teeth, he flicked his head rapidly back and forth, beating his neck on both sides with the towel. "I don't dare grab it until he's done," said Oswaldo as he watched. "And even then, I have to trick him with a new one." He was holding a second wrapped towel behind his back.

"I'd say that was a good alert. Whatever it is, it's in there," Oswaldo remarked as he pointed at a duffel bag he could see on the bench seat through the tinted side door window. Ruud spotted a shady spot of ground in the shadow of a 1950s road grader, circled, settled, and began pulling the towel apart with his sharp front teeth. Oswaldo walked in his direction.

Scott pulled out his cell phone, called Tyrus, and briefed him on the new discovery. He then walked to the Crown Vic, took the camera kit out of the trunk, handed the keys to Adrian, and told him to rally the troops and hit dorm 3 with a vengeance. "You mean dorm 5?"

"Dorm 3, Adrian, and take all the personal keys from the dorm 3 officer and open everything that has a lock on it. If he doesn't give you his keys, use the bolt cutters. Oz will be with you. Be thorough, Adrian. We will join you as soon as we can." The only thing on earth with more fury than a woman scorned was a dorm 5 inmate who wasn't allowed to benefit from the exploits of a corrupt, compromised, or dirty cop in dorm 3.

The assembled group standing behind the pricey pickup was composed of Garage Manager II Ben Prado, Commercial Truck Driver I Alfredo Garza, Investigative Lt. John Templeton, Investigative Sergeant Tyrus Phillips, and Investigator Scott Doggett. Lieutenant Templeton explained to Alfredo his obligation as an employee of the department of corrections and rehabilitation to cooperate with the investigators and the order of the warden that his truck and its contents would be searched regardless of his objections. If he refused to surrender the keys, the warden instructed his investigators to "breach the doors with the minimum amount of force necessary to gain entry." Of course, "minimum amount of force" did not exclude an angle grinder or crowbar, provided it was "necessary." Lieutenant Templeton explained a search warrant was not required as any vehicle, person, or property on state prison grounds was subject to search and by the order of the warden.

Alfredo resigned himself to his fate, surrendered the keys, and asked only that he be allowed to call his wife "before." He did not elaborate on exactly what the "before" would be "after."

"Cell phones, tobacco, marijuana, and . . ." Scott paused as he pulled a plastic-wrapped black tarlike substance from the interior of the duffel bag. "What I suspect is the black tar heroin from the tin can at Rose's house."

Alfredo's head was down, and he was looking at the dirt directly in front of him. Suddenly, he looked up and said, "I can explain."

After twenty years of being a criminal investigator, Scott understood that the words "I can explain" meant your suspect had just thought of a lie. "Alfredo, I take no pleasure in charging you with a violation of California Penal Code section 4573, possession of controlled substances on state prison grounds, a felony, and section 664/4576, possession of cellular telephones with the intent to smuggle/provide to the inmate population, a misdemeanor. You are under arrest at this time. Please go with Lieutenant Templeton and Sergeant Phillips to the internal affairs lieutenant's office. Oh, and, Alf, I'm taking this tire as evidence," Scott advised.

Tyrus whispered to Scott, "Why the tire?"

Scott turned to Tyrus and quietly said, "Because he's also guilty of the murder of Inmate Weller. Oh, and, Ty, according to this text message from Oz, one of us needs to go to dorm 3. I believe we will be charging the dorm officer with a violation of California Penal Code section 67.5, bribing a public official, one of the elements being the public official accepts the bribe." Scott explained the tip from the inmate worker, and his decision to raid dorm 3 instead of dorm 5 as planned. Apparently, Oswaldo and Adrian recovered a bounty of illicit and contraband items, including drugs, cell phones, inmate-manufactured weapons, smuggled electronics, and tobacco hidden in two lockers under the control of the officer. He also asked Tyrus to be certain Alfredo was only interviewed by the internal affairs lieutenant regarding the items in the duffel bag and not the murder. Scott wanted to conduct that interview himself. Tyrus agreed and said he'd take care of dorm 3 after talking with Lieutenant Templeton about the interview and the corrupt dorm officer.

As Scott removed a bumper jack and tire iron from underneath the bed of the pickup, he suddenly remembered something he wanted to ask his partner. "How did the interviews of our recycling plant inmates go?"

"Gottfried outlined the smuggling operation with Mr. Graves, Alfredo, Weller, and Martinez. He said Mr. Graves was against the whole thing and tried to persuade Weller not to continue his participation, but Weller needed money to get his girlfriend to another state, like Utah. Gottfried, of course, said he had nothing to do with it but just kept his ears open. He said he didn't know anything about the gun but said he 'wasn't surprised.' Morton said he was working with Duane and Ron to figure out what was going on out there and dropped them a note with the information he discovered. He wants to go back out there as soon as we release him from ad seg. He says it's the best job he's ever had. Martinez asked for a lawyer straight up. Dog, how do you know Alfredo killed Weller?"

"A tire, a top-break antique revolver, and this," Scott said as he retrieved Alfredo's cell phone from a cubbyhole in the dash of the extravagant pickup truck. "We need to make a trip to Rose, Veronica Mendez, and the dealership of this fancy ride, and all will be made perfectly clear, Tyrus."

Chapter 17

Earthlier Happy Is the Rose Distilled

"Alfredo made bail on the dope charge this morning. He called the warden to see if he can pick up his truck today," Scott informed Tyrus.

"Damn, Dog, how much was the bail?"

"Ten percent of $25,000, and, Ty, it's a good thing. It means I can interview him at his house without an attorney present, and it means we have more time to get him on the murder charges."

"Where to first, Dog?" asked Tyrus as they entered the freeway at speed.

"The dealership in Salinas with this administrative subpoena."

Tyrus studied the document signed by the warden requesting financial information regarding the purchase of the truck. "And then where are we going?"

"Richard Rainwater with a petition for an electronics search warrant for Alf's cell phone. He's already approved the warrant, and I've got a call in to the search warrant desk for a judge. And before you ask, Ty, it's off to Pacific Grove."

"Good, Dog. If we have time, we need to stop by the Pacific Grove Police Department. They have video of a nice, new, and shiny big white truck with a large man in the driver's seat turning right onto the street where Rose lives. It was from the convenience store. Oh, and they want to know if we took the shovel."

The dealership was exceedingly helpful and honored the administrative subpoena. Scott and Tyrus exited the business with a photocopy of a cashier's check for $72,718.48. Alfredo paid cash for the truck. Scott called Lieutenant Templeton with the information and asked that the truck be seized as the ill-gotten gain of a criminal activity. The warrant was signed by a judge of the superior court and recorded with the clerk of the court. Scott delivered Alfredo's cell phone to the district attorney's office, investigations division, computer and electronic device analysis unit. The analyst promised to make it a priority since it was a murder investigation. Scott would have his information by day's end.

Tyrus and Scott were once again on Highway 68 toward Monterey. "It's lunchtime, Dog. You know what that means," reminded his partner.

"Next stop, Papa Chano's."

While they ate, Scott asked Tyrus what Alfredo told the internal affairs lieutenant during the interview. Tyrus detailed the implausible story of how Alfredo saw the duffel bag sticking out of some bushes near the entrance of the prison when he drove in to work that morning. He put the bag on the back seat of the truck. He intended to call them and report his find but completely forgot. The best part was he said he never looked in the bag.

"Really," Scott remarked in a slow expression of disbelief. "So let me get this straight, Ty. He sees a duffel bag in the bushes not twenty yards from an armed gatehouse. He parked the big truck, got out, picked up the duffel bag, and carried it back to his truck. He put it on the back seat, drove past the gatehouse officer, and didn't bother mentioning it to him, even though he was required to stop and show the officer his identification card. He then drove past the entrance building, two towers, and one sally port officer. He parked his truck, got out, and walked to tower no. 7, where he exchanged a chit for a set of keys to the garbage truck. Three hours later, I am engaging him in a conversation at his truck. Never once did he think to tell any of those officers he passed or engaged in conversation that he found a duffel bag full of dope and contraband?"

"That's his story, and he's sticking to it."

"Good luck with that, Ty. Good luck with that."

As the old Crown Vic winded its way around the Holman Highway, Scott attempted but failed to remove a spot of salsa from the breast pocket flap of his uniform. This included pouring water from his water bottle directly onto the shirt, which ran down and around Scott's right leg. Tyrus just stared at him, shook his head, and asked, "What are we going to talk to the Mendez girl about?"

"Loose ends, Ty, just tying up some loose ends."

"Like?"

"The need for a gun, Tyrus, more specifically, the need for a gun from Mr. Graves and a note she gave to an old black man about Spider."

"You've lost me, Dog."

"All will be clear, Tyrus. All will be clear. We're almost there."

Carolyn Mendez opened the door to the beautiful Pacific Grove house. Her husband, the doctor, was not home. She called to Veronica to descend the stairs and speak with Tyrus and Scott. Everyone was cordial, and Scott reminded Veronica she was not in any trouble or under arrest. He inquired about her general health and emotional state with a genuine frankness and concern for a person grieving. If anyone knew about grieving, it was Scott. She said she was "coping."

Scott began his inquiry. "Veronica, did you take these photographs at the party in the park?"

The answer was in the affirmative.

"How did you know Alfredo?"

She didn't. She was asked to the park by Mr. and Mrs. Graves. She met Alfredo there.

"Is that where Alfredo proposed the smuggling operation?"

Yes, but she was assured she would never actually smuggle anything into the prison itself, just receive packages that people would deliver to her and collect the money. Either he or Mr. Graves would collect the items from her. She could keep a percentage of the money they collected.

"Did Mr. Graves ever collect money from her?"

No, only items. He never asked for money.

"Did you give Mr. Graves a small handgun to give to Spider?"

No, she gave it to Alfredo.

"Did Mr. Graves know about the gun? Was that in the note Richard gave you to give to Mr. Graves?"

Yes, it said Spider had a gun, and he was scared. Mr. Graves was very upset. That was when Mr. Graves said everything had to stop.

"Did Inmate Weller say he would no longer participate in the smuggling operation?"

He said they were going to stop what they were doing, and he said he asked the officers at his work to let him stay up near the front of the recycling plant where the tower officer could see him.

"Did you give Mr. Graves a small tin box that contained black tar heroin?"

Yes, the day before he and Richard died.

"Thank you, Veronica. Do you have any questions for me?"

"Yes. Do you think Mr. Graves and Richard went to heaven together?"

"Of that, my dear, I am most certain. They both died with love and goodwill in their hearts." Veronica cried and hugged Scott, who whispered into her ear, "None of this was your fault. Nothing you could have done would have prevented this. You must live your life to the fullest and never forget him, or Mr. Graves, ever. Find that one thing that you most admired about both of them and make that characteristic a part of you, in loving memory, always. Forget the bad things and remember only the good. Carry Richard with you in your heart forever."

With that, he secretly passed her a small locket on a silver chain that contained a facial photograph from the identification card issued to Inmate Weller and said, "Keep this from your mother until she is willing to accept he loved you."

Scott and Tyrus thanked Mrs. Mendez for her hospitality. Scott reminded Veronica she may be called up to give testimony in court but as a witness and not a suspect. Tyrus and Scott walked down the long walkway to the car. "What was that about, Dog? I saw the locket. He was a child molester."

"Yes, Ty, he was by today's standard. But when it comes down to it, he didn't use her to satisfy some perverse, lustful desire. He actually loved her. There is no way you will ever convince that girl what he did was immoral, unlawful perhaps but never immoral." Scott stood for a moment and looked to the northwest. From where the Crown Vic was parked, they could actually see the ocean. "I only hope to God she doesn't throw herself into the surf during a night of deep despair."

"Knock, knock! Rose, are you in?" called out Scott as he peered through the open front door of the small bungalow.

"Who's that?" came a voice from within.

"Ty and Dog, Rose. We've come to visit," answered Tyrus.

"Oh, boys, come on in here and have a seat. How are you, Sergeant Phillips and Mr. Doggett?"

"Rose, I do believe you have been drinking," replied Tyrus.

"Just a little tonic, Sergeant Phillips. I am guilty as charged."

"Nothing like a little day drinking," he replied.

"You know, I got this bottle of white wine at Trader Joe's, and I was only going to have one small glass with my lunch. I had a nice chopped salad. Well, I don't think there's anything left, or I'd offer you some. I wouldn't tell anyone you boys was in uniform."

"Thank you, Rose, but our lieutenant frowns on day drinking, although I bet he's a firm believer in it himself," replied Scott.

"How can I help you, boys?"

"Ty and I came to check on you and to ask you just a few questions. Do you feel up to it?"

"Probably more so now than ever," she replied with a wink as she lowered herself down to the corner of the sofa.

"Mr. Prado sends his regards. Rose, has Alfredo called you?"

"Yes, Mr. Scott, he called me this morning. He is a bad man, Mr. Scott. He is an evil man. I pray to God he takes that man soon. He killed my Walter, Mr. Scott, as sure as he did it himself."

"Rose, did Walter bring a small tin box into the house recently?"

"He didn't think I saw him, but I did. He brought it in and hid it in Christopher's room. Christopher was my son. He passed too when he went to college. He fell off an elevated parking garage. They said he was drunk and leaned too far out. Ten years ago, but it is still like yesterday to me. We haven't done nothing with that room since. Walter would go in there, sometimes sleep in there on his old bed."

"Yes, Rose, I remember when it happened," comforted Tyrus. "Daughter too, yes?"

"Shauna, Sergeant. She grown now, living in Los Angeles, married with three beautiful kids."

"Rose, tell me about the old revolver," encouraged Scott.

"He said he was going to give it to that Weller boy. He knew it was against the law, but he was going to do it just the same. My Shauna used to babysit that boy. We know the Mendez girl too. We've known the family for years. They is good folks, good church folks too."

"Why would he give the gun to Richard?" continued Scott.

"Alfredo gave a gun to some inmate named Bug or Scorpion or Insect, Spider, or something. He was going help that inmate escape, but they was going to kill Richard because he knew what they was going to do, and Richard said he would go to Mr. Parkinson or Mr. Richmond and tell them what they was doing with the drugs and everything. Walter said he was going to give him his old revolver so he could protect himself. It was stupid. I told him not to do it and to go tell you or Sergeant Phillips what was going on. He sure did like you both. My poor Walter, I never got to say goodbye. I never got to say how much I loved that old fool. I begged him to stop working. That man and his pride."

"A man must work, Rosie. A man must work," replied Tyrus.

"I knew he would work until the day he died, or the warden said he had to stop, but that would have killed him too."

"Rose, are you willing to testify to what you told me in court as a witness?" asked Scott.

"Walter would have wanted it that way," she replied.

"Rose, there is a very young lady who is grieving and is in need of a kind, understanding grandmother. I'm going to ask you to help her.

The support you may give may just make two fractured victims whole again, you and her."

"You know you are right, Mr. Doggett. I will do just that, after my day-drinking nap."

Tyrus and Scott thanked her for her assistance and quietly got up to leave. Rose wasn't napping. She was crying. As they got to the door, Tyrus asked, "Should we leave, Dog?"

"She'll be fine, Ty. A wise man once said, 'To weep is to make less the depth of grief.' Close the door behind you."

"The gun, Dog, how did you know?"

"To quote another wise man, 'Because I was looking for it.'"

Scott checked his email as they both sat in the car. He looked at Tyrus and said, "The DA's office dumped all the data from the cell phone. If we hurry, we just might make it there before they go home for the day." They first drove to the Pacific Grove Police Department to retrieve the video and explain how the prison managed to come into possession of the shovel. Scott excused himself and stepped into the public restroom. He reappeared a few minutes later. The breast pocket and flap of his uniform was saturated with water but absent one salsa stain.

Chapter 18

"Elementary," Said He

"Excellent!" exclaimed Tyrus as he looked at the text message the analyst from the district attorney's office found in Alfredo's deleted messages file.

"Elementary," said Scott in reply.

"Don't tell me you were looking for that too." Tyrus smirked.

"You won't believe me, Tyrus, but yes, I was, and I believe that closes the case of the murder of Inmate Weller."

"What's that, Scotty?" asked the anxious Oswaldo.

"It reads, little buddy, 'Meet me at the truck when Graves goes to the firehouse for coffee.' Sent from Alfredo's phone to a number provided to me by Veronica Mendez that belonged to the bootlegged telephone possessed by Inmate Weller before his untimely demise. The message was sent at 0705 hours, ten minutes before his death."

"That explains the tire tracks next to those of the garbage truck. But why did he go back later?" asked the inquisitive Oswaldo.

"To throw the heroin over the fence to Martinez, that is, after he hit Rose in the head with the shovel and ransacked her house looking for it. He paid $800 for that dope, and he wasn't about to let Mr. Graves get away with not delivering it as promised. There's a text message chain to that effect to the phone Adrian got from Martinez. Oh, and the call Alfredo was making when I walked up to him in the truck was to the cell phone of Inmate Martinez. He got no answer, so he sent a text message that read, 'Where you at? I got the stuff.' He apparently didn't know we had Martinez on contraband watch. The DNA swabs from the Glock came back positive to Martinez as did ridge-print impressions I developed on the extra magazine. Veronica, Weller's girlfriend, said she gave the gun to Alfredo. Text messages to Martinez on Alfredo's phone confirm the delivery of 'baby G' to Martinez. Baby G, Ty, is the Glock."

"What about the escape plans?"

"Sadly, Oz, we have nothing but the testimony of Veronica. I'm afraid we will not be able to charge that crime. It is, however, the least of their troubles. I just received the response to the financial records warrant I sent to the bank that issued the cashier's check to the dealership. Alfredo managed to amass nearly $100,000 in this 'special' account, which differs from the account he gave to his personnel specialist for the direct deposit of his paycheck. The DA's office will seize what is left for ill-gotten gains. They have subpoenaed the income tax records for Alfredo, and I wager he neglected to claim his extra income.

"Oh, and my favorite part is the club used to separate young inmate Weller from this world. The blood matched the DNA of our victim, and Alfredo will be shocked to know, although he wore latex gloves, he wore the gloves too long, and his sweat managed to permeate through or around the protective barrier. There were no prints, but his sweat managed to deposit itself on the handle, perhaps as he handled the weapon after struggling to push Weller into the bowels of the garbage truck or as he concealed it before tossing it into the newer garbage truck for its ride to the dump. I am certain the defense will challenge the results owing to some contamination or other. As I say, they can take one piece of the finished puzzle, but a good jury can still see the picture that remains. Let's just say that Richard Rainwater is extremely pleased with our investigation. He has issued an arrest warrant for Alfredo for the murder, and Tyrus and I will be paying him a visit in just a few minutes.

"Oz, take Adrian to the armory and draw your weapons. Stand by for us by the gatehouse. We shall join you shortly. Alfredo lives in

Greenfield. We'll stop by the police department first to let them know we will be serving an arrest warrant in their city."

"Squared away, Scotty. Good as gold."

Tyrus walked into Scott's office with the operations plan for the arrest of Alfredo Garza in hand. "Lieutenant approved the ops plan, Dog. Man, I cannot believe all that has happened. Dog, we've known Alfredo for almost twenty years, Mr. Graves too. If you asked me two months ago if they were going to end up like this, I would have said you were crazy."

"Tyrus, I will tell you something. I didn't believe any of it until I saw one thing."

"What's that, Dog?"

"Look at this photograph from the barbecue at the park. What one thing do you notice?"

"What am I looking for, Dog?"

"Alfredo in the Hawaiian shirt. What is he holding in his left hand?"

"A bottle of some kind."

"A tequila bottle, but here, use this loop magnifier. Can you make out the label?"

"I can see the colors of the label, but I can't make it out," replied Tyrus as he squinted into the loop.

"It's Jose Cuervo Especial. It's the same as the bottles Duane found at the recycling plant raid, Ty, and it's Alfredo's favorite. It all just fell into place from there."

"Let's get this over with then, Dog."

Within twenty minutes, both Crown Victorias were in the parking lot of the Greenfield Police Department. The watch commander was advised and agreed to provide a marked unit for the arrest warrant in case Alfredo made a run for it. The three cruisers drove southbound on El Camino Real to Oak Avenue, turned right, and proceeded to San Antonio Drive. The two white Crown Victoria vehicles pulled up in front of Alfredo's house. Two cars were parked in the driveway. Oswaldo and Adrian walked to the side of the house and prepared to chase Alfredo if he ran out the back door, even though Alfredo tipped the scale over three hundred pounds and was long past his running days.

Tyrus and Scott stood on each side of the front door and knocked. They could hear a television in the background and the sound of approaching feet. The door opened, and Alfredo looked at the two investigators with a confused expression. "Alfredo Garza," began Scott, "I have a warrant for your arrest for the murder of Richard Weller, an inmate at the California State Prison–Gabilan, and the assault and battery of Rose Graves. You have the right to remain silent. Anything you say can and will—and down he goes." Alfredo collapsed to the floor.

"Dear god, Dog, we've killed another one!" exclaimed Tyrus as he assumed the kneeling rescue position and checked for a pulse. "No, he just fainted."

"Roll him on his side and cuff him before he comes to, Ty. Here, use two pairs."

Tyrus skillfully placed the linked pairs of handcuffs on the now prone garbage truck driver.

"Roll him on his side, Ty. He's coming around. Where was I?"

"Anything you say."

"Thank you. Anything you say can and will be used against you in court. You have the right to an attorney and to have an attorney present during questioning—and he's out again. Save my place, Ty. I will be right back. Oh, what the heck, if you cannot afford an attorney, one will be appointed to you free of charge. I'll ask him if he understood his rights when I get back."

Tyrus gave him a scowl.

"I know, I'll read them again, Ty, later." Scott walked to the driveway and hollered for Oswaldo and Adrian. "We're code 4. Ask the Greenfield unit to call for an ambulance. Alfredo appears to have fainted twice."

He returned to the doorway, where Tyrus was fanning the moaning in-custody suspect with the arrest warrant. Scott looked in the living room and spied Alfredo's wife, Isabelle, and his mother-in-law standing with their hands to their mouths. "I'll let you handle this, Sergeant. I'll just wait here for the ambulance." Tyrus stepped into the house and approached the shocked spectators. Scott keyed his radio. "Squad 2, Squad 12. One in custody. Ambulance requested as a precaution."

The ambulance arrived, and Alfredo was strapped into a gurney and wheeled into the back of the van. Oswaldo jumped in, and Scott and Tyrus followed the ambulance to Mee Memorial Hospital in nearby King City. Once Alfredo was sufficiently in possession of his senses, Scott again advised him of his rights pursuant to the *Miranda* decision. Alfredo acknowledged these rights and said, "I can explain." He rambled on about Inmate Martinez blaming him for everything that transpired.

Scott listened intently and said, "It's a good story, Alf, but you forgot one thing. Inmate Martinez was still at the farm gate when you bashed in the head of Inmate Weller."

The hospital staff cleared Alfredo for placement in the county jail with a caution for high blood pressure. Scott and Tyrus transported him to the Monterey County Jail in Salinas. Oswaldo and Adrian returned to the institution.

Chapter 19

The Coda

Isabelle Garza hired an attorney to represent her husband at trial. The district attorney had requested the death penalty, and the case was presented at the preliminary hearing. Scott gave testimony as did Tyrus, Rose, Oswaldo, and Veronica. The hearing lasted three days.

Forensic technicians from the district attorney's office testified to the information extracted from the cellular telephones of Alfredo and Inmate Martinez. Records were produced for the telephone number belonging to the cellular telephone once possessed by Inmate Weller. Scott tried to extract the information from Weller's cell phone, but it was an old flip phone, and Weller was adept at deleting all data each time he used the device. The defense made a big deal of the absence of this data on Weller's phone. Richard Rainwater was unconcerned. He'd fix that at trial.

Laboratory technicians testified about the soundness of the DNA evidence but agreed the pipe used in the killing was heavily contaminated from its ride in the garbage truck, or Alfredo may have touched the mop bucket handle before another person removed it from the bucket, and the shovel lacked fingerprints or DNA associated with the defendant. Again, Deputy District Attorney Rainwater was unconcerned. That too he would fix at trial.

Testimony regarding the Glock pistol was provided. The defense attempted to disqualify the admissibility of the evidence for cause. The gun was not used in the murder, and its admission as evidence would be prejudicial to the jury. The judge allowed the pistol for the preliminary hearing but warned the prosecutor he would need to show a link between the murder and the gun at the jury trial. In the end, the judge held Alfredo to answer and allowed the trial to proceed as a death penalty case but warned the prosecutor the death penalty might "complicate the state's case unnecessarily." In a brief, Richard Rainwater successfully linked the smuggling operation with the gun to the murder.

The high-priced private attorney, having lost every motion to suppress evidence or to dismiss the charges, persuaded Alfredo to accept a plea agreement to fifteen years to life with the possibility of parole when he turned sixty-five. Subsequently, he also entered a guilty plea to the possession of narcotics with the intent to smuggle to the inmate population, for which he received an additional sentence of six years to be served consecutively to the murder conviction. Even if he received a parole date on his sixty-fifth birthday, he would still be required to serve the additional six-year sentence.

He was, of course, terminated from state service. His pension was surrendered except for the money he contributed, which wasn't much after the lawyer took his share. Isabelle was forced to work at a vegetable processing plant as a quality control manager. Alfredo was transferred to San Quentin State Prison, where he suffered a stroke. He was transferred to the California Medical Facility–Vacaville, where he remained. Isabelle visited when her job permitted. His fancy truck and secret bank account were seized by the state as proceeds from unlawful activities. The prison eventually received a check for $5,000.

Somehow the money held in the account of Veronica Mendez was overlooked. Scott thought it was for the best; the poor girl had suffered enough. Walter Graves died before he could be separated from state service for his participation in the criminal enterprise. Warden Brown attempted to have his state service discharge designated as dishonorably separated, but Lieutenant Templeton managed to convince him that poor Mr. Graves was not capable of defending himself in the adverse action and therefore could not prove his innocence. His separation from service was documented as "deceased," and Rose was allowed to collect his pension.

Inmate Spider Martinez was charged with possession of controlled substances and narcotics for the purpose of distribution. He was also charged with a violation of California Penal Code section 4502(a), possession of a deadly weapon by an inmate, and for being an ex-felon in possession of a firearm owing to his previous prison terms. Although proclaiming his innocence, he agreed to a plea agreement for eight years to be served consecutively to his current commitment. He was looking at twelve years if he went to trial. Scott thought the sentence was light and that somehow he had not seen the last of Spider Martinez.

Scott prepared a lengthy report in the matter of the murder of Inmate DeSantos. The report included a detailed bloodstain pattern analysis of the crime scene and suspect. The office of the public defender paid a private certified bloodstain expert to conduct an independent analysis using crime scene and autopsy photographs. The "expert" submitted a nine-page report excoriating Scott as an incompetent bloodstain pattern analyst. Richard Rainwater called Scott to his office and presented him with the defense response to his analysis. Scott read it intently and, after the eighth page, discovered one brief paragraph with the summary that was in complete agreement with Scott's analysis. He looked up from the report and said, "So if I read this right, I am a colossal idiot, but I managed to get the analysis spot on."

"In a nutshell, Scott," was the reply. Richard added, "The best part is that is exactly what I told the judge. Their expert will not testify, but you will. I'm sure he pocketed his $5,000 and went on his way satisfied."

Scott gave evidence in the preliminary hearing and later in the jury trial. It was the fastest homicide trial he had ever participated in as the primary and expert witness. The jury was seated on a Monday. The evidence was presented on Tuesday morning. Expert witness testimony and forensic laboratory technician testimony was completed by Tuesday evening. Closing arguments were completed early Wednesday morning and the jury instructions completed before lunch. By four fifteen in the afternoon of Wednesday, the jury had returned a verdict of guilty as charged.

Inmate Cooper smiled broadly at Scott throughout the trial, a childlike, almost impish smile. He listened carefully to the bloodstain pattern testimony, nodding in agreement when Scott pointed to various patterns on images depicted on the large screen as if to say, *That's exactly how it happened.* When the verdict was read, Inmate Cooper nodded as if he would have rendered the same decision and mouthed the words "thank you," causing a raised eyebrow from the judge. He was transferred to Corcoran State Prison with an additional twenty-year-to-life sentence.

He would never again be housed with a cellmate. It was said he was never the same. He seldom spoke. He took up drawing and even had made several lifelike drawings of the facial features of his former cellmate from memory. He kept his cell immaculately clean and spent hours on end hand-polishing his floor. He fell out of favor with the gangs and never killed again.

Scott and Tyrus took up a collection at the prison and raised $2,900 from friends and coworkers to buy a marble tombstone for Mr. Graves. They arranged to meet Rose at the Pacific Grove Cemetery, where he was interred with military honors. Rose was accompanied by Veronica Mendez, who wore the locket proudly on the chain Scott had given her. They were both tearful but not in a sad way. Rose pointed to the grave next to her beloved Walter. The simple tombstone read "Richard Weller, rest in peace."

The cemetery staff uncovered the recently installed tombstone of Mr. Graves. "Oh, it's beautiful!" exclaimed Rose as she looked at the marble tombstone of her departed husband.

After a few minutes, she pointed at an object embedded into the stone. "What on earth is that?" she asked.

Tyrus chuckled and looked at Scott. "Perhaps you should explain, Dog."

"Well, Rose, that's the gearshift knob from the old garbage truck. I kinda purloined it as it was being towed away to the scrapyard."

"Yes, he did," said Tyrus with an enormous grin.

"It's beautiful," repeated Rose with a tear.

The End

Prison Jargon

ABFO scale—An L-shaped ruler used for photographing injuries as designed by the American Board of Forensic Odontology.

ad seg—The administrative segregation unit is a prison within the prison where all inmate movement is restricted. It is referred to as "the Hole" by the inmate population.

B or Baker number—Inmates are assigned alphanumeric numbers for identification purposes. The alphanumeric system includes one or two letters, followed by a series of numbers, such as B-12345. B numbers were issued in the late 1970s and early 1980s, followed by C (Charlie), D (Delta), E (Edward), and so on. It is possible for an inmate to parole, return to custody, many years later and retain his or her original number (also known as CDCR nos.).

boneyard—A series of apartments used as conjugal visitation areas for inmate with privileges. Inmates can visit with relatives for a period longer than typical visitation.

canteen—A store of sorts where inmates can buy personal hygiene items, snacks, sodas, and stationary using script.

central file—A large file containing the inmate's criminal history, assignment history, court and classification information, confidential information, etc.

chrono—Short for *chronograph*, a paper used to document events during an inmate's incarceration, such as behavioral issues, assignment changes, classification changes, property, and medical issues.

close B custody—A classification that requires an additional inmate count during the   day.

control room—A highly secured building where equipment is issued, the count is recorded, alarms are announced, and movement is controlled.

count—Several times each day, the entire inmate population is counted for accountability purposes with one standardized positive standing count where all inmates are seen standing, alive, and well.

DO or dropout—An inmate who has left the allegiance of a particular street disruptive group or prison gang.

ducat—A pass provided to an inmate instructing or allowing him or her passage through the institution to an appointment, interview, job, or special program.

farm gate—A building at the minimum support facility where inmates who are assigned to jobs outside the secured perimeter are processed.

floater—A television or electrical appliance that has been left behind by a departing inmate and does not appear on the current possessor's list of authorized property.

fish—The name given to a newly arrived inmate at a prison by other inmates. A fish bundle is an issue of linen, underwear, and a blanket issued by the clothing room to a newly arrived inmate. The senior officers at the prison refer to new officers as fish cops.

entrance building—A building outside the secured perimeter controlling movement in and out of the institution, as well as processing official and inmate visitors.

fishing—A technique used by inmates to recover items outside their closed cell doors by tying a hooklike paperclip with a small weighted item to a long string and casting the "fishing line" under the door, generally toward the cells of other inmates who have items they desire. Once the item is hooked, it is pulled back into the cell from beneath the door.

garrote—A length of cord or wire used to wrap around the neck and restrict breathing.

grille gate—A grille gate is a movable gate constructed of bars that allow an officer to limit inmate movement between two areas.

Hole—A euphemism referring to the administrative segregation unit, the prison within the prison where inmates are secluded from the mainline inmates.

hot room—A secured area of the housing unit for the temporary storage of contraband or other prohibited items where inmates are not allowed.

housing unit—A building containing cells, generally with several tiers, where inmates are housed.

pin joint—A very thin and small marijuana cigarette that is exhausted in one or two puffs. This allows the inmate to avoid detection by using the quantity quickly and immediately changing their location.

R&R—Receiving and release is the unit responsible for the documentation and control of new inmates or inmates transferring from other facilities or prisons, departures to parole, other facilities, or temporary release to court and medical appointments. This unit maintains the records of all inmates' authorized property lists.

sally port—A sally port is a controlled area where movement can be made without a breach of a secured perimeter as it allows only one gate to be opened at a time.

shank—A handheld, inmate-manufactured, improvised stabbing or slashing weapon.

shot caller—An inmate bestowed with authority over other inmates in a gang or group by the hierarchy of that gang or group.

skinhead—A person who believes in the supremacy of the Caucasian race over all others. The skinhead movement began in London, England, in the 1960s and is characterized by shaved heads and working-class clothing. The skinheads embrace neo-Nazi ideology and racist beliefs.

state blues—Inmate clothing defined by a blue chambray shirt, blue denim jeans, a blue nylon jacket, and brown boots.

yard gloves—Cloth or leather gloves left on the yard by a group of inmates for communal use by inmates of the same race or gang.

X Wing—A housing unit for newly arrived inmates and an overflow for ad seg.

Lightning Source UK Ltd.
Milton Keynes UK
UKHW010048300520
364134UK00004B/69/J

9 781984 580122